Beneath the Surface

EMILY MCINTIRE

Beneath the Surface
(Sugarlake Series, Book Four)
By: Emily Mcintire

Copyright © 2021 by Emily McIntire

Cover Design: Emily Witting

Editing: Ellie McLove (My Brother's Editor)

Proofreading: Rosa Sharon (My Brother's Editor)

Paperback ISBN: 978-1-7349994-9-5

Hardback ISBN: 978-1-7375083-0-4

Ebook ISBN: 978-1-7375083-1-1

BENEATH THE SURFACE
PLAYLIST

Sober - *Demi Lovato*
Broken - *Jonah Kagen*
Closer - *Nine Inch Nails*
Use Somebody - *Kings of Leon*
Shallow - *Lady Gaga, Bradley Cooper*
You and Me - *Lifehouse*
As I Am - *Justin Bieber (Feat. Khalid)*
River of Tears- *Alessia Cara*
Fix You - *Coldplay*
Wonderwall - *Oasis*

For Survivors.

(And for Sav. This series wouldn't be what it is without you. Mason is yours.)

Out of suffering have emerged the strongest souls; the most massive characters are seared with scars.

— KAHLIL GIBRAN

AUTHOR'S NOTE

Beneath the Surface features mature and graphic content.
READER DISCRETION IS ADVISED.

If you would like a detailed content warning list you can find
it HERE

Beneath the Surface is the fourth interconnected standalone in
the Sugarlake series. While not necessary, it is HIGHLY
recommended to start with book one and read in order for a
full reading experience.

Read Book One: Beneath the Stars

Join Emily's Facebook Group THE MCINCULT to chat
while you read!

PROLOGUE

LILY

I remember the wind.

The house we were in was sturdy, but that night, I thought it might tumble down. There wasn't any storm, no pitter-pattering of raindrops against the roof's shingles. No thunder to accompany the hole being ripped open in the middle of my chest.

But there was wind.

And it was howling.

Thinking back, I like to pretend it was Mother Earth's way of crying, guttural groans against the brick, while a meaty hand that smelled like beef jerky and stale cigarettes muffled my voice.

Not that I would have made any noise anyway. My older brother, Chase, was right next door, and I knew that if I woke him up, he'd come charging in, getting us both in trouble.

And more than anything else, I was terrified of being separated. Chase always told me it was us against the world. Forever. But I heard our caseworker say we were one of the lucky ones—that usually siblings were split apart.

If I didn't have Chase, then I wouldn't have anyone.

So, instead of letting out a sob, my fingers dug deeper into my stuffed bunny rabbit, gripping it as tight as possible, while my foster father stole my innocence.

I was nine years old.

We were with them for over a year.

I've blocked out a lot from that time, and the memories I do have, I've doused in black tar and liquor, but there're some things that just can't be erased—tattoos that get etched beneath the surface, carved so deep they brand your soul.

And I remember the wind.

1

LILY

"Johnny, there're a couple of guys who just walked in, I'm about to send some orders," I holler at my manager.

He sighs, leaning back in the rickety office chair, his normally spiked blond hair matted against his head, and his Dina's Diner shirt crinkled and stained. Our cook never showed up today, so Johnny was stuck on the line, frying up eggs, and overcooking bacon for the truck drivers that stop through.

We don't get a lot of regulars here—other than Barrie—a man in his seventies who shows up every morning like clock-work, sipping on his coffee and working on his crosswords.

We're close enough to the big city for a night on the town, and far away enough to be considered the middle of nowhere. But we're right on the edge of State Route 60, so we get plenty of people passing through on their way to Phoenix.

My foot cramps against the linoleum floors, and I cringe, the tray of Coke tipping slightly in my hands. Pasting on a smile, I rebalance the weight and make my way over to the table of three grungy men who stumbled in fifteen minutes ago. They're the only ones here, other than a lone customer in the back booth, tucked away in the corner.

My eyes flick to him. He's been drinking coffee and reading *The Art of War* since he walked in three hours ago, and he hasn't said a single word the entire time I've served him.

"Y'all ready to order?" I slide the Cokes down the table, grabbing my notepad from my apron and smacking my cinnamon gum.

"That depends, sugar. Are you on the menu?" The man closest to me leers, his stringy black hair falling over his bushy eyebrows, his mud-caked nails absentmindedly scratching against his forearm.

I smirk, playfully rolling my eyes, pretending like I haven't heard some variation of the cliched phrase a million times. "Did no one teach you how to read wherever you're from?" I ask, my head tilting to the side.

His smile drops and his hand stops scratching against his raw skin long enough to reach out and wrap around my wrist.

My body freezes, ants skittering up my arm and dropping into my gut—thousands of tiny legs crawling around inside of me. Just his touch has transferred the itch, and now *I'm* the one who needs to be scrubbed clean.

"You've got quite the mouth on you, *bitch*," he spits. "I've got a nice way to shut you up." His free hand gropes at his crotch, humping the air lewdly. His friends break out in raucous laughter.

I swallow, my eyes glancing around, not wanting to cause a scene. Whether I like it or not, I need the tip this guy and his friends will hopefully still leave.

Besides, it's not the first time someone less than appealing has thought to take advantage of me.

My eyes lock on the lone stranger in the corner, and my stomach flips. He's *intimidating.* And for the first time since he walked in, he's staring right at me. My breath catches in my throat at the intensity in his gaze, his eyes almost an unnatural golden brown, and I watch as they drop to where the grease-ball's slimy fingers are wrapped around my wrist.

His grip tightens, drawing my attention back. I lean in close until my lips are just a breath away from his ear. "Sorry, *sugar*, but I'm a special service. Only available for those who know how to eat me properly."

His muddy brown eyes flare, his mouth opening to say something, but before he can, a shadow falls over the table. I glance up, my breath sticking in my throat as I crane my neck to see who's towering over us.

It's the stranger from the corner. He's taken off his black leather jacket, and my eyes trail along the rainbow of colors that cover every inch of his tan skin.

Who is this guy?

He still doesn't say a word, the veins in his forearms popping as he crosses them and continues to stare down the table. Slowly, I feel the grip on my wrist loosen until it disappears completely.

"Whatever. None of this is worth the trouble. The food *or* the used up pussy," the wrist grabber huffs. He jerks out of the faded red booth, shouldering past me and stomping out of the door. His friends follow, and as I stare after them, the only thought that rushes through my mind is who will end up paying for the Cokes. No way Johnny lets it go, money's tight enough around here as it is.

Just fucking great.

I spin, my eyes narrowing. "You scared them off."

The tattooed stranger smirks, his golden eyes sparking, and it makes me want to smack the pretty right off his face—watch his cheek grow pink from the sting of my hand.

"I did you a favor," he responds.

My breath stutters, not expecting the deep rumble of his voice. Like it scraped over gravel before it passed his lips, creating a rough, but oddly enticing sound.

I scoff. "I've had enough *favors* to last a lifetime."

"Is that your way of saying thank you?" he asks, his brow arching.

"That's my way of saying, mind your fucking business." I smile wide as I hiss through my teeth.

He cocks his head, and I lift my chin, refusing to fidget under his gaze.

It's absolutely ridiculous how tall he is. I feel small enough on a normal day—barely passing five foot two—but with his frame, he could pick me up and put me in his pocket, or break me in half without even trying.

"I'm adding their drinks to your bill." I slip my pad of paper back in my apron.

He grins slightly before something passes over his face, making his entire demeanor change. With a sharp nod, he spins, walking back to his table and picking up his book.

Good. Prick.

An hour later, he finally leaves. I walk over to his booth, cleaning up his dirty mug and wiping down the table. He was the last person here, but he never said another word after our encounter, and now that my irritation has died down, I feel like a bitch. He was only trying to help.

That guilt triples when I lift his mug and find a crisp one-hundred-dollar bill underneath.

My chest squeezes, and maybe I should feel guilty for what is clearly a sympathy tip, but I don't. Because this means I'll be able to put food on the table. *Real* food.

Realistically, I should be putting that money straight into savings. There isn't a bill that exists in this town without my name on it. But I can't stop myself from dropping by the twenty-four-hour corner store and picking up some treats. Ingredients for homemade pancakes, Cool Whip and chocolate chips. And then I grab some cookie dough ice cream, too.

Just because.

My legs ache as I walk the six blocks home, and there's a crick in my neck from the long hours and the lack of adequate sleep, but I ignore it as I knock on Susan, my next-door neighbor's, front door.

"Hey, Susan. Sorry it's so late," I speak low.

Susan yawns and smiles. "No worries, honey. Good night?" Her brow raises as she glances at the few bags dangling off my arm.

I shrug, the corner of my lips twitching. "Yeah. It was a good night."

"Well, he was an angel, as usual." She yawns again before disappearing.

My heart swells three times its normal size when she reappears, my gaze soaking up my baby boy. I miss him so much when I'm gone. His little fists rub into bleary eyes, his black hair, identical to mine, sticking up in random patches. His gaze swings around and locks onto me.

"Mommy!" he squeals, jumping into my arms. I stumble back, trying not to drop the bags as I wrap my hands around him.

"Hi, baby." I kiss his forehead.

"What's that?" He peers down at the bags on my arm.

"It's a surprise." I widen my eyes. "Only good three-year-olds who brush their teeth, and go straight to bed get to find out what it is."

"*I'm* thwee!" he whisper-shouts.

I nod, juggling both him and the bags in one arm, unlocking our front door with the other. "That's right. I guess you better be good."

"Okay!" He shimmies down, racing to the bathroom, water turning on before I even make it to the kitchen.

After brushing his teeth, I settle him into bed, picking out our favorite nighttime story. The one I've read every single day since we came home from the hospital. He snuggles under his Spider-Man covers, his fluffy head resting against my side. He's asleep before we even hit the fifth page.

"I'll love you forever, I'll like you for always. As long as I'm living, my baby, you'll be." I whisper the last lines of the book, closing the pages delicately as his soft snores fill the room, and just like that, everything drains away.

My throat swells with gratitude. I may have been a bitch to the stranger, but I'm not too proud to acknowledge help when I get it. I don't know who he was, but he's the reason my kid is smiling tonight, and the reason he'll be smiling tomorrow, with a full belly and chocolate chip smudges on his face.

A treat we don't ever get to have.

In moments like these, in the deep dark of night, right after I put my baby down to sleep and am feeling the sting of loneliness—that's when I miss my brother the most. When I regret running away the way I did all those years ago.

Thoughts creep into the forefront of my mind and I wonder where he is, what he's doing… if he still thinks of me.

I wouldn't blame him if he didn't.

Running my hand over my baby boy's hair, I lean down, kissing his forehead.

"Good night, Chase. Sweet dreams."

2

MASON

That was stupid.

And I had been doing so well. Keeping my distance. Watching her. Taking notes. Collecting data. Hiding in the shadows, the way I'm supposed to. The way I'm being *paid* to.

But today, something fogged my logic. This stupid fucking need inside of me, wanting to see Lily Adams just a little bit closer.

When I took the job six months ago to find her, I expected some used-up druggie on her last leg, needing to be saved. That's what her brother, Chase, made it sound like, at least. But what I've actually found is someone completely different, and after watching her for the past two months, I've formed a bit of an infatuation.

And *that* is a fucking problem.

But she's just so… different than what I was expecting.

She whips around the dingy diner she works at with a smile on her face, jabbering people's ears off, and acting like there's nothing that can bring her down. But I see her as she counts her money at the end of the night. I watch the world settle on her shoulders when no one is around to notice her slump from the weight.

There are secrets in her eyes, and hidden behind the tattoos on her arms.

I haven't told Chase that I've found her. Unprofessional as fuck, but honestly, I don't really care. Instead, I've been collecting as much information as possible, so that once I pass it along to him I can leave and never come this close to the West Coast again.

He's lucky I took the job in the first place.

But there was desperation sparking off his skin, and I could tell that his need for finding her was genuine. And I respect that. I'm not like other private investigators. Most work within the parameters of legality, running alongside the law. But, I've spent too many years of my life living within boundaries, while watching the people who make them dance outside of their edges.

Rules for thee and not for me.

It's all bullshit.

I'm not a bad guy, just someone who knows how both sides work. And I *know* that just because we don't see the cage, doesn't mean we aren't chained inside of it.

Meeting my mentor, Don, ten years ago was fortuitous. He took me under his wing and taught me everything I know. How to find people. Like Lily. And how to make them disappear. Like me.

He taught me that you see the soul of a man by looking in his eyes, and I've been a big believer in only helping those who I know are pure in their intentions.

Chase's intentions are honest. And the heat spiraling through my insides as I watch his little sister lets me know that mine are not. And while normally, I would drop her location and be on my way, my loyalty to my paying customer is skewed by whatever this *thing* is swirling up inside of me.

But going in and meeting her was fucking stupid.

I perk up from where I'm slouched on my Harley, slipping

off the seat and standing, my coffee cold in my hand as Lily walks out the front door of her apartment.

Her complex is in the worst part of this do-nothing town —a small, run-down building with faded yellow siding and garish red front doors. She lives on the second floor, the cement hallways that line the apartments stained with dirt and memories from a thousand different struggles.

It's a shithole.

But there's a smile on her beautiful lips as she grabs her little boy's hand, his face beaming up at her as they head down the street. It's Wednesday morning, and I know without following that they're on their way to the playground.

She doesn't have a car, and she doesn't really have any friends, so she rarely travels outside of the two-mile radius between her home and her work, but every Wednesday morning, like clockwork, she takes her little kid to the park on the edge of town. It's not kept up well by the state—*no surprise there*—the colored metal of the monkey bars chipped and faded, and the swings squeaking with rust, but that boy's face lights up when they go. Like it's the best thing in the world. A simple type of joy that somewhere along the way we lose. Either because we become conditioned to view the world through a certain lens, or because it's beaten out of us by the harsh realities of our lives.

Maybe it's a little bit of both.

My chest tugs as I follow them, my stomach flipping. My hand grips the cold coffee tighter, my teeth grinding as I get lost in my head, visions of a different little kid running around a playground, looking at *me* the way this boy looks at Lily.

When I come back to myself, Lily's staring right at me.

Fuck.

Twice in two days, I've slipped up, and I curse myself as her brows draw in and recognition flickers over her eyes. I don't exactly blend in, but I meant to keep to the shadows.

She was never supposed to know who I was.

She glances back at her kid before taking a hesitant step toward me. My mind races trying to figure out whether I should turn tail and leave, or play it off like a coincidence.

It's not usual for a grown man to be watching a playground on a Wednesday morning. I cringe. *This doesn't look good.*

Sure enough, her eyes narrow, body growing rigid as she stares me down.

Blowing out a breath, I make my way over, and while I know I shouldn't be talking to her again, the thought of her thinking the worst is a dull blade prodding down my middle.

I don't *want* her to think of me and feel disgust or fear.

I *shouldn't* want her to think of me at all.

Taking a slow sip of my coffee, I walk toward them, noticing quickly how her back straightens as she moves her body to face me full-on, her chin sticking out. Despite how small she is, she looks intimidating. But most of my life was spent under intimidating people's gazes, so it doesn't have the intended effect.

I reach her, stopping when I'm a little over a foot away.

"Hi." I smile.

Her eyes are weary, face tilted high, and even though I'm six-six, and she can't be barely over five foot—with the aura she's radiating, she feels bigger than life.

She tilts her head. "Hi back."

"Funny running into you here." I smirk.

"Is it?" She crosses her arms, her eyes glancing behind her.

Internally sighing, I realize this truly does come off as creepy. Borderline stalker. And while technically, I *have* been stalking her for the past two months, it's not the way it looks.

Not that I can tell her any of that.

"I like to get outside in the mornings, get some coffee." I lift my cup. "Some fresh air. Saw you over here, and thought I'd come by. Apologize for yesterday."

She sucks on her teeth. "You get your fresh air around playgrounds a lot?"

My eyes glance around, quickly taking in our surroundings, snagging on the Motel Eight. I nod my head toward it. "I'm staying right over there."

Her eyes follow, her right hand absentmindedly rubbing the wrist of her left arm, right over one of her tattoos. Finally, her eyes soften and she nods.

"There's nothing to apologize for," she sighs. "I was in a mood yesterday, and you were only trying to help. I was being a bitch."

My lips twitch as I lean back in my boots and take her in.

"I'm Lily, by the way. If you're gonna be stalking me, you might as well know my name." She grins.

"I know. You told me yesterday when you poured my coffee." I wink. "I'm Alex."

Fuck. The name slips out before I can stop it, my mouth speaking before my brain can finish the thought.

She runs her fingers through her silky dark hair. "Alex." She bobs her head. "Well, it's nice to meet you, Alex. Maybe I'll see you around again." She glances to the motel before looking back at me, a cautious smile on her face.

Did she just dismiss me?

I stifle the amusement that's trying to break free at the thought. This woman is so different than what I expected, and I'm a fucking moron for letting her see my face. But I'm nothing if not adaptable.

"Only so many places around here to get hot coffee and good service." I grin. "Have a nice day."

I spin, walking across the street toward the Motel Eight that I definitely am *not* staying at, and tell myself that I didn't just monumentally fuck up. That this might work in my favor. Chase seems like the kind of guy who won't be satisfied with a simple location, and this will allow me to get closer—gather more information to pass off.

Technically, my job is done. I found her. And if I was smart, I would leave the West and everything that comes along with it as quickly as possible.

Go back to Nashville where it's safe.

But as I look back one last time, there's a burn simmering low in my gut, and I know I won't be leaving.

Not yet.

Lily Adams is still too much of a mystery. And I'm desperate to uncover her secrets.

3

LILY

I brush off the chill that's been sticking to my back ever since I saw the same stranger staring at us from across the playground.

Alex.

He doesn't look like an Alex.

I should have asked him what he's doing here in Raindale, Arizona. It's not exactly a place people come to stay. Other than a few gas stations and fast-food restaurants off the highway, plus a small church in the middle of town, there isn't much else. Which is exactly why it's the perfect place for me.

Gripping Chase's fingers tighter in mine, we walk the few blocks back to our apartment. After giving him pancakes this morning, I knew the playground would be the only way to get out his energy. We go every Wednesday since it's my only morning off work, and even though there aren't many kids around his age in this town, I find myself continually hoping that one day, we'll show up and he'll be able to make a friend. It hasn't happened yet.

But at least we have each other.

A pang hits the center of my chest as I look down at his smiling face, blooming with the innocence that only exists when experience hasn't railroaded its way into your life, and smacked you upside the head. I bask in his naivete, gripping on tightly and praying he never lets go, because once it's gone, there's no getting it back.

I lost mine far too early. And so did my brother.

Shaking off the thought, I grip Chase's fingers tighter as we cross the street.

"Mommy, who was dat man?" he asks.

My stomach flips. I should have known he would ask. For a three-year-old, he's very aware of his surroundings. Inquisitive. Not afraid to walk up to someone and ask them a million questions before they can even get a word out. I don't have enough experience with kids to know whether that's a normal toddler thing, or if it's something that was passed down from me.

Growing up, I always had a problem with being too nice to strangers. It's terrifying having him so easily trusting people the way I did. My chest pulls tight as I think about the example I set today. Having someone walk up on the playground, and me, engaging in conversation like it was no big deal.

It's always a big deal.

"That was Mommy's friend," I rush out quickly. "Someone I know from work."

"Oh." He nods his head. "He didn't wanna say hi?"

I glance down at him. "To you?"

He nods again.

"Well…" I pause, trying to think of something to say. "He didn't want to scare you. Some people are afraid of him because of his size and the drawings on his skin."

Chase's chest puffs out as we stop at the crosswalk. "Not me."

"No?"

"Uh-uh. His skin looks like yours. And he looked nice. I can tell."

"Oh?" I grin, my chest warming as I glance at the tattoos scattering my forearms. I'm not covered like Alex, but I have enough to hide what I don't want to show. "Well, you're pretty brave."

He's right. Alex does seem nice. Almost too nice. But any man will act friendly to get what they want.

Glancing at the clock when we get back to our apartment, I put on a cartoon and go to make an afternoon snack. We don't have too much, just some apple slices and peanut butter, but it's enough to get Chase through until I make his lunch.

I never knew that having a kid meant they ate you through house and home. My stomach squeezes as I think back to my earliest memories. The ones that are foggy and scattered because of how young I was, not because of the drugs I used to shade them.

There were so many nights my brother gave me the only thing we had in the cupboards and went hungry himself, just so I could eat. Countless times, he would hold me in his arms —while our mom was in the living room with a man, or with a needle stuck up her arm—and promise that everything would be okay.

"It's us against the world, Lil. Forever."

My throat swells, and I push the thought away, but it doesn't go far. It never does. Chase is always there in the back of my mind, drowning in the well of guilt that I also keep hidden in the shadows.

It's been almost a decade since I've seen him. Spoken to him. Ran away from him and the life that we always promised each other.

But I was young, and stupid, and desperate to forget. Blinded by the demons that crawled into my throat and blackened my lungs, swirling poison through my veins. Even the thought of it now makes my stomach cramp, an uncomfortable itch skittering along my skin, my chest tightening as my body tries to trick my mind, whispering to just give in to the craving.

I don't think there will ever be a day I don't have a physical reaction to the thought of drugs. But all it takes is one look at my baby boy, and the feeling is capsized and washed away by my love for him. I would do *anything* to give him the life he deserves. The life I never had.

He's why I got clean in the first place.

And he's why I can never go back home.

A few hours later, I'm fresh out of the shower and about to wake Chase up from his nap. I need to get him ready to go next door to Susan's, so I can head to work for the night shift. My stomach tugs, wishing like hell that I could call off and curl up on the couch with him instead. Watch silly movies and roll around in his giggles, let them serenade me into being happy with my life.

I grab the Play-Doh off his toy shelf, glancing down at the lid, popping the top and reaching in until I'm squeezing it through my fingers. Over and over again, I mold the dough, allowing the feel of it pushing between my palms to calm me.

The shock of seeing Alex at the playground has my nerves frayed and on edge. The fact that my child saw him, and the way my memories are playing like a TV show when all I want is to see static, has my mind desperate to find a way to numb the pain.

And when it gets like this—when the cinnamon gum, and the thought of being the best mother I can be isn't enough to curb the craving—I grab onto my son's Play-Doh and squeeze it between my hands. Something about focusing on the silky texture as it molds under my fingers reminds me that everything is reshapable. Nothing is permanent. Things are always under my control, and I can *choose* to do things however I want.

That's all anything is, really. A choice.

Breathing deep, I shake off the ache that's filtering

through my bones, whispering a want so visceral, that even after almost four years, my muscles stiffen and my lungs lock up tight.

Grabbing my phone, I pull up the only number I have in time of emergencies, when the feeling becomes too much and I feel like I might drown from its weight.

Derek.

"Hello?"

I breathe out a sigh. "Hi, Derek. I'm sorry to call but—"

"Lily," he breathes. "Don't you ever apologize for callin'. Talk to me."

Derek Andrews is my sponsor, of sorts. I've never been to rehab. But I *have* been to a meeting. Just one. And that's where I met him.

He's saved me countless times from falling off a deep, dark ledge. Picked me up off dirty bedroom floors in rotting, drug-infested houses when I couldn't stand to stay sober, and he's talked me down every single time I've wanted to relapse—my body speaking lies to my mind, making me feel like I'm not strong enough to survive the words they spit.

He lives in Sweetwater, Tennessee. And he's one of the only people who knows where I am.

"I just..." I blow out a breath, watching as the red clay oozes between my fingers. "It's a rough day," I whisper.

"So make it unrough."

Laughing, I lean back against the shelf of hand-me-down toys and stare up at the popcorn ceiling. "Your amazing ability to see through bullshit astounds me, Derek. Calling you *is* me making it unrough."

He chuckles. "Listen, you're a strong woman. And you're a hell of a mother. The urges that are spinnin' through you right now? They're liars, and they're testin' your strength. But just like you do every other time, you're gonna prove them wrong."

Closing my eyes, I swallow around the knot lodged in my throat. "Okay." I nod.

"You're gonna choose to be strong today just like you did yesterday, and the day before, and every day before that since the moment you walked into that clinic and realized you had someone else to live for."

I close my eyes, memories of when Derek took me to the walk-in clinic four years ago flashing through my mind. I had tried at that point—unsuccessfully—to get clean. But my boyfriend at the time, Darryl, always managed to drag me back. And like flycatcher's mud, my vices wrapped around my legs and sucked me down until I was covered in their thick, wet dirt, unable to pull myself out.

I was scared, desperate, and *high*. Living on the streets of Tennessee, hiding in plain sight, making sure that my family and friends could never find me.

But I remember waking up that morning, throwing up the bile and acid that lined my stomach. I assumed it was withdrawal. It's how I usually woke up—with the shakes setting in, desperate for the chemicals I had trained my body to need. So while it seemed a little aggressive, I did what I *always* did to take away the pain.

But two hours later, with half an eight ball of coke swimming through my veins, and a rock inhaled into my lungs, I still felt like death. So my friend Amy grabbed up all the spare change we had, and went with me to the store to get some medicine. And when we were there, I walked past the feminine aisle, and something made me stop, a sledgehammer knocking against my insides, threatening to smash everything to bits.

I knew it before I even took the test. Even with snow flowing through my veins, my intuition was rarely wrong.

Pregnant.

And a junkie. Just like my mom.

4

MASON

Glancing around the motel room, I sigh. After telling Lily that I was staying at the Motel Eight, I felt like a piece of shit for not *actually* staying there, so I checked out of the room just outside of town and checked into this shithole instead.

Lily's morning shift started two hours ago, and I want to give her a couple hours before I head in to see her. At this point, I know her waitressing schedule like the back of my hand. It never changes. She works Thursday through Tuesday, taking Wednesdays for herself.

Flicking on the TV while I get changed and ready, I turn it to the local news—not because I actually give a damn about what's going on in the world, but because the quiet is stifling. Silence allows the ghosts from my past to whisper in my ear, and the noise takes it all away.

Usually.

Grabbing my rings from the counter and slipping them on my fingers, I plop down on the stiff mattress, sighing again when I realize I'll never be able to get a decent night's sleep with a bed that's half the size of my body. But that's alright, I've slept in much worse places for longer.

The bed frame creaks under my weight as I lean forward to lace up my black boots, rolling a toothpick between my lips.

"In presidential news, there are a few surprising hopefuls putting their name into the ring."

The TV drones and I roll my eyes. Of course this is what they're talking about. Fucking politics. I've never understood why we have to start hearing about presidential candidates nineteen months before they actually *become* president. Who fucking cares?

Blowing out a deep breath, I push down the disgust that's crawling through my stomach.

This is why I never watch TV.

Before leaving to head to the diner, I grab my phone and check my email, seeing one from Don, asking how things are going. It's vague, because he knows better than anyone that we can't speak about anything work related on an unsecured email. Besides, I wouldn't know what to tell him anyway. No way in hell I'll let him know I've found the mark and am doing fuck all with the information, choosing to stick around and get to know her instead of collecting my cash and moving on.

Don is the one who taught me about this business, and I owe him... everything. He retired two years ago. Fell in love with a dime piece from Nashville, whisking her away to some small tropical island off the Caribbean, and hasn't been back since. But every once in a blue moon I'll get an email or a phone call. It's nice to know that he still cares, because whether I want to admit it or not, sometimes, I miss the hell out of him. This life is a lonely gig.

But I'm okay with solitude.

Grabbing my wallet and keys, I swing my legs over the seat of my bike, revving the engine and heading to the diner. As I ride, a new plan formulates in my mind over how to handle the Lily situation.

I can't believe I told her my name was Alex. Fucking ridiculous.

If I was a smart man, I would stay away. My line of work —my life in general—demands it.

Parking my bike, I glance up, *Dina's Diner* flickering in yellow against the faded lime green sign, my new plan slotting into place in my brain.

I'll watch Lily in plain view from now on. Just for a little bit, so I can make sure that giving up her location is what's best. Normally, I wouldn't give a damn. My loyalty only lies with the person who's paying me, but there's just something about this girl that I can't let go of. I need to make sure that calling her brother won't be detrimental to what she's got going on here.

And that's yet another glaring red flag blowing in the breeze. Don would tell me to get my shit together before things come back and bite me in the ass. I don't *do* personal relationships. I don't *feel* things for anyone. It's the only way to ensure everyone's safety. The last thing I'd want is to drag somebody into my murky past—get them tangled up in webs they have no business being in. The same webs I've tried to keep from being caught in for the past decade.

I don't even know this girl, but yet, here I am, my chest pulling tight as I walk through the doors and she comes into view. Her eyes narrow as she notices me slipping into the booth in the corner, pulling my paperback from my jacket and laying it next to me.

She walks up, a fresh pot of coffee in her fist, her dark hair contrasting vividly against the mustard yellow of her *Dina's Diner* polo shirt.

"Back again, I see." She props her hand on her hip, smacking the gum in her mouth.

I smirk. "Is that a problem?"

Her eyes trail down my body, lingering on my exposed arms, her gaze like a needle, reopening my scars until the ink bleeds. I shift, suddenly uncomfortable under her scrutiny.

"That depends… coffee?" She lifts the pot and I nod, flipping over the mug that's upside down on the table. She hums as she pours and I attempt to keep my eyes on the steam that's swirling from the liquid, instead of on her.

Finally, I tear my eyes away and glance back to her face. She fidgets and pastes on a grin. "You gonna eat today or just lurk in the corner reading that old paperback?" She nods toward my book on the table.

The Art of War. The first book I read after leaving home, and the only one that has stuck with me years after. "Maybe *you* should read it. It's a good book."

She shrugs. "I'm not much for reading."

"What *are* you much for?"

Her lips twitch and she bounces a bit on her toes. "Plenty of things."

My brow raises, and I grab a toothpick from my pocket, unwrapping it and rolling it between my lips. "Care to share with the class?"

She tilts her head, blowing a bubble with her gum, the faint scent of cinnamon wafting from her mouth and into my nostrils.

"Nah." She shakes her head. "I don't tell my life story to strangers."

I take a sip of my coffee, the heat scalding my tongue. "And we're still strangers?"

She frowns. "Yes, Alex. We are."

The name splits my chest and twists my heart, showing me just how right she is.

I nod, leaning in. "Well, what do I have to do to *not* be a stranger?"

Her eyes narrow. "Are you hitting on me?"

I grin, amusement swimming through my veins. "You're cute as hell, but no, I'm not hitting on you."

She purses her lips. "I don't need a friend."

"Everyone needs a friend."

"And you think that person is *you?*"

I shrug. "Why not?"

"Lily. Order's up. Let's go." The gruff voice cuts into the moment, and she glances behind her, cringing before twisting back to face me. "Gotta go. Let me know if you get hungry."

And with that, she bounces away, a lightness in her step and a grin on her face that hides the history of someone who ran from their family.

A history that I'm suddenly dying to know. And once my curiosity is sated, *then* I'll tell her brother and get the fuck out of Dodge.

5

LILY

I don't have many friends, unless you count Annabelle, a server who works with me at Dina's Diner. But we're more acquaintances than anything, and we honestly have nothing in common other than living in the same town, running away from everyone we know back home. Although her idea of running is thirty minutes outside of Phoenix where she's from, and mine is disappearing for good and hoping they think I'm dead.

Other than her, I'm all alone. And even though growing up I surrounded myself with people and parties, I've come to appreciate the solitude. Besides, working my fingers to the bone just to put food on the table doesn't leave a lot of room for things like going out and meeting people.

And I'm okay with that.

There's not much you can say to convince me that friends are worth it in the end, anyway. So, when Alex decides *he* wants to be my friend, I'm taken aback. And I'm not going to let it happen. There's no point. I don't need friends, and he's really nothing special, other than the fact he's the first man in years who doesn't make my skin crawl just by looking at me.

I'm not really sure what to do with that realization other

than acknowledge it, and let it go. But he's the first man that I've felt that way about *ever*. Even when I was dating Darryl, it wasn't because of his good looks or his charm.

I was groomed by him.

A naive fourteen-year-old girl who was desperate and stupid. And Darryl was a twenty-year-old drug dealer pedophile who knew he could drag me down and keep me in chains. My stomach rolls as I think back to how we met, and all of the years after. *All of the years before.*

I must wear my weakness like armor—my shield a magnet, drawing up evil that lurks within everyone who dares to get too close.

And it's not just men. My childhood best friend's greed and selfishness sprouted wings and took flight whenever I was around, too. I was just blind to it, fooled just like the rest of the town with her girl next door act.

But instead of being loyal to me, she *used* me to get to my brother. She pushed me out of the chambers of his heart, made him forget all the words he said to me growing up. Made him forget that he was my home. Until suddenly, he didn't see me at all.

He only saw *her*.

So fuck having friends. Been there. Done that. Bought the getaway ticket. I have zero interest in uncovering Alex's fatal traits.

It's a few hours later when I'm refilling the sugar caddies, getting ready to be off my shift for the night, that I hear it.

Annabelle's tinkling laughter coming from the corner booth.

My head snaps up, my chest pulling tight when I see her standing next to Alex with a hand on her hip and a beaming smile on her Maybelline-caked face.

Good. Maybe his attention will leave me, and end up on her, and I won't have to focus on how much he unsettles me.

He grins at her, his expansive arms stretching against the

back of the booth. My heartbeat picks up speed, my breath lodging in my throat as my eyes flick back and forth between them.

Her hand reaches out, her bright pink press-on nails wrapping around a laminated menu, her breasts practically grazing his face, when suddenly his eyes snap over to me.

I jerk, the sugar packets falling from my hand and onto the table. Heat rushes into my cheeks as I clear my throat and glance down, scrambling to pick up the pink and blue packets and place them in the caddie.

Ugh. Great. Quit looking, Lily.

But a few seconds later, I can't stop myself from glancing up again. Annabelle's hand has now latched onto his forearm as she leans across the table and points to something on the menu.

Oh, so now he's hungry.

Finishing up the rest of the table fills, I head over to where Annabelle is standing, knowing that I shouldn't interrupt. That I shouldn't care. But I do it anyway. I feel weirdly possessive over this stranger that I've shared nothing more than a few moments with.

But they were *my* moments, and my chest squeezes at the idea that maybe she'll get them too.

"Annabelle, I'm off for the night. Everyone's cashed out except for the guys at table three, but I'll just transfer them."

She turns to me, her auburn hair swinging in a high ponytail, a genuine smile gracing her face. "You don't want the tip?"

I shrug, feeling Alex's eyes burn holes into the side of my face. "I want to go home more."

She nods. "I get it. No problem."

"You never cashed *me* out," Alex's voice cuts in.

Annabelle glances at him. "Oh, I have zero problem taking you over."

His eyes flick to hers before coming back to meet mine.

"Well, that wouldn't be very fair. I was hers first." He smirks like he's teasing, and a nervous twinge spikes low in my belly.

I bite the inside of my cheek and smile big. "Oh, I don't mind."

His grin dims just a bit. "You sure?"

"You tipped me more than enough yesterday to last a lifetime."

It's not true. That money is already gone, sucked down into the hole I can never climb out from, but I need him to get the picture that whatever he's trying to accomplish with me—whatever it is he *thinks* will happen, won't.

The only reason someone comes to Raindale is so they can disappear. And he couldn't disappear if he tried, so I'm wary of why he's even here in the first place.

His brows draw in, a toothpick rolling back and forth over his lips, and my cheeks hurt from the strain of keeping a chipper face in place.

"Okay, Lily." Annabelle's eyes widen as she looks at me. "Have a good night."

I nod, relief loosening the knot that was forming in my stomach, and I turn around to do my check out and get home to what matters. I'm just grabbing my purse from the back office when the door busts open, and Annabelle comes rushing in, her cheeks flushed and a smile high on her lips.

"Oh my *God*, Lily, can you believe someone that fine is here?"

I laugh, rolling my apron strings up and tucking it away in my purse. "He's different, that's for sure."

"He's a work of art. Fucking gorgeous." She swoons. "I wonder if he lives in Phoenix. That's not too far, I could totally convince him to let me come down for the weekend."

I shrug, ignoring the pinch in my chest. "Says he's staying at the Motel Eight here in town."

"Oh, *really*? That's even better." She pauses. "Hey,

speaking of Phoenix, me and some of my hometown girls are going out this weekend. You should come."

I cringe. "Uhh… no thanks, I don't have anyone to watch Chase."

She pouts. "Can't your neighbor do it? Just one night, Lily. You're this big ball of energy, but you never do anything fun."

I laugh, my brow rising. "You ever live with a three-year-old?"

Her nose scrunches as she shakes her head.

"Exactly. Try that first, and then come back and tell me my energy doesn't have an outlet."

"Well, whatever. I'm gonna keep pushing until you give in."

"Good luck." I walk out the door, waving at her behind my back.

As I head home, a tendril of sadness weaves its way around my heart, because Annabelle isn't wrong. I don't go out at all anymore. Don't have any money, or any time to do it. Shots of my old life flash before my eyes, back when I used to be the life of the party. Before things got so bad I couldn't fake it.

Sometimes I miss that life.

But then I shake my head, reminding myself of how far I've come, and I go home and pick up Chase, cuddling him on the couch while we watch an old Disney movie and fall asleep.

This is all I need.

Right here.

Friends are overrated.

6
MASON

I watch Lily leave just as a plate filled with steak fries and a turkey club is plopped down in front of me. I wasn't planning on eating here, but this new waitress, Annabelle, is persistent and I can't survive solely on black coffee and the craving for nicotine running through my veins.

The toothpicks are my half-assed attempt to curb the habit, but I'll be honest, they don't really do the trick. I've always been one to give into my vices. One of which is being offered to me on a very obvious silver platter in the form of a curvy, redheaded girl who I've seen in passing but never paid any mind to until this moment.

I've always had a thing for redheads.

"So, what ya in town for?" Annabelle asks, leaning her hip against the side of the opposite booth.

"Work," I grunt, diving into my sandwich and taking a bite.

Her face scrunches up and her head tilts. "What kinda work is here in Raindale?"

I arch a brow. "The *work* kind."

"Oh. Okay then." Her mouth thins. "Well…" She leans in, her polo stretched tight across her chest, and my eyes drop, my dick twitching at the sight. "If you need some company while you're here, you know where to find me."

Her voice is low and breathy, and blood rushes into my cock, hardening it further. *Fuck, I need to get laid.*

Setting down my sandwich, I wipe my hands on a napkin as my eyes take her in, trailing up her curves and considering her offer.

I smirk. "I'll think about it."

The bell above the front door chimes letting us know that customers are walking in. She clears her throat and straightens, running a hand over her ponytail.

She's occupied for the next few minutes, and after I finish my food, she comes back around to set down my bill.

She leans in much farther than necessary, her tits grazing against my forearm. "Don't think too hard, handsome. Be a shame to miss out on a golden opportunity."

I grace her with a wink and drop some cash on the table.

When I'm back at the motel, I fire up my laptop, pulling up the file I keep on Lily. Bypassing the photos I've taken— her walking with her son, and working at the diner—I drop down to the bottom of my notes and type in the new information.

My phone vibrates across the desk and I pick it up without looking. "Yeah," I bark.

"What's up, kid?"

A grin twitches at my lips. "Don, you big bastard."

"Only big where it counts." Amusement lines his voice.

I chuckle. "How's retired life?"

"Boring as shit." He sighs. "But the lady likes it, and if she's happy then I'm happy."

Rolling my eyes, I lean back in the chair. "Sounds *thrilling.*"

He laughs. "You're still young, Mase. You'll learn. How are things there?"

My eyes creep over the black-and-white photos of a

younger Lily. Ones that her brother sent me. "Things are just fine."

"Everything going okay?"

My stomach tightens. "Everything's *fine*."

"Mmhm." He grunts. "You find what you were looking for?"

My jaw clenches. "Yep."

"You on your way home?"

My chest pinches. "Nope."

There's silence on the line for long, stretched moments. "What do you mean, 'nope?'"

"I *mean* there are some loose ends for me to tie up still. Some more information."

"Ah, I see. He paying extra for that?"

My heart falters and for the first time, I consider lying to Don. But *why*? He's retired. I can run things however the hell I want.

I clear my throat. "No. This is just to make sure he deserves to know where she is in the first place."

Don sighs. "Kid, that's not your problem."

"Well, I'm *making* it my problem," I snap back.

"Jesus. Fine." He chuckles. "What is it you need to know that you haven't figured out?"

Defensiveness swirls in my gut. "If I knew then I wouldn't still be here trying to find out."

He chuckles again and irritation snaps at my back. Most likely because he's hitting me with valid questions that I have no answer for and we both know it. There's no *real* reason for me to stay. There are a million reasons why I should leave. I'm being a fucking moron.

I groan, lifting my head to the ceiling. "I met her."

"Yeah, and..."

"No." I pinch the bridge of my nose. "Like... I fucking *met* her, Don. She knows who I am. She knows my face. Her fucking kid saw me."

"What?" His voice is low and surprised. "How the hell did that happen, Mason?"

My chest pulls. "I don't know it just... did."

"You need to leave." His voice deepens, a serious note taking over the timbre. "What the hell are you doing?"

I run my fingers through my hair, tugging on the strands. "Yeah, I don't know."

"Is there something you're not telling me?"

I sit up straighter. "No, why would you think that?"

"Because this isn't like you, Mason. You *always* know. You *always* have a plan of action. You never let emotions get in the way. Hell, I'm surprised you have any at all, to be honest. Your lack of them is what makes you so damn good at what you do."

My teeth grind. There's a difference between not having emotions and not showing them, but I don't need to tell him that.

"You've always been thorough," he continues. "But how much more can you even find out about her? And now she knows who you are? That's a recipe for disaster and you know it." He hesitates. "How long has it been since you've been this close to the West Coast?"

My body stiffens, squeezing the breath from my lungs. "Since I met you."

He hums. "You watched the news lately?"

My eyes flick to the TV. "Not if I can help it."

"Hmm."

A tingle of warning skates down my skin. "Why, should I?"

He's quiet, and I can picture his fingers rubbing across his bushy brows, trying to figure out how to talk some sense into me. "I think you should get out of that town and go back home."

"You're right," I sigh.

"Always am. You need to be smart here, Mason. Don't

fuck around. Nothing good will come from talking to this girl, okay? What are you gonna do, tell her you've been hired to spy on her?" He huffs out a laugh, and my stomach sinks. *What the fuck am I even doing?*

"Listen, I gotta go. But be smart. And safe."

I grumble a response.

"Talk to you later, Mase."

He hangs up and I blow out a breath, my eyes still locked on the grainy photos of Lily. Don's right. I don't have any reason to stay here, other than the flimsy excuses I've made. And for what—to justify my curiosity?

But she *knows* me now. And that's not a good thing, no matter how I try to spin it. That's just me being shitty at my job.

I'll call Chase in the morning and then I'll leave.

Reaching in my pocket, I pull out my receipt from the diner, my thumb brushing over the phone number written hastily in ink. *Annabelle.*

If I'm leaving anyway, I might as well have some fun.

7

LILY

I don't know how Annabelle talked me into coming out. All I know is that it's Friday night, and instead of being home cuddled up with my baby boy, I'm in downtown Phoenix, cuddled up to strangers.

I'm uncomfortable.

There's a reason why I don't go out anymore. I've found that it's much easier to avoid temptation if I don't place myself in front of it. But it's been almost four years, and I convince myself that one night out won't hurt. Even though I told Alex I didn't need them, the truth is that I'm desperate for some friends, no matter how much I try to fool myself into believing I'm not. And Annabelle is as good as it gets in this new life of mine.

"Have I told you how *fantastic* you look?" she asks from across the high-top table, her eyes trailing my body. A grin creeps on my face, not because she's looking, but because it's been so long since I've had anywhere to dress up for, and I had forgotten how much I enjoyed it.

I remember being at the last foster home—before my parents, Sam and Anna, adopted us—stealing Fashion Weeklys off the coffee table and hiding them under my bed.

Whenever I needed an escape, I'd drag those magazines out, staring at the fabrics and dreaming of a different life. One where I could be the name gracing the labels, so important and powerful that nobody could ever take advantage of me again.

But amazing things belong to amazing people. And I've never fit that mold.

Shaking out of my reverie, I glance around, taking in the bar. I won't lie and say it doesn't feel good to get out of the house for something other than work. As much as I miss Chase, I know he's in good hands with Susan, and it's been years since I've had a night out. My soul aches for the socialization.

I *used* to be the life of the party, getting high off the buzz from the crowds and snorting lines in the bathrooms. Back then, I had to sneak away, because no one knew what I was doing.

Of course they didn't.

Even when I've tried so hard to be seen, I've always been invisible.

But then Darryl came along, and he showed me a way to feel better. A way to make my festering insides match my sparkly outside.

And I was so *tired* of faking it.

Neither of my best friends, Alina May or Rebecca Jean, would have gotten it. The most they did was steal sips of liquor from Becca's mom's hidden cabinet. And Chase definitely wouldn't have. He's always been against drugs, ever since we were thrown into the foster system and left to rot.

And rot I did. A pretty shell with a hollow center, mold growing from the inside out.

But unlike my brother, instead of cringing away from it, I leaned into it. After all, it must have been something special to make our mom choose it over us, and I was desperate for something to numb the memories.

Chase's biggest demon was living with our mother.

Mine was after she left.

"What are you thinking about so hard over there?" Annabelle's friend, Natalie, asks.

I shake my head, pushing the thoughts down deep and pulling up the husk of happiness that I've worn my whole life.

"Nothing." I smile, shaking my head. "It's just been a while since I've been out."

Annabelle squeals as she looks toward the front door, her face breaking into a beaming smile. "He made it!"

Her eyes sparkle with excitement, a blush skimming over her cheekbones. I'm about to open my mouth and ask *who* made it, but heat trickles down my back, making the words stick in my throat. There's only ever been one person that makes the air shift just by *being* in it, and I haven't seen him in three days.

I assumed he was gone.

Annabelle's grin widens as he approaches the table, and she stands up, practically jumping in the air to throw herself around Alex's body. "You're here!"

The hairs on my arms stand straight, my stomach roiling with an unfamiliar sensation. He's loosely wrapped around Annabelle like decoration—a garland of color and art swirling over his veiny hands, disappearing under the sleeves of his long-sleeved Henley. But his dark gaze is on me.

My chest pulls, but I shake it off, smirking. "Well, hi there, *friend*."

He releases Annabelle, sitting down, his long legs taking up all of the empty space left under the table. "Hey, little bird."

My nose scrunches. "*Little bird?*"

He doesn't respond, only grins.

"Haven't seen you in a while," I continue. "I thought you were gone."

LILY   49

His eyes spark. "Is that how you see me? As someone who would leave without saying goodbye?"

My stomach flips, my heart cinching tight. "I don't know *what* you seem like. We're strangers, remember?"

He tsks, a smirk pulling up the left side of his face. "You just called us friends. You can't take that back."

My brow quirks. "Says who?"

"So, you two *clearly* know each other," Natalie interrupts. "I'm Natalie, by the way."

He gives her a chin nod, and Annabelle forces a laugh. My eyes volley between them as her hand presses against his forearm. "He *was* planning to leave, but I convinced him to stick around a while."

I ignore the sudden pinch in my chest and force a laugh. "You've always been a good salesman."

Alex clears his throat and shifts, his calf brushing mine just slightly under the table. Electricity races up my leg.

I sip from my water. "It's a good thing you started showing up to our diner then, huh, Alex?"

"It *definitely* is." Annabelle's fingers tighten on his arm as she looks up at him adoringly. "Thanks for coming out, I didn't know if you would."

He shrugs. "Had some business in Phoenix this weekend, anyway."

My eyebrows draw in as I wonder what he does for a living. As I wonder, for the thousandth time since he walked into my restaurant and sat down in my booth, why he's here.

Annabelle leans in, whispering something in his ear that makes him grin, and I force my eyes away, not sure why the image of them together makes nausea churn in my gut.

Natalie smirks as she watches me from across the table. "Wanna go grab some drinks at the bar?"

My heart pounds faster against my ribs, and my hands grow clammy. "Oh, I don't drink."

Her smile falters. "What? Like... not at all?"

Gulping down air, I suck my teeth. "Not at all."

And *this* is the other reason I don't ever go out. Because I don't particularly like being put into situations like this, where people expect me to cave in to societal norms. To live and breathe the pastime that gives them a simple night of fun, yet leaves me teetering on the edge of a crumbling cliff.

"Oh well that's… boring." She frowns.

The smile on my face grows as I push down the ache that's splitting my chest. *I shouldn't have come tonight.*

"Oh, I don't know." I sigh, running a hand through my hair and sitting up straighter. "I like to think that I'm a naturally fun person."

She makes a face, but doesn't try to keep the conversation going, and a sour feeling swirls in my stomach. This is awkward. I haven't *people'd* in a long time, and where I used to be a natural, now it just feels… forced.

Maybe I'm just out of practice.

"You don't drink?" Annabelle asks.

I shake my head. "Nope, not for years."

"How come?" She tilts her head.

My fingers scratch at my wrist.

"Who cares?" Alex cuts in. "I don't drink either."

My breath whooshes out, and Annabelle's head snaps to him. "What?"

His brow rises. "Is that a problem?"

"N-no," she stutters. "I just assumed, I guess. Most people do, and—"

"So because *most* do that means *everyone* should?" he presses.

A warmth unfurls through my chest, and I soak him in greedily while his gaze is stuck on her.

He definitely looks like a drinker, but I learned a long time ago that first impressions never tell the true story. Curiosity over what *his* story is wraps around my edges.

Annabelle shakes her head. "No, I—"

"Why the hell would you two come to a bar on a Friday night if neither of you drink?" Natalie cuts in.

"Because we were invited," I say. "And like I said... I'm the life of the party. Who *wouldn't* want me here?" I wink, trying to avoid the heat of Alex's stare, but my eyes are drawn back to him anyway.

He didn't have to speak up when he did, and maybe it's a coincidence, but I can't help feeling like he was trying to make things more comfortable for me. Pinpricks of energy lance off my skin and race down my spine as I hold his gaze. It's uncomfortable, and I want to look away but... I can't.

Turns out, I don't need to.

Because he does.

And then his big hand reaches out, the lights bouncing off his jewelry as he grips Annabelle's upper thigh. Just like that, all the electricity is zapped from my body, and I'm left feeling cold, and wanting to go home.

8

MASON

Swear to God I was planning to leave town. I took everything Don said to heart, reminding myself of all the reasons why staying was a colossal waste of time. A *stupid* decision. I got as far as picking up the phone and calling Chase, ready to let him know everything.

I found her. Boom. Done. That's it. Time to collect my money and leave, the way I do with every other job.

But Chase didn't answer, and by the time his voicemail beeped, my attention was stuck on the TV, bile burning the back of my throat while flashes of a previous life played on the screen. A life that I would rather die than live again. And that made Lily and her kid run through my brain, wondering if she feels the same.

So I stayed. Because for some reason, I *can't* just hand her over without knowing why she ran.

A hand trails up my thigh, and I smirk when Annabelle's fingers rub against my cock under the table. She's brazen, and honestly, a little fucking annoying, but in the grand scheme of things she's harmless. She knows not to expect anything other than a free ride on my dick.

Besides, being close to Annabelle means being close to Lily without her questioning why.

I lean in, brushing my lips against Annabelle's ear. "Watch those hands."

She blushes, but her hand drops.

I'm into a lot of shit, but voyeurism is not my kink. And even if it was, having a hookup jerk me off while the girl I'm stalking sits across the table isn't something that appeals to me.

But is it really stalking if you're getting paid for it?

My gaze snags on Lily's. Her head is tilted as she stares, curiosity brimming through her eyes, but I can tell that she's still cautious. She *should* be wary of me. I'm not the good guy in this scenario.

I haven't been the good guy for a long time.

My chest pulls tight and I reach in my pocket for a tooth-pick, unwrapping the plastic and rolling it between my lips.

Damn nicotine cravings.

I wasn't sure about coming tonight, Phoenix is about thirty minutes out from Raindale, but when Annabelle mentioned she had convinced Lily to go... the rest is history.

Lily sips from her water, her thick silver bracelets clacking together with the movement. If I were a chick I'd say they were fashionable, but I know why she's really wearing them.

Sometimes we cover our skin to hide the sins of our past.

She's practically vibrating in her chair, dark hair bouncing off her shoulders, an anxious energy seeping from her pores. I find myself wondering if she's always been this energetic, or if it's a recent development. A bird flapping around her self-imposed cage, wanting to spread her wings and soar, but knowing she can't.

My eyes glide back down to her bracelets. To the tattoos covering her arms.

Or maybe she already did.

"Well this is way more boring than I thought it would be,"

Annabelle's friend, Natalie, complains. "I thought we'd be at a club, not this lame-ass bar."

Annabelle shrugs, pushing her auburn hair off her shoulder. "I don't like clubs."

"You used to," Natalie retorts.

"Yeah, when I was nineteen and too young to even be in them." Annabelle scoffs. "I'm too old for that shit."

"I've never liked clubs either," Lily pipes in, smiling at Annabelle.

I'm not sure what to make of their relationship. They seem friendly enough, but this is the first time I've seen them interact in the two months I've been here. Honestly, I've never seen Lily spend time with anyone other than her kid or the patrons in the diner.

Natalie huffs a laugh. "That's not surprising, Miss 'I don't drink.'"

Lily's head cocks. "And there's a problem with that?"

Annabelle chuckles, but it comes out pinched. "Come on, guys."

Natalie takes a drink from her martini. "I mean... don't you ever want to have some *fun*?"

Lily laughs, the sound hollow as it rings through the air. "I've had enough fun to last me a lifetime."

"Yeah, I bet." Natalie rolls her eyes.

My stomach sours. "Annabelle, are *all* your friends gigantic cunts?"

Natalie's head whips toward me. "*Excuse* me?"

"You're a bitch." I shrug. "I'm just trying to figure out if it's because you feel threatened by her." I nod my head toward Lily. "Or if it's just woven into your personality." I rest my elbows on the table. "Let me clue you into something. The only reason we aren't having any *fun* is because you're here."

Natalie's jaw drops and she looks to Annabelle. "*This* is the company you're keeping these days, Belle?"

Annabelle glances at Lily, then me, and then back to Natalie. "They're my friends," she says slowly.

Natalie's lips thin. "*Jesus*, when did you turn into such a drag?" She slams the rest of her drink before standing and grabbing her purse.

Annabelle nods, exhaling a slow breath. "Before you go… it's only fair you know the answer to his question, in case it ever gets brought up again. You are definitely *always* a bitch."

Natalie's eyes turn into slits. "You're pathetic. *Don't* call me again."

She leaves and for a few moments the table is silent. Then, Lily drops her head in her hands, shoulders shaking, a bubbly sound coasting through the air and wrapping around my insides. She looks up, tears streaming down her face from how hard she's *laughing*.

A grin breaks across my face, and I grab the toothpick from my mouth, pointing it at her. "You always cause this kind of trouble?"

"Me?" She points to her chest, speaking through her giggles. "What did *I* do? You're the one who… who called her a—a cunt."

Annabelle chuckles, reaching over and grasping Lily's hand across the table. "I'm sorry she was such a bitch to you." She glances toward the door. "She used to be alright. I don't know what happened to make her so bitter."

Lily sighs, wiping her face with the back of her hands, the laughter dying down. "It's okay. I'm sure it had more to do with her than me. There's bitterness in all of us."

My head tilts, curiosity a blazing inferno rising inside me.

"Well… tonight was a bust, huh? Sorry we drove all the way down here." Annabelle sighs. "We can go back to my place and watch a movie or something if you guys want?"

"Sounds good to me," I say.

Lily's gaze narrows. "I thought you said you had business in Phoenix."

I shrug. "And?"

"And you're just gonna hop on that bike and follow us back to Raindale when you're already down here?"

I spin my ring around my finger. "Are you saying you don't want my company, little bird?"

Her lips twitch. "That's exactly what I'm saying."

"Well... tough shit." I shrug, biting back a grin. "Maybe I want yours."

Her smirk softens into a small smile.

The bill shows up and I grab it before anyone else can, paying for the two Cosmos Annabelle and her friend drank.

It's not until I'm on my bike, the vibration of the engine rumbling underneath me, that I question what the hell I'm doing. There's something foreign thrumming through my veins. A craving to spend more time with Lily, unwrap her layers one by one until I can figure out what the hell it is about her that makes her feel so goddamn different.

But when I get to Annabelle's she isn't there.

And later that night when I'm back at the motel, I wonder why I pictured hazel eyes staring up at me instead of Annabelle's browns.

9

LILY

L ast night in Phoenix wasn't what I was expecting, but it wasn't a complete bust either. I've found a camaraderie in Annabelle that up until this point, I haven't allowed myself to have. We've worked together for two years, and she's tried consistently to become my friend, but I've pushed her to the side.

Being alone is safer. Smarter.

It still is, that hasn't changed.

I doubt I'll ever be the type of girl who goes out for brunches and sips on fizzy drinks, but after last night, there's a crack of light filtering through my dark and heavy.

"So, how are things with your kid? Chase, right?" Annabelle asks while we roll up silverware.

"He's doing fine." I clear my throat. "Good. I'm just... he's almost four now, and he needs to be starting preschool, but I don't really know where to put him or how I'm gonna pay for it."

She sucks on her teeth. "There's that KinderCare off Route 60 you could take him to. Don't they do preschool?"

They do, but the thought of having him around strangers all day and having to acclimate to a new place—having *me* acclimate to new people to trust him with—is a bitter pill I'm not sure how to swallow. Instead, it just sits on the back of my tongue, slowly dissolving like chalk.

I've been putting aside every spare penny I can to enroll him in a preschool. The options around here are limited, but I know he needs socialization with someone other than my fifty-year-old neighbor. I need to give him some other kids to play with and let him spread his wings.

Nerves tumble through my stomach at the thought.

"Yeah, maybe." I sigh.

The deep growl of an engine distracts me, and my heart skips when I see Alex's Harley pull into the lot, his leather jacket framing the tattoos that run up his neck.

"Your man's here." I nod toward him.

Annabelle smirks, placing a silverware roll-up in the wire basket. "Don't let him hear you say that. He'll think I'm going around trying to 'claim him.'"

Her words are soaking in familiarity when she speaks about him, and for some reason, it makes my chest burn. "Are you two *not* hooking up?"

Her grin widens. "I didn't say that."

"Well…"

She shrugs. "Well, he's just… not here for a relationship, you know? Honestly, I can't really see him in a relationship at *all*."

"No?"

Her eyes flick to him as she bites her lip and shakes her head. "Nah, he isn't really the *feelings* type of guy."

"So you guys are just what? Friends with benefits?"

"We're just…" She twists around when the bell dings over the front door. Alex ducks to walk through the entry, a book in his hand, his eyes scanning the restaurant before going to sit in the corner booth.

"He know you're about to leave for the day?" I ask.

She sighs. "Probably just waiting on me to finish. I'll be back."

"Have fun." I wave her off, ignoring the way my insides twist as she walks over to him.

He strips off his leather and lays it in the booth next to him, setting his book on the table. He smirks as Annabelle approaches, but when she speaks he shakes his head. Her posture droops the tiniest bit as she turns and walks back over.

"Hey, girl. I'm gonna head out, you good here?"

I glance around at the empty booths. "Yep. Does he need food?"

She presses her lips together in a close-lipped smile. "Guess so. He isn't here for me, that's for sure."

I scrunch up my nose.

"It's fine." She waves her hand in the air. "Like I said, it's not like we're in a relationship. Just a good time. It's for the best anyway to keep it casual. He doesn't even live here."

I glance back at him, my heart jumping when our eyes meet. "Where *does* he live?"

"I've got no idea."

My eyes swing to hers. "You guys don't talk?"

She smirks. "He isn't really the *talking* type."

My chest tightens, and I force a grin, even though I disagree. When he's around me, he never shuts the hell up.

She smiles. "Enjoy your shift. Hope you make a million dollars. Johnny's a bitch today, so try not to piss him off."

Nodding, I watch as she ducks down behind the host podium and grabs her purse before walking out the front door. My eyes slide back to the corner booth. Sighing, I stand, brushing off my apron and making my way toward his table, an annoying buzz simmering deep in my gut.

"Back again?" I ask.

He smirks, running his hand through his wind-tousled hair. "Did you miss me?"

"Like a hole in the head."

He hums as he stares, the silence wrapping around me until I grow heated under his gaze.

My fingers scratch at the inside of my wrist. "You hungry?"

He nods. "You definitely missed me."

My stomach flips. "I don't even *know* you. Are you hungry or not?"

"Not yet. But I have some stuff to do so I'll probably want something in a bit."

My brow raises. "Stuff?"

"Yeah… work stuff." He shifts in the booth.

I peer down at his book. "And what is it you do for work again?"

"I'm an independent contractor."

"Hmm…" I rest my hip against the side of the booth. "And what do you 'contract?'"

"Whatever I'm needed for."

I roll my eyes. "That's extremely vague."

He shrugs. "NDAs."

A shiver skates its way up my spine and I step back, suddenly on edge around him. His avoidance of actually answering any questions throws me off-kilter, like there are secrets about him that I'm not sure I want to unravel.

"Lily?" Johnny's voice yells from the back.

I look behind me before glancing at Alex again. "Okay, well let me know if you need anything, *friend*."

He jerks his chin and then his attention is gone, his eyes locked on the pages of his paperback.

Saturday afternoons are our busiest times, lots of travelers stopping through, grabbing a bite on their way to somewhere bigger and better. So it isn't until I have a second to breathe—when my shift is winding down—that I acknowledge Alex is *still* here, sitting in that same booth, garnering stares from everyone who sees him.

The bell above the door chimes, and I turn toward the noise, wondering who would be here at nine p.m. when we're about to close. Susan comes whirling in, a wild look in her eye. My heart stops, free-falling to the floor when I see a sleepy Chase in her arms, gripping his stuffed Spider-Man tight. I drop the wet rag from my hand and rush over.

"Susan, what's wrong?"

"Honey, I'm… I'm so sorry, but my sister's in the hospital in Phoenix. Some idiot slammed into her, and I'm the closest family she's got. I tried to call first but Johnny said you were busy, so I'm just here to drop off Chase."

I nod, tension cinching my gut. "Okay, of course. No problem, thanks for bringing him by. I'm so sorry about your sister."

She nods, tears lining her eyes as she transfers Chase to my arms and rushes out the door. Chase mumbles, his sleepy eyes opening as he peers up at me. "Mommy?"

I brush my hand across his forehead. "Yeah, baby. I'm here. You're gonna have to hang out at Mommy's work for a while okay?"

His bottom lip turns down. "Why?"

"Because Susan had to leave, and you can't be alone."

"Why?"

"Because I said so." I boop his nose.

Chase's nose crinkles and I glance around, wondering where I can place him while I finish up for the night. My chest pulls tight as my gaze locks on Alex.

His head is angled down, and he seems completely oblivious to what's going on around him. The thought of putting Chase with him makes me uncomfortable, but not as uncomfortable as leaving him alone.

Time to swallow some pride.

Chase fidgets, his body wiggling against me until I set him on the ground, grabbing his hand instead as I walk us toward the back booth.

Alex's head snaps up as we approach, his eyes bouncing between us.

"Hi," I say.

He runs a hand through his hair, the fluorescent lights glinting off his jewelry.

I sigh. "Can he sit with you?"

Alex's jaw tightens, and for just a moment, I think he's going to say no, but then his eyes leave mine and land on Chase's, and a blinding smile lights up his face. One that catches me off guard and slugs me in the chest.

"Of course," he says. "I'm lonely over here being ignored by you, anyway."

"I'm not *ignoring* you." I scoff. "I'm working."

I crouch down in front of Chase. "You're gonna sit with Mommy's friend while I finish up, okay? Do you remember asking about him?"

Chase's eyes trail to Alex and he nods.

"Remember how brave you said you were?"

His fingers tighten on mine as his chest puffs out. "Yeah."

"That's right. You're the bravest boy I've ever known."

"I know." He beams at me before scrambling into the booth, resting his Spider-Man stuffy on the table and staring at Alex.

"Hi," he says.

Alex smirks. "Hi back."

"I'm Chase. I'm thwee and you got cwayon on your skin just like Mommy."

My chest warms, and I bite back my grin.

Alex glances down at his tattoos and bursts into laughter. "I'm Ma—" He clears his throat. "Uh… Alex. I'm twenty-nine. And you're right, I do. You wanna see?" He holds out his arms.

Chase's eyes widen as he nods, leaning over the table. My heart pounds so hard I think it might explode, guilt pumping through my bloodstream. This is one of the first major interactions Chase has ever had with a man. I've kept him from all the strong male influences that could have been in his life. But there's a good reason for it. And I'd do it a thousand times over if it meant saving him from the one man who I hope never knows he exists.

10

MASON

"What's dat one?" A sticky finger presses on the inside of my forearm. We've been at this for the past hour, Lily's kid pointing out my art and asking about each individual one.

He's a cool kid. Polite, listens, and I can understand about sixty percent of what comes out of his mouth.

My eyes widen. "That one?" I blow out an exaggerated breath, my cheeks puffing from the motion. "That's from when I met my first dragon."

He sucks in a breath. "A *dwagon?*"

I nod slowly. "Yeah, dude. A big one. A mama. I was traveling off the coast of Spain, and went cliff diving."

His nose scrunches. "What's dat?"

I cock my head. "Cliff diving? It's where you stand on the edge of a tall rock and jump off."

His eyes widen.

"Anyway, after I dove into the crystal waters below, I saw an opening."

"You *did?*"

I nod. "Mmhm. A secret one…" Movement from my peripheral catches my eye and I glance over to where Lily is leaning against the booth across from us. There's a small smile on her face as she pushes her purse up her arm and waits patiently for me to finish my story.

"Naturally, I had to go explore," I say, leaning back against the booth and stretching out my arm. "And guess what it was?"

"What was it?" Chase whispers, staring down at the dragon breathing fire that decorates my arm.

I lean in. "A *cave*."

He sucks in a breath.

"That's right. And there was a beautiful dragon inside. Gorgeous."

"Dwagons ugly, though."

I shake my head, tsking. "Noooo, who told you that? Dragons are beautiful." My eyes jump back to Lily's. "Strong. Independent. *Fierce*. Especially this one. She was a mama dragon, and there's something special about mamas."

"Like mine?" Chase asks.

Lily grins, a glossy sheen coasting across her eyes.

I nod again. "*Exactly* like yours."

Chase's finger trails up my arm and stops on a different one, pressing down. "Thwee. One. One." My eyes drop, but I already know what tattoo he's reading before I look. A weight drops in my gut, pain lancing through my esophagus and wrapping around my throat. He asks something else, but I can't focus enough to decipher his toddler talk.

"What?" I rasp.

I see Lily walk closer from my peripheral, scooching into the booth on the opposite side. "He's asking what the numbers mean."

My heart stutters. "They don't…" I clear my throat. "They don't mean anything."

Her mouth opens and closes, her eyes searing through the ink on my arm. But she nods and focuses her attention on her kid.

Chase.

It's no coincidence she named him after her brother, which makes me wonder why the hell I'm still fucking around here instead of just reuniting them. But I *need* to know why she left and hasn't gone back.

"You ready to go, baby?"

I smirk. "Well, we went pretty quick from strangers to pet names, but I'm ready whenever you are."

She frowns, but there's a twitch at the corner of her lips. "I was speaking to my son, dummy."

My grin grows. "Whatever you say, little bird."

"Speaking of pet names... why do you call me that?"

I shrug. "Why not?"

A giant sigh coming from next to me interrupts our conversation, and both of us turn our attention to Chase, who is yawning and rubbing little fists in his eyes.

"Okay, sleepyhead," Lily says. "It is *way* past your bedtime. Let's get you home."

"I'm too sweepy to walk."

She stands up, leaning down and gathering him in her arms. "I'll carry you."

My brows shoot to my hairline. "You're gonna carry him all the way to your place? That's like half a mile."

"So?" She cocks her head. "How do you know where I live anyway?"

Shit. "Just a guess. There're only so many square blocks in this town."

"That's true." Her eyes are calculating. "Why did you say you're here again?"

"I—"

Another yawn interrupts me and she runs her hand over Chase's back. "Never mind." She turns to walk away, but then turns back. "You have to come with me you know. We're closed."

"Oh, shit—*shoot*—my bad." I jump up from the booth and follow her out.

She stops on the sidewalk, glancing at me and pursing her lips. "I guess I'll see ya when I see ya."

"Don't miss me bad while I'm gone." I grin.

She rolls her eyes and starts to walk down the street.

I head to my bike, but turn around at the last second, something tugging at my insides. "Hey, wait," I huff out as I jog to catch up to her.

Damn, she's a fast walker.

She spins around, Chase already asleep on her shoulder.

"Do you have a phone?"

She shakes her head, her jaw tightening.

"Okay, well… hold on. Just… wait a minute." Rushing back to my bike, I dig in the side satchel, finding a spare piece of paper from my notebook and a pen, scribbling down my number and then walking it back to her and pressing it into her hand. "Here's my number."

She glances down at the crumpled paper. "And what do you think I need that for?"

I shrug. "Just in case."

"In case of what?"

I shrug. "Anything."

She nods and then leaves, and I stand at the corner of the diner watching until she turns the corner and disappears from my view. A strange sensation fills me up once she's gone.

Something I've only felt once before.

A thick, tumultuous wave of protection crashing through my insides.

There's just… something about her that won't let me treat her like everyone else. And now that I've met her kid, well…

Turning around, I slide onto my bike, the roar of the engine loud against the still of the air, calming my senses and letting me sink into familiarity—which is what I need right now, because the way Lily and her son make me feel are anything *but*. They bring up emotions I'd thought I had buried when I left who I used to be and everyone in it.

I wait a few more minutes before leaving the lot, wanting to be able to drive by Lily's apartment and make sure they got home safe, without her seeing me. Once I see the light flicker on through her apartment window, I head back to the motel, going straight to my room and pulling up my computer to open her file.

And then I jot down everything that happened tonight.

I still have a job to do, after all.

11

LILY

The next morning I call Annabelle to cover my shift.

I know Johnny will be pissed, but I don't have a choice. Susan still isn't back in town, her sister is in rough shape from the accident, so she's staying in Phoenix for the week. And while I understand, I don't really know what to do. I've never had a backup plan in place for Chase.

It makes the mom guilt hit hard, flooding through me and choking my chest, making me think of all the ways I should be doing things differently. Making me second-guess every choice I've made as a mother.

I don't know what the hell I'm doing.

Johnny will most definitely fire me if I don't show up for the next week, but there's no one else around here I trust. And no one that I could afford even if I did.

There's a loud knock on my front door, and I glance back to where Chase is sleeping for his nap, hoping that the noise doesn't wake him up.

Who could that be?

The only people who know where I live are Annabelle and Johnny, no one else in this town even cares to ask my name. Swinging the door open, my breath whooshes out of my chest.

Alex stands there, towering in the entryway, his arm leaning against the top edge of the frame.

"Wha—" I start to say.

His finger jumps down and presses into my lips. "Sssh. Don't ask questions you don't want the answer to."

My brows scrunch. "But I *do* want the answer."

He shakes his head. "You really don't."

Brushing by me, he walks inside, stopping in the middle of the living room and glancing around. "I'm here to help."

"Help *what?*"

"You, obviously." He spins, his hands on his hips. "I don't want to brag, but I think your son might be a little in love with me, and because I can't help the charm that oozes from my pores, I guess I'll have to stick around and keep entertaining him."

I roll my eyes, my stomach clenching tight. Alex walks over to the couch and sits down.

"No, please, make yourself at home," I snark.

He smiles. "Do you or do you not need someone to help take care of Chase?"

My brows furrow. "How do you—?" I shake my head. "Well, I *do* but not you."

He frowns. "Why *not* me?"

My muscles tighten. "Um, because I don't know you? Because it's super fucking weird that you're just showing up *everywhere* I am for the past few weeks, and now suddenly you want to just watch my child? Because you're a man who I can't trust?"

Alex's face turns down more with every word, and he sighs, tugging the toothpick out of his mouth. "Annabelle told me where you lived when she was leaving my room... to cover *your* shift. I just thought you could use the help."

My stomach curdles knowing that Annabelle gave up my address so easily, and a flash of them together, having pillow talk about my issues makes my insides pull.

"Oh." My shoulders slump.

The corner of his mouth lifts. "Yeah, *oh*."

My fingers scratch the inside of my wrist as I walk to the high counter that separates my tiny kitchen from the living space, grabbing a piece of cinnamon gum and popping it in my mouth. "I appreciate you stopping by Alex, but it's fine."

"Okay." He nods. "So what are you planning to do tomorrow, or the next day?"

I cringe.

"Right." He smacks his knees with his hands as he stands. "That's what I thought. I'm here. I can do my work from anywhere. Let me help."

My stomach muscles seize at the thought of trusting him. Of leaving this virtual stranger alone with my toddler.

I shake my head. "I don't even *know* you."

"So get to know me." His arms raise to the sides.

"What, right now?"

He shrugs. "No time like the present."

I'm quiet, the cinnamon flavor of the gum singeing my taste buds. "Okay. Where are you from?"

"Originally? Oregon." His mouth tightens. "Next."

Oregon? "Where do you live now?"

He grins. "Wherever the wind takes me."

I scoff. "See? This is my point. You don't *give* me anything. Christ, it's like pulling teeth trying to form a complete image of you in my head."

"Okay, fine. I live in Colorado. But like I told you, I'm here for work. I travel a lot."

My brow rises. "And what is it you do again?"

He shakes his head. "I've already said all I can with that. I sign multiple contracts when I take on clients."

Blowing out a breath, I attempt to shake off my anxiety and bob my head. "Okay."

He moves toward me. "Let's just chill today before you

make any decisions." He keeps walking until he's directly in front of me, my eyes meeting the space just below his chest.

Jesus, he's tall.

"Spend some time with me. Let Chase spend some time."

Glancing at the floor, my tongue swirls around the cinnamon gum, unease chomping at my back. His finger presses under my chin, lifting my face to his, the cool metal of his ring sending a chill down my spine. "I understand you don't trust me. Honestly, you shouldn't."

I huff.

He chuckles. "I just mean it's smart. It makes you a good mom. But, Lily, what are your other choices?"

Hopelessness stretches across the middle of my chest as I admit to myself that he's right. I have no options—stuck between a rock and a hard place. I've backed myself into a corner by only trusting Susan, because now, there's no one I can call when I need a hand. It's so *incredibly* stupid to become dependent on one person when there are so many things that could go wrong.

But I'm always trusting the wrong people.

I exhale, my anxiety ramping higher with every second. "Look, it's not that I don't appreciate you showing up. But as much as you wink, and flirt, and charm your way into my thoughts, I *don't* know you. You're... mysterious, and aloof, and any time I've ever tried to ask you *anything* you evade the question, which tells me you've got practice in avoiding answers."

He smirks, his finger moving from under my chin until his entire palm wraps around my jaw. A flare of heat spikes through me at the change in position.

"You're like a damn politician."

His smile drops, his body pushing into me harshly. I stumble, the counter digging into my lower back as his hips pin mine.

"Take it back," he rumbles, his eyes sparking.

"Which part?" I breathe.

He leans his body weight into me farther, and my stomach jumps into my throat. His mouth grazes my ear, his hand squeezing my jaw until it hurts, the smell of leather and birch-wood lighting up my senses. An ache settles between my legs from how roughly he's handling me.

It's sick, what turns me on.

His head angles down, his nose barely skimming the length of my neck, making goose bumps sprout along my arms. My heart steals my breath from how fast it's pounding.

"I'm a lot of things, little bird..." His voice vibrates against my skin. "But I am *not* a politician."

"O-Okay," I stutter, trying to keep the heat from spreading through me at his touch. At the way his body has me completely immobilized against the counter.

My hands come up to push against him, but he doesn't budge.

"Say it," he rasps.

"You're not a politician," I whisper.

He's still for a few long, tortured seconds, his breath puffing out against my throat, before he snaps back, running a hand through his tousled hair.

"Good." He smiles wide. "I *am* your new babysitter, though." He winks.

The corner of my mouth twitches as I bite back a grin, attempting to shake off whatever the hell just happened.

This is a terrible idea. I *don't* trust him, and I definitely don't trust myself around him... but he's right.

I have no other choice.

12
MASON

*T**his is the stupidest thing I've ever done.***

Don called me again this morning, and for the first time in ten years, I declined his call. I know he'll talk some sense into me, but I don't feel like listening to all the ways I'm being dumb as fuck.

I shouldn't still be in this town.

I shouldn't have talked to Lily in the first place.

And I *definitely* shouldn't be sitting in her cramped living room, acting like a stand-in boyfriend, wanting to take care of her when she hits a rough patch.

But here we are.

Annabelle spewed Lily's personal problems without a second thought, apologizing for having to leave before she could ride my dick, but saying she couldn't turn down the shift.

And even though I tried to talk myself out of it a thousand times—even though I'm sure Don calling was a sign from the universe, begging me to be smart—I ignored it. Apparently, the need to help Lily and her kid overwhelms logic and common sense in my brain.

Like I've said before, I've never been good at staying away from my vices.

The most surprising part of my morning is how hard Lily has been fighting against the idea of my help. Honestly, I thought she'd be thankful, since she doesn't have anyone else to call. But it's obvious she doesn't trust me. Not that she should.

I shouldn't fucking be here.

The words filter through my brain for the thousandth time, and I know her resistance is the perfect out—a way to stop my descent before I've gone down the whole slide—but I don't listen.

"Chase," she says.

My heart stutters. *Is she talking about her brother?* "What about him?"

Lily's eyebrows scrunch, and I realize two seconds too late that she *isn't* talking about him. She's talking about her *kid*.

"What do you mean, what about him? He's gonna wake up any minute, and there's never been anyone in the house when he does..." Her fingers scratch her wrist and my eyes follow the movement. "Maybe you should just leave."

"He's *never* had anyone else here?" I don't know why that makes my stomach clench tight, but it does. Thoughts of a three-year-old not having anyone besides his elderly babysitter and his mom is a sad reality. One I won't make better by coming into their lives when I'm only going to leave again.

But if I don't, then she'll go back to having absolutely no one. And I think that's worse.

"No, not really... we don't—" she starts.

I shake my head. "I get it."

Her eyes scan my body. "I highly doubt that."

Smirking, I lean against the wall. "Chill out, little bird. We're just gonna hang today. Let me help you."

A noise comes from down the hall, and I glance in that direction. "Which room is his?"

"The only room there is. The door on the left."

I lock my eyes back on hers. "What do you mean the only room? Where do you sleep?"

Her cheeks tinge pink as she nods toward the couch.

"You sleep on the *couch?*"

"It's not so bad." She shrugs.

I'm not sure why I'm surprised, I know her financial situation, and I've seen people live in much worse conditions. But the act of her giving up the room just feels so... selfless. I hope one day her kid looks back and realizes he chose a good mom when he came into this world.

"Don't look at me like that," she snaps.

"Like what?" My brows raise.

Her hands go to her hips and I bite back a smile. She's *so* feisty. All five foot two of her.

"Like you don't approve of our living situation."

"You have no idea what I'm thinking." My grin widens.

"Let me tell you something, *this*—" She waves her arms around the room. "I know this doesn't seem like much. But this is incredible for me." She takes a step closer with each word, until she's standing so close I can feel the heat sparking off her body. Her neck cranes so she can see my face. "I've slept on frozen street corners, and I've lived on filthy floors. So you don't get to come in here and judge us. Judge *me.*"

My heart dives into my stomach, sinking like a rock. *Is that what she thinks?*

Reaching out my hand, I tuck a loose strand of hair behind her ear, grazing her jaw with my fingers. "Believe me little bird, the last thing I'll ever do is judge you." My eyes track down her body, her chest heaving under her oversized Nirvana shirt. "I think you're fucking incredible."

She sucks in a breath.

"So." I clear my throat. "What's on the agenda for today?"

Her body shifts, and she backs up a couple steps. "Absolutely nothing."

I nod my head. "I can dig that."

She smirks. "You can *dig* it?"

Something light flows through my chest. "Are you making fun of the way I talk?"

"Mommy." The voice startles me, and I jerk around, my eyes coming face-to-face with Chase.

His eyes bounce between us, confusion swimming in his gaze, and Lily rushes over, picking him up and setting him on her hip. "Hey, baby. You remember Alex?"

My chest twists, the way it does every time she says that name. *Alex.*

Chase rests his head on her shoulder, his little legs dangling down her body as he nods.

"Is it okay if he hangs with us today?" she asks him, her hand swiping over his dark locks.

He stares at me in silence for a few long, stretched seconds, and finally nods, his chubby arms squeezing her tight. "Otay," he whispers. "Can we have pancakes?"

She nods and he continues, "The good kind though, not the ones fwom the box."

Her eyes dim, the muscles in her face pulling tight. My stomach sinks because I know before she even says it— pancakes aren't an option.

And that breaks my fucking heart in half.

"We can go to IHOP if you want. My treat," I say.

Lily's mouth snaps closed, her gaze swinging to mine.

"What's IHOP?" Chase asks.

I smile. "A magical place full of whipped cream and never-ending pancakes."

His eyes widen. "That sounds *awesome.*"

Lily laughs. "How are we gonna get there, Einstein? You gonna load us up on the back of your bike?"

Shrugging, I pull out my phone. "I'll call a cab. You just say the word."

She gazes at me until Chase's little fists pull on the front of her shirt. "Mommy, pwease. I want pancakes."

"Yeah, Mommy," I say. "And *I* want whipped cream."

Her eyes narrow on me, but she pats Chase's back, setting him down. "Go start getting ready, and I'll be in to help brush your teeth."

"YES!" he squeals, racing down the hall.

The grin cracks my face as I watch him run away. *He's a cool kid.*

"You don't have to do this, you know?" Her voice is low.

My brow quirks. "Do what?"

"Buy his affection… or mine."

My stomach tightens at her words and I step into her, forcing her back until she's flat against the wall. The second our bodies touch, heat spirals through my veins.

"Is that what you think I'm doing, little bird?"

Her breath falters, her palms coming up to rest against the cotton of my shirt. "Isn't it?"

"If I wanted your affection…" My hand slides up the side of her body, skimming against the tight curves hidden beneath her oversized shirt. "I'd take it."

She scoffs. "You can't *force* affection."

My palm continues upward until my fingers wrap around her neck, my thumb resting under her chin. I squeeze firmly, tipping her head back. "Who says I'd have to force it?"

Her eyes flare, her body arching into mine. My stomach flips, my cock straining against my jeans. *Christ, she's sexy.* I'm three seconds away from wrapping her legs around my waist so I can slip between her thighs, but her fists press against me, and I allow her to push me away.

"I need to go check on Chase."

And with that she scurries down the hall.

Fuck. I'm in trouble.

13
LILY

My chest warms as Chase stuffs his face with chocolate chip pancakes and chocolate milk. He's about to have a horrible sugar crash, but I don't even care.

He never gets to enjoy things like this.

I never get to enjoy letting him *have* things like this.

Gratitude overflows from the tap, soaking into my bones, as once again, this giant tattooed stranger has barreled into my life and made my kid smile. I don't know where he came from, or why he's here, but I know at this point, I'm going to let him stay because he just does these things... these incredibly nice things.

"Take a breath, dude." Alex's voice filters across the table, as he stares at Chase with a disgusted look.

Chase smiles, bits of pancake peeking through his teeth, and Alex cracks a grin, chuckling. "You're supposed to savor this shi—stuff."

I huff. "Kind of rude to assume he *isn't*, just because he eats them differently than you."

His eyes sparkle as he looks at me. "He isn't. I can tell."

"How's that?" My stomach flips.

"Because when you *savor* something, you take your time."

He leans forward, his elbows resting on the table, his eyes branding so deep they sear my soul. "You let it rest on your tongue until all you can see, think... *feel* is how lucky you are to have it touch your mouth in the first place."

My heart pounds against my chest, a rush of arousal spreading through my body. I cross my legs under the table, squeezing my thighs to stem the ache. *Jesus.*

"I'm savowing," Chase responds. His cheeks bulge from where the food sits, and I giggle, trying to brush off the way Alex just made me feel and focus on my kid instead.

"You can savor all you want, but we don't talk with our mouth full."

Chase nods, his face blooming red.

"That's more like it, my guy," Alex cuts in. "No need to rush. We've got nowhere to be."

Alex drapes his arm over the back of the booth. I smile as I watch him, taking a sip from my coffee and letting the warmth seep through my hands. This is... nice. "So, how are things with Annabelle?" The question rushes out before I can stop it.

He bites his lip. "Why?"

Because even though I have no reason for it, I hate that you're together.

"Just curious. You two seemed to hit it off."

He shrugs. "She's a nice girl. But she's just stress relief."

I nod slowly, sipping from my coffee. "Sounds like something a d-bag would say."

He smirks. "A d-bag?"

"Yeah." My eyes slide to Chase and back to him. "Don't make me say it, you know what it means."

"I think you may be trying to insult me, little bird. Are you jealous?"

My chest burns.

"Mommy's a bird?" Chase interrupts.

Alex smiles, his gaze leaving mine. "Your mommy's a lot of things."

His eyes flicker as he glances around the room, zoning in on something behind us.

And just like that, his entire body stiffens, his face dropping into a hard mask. The sudden change is striking, and as a result *my* body flies into fight-or-flight mode, the hairs on my arms standing at attention. "What's wrong?"

His jaw clenches tighter with each second, but he ignores me. Or maybe he doesn't hear me at all.

I twist around to see what he's looking at. A TV. *What the hell?*

"Alex."

"Don't call me that," he snaps.

My brows scrunch, my insides cowering at his tone. "What? That's your name, crazy."

He moves his gaze back to mine, his eyes fogged over. *Something isn't right.*

Without a second thought, I reach my hand across the table to cover his. "Hey… are you okay?"

Suddenly, he shakes himself out of his stupor, pulling back and drawing a toothpick out of his pocket. "I'm just fine, little bird. I'm sorry, you sounded like my mom for a second." He taps his head. "Flashbacks."

He grins, but it doesn't reach his eyes.

And I drop it, not wanting to ask.

*

ALEX NEVER LEFT, and Chase took to him like a duck to water. I can't decide whether it was because he actually likes him or if he's been starving for a male role model. Guilt wraps around my throat and squeezes.

"What's wrong?" Alex's voice pulls me out of my

thoughts, but the feeling stays, simmering in my stomach, threatening to scald everything it touches.

I shake my head, my fingers scratching at my wrist. "Just thinking."

Pushing the hair off my face, I grab a glass from the cabinet and fill it with tap water. My hand shakes as I bring it to my lips, and the glass slips from my fingers.

Alex's hand shoots past me and catches it before it smashes on the counter. "Careful." His voice is low and raspy, the heat from his body skimming across the back of my shoulders.

"Why are you shaking?" His breath tickles my neck.

My mouth parts and my fingers pick at my wrist, trying hard to focus on *anything* other than the way I feel. The way he *makes* me feel. His body presses against my back, his hands resting on my shoulders, goose bumps sprouting along my spine. "Lily," he whispers. "Relax."

My fingers grip the edge of the counter and I close my eyes, arousal rising through me like a heatwave, scorching my skin. He squeezes and my head drops, the pressure of his hands against my muscles making me groan. It's been years since someone has touched me. It's been forever since I've actually *wanted* to be touched.

"Talk to me. What's wrong?"

I spin to face him, his hands leaving my shoulders to rest on the cabinets behind my head. The way he cages me in makes my lungs compress. "N—nothing's wrong."

He cups my jaw, his thumb brushing against my bottom lip. "This mouth looks pretty when it tells me lies." His other hand leaves the cabinet, his fingers sweeping across the corner of my eye. "But your eyes show the truth."

My body is frozen in place, sparks flying off my skin from his touch. I swallow, my heart slamming so hard against my chest, I'm afraid it might break.

He hums, tracing designs along the side of my face. "Are you afraid of me, Lily?"

I should be. I've been scared of almost every man in my life at one point or another. But for some reason... I'm not.

"No," I whisper.

My breath hitches when he moves forward, his body suddenly flush against mine as he pushes me into the counter. His hand moves into my hair, gripping it firmly, dragging my head backward until my back starts to bow. His lips skate across my cheek. "How about a secret for a secret, little bird? Do you want to know something true?"

I attempt to nod, but his hand tightens in my strands, making the root pull. Tingles flood through me, pooling between my thighs. "Yes," I breathe.

His lips move from my cheek until they're resting just above my lips. "I don't enjoy kissing. It's never been my thing."

My stomach jumps into my throat, my knuckles tight from where I'm gripping the counter.

"But I swear to God, I'd let the world burn if it meant I could taste your lips."

My heart free-falls into my stomach, my brain waging war against my body. My hands come up to push against his chest, but he doesn't budge. He shakes his head. "Don't do that."

"Do what?" My tongue peeks out, swiping across my mouth.

"Don't push me away." His hips press into mine, the outline of his erection thick and hard against my stomach. "Tell me you don't want me to kiss you," he speaks against my lips. "Tell me you don't feel this."

I take a deep breath. I *do* want him to kiss me. The truth is, not many men have. No need for an intimate act like kissing when the person you're fucking is just a prop.

Pinpricks of energy spark off our breath, drawing us together, begging me to give in. To move forward and let him taste all the ways he makes me feel. But then I remember

Annabelle. The one person in my life I can *almost* consider a friend, and I pull back.

My chest wrings tight, the sad reality of what I almost did making my gut heavy.

"I don't want you to kiss me."

Just like that, his touch disappears, and he doesn't try again for the rest of the night.

14

MASON

It's been two weeks of watching Chase. Of spending time with Lily when she gets home from her shift, letting her decompress and tell me about her day. It feels oddly domesticated, and while I've been running from that feeling for years, in this setting, for some reason, it doesn't bother me. And as the days wear on, I find myself looking forward to the little moments.

I've only had one serious relationship. It was with a girl named Olivia, and it was a lifetime ago. Part of my past that I like to keep hidden away, buried deep where not even my subconscious can access it. But lately, it's been creeping back into the limelight, showing me all of the things I was missing back then. When I thought Olivia was where I'd spend my forever. Because even though I was with her for years, she never made fireworks explode inside my chest with a single look. My stomach never flipped and turned with anticipation, just at the thought of seeing her face, even for a second.

And I almost *married* her.

Meanwhile, Lily won't even let me past the friendship stage, and she barely lets me get to that. She constantly reminds me that I'm only helping her out with Chase.

That's true, I am. And like everything else that I've been doing since I've been here in Raindale, I've made a giant mistake.

Because now I fucking love this kid.

He's smart. And polite as hell. And just… he's everything that I thought I would have once upon a time.

My heart cinches in my chest.

"What's that face for?" Lily asks, dropping down on the couch. She sighs, her fingers reaching down to grab the soles of her feet, most likely tired from her day at work.

"Nothing." I grab her legs and pull them onto my lap, taking over from where she was rubbing. A thrill races through me when she doesn't put up a fight, and instead leans back against the cushions, groaning as I work the stress from her body.

"Thanks for watching him." She yawns.

I smile, my thumb pressing into her arch. "You've gotta stop thanking me. I told you I'll do it for as long as you need."

Her head tilts. "Oh, yeah? You gonna move here and babysit forever?"

I smirk. "I don't think I can commit to moving here permanently. Not when I can't even get you to watch a movie with me after Chase goes to sleep."

She rolls her eyes. "I don't even *have* any movies other than a few Disney ones."

"So you're saying if you *did* have one, then you would?"

She frowns. "I guess."

My chest warms. I've been trying to get her to relax around me for the past two weeks—ever since she pushed me away when I was two seconds from fucking her against the kitchen counter. "Lucky for you, I brought some."

She huffs out a laugh. "Of course you did."

"I wasn't sure what type of movie buff you were, so I brought options." I wiggle my brows. "Horror. Rom-com. Action. You pick it, we'll watch it."

She bites her lip. "You don't seem like a rom-com kind of guy, no offense."

Her leg jerks when my thumb presses against a tender spot. "I mean, I'm definitely offended, but it's fine."

She giggles. "Well, *I'm* not a rom-com kinda girl, so let's do action."

I nod and smile, knowing this is when I should go get the movie. But I don't move from my spot, afraid that once I do, she won't let me touch her again.

She watches as my hands work from her feet up to her calves. My heart speeds up, banging against my ribs.

"How come you don't like rom-coms?" I ask.

"How come you *do*?"

I shrug. "Sometimes you need something light. Something ridiculous and fluffy, so you can forget the world is so damn heavy."

She nods. "It's just a little unrealistic, don't you think?"

"Isn't that the point of movies? To escape reality for a little while?"

"Maybe." She takes her hair out of her ponytail, running her fingers through the strands. "But I don't need more reminders of all the love stories I'll never experience."

Her legs shift in my lap, and even though we're having a serious conversation, my body takes notice. It *always* notices her.

"Bad relationship?" I ask, my heartbeat climbing so high I hear it in my ears. This is my moment—my in. A chance for her to tell me all the things I already know, and hopefully the pieces I don't, so I can ease my guilty conscience and leave before things get too complicated.

Before I become too attached.

I'm already walking a dangerous tightrope, teetering on the edge.

"Yeah." She laughs. "I guess you could call it that." She rests her head on the couch cushion, her eyes softening as she stares at me, the silence stretching. I let it linger. Let it fill up all the cracks in the space between us, leaving the moment pregnant with expectation.

"I've only been in one…" she finally says. "If you can even call it that. Darryl. I met him in the airport of all places, coming back from Florida with my family."

I already know about Darryl of course, but I was born into a family where "poker face" was a birthright, so even though my chest is burning from the knowledge, I master the neutral stare with ease.

She cringes. "He was twenty. I was fourteen. It wasn't—" She shakes her head. "I was young, and stupid, and groomed for bad situations. My mind was twisted, and warped into thinking it was normal. That it was something I wanted."

Nausea swirls through my insides. I've been wanting her to open up, but the way her body coils tighter with each word has tension painting itself across my skin, pulling it tight.

"How the hell did your parents let you get away with that?"

Her eyes gloss over at the mention of her parents, and the look has guilt dropping like a boulder in my gut. I knew this question would make her uncomfortable, but I'm not *supposed* to know that, so I press on.

"They never knew. No one ever knew except a couple of m—" she hesitates, clearing her throat. "My friends. My parents were…" She sighs. "I was adopted, and they were so happy to even *have* kids that they never wanted to do anything to push us away. I took advantage of that."

She pauses, her fingers jumping to her opposite wrist, scratching against the skin.

"They were… *everything* I ever wanted," she continues. "And I was a fucked-up kid, hiding behind a big smile and a fake personality." She shrugs. "I was the *good* kid. It was m—" she hesitates again, swallowing around her words. "It was my brother who they thought would cause all the trouble."

My heart pounds, my fingers stuttering from where I'm massaging her leg. "You have a brother?"

"Yep." Her jaw tightens. "What about you?" she asks.

I grow dizzy from how fast my stomach flips, nausea racing up my esophagus and burning the back of my throat. I grind my teeth. "No. No siblings."

She frowns. "How about relationships? I mean, I know about Annabelle, but before that. Anything serious?"

My grip tightens on her legs. "How many times do I have to tell you Annabelle and I aren't in a relationship?"

She lifts a shoulder. "You're still *with* her even if you don't put a title on it."

I shake my head, something heavy settling in my gut. "No, I'm not. I haven't even *seen* her since before I started watching Chase."

"Hmm," she hums. Her eyes are critical, like she's debating on whether to believe me. And for some reason, I *need* her to believe me. I move quick, jerking her legs so her body slides closer, my hand gripping her hips tightly as I settle her across my lap. My palm wraps around the nape of her neck and drags her face toward mine, our noses brushing from the movement.

"If I was in a relationship, I wouldn't do this," I whisper.

My lips meet hers hard, my tongue licking the breath from her mouth until I'm drowning in her taste.

She melts into me immediately, her fingers tangling in the strands of my hair. I groan, my palm tightening on her neck. And then... she fucking bites me. Her teeth sink into my bottom lip and pull, the sting sharp and sudden, my cock jerking underneath her. Copper floods my tastebuds, and I rip her head away, my hand leaving her hip to swipe at the blood that's dripping down my chin.

"That wasn't very nice."

She grins. "Maybe I don't like nice."

Arousal spreads through me like smoke, suffocating my

logic. I lean back in, pressing my mouth to hers again, the taste of blood mixing with the sweetness of her breath. She breaks her lips away and moans, the sound a straight shot to my dick, making it throb painfully.

"Fucking *Christ*, Lily."

Her body freezes, and the icy tendrils shoot from her and spear me in the chest. She jumps up and I let her, even though every inch of me is begging to pull her back in.

Her fingers press against her mouth. "You can't just... you don't get to... ugh!" She grips her hair, the strands mashing against her fingers. "Why would you *do* that?"

I smirk, amusement dancing through my chest. "You were a pretty willing participant, little bird."

"But you're not *mine*. Now I'm gonna feel like a home-wrecker when I see Annabelle. You may not think she likes you, but she *does*, Alex."

Alex. Reality crashes back through me at the name.

"She doesn't even *know* me," I snap.

"Oh, and I do?"

Irritation floods my veins.

From her questions.

From the fact that I lost myself in her.

From the fact that I want to *keep* losing myself in her.

I spring from the couch and walk straight into her, pushing until she's flat against the wall.

My hands come up and grip her face tight, forcing her to meet my eyes. My body is flush against hers, and I swear I can hear her heart racing. I wonder if she can tell that mine's beating just as fast.

"I. Am. Not. With. Annabelle." Moving one hand from her jaw, I grab her fingers, pressing them against my chest. "You feel that?"

Her eyes blink rapidly, her breaths coming in short pants as she nods.

"No one has *ever* done this to me. Like my body is revolting against me just from being next to you. Just from the fucking *thought* of touching you." My thumb rubs against her cheek. "So, no, Lily. Maybe you don't know me. But you know *this*." I press her hand harder against me. "And you know you feel it too."

I dip back down, brushing my lips across hers one last time, before releasing her and turning away to walk out the door.

15

LILY

Chase's tinkling giggle filters through the air and falls on my ears, my chest warming from the sound. It's been a little over two weeks since Alex started watching him, and while I've been on edge, things have gone better than I expected.

It's hard for me to let someone in. But Chase... he *loves* him. He hasn't been around many men, or many people in general. The constant knot in the center of my chest tangles him up and forces me to keep him close.

I do the best I can, but it doesn't stop the regret from slamming into me in the silent moments.

This is good for him.

Alex is good for him.

And that terrifies me, because Alex doesn't live here.

"How come you never told me that he was watching your kid?" Annabelle asks, her eyes bouncing to the corner booth and back to where we're doing side work.

The middle of my throat swells with guilt, my lips tingling from the memory of Alex's lips on mine. I wanted it, which is... surprising, to say the least. Sex has never held much importance for me. When I was young, I didn't understand why people put so much value on it in the first place. They protected their mythical "virginity" like it was something to be proud of keeping. Like it was shameful *not* to have it.

But I hadn't had mine in years, and when something is taken before you even know you're supposed to keep it? Well, that can fuck with your vision a bit. Skew things until up is down and left is right. I never "lost" my virginity, because I never knew to look for it in the first place.

By the time I was with Darryl, I was so used to laying there and going to the dark corner in my head, it wasn't even a second thought. But there's never been any good feelings involved. The guys I've been with were never interested in *my* pleasure.

But for some reason, Alex is different. That dark corner still exists, but when he touches me, my body sparks alive instead of cowering to hide. Everything buzzes, a live wire waiting to explode.

That doesn't change the fact that Alex isn't mine, and while he says he isn't Annabelle's either... the way she's looking at him right now makes it feel like he is. And while I may not owe her anything, it still feels like I'm being a shitty friend.

I finish scooping the coleslaw into the ramekins, avoiding eye contact, worried she'll be able to see the guilt seeping from my soul. "I figured you knew."

"Nope. I haven't even seen him since the morning I picked up your shift. I've called and texted a couple times, but he usually doesn't even respond." She shrugs, shaking her head. "Men. Am I right?"

Satisfaction trickles through my insides at her words even as I roll my eyes and agree.

She sighs. "It's fine though. I mainly just miss his dick."

I force a chuckle through the squeezing of my chest.

"Ricky's back in town, anyway," she continues.

"Am I supposed to know who that is?" I ask.

"I guess not." She stops what she's doing and turns toward me completely, her hip settling in against the metal table where we're doing side work. "How come we've worked together for so long, and we're only just now becoming friends, huh?"

"I don't... uh... I don't know." Her question makes me uncomfortable. There are so many different ways I could answer.

Because I don't like making friends. Because being alone is safer. Because the fewer people who know things about me means the less chance of *him* finding me.

"Well... Ricky lives in the 'burbs, where I grew up. We've been on and off since high school."

"Why do you live in Raindale, if you've got family and friends so close?"

I don't know anyone who would willingly live here. There's a reason I picked Raindale, and it isn't for its beauty or its amenities.

She shrugs. "Sometimes you need to get away. *I* needed to get away, somewhere people wouldn't look, but... I'm kind of a pussy. I couldn't make myself go too far." She smiles. "And obviously, everyone knows now anyway, because I tucked tail and went home to my folks last year. But staying here just fits for now. Gives me some separation." She glances at me. "How about you?"

My stomach somersaults between not wanting to tell her and wishing I had someone to confide in. But I just don't trust her enough. My gaze flings to Alex, the colorful ink on his skin contrasting against the black of his shirt, his broad shoulders tensing while he colors with my son.

The scars on my wrist itch as I give my attention back to Annabelle. "We've all got things to run from."

Her lips tilt. "That's the truth."

Chase giggles again, the sound light and fluttery as it floats across the restaurant and sinks into the center of my chest.

Annabelle smiles slightly. "Why don't you go ahead and take your boys home? I'll finish up here."

My body stiffens at her insinuation. "I don't—we…"

She laughs, her hand coming out to rest on my arm. I jerk away, not liking the way it feels to have her hands on me.

"It's okay, girl. Like I told you, things with me and Alex were just a good time."

I narrow my eyes. "You seemed *super* into him."

She shrugs, her eyes flicking toward him before landing back on mine. "He doesn't look at me the way he looks at you."

My stomach slingshots into my throat as I look down at the ramekins and shake my head. "He doesn't look at me."

Annabelle huffs out a laugh. "He's looking at you right now. You make a habit of lying to yourself?"

I glance toward the back booth, my eyes colliding with his golden gaze, as they pierce through my chest and pull heady sensations from the deepest part of me.

He winks, and a small grin makes its way onto my face, my heart skipping. Breaking our stare, I give my attention back to Annabelle.

"Only when it keeps me safe."

16

MASON

"No, do it like this."

Chase's voice snaps my eyes away from Lily, and I look down at the dinosaurs printed on the kid's menu—the fifth one we've gone through since getting here half an hour ago.

It hasn't been a good day. I've never had an issue with Chase; he's always been a laid back, chill kid, but today he was crying for Lily the second he woke up. We played Monster trucks and sang "Baby Shark". Built Legos and made castles out of Play-Doh, but still, he just wanted his mom.

I can relate.

So, I packed him up and we made the trek to *Dina's Diner.* I should have brought him here earlier. It's a win-win situation. He's happy just by being able to see her, and *I'm* happy watching her blush every time I catch her stealing a glance.

I haven't stopped thinking about the way her lips felt on mine since the moment it happened. Jesus *fuck*, I can't get it out of my damn head. The past twenty-four hours have been filled with vivid images of filthy things.

Things I'm not sure she'll let me do.

Things I should know better than to even *want* to do.

My eyes drop to my cell on the table, the missed call log filled with messages from Don. He usually isn't so persistent, but I've also never avoided him like this. If I answer, I'll have to own up to the fact that I'm breaking the cardinal rule.

Never interact with the target.

And definitely don't get them alone, press them against a wall, and slide your tongue in their mouth. My stomach tightens at the memory.

Lily bounds from around the corner and prances over, making my pants tighten and my heart skip like a schoolboy with a crush. She seems light today, and a smile cracks my face before I can stop myself. Whether I want to admit it out loud or not, the reason I'm avoiding Don is because of *this*. Because when I'm here, all I can focus on is how nice it is to be with her. To be with her kid. To be part of something that feels so goddamn real. And *that* makes me a pussy, because it's not something I should be thinking. Or wishing for. I gave up rights to that life a long time ago, and I haven't looked back since.

I haven't *let* myself look back.

But suddenly, I can't figure out how to separate thoughts of my past from the feelings in my present, and every time I'm around Lily they start to creep back in.

Would I have been a good dad?

"Mommy!" Chase drops the purple crayon from his fist, launching himself into Lily's arms. My splintered chest aches.

"Hey, baby." She rubs his back. "What are you two doing here?" she asks, her eyes darting everywhere except for my face.

Slinging my arm across the back of the booth, I grin wide at her, letting my gaze linger. If she isn't going to look at me, I can at least make sure she *feels* me. I've been ready to explode ever since I felt every inch of her delicious body pressed against mine, and now that she's standing in front of me, I can't help but want to eat her fucking whole. Devour her until she doesn't know up from down and left from right.

Show her what it's truly like to be worshiped by a man.

I doubt she ever has been.

Her discomfort makes my cock harden, desperate to see her squirm underneath me instead of somewhere I can't reach. Grabbing a toothpick from my pocket, I slip it between my lips, the sudden craving for nicotine swimming through my veins and tightening every nerve.

I nod my head toward Chase. "He missed you."

"I had a bad dweam," Chase whispers, his head resting on her shoulder. "And when I woke up, you wewen't there."

She brushes her fingers over the back of his dark hair and squeezes him to her tighter.

"Well, I'm here now, baby. You ready to go?"

He nods, pushing his head farther into her neck. I watch, fascinated and oddly, a bit jealous at their closeness. A blind man could see it's the two of them against the world, and while my chest expands with warmth knowing they have that with each other, it also makes me feel like shit.

Because here I am, worming my way in, just to implode their world apart by telling her brother where she is.

But I always finish my assignments. So no matter how much I like this girl, no matter how much I care for her kid, I can't get attached. The thought is a rock slicing down the middle of my stomach, making my insides heavy.

"You okay?" Lily asks.

"Yeah." I clear my throat. "Everything's great, now that you're here." Standing up, I step in close, running my hand over the top of Chase's hair. "He wanted his mommy, and so did I."

Electricity zings around my chest when her eyes spark, the apples of her cheeks flushing hot. *Fuck*, I have no control, but it's so damn satisfying to get a response out of her.

Chase wiggles in her arms, and she lets him down until

he's standing with his back to us, his eyes scanning the room.

My body presses against Lily's back, her ass brushing against me with every inhale. "We missed you," I breathe against her neck.

She shivers and it sends a thrill racing down my spine.

"Well, thanks for bringing him," Lily says, twisting to face me.

My stomach flips when her dark eyes meet mine. "I'll walk you back."

She shakes her head. "We're just fine." She reaches out, grabbing Chase's hand. "Isn't that right, baby? You're the only man I need." She looks down to Chase who beams up at her with a toothy grin.

"I wanna pway with Awex."

My heart fucking skips in my chest, a smirk sliding on my face. "You hear that? He wants to play with *me*." I wink, pointing to myself.

I move toward the front door, but before I get far, a small palm reaches out, stopping me in my tracks, my breath sticking in my throat.

Chase's tiny hand grips mine, his sticky fingers the glue keeping me in place. Tethering me to this picture-perfect moment—an innocent kid between two people, excited as hell to do a simple thing like walking home.

My chest pulls when I think of all the hours I wasted once upon a time, imagining a moment just like this. Looking forward to simple seconds that ingrain themselves into your soul forever. Future memories that were stolen from me before I ever had the chance to see them through.

My heart stutters and twists until the burn radiates through every part of me. I shake my head and twirl the toothpick around with my tongue, brushing off the almost overwhelming urge for a smoke.

That was a lifetime ago, and I don't think about the past.

It's too dangerous.

17

LILY

We're sitting on my couch when it happens—my past coming back to haunt my present.

It's late, Chase is already in bed, and I'm here with Alex, my stomach clenching tight from how obviously attached Chase is getting. Alex doesn't even *live* here. I don't know his last name or where he's from. He's a mystery that I haven't unraveled because I'm afraid once I do, I won't like what I find.

And it's been so long since I've liked someone.

I'm also terrified he's planning to leave, and that when he does, my child will be a broken mess on the floor. My heart splinters from the thought.

"What are you thinking about so hard over there?" Alex reaches out and grabs my leg, but I jerk it away, my stomach jumping into my throat.

Not because I mind his touch, I don't.

And that's the problem.

It's unusual not to have a visceral reaction from another person's touch. It's even more unusual to *want* the feel of them on my skin. Past experiences have rewired my brain. Criss-crossed all the wires and neurons until the very thought of someone coming near makes me feel like I might puke. But I learned at a young age that fight or flight doesn't work, so instead, my brain hides in a corner where it knows I'll be safe. Sometimes when I come to, I couldn't tell you who or what happened.

That doesn't change the way my body wears the trauma like a second skin.

I shrug. "Just thinking."

Alex scoots in closer, reaching for me again. This time, I let him pull my arm into his lap and dance his fingers along my surface, pinpricks of pleasure floating through me. I close my eyes and let the feeling wash over me. Let it sink into my pores and fill me up with an energy I haven't felt from a man's touch in... ever.

"How did you get these?" His voice is soft as his fingers trail over scarred flesh, but I stiffen in his grasp.

I try to move my arm, but his grip tightens around my wrist and brings me back in. "Don't hide from me, little bird."

My lips part and I blow out a slow breath, my stomach in knots at someone acknowledging the marks on my arm that mirror the bruises on my soul.

"You mean my tats?" I force a grin.

His brows draw in, his thumb running circles over the ink, my insides coiling tighter with each pass of his thumb.

"Sure. That's a good place to start." He smirks.

I drop my gaze, staring at the tattered gray bunny on my arm—stuffing coming out of the sides, and a gaping black hole where the heart should be. A burn chars the center of my throat and I swallow around the tender tissue.

"Growing up, I had a stuffed animal." My words catch.

"A bunny?" he guesses.

"Yeah." I nod. "I kept it for way too long, but it was always my sense of comfort. My brother and I, we moved around a lot. Wiggles grounded me." I frown. "But eventually, I lost him."

Alex smiles, his white teeth blinding against his tanned skin. "So why the ink?"

"To feel safe, I guess?" My shoulders lift. "Whenever things happen I don't want to think about, I can touch it here on my arm and, I don't know..." Embarrassment floods through me as I talk, worried he'll think I'm stupid for caring so much about a stuffed animal.

"It makes you feel safe." His thumb presses into my skin.

"Yeah," I mumble.

I expect him to dig deeper, to ask about the rough edges of my skin, puckered and raised underneath the ink, but he surprises me by simply nodding and then raising his eyes to meet mine. There's a depth to his gaze that I haven't seen before. Like he's stripping me bare and looking at every used up part of me.

It's heady and intoxicating.

It's *terrifying*.

And even though a large part of me wants to cower away, there's another part that whispers to let him in. Let him *see*. But I've never been asked to share a piece of me before, and I'm worried he'll take it with him when he leaves.

Alex moves, scooching closer on the couch until our thighs are pressed together, the heat of his body blazing next to mine.

I sink into it, sink into *him*.

He grabs my fingers, trailing them along the bright colors that cover every inch of his skin. My gut jolts when we stop moving, my hand touching raised flesh. My eyebrows draw in, confusion swimming through my veins, and I lean in closer, eyes straining to see what it is I can feel.

A raised, jagged line.

"The first time I cut, I was eleven."

My heart jumps into my throat and I swallow around the lump.

"My parents were..." He clears his throat. "Different than

most. Controlling. Image was absolutely everything, and because of that, I never had a choice in what mine would be."

My stomach twists as he speaks, but I'm enraptured by his voice. By his story. I've never had anyone share their scars to help me find comfort in my own.

"I don't even know what made me do it that first time. I can't remember ever seeing anything about it, or... thinking beforehand. I just remember it had been a good day." He shakes his head. "Art was my favorite subject, and I spent that entire month working on a piece to bring home. It was of my dad." His voice pinches. "How I saw him at the time, anyway."

Curiosity at who his parents are, brims inside me like water overflowing from the tap.

"My art teacher, Mrs. Mayberry," he continues. "She told me how gifted I was. How proud they would be. She wanted to feature the drawing in an upcoming community art show. I went home and was *so* fucking excited. Everyone in my family had a path, you know? And I just knew it in my bones that this was mine."

"At eleven years old?" I ask.

"When you know, you know." He shrugs. "But my dad disagreed." His jaw clenches. "Tore up the canvas right in front of me. Called it a waste of time."

I scoff, an ache unfurling in the center of my chest for Alex being told his dreams didn't matter. "He sounds like a dick."

"He most definitely was," Alex chuckles. "Anyway, I was upset and started to cry. Which my father *also* didn't like." He moves my hand down to his, our fingers locking together. "Suffice to say, the family I came from didn't appreciate emotion. And they also didn't appreciate me going against the grain. Against what was *expected*. They were the masters driving the carriage, and they gripped the reins tightly. So I hid where no one would see—" He nods toward his arm. "And I controlled what I could." Sighing, he shakes his head. "And that control was addicting."

Tears spring behind my eyes at his story. At imagining someone just a few years older than my baby boy, crouching in a corner and putting a blade to their skin.

Alex's free hand moves up, gripping my chin and turning it until our eyes catch. Until I'm *hooked* in his gaze.

"My point is, little bird, I understand hiding your past beneath the surface—under pretty colors and inked up skin."

He leans in, his mouth grazing against my neck. My stomach flips. "You can tell me all your secrets, Lily," he whispers into my skin. "I promise I'll keep them safe."

My heart stutters in my chest, fighting against the urge to believe him. It's easy for someone to say words, easy to think they want to know what I've been through. But even *I* don't want to know. Even *I* ache to forget. My life is the type of movie you only watch once, and then warn others not to waste their time.

So I won't tell Alex all my secrets.

But I'll keep his safe all the same.

18

LILY

Some scars are too deep to show.

The slightest tug makes them rip, fester, and ooze all over again, and I've worked too damn hard over the years trying to staunch the bleeding and numb the ache. Still, Alex gave me something of himself, and my stomach jumbles around, wanting to give him something *more* back.

"I'm a drug addict." My words sound harsh in the still air, and my eyes bounce from him to the cinnamon gum on the kitchen counter—my insides sizzling with need, my body physically begging for something I'll no longer allow it to have.

I don't think it ever goes away. The craving. Gets easier over time, sure, but it's always there in the background, like a lion hunting prey, waiting for the opportune moment to pounce.

And it *always* pounces.

Sometimes it's the smell of a pan on the stove, so similar to the stench of burning foil. The kind I used to freebase, sucking cocaine and baking soda vapors through a metal straw, or a dirty dollar bill.

Other times, it's a simple thought that does it. Secretly, I worry that one day, my love for Chase, and my willpower won't be enough.

Alex's fingers caress the scattered marks along my arm, hidden from the eye but easy to feel when you press a little deeper. Heroin was something I fell into after I ran away from home, when the misery of losing my family was salt pouring into my infected wounds, making the pain too much to bear.

"I never thought I'd be *that* girl, you know?" I continue.

He shakes his head. "*What* girl?"

Irritation prods at my nerves and my tone comes across harsh. "A fucking junkie. What do you think?"

Disgust crawls up my throat, wrapping around my esophagus like a noose. "You talked about your family being controlling and caring about image, well—" A bitter laugh escapes my lips, my chest cracking from the memories. "My birth mom was the opposite of that."

"She had a drug problem?" he asks.

I nod. "I—my memories of her are faded. But I remember what it did to my brother. What *she* did to him. What..." My voice fades, but the unsaid words linger in the air.

What I did to him.

The thought of my brother is a tidal wave of grief rising up like a storm surge, pulling me under until I drown.

"Is Chase why you got sober?"

My stomach twists, but then I pause, realizing he doesn't know *that* Chase. He's obviously asking about my baby boy.

My tongue sticks to the roof of my mouth as I nod. "The thought—" My voice catches on the rough edges of my words, and I take a deep breath to try again. "The thought of something similar happening to Chase, because of me, makes my heart feel like it's splitting in half."

He hums. "You're a good mom."

I huff out a breath, reaching over to rub at my opposite wrist. I hit Alex's hand instead, and he grabs on, interlocking our fingers.

"You think?" My throat swells. "Sometimes I think about how easy it would be to become a bad one."

His hand squeezes mine, and maybe it's because he's not judging, or maybe it's because it feels good to *finally* talk about it, but I can't stop the next words from spewing out of my mouth. "It was just coke at first. A line here and there to take the edge off. But then... you know how it goes." I shrug.

He cocks his head. "Why don't you tell me, anyway?"

I stare down at our entwined hands, not wanting to look him in the eyes as I talk, too afraid of what I'll see. "I liked the way it felt. Suddenly, I didn't have to pretend, you know? Didn't have to consciously put the extra bounce in my step or the gigantic smile on my face, because it was just there. And after years of pretending, of being this gigantic bubble of energy, it was relieving to have something else holding the mask in place. To hide the pain somewhere even I couldn't reach."

"Pain from what?" Alex whispers.

I open my mouth but emotion clogs the airway, a phantom pain rippling across my chest.

"I don't wanna talk about that." I shake my head. "I *can't*."

He nods, bringing my hand to his mouth.

His lips are surprisingly soft when they graze against my skin, but the impact is the harshest I've ever felt. It creates an inferno of fire that rages through my veins, melting away the chains that lock up my vulnerabilities, keeping them in the dark.

Alex's lips move farther, skimming across my wrist, and I collect his kisses like candy. One for every scar. One for every mark.

It's minimal what he's doing, but really, it's fucking *everything*.

My body vibrates, regret for my weakness, and arousal from his attention spinning a twisted, sick web inside of me, tossing my stomach and creating an ache between my thighs.

"Wh-what are you doing?" I stutter.

"Kissing you," he replies, his voice deep.

"Why?" I choke out.

He pauses, his breath hot as it wafts over my wrist, his eyes gazing up at me from under his lashes. "Because you deserve to be kissed."

My heart catapults, smashing any restraint I had on the way down. I yank my arm free and grab his face, pulling until the top half of his body hovers in front of mine, my hands framing his jaw.

His free hand comes up, his thumb pressing firmly against my bottom lip. "I plan to kiss *every* part of you, little bird."

I suck in a breath, the moment tense and strained, my eyes darting between his, searching for the truth in his words. I'm not sure if I find it, but something snaps inside of me—a dam that's been fracturing for weeks—Alex the culprit behind the break. And as the water floods through my system and drowns my reservations, I surge forward, our lips meeting in a frenzy.

He groans, the sound deep and gravelly, scraping along my insides and lighting my nerves on fire. My fingers thread through the hair at the nape of his neck, needing *something* to grasp on to.

Wrapping his arms around my middle, his calloused palms slide underneath my shirt, the cold metal of his rings a shock to my heated skin. He jerks me roughly until our bodies are plastered together, our chests dancing with heavy breaths. His tongue darts out, swiping at my bottom lip, and I moan, sucking it into my mouth and twirling it around my own, the base of my stomach crackling with sparks that send shock waves through my body.

He leans farther into me, forcing me to lie back on the couch, his hand slipping around my head until his fingers thread through the strands of my hair.

And then… he pulls.

The sharp sting is a jolt to my system, causing a gasp to leave my mouth. The harsh tugging causes a flood of desire to shoot through my veins and pool between my legs.

"How do you like it, little bird?" he rasps against my ear.

"Rough." The word tumbles out before I can give it a second thought, and while maybe I should be embarrassed admitting my fantasies, I'm too turned on to care.

He smirks, and it sends a thrill spiraling through me. I've never told anyone what I think about when I'm at the height of my own pleasure, and I know that after the high wears off, I'll come back down to earth and I'll be disgusted with myself. With my sick thoughts, stemming from something that happened once upon a time.

What the fuck is wrong with me?

Still, Alex makes me feel safe. Makes me feel like he can be trusted. The pulsing of my clit, and the throbbing of my womb has me whispering more secrets than I intended to spill in the space between us.

He pulls back, staring down at me, his eyes flaring with so much heat they singe my soul.

His hips press into mine, the thick outline of his cock lining up perfectly against my center.

My heart rams against my ribs, and the little bit of logic I had left flees, replaced with the anticipation of him giving me what I want.

What I need.

His lips dip down again, his teeth biting into my collarbone hard enough to bruise, and he thrusts.

"Oh, *God*," I pant.

"There's no God here, little bird. It's just you and me."

His palm runs up the outside of my thigh, goose bumps

springing all over my body. He continues his trek over the top of my leg, grazing the line just above my pants and then working his way down until he cups my pussy over the fabric. "Do you want me here?"

My lungs compress until I'm dizzy from the lack of air, and I nod.

"Use your words. Tell me you want my cock or you won't get it."

"I want you to..." Heat floods my cheeks, and I turn my head to the side.

His hand shoots to my face, gripping it tight as he turns it back toward his. "Don't hide from me, Lily." He drops his body weight until it rests fully against mine, his breath tickling the hairs on my neck as he leans in close.

"Tell me all your secrets, little bird," he whispers in my ear.

It's the same thing he said earlier, and while I won't tell him everything, maybe I *can* tell him this.

My stomach shoots to my throat, my hands suddenly clammy, anxiety wringing my insides tight. But then his fingers squeeze my jaw, forcing me to lock onto his gaze, and a calmness washes over.

And that makes the words flow off my tongue. "I want you to *take* it."

Quick as a flash of lightning his demeanor changes, his body somehow growing larger as his hand leaves my face and moves down. His fingers wrap around my neck, my pulse jumping under his palm.

He squeezes.

A sharp shot of arousal spikes through my middle and my mouth parts on a gasp.

"So responsive." He smiles.

"You made me." I laugh.

His grip tightens again and my giggle cuts off from the pressure.

"I'm starting to think you were made *for* me," he says.

And then he leans in and steals my shocked gasp with a kiss.

19

MASON

S he's so fucking sexy.

If lust wasn't swimming through my veins and twisting up my logic, maybe I would stop whatever is happening and *think* about what she's asking. But it's no surprise I don't, because truthfully, I haven't been thinking straight since the moment I saw her—long before she ever knew of me.

The taste of her mouth makes me woozy, and my tongue presses deeper, trying to dive inside her body and let the feel of her ground me. I start a slow grind, my hips pressing into the space between her legs, the tension in my abdomen coiling tighter with each thrust against the thin material of her sweatpants.

My hand wraps around her throat, her pulse jumping erratically beneath my thumb.

The harder I squeeze, the more responsive she becomes.

"I want you to take it."

My palm moves back, slipping into the strands of her hair, pulling sharply until her lips separate from mine mid-kiss. Tugging her head to the side, my teeth graze against her neck, my free hand moving down the column of her throat until it reaches the top of her chest.

She squirms underneath me, and my grip on her hair tightens, causing a whimper to escape her lips. My eyes flash to hers, a sudden tightening in my chest, urging me to make sure she's still with me. That when she asked for rough, she meant it.

I'm testing the waters, not sure she understands just how *rough* I can get.

Her eyes are heavy, and her cheeks flushed.

So fucking beautiful.

My fingers continue to slip down the small frame of her body, grasping the hem of her oversized band tee, and pushing it up. My already hard cock stiffens further as she moans, grinding herself on me.

When my gaze falls to her chest, my lungs squeeze tight. Her breasts are bare, nipples pebbled, begging me to make them swollen and tender from abuse. I lean down, sucking the peak into my mouth, swirling my tongue around the bud before my teeth clamp down slightly, tugging enough to cause a gasp. My stomach tenses and I swallow a groan.

"Oh, God," she moans.

"What did I tell you about saying that?" I respond, my fingers coming up to her other nipple and pinching.

She gasps, her back bowing, hands shooting up to dig into my shoulders.

Leaving her chest, I work my way down, my hand following the path of my mouth until I reach the top of her sweats. Pulling them off her legs, I toss them to the side. My heart skips so hard at the sight of her bare pussy it feels like it might break, but I swear to God if I die, this is how I want to go out. Right here, staring at Lily in all her beauty—her taste on my tongue and her body a vision, skin flushed and glistening, begging me to do all the things I've dreamed of.

She fidgets and my arm jumps up to her midsection, pressing down firmly to pin her in place.

I may not be an expert in emotional connection, but one thing I *do* know is how to fuck. How to draw out the hidden deviant living inside, so you can enjoy the pleasure of submerging in your darkest desires.

And Lily Adams likes dark things.

My free hand moves down, pushing against her thigh. She resists, her legs tensing, and my eyes glance at her face. I smirk, my dick jumping at her refusal. I put more pressure, prying her legs apart, smacking the inside of her thigh once they're forced open, her pussy glistening and on display.

The sight of the red print left behind makes precum leak from the tip of my cock, wetting my boxers. "Don't pretend you don't want my tongue on your pussy."

Her fingers reach up and grasp my hair so tight there's a sting at the root. "No one has ever——"

My heart stutters, mouth watering; a thrill surging through me like a tidal wave.

I move closer, my arm still pinning her down by her stomach, blowing my breath on top of her already swollen clit. "Shame for them then. A fucking pleasure for me."

And then I lap at her pussy, groaning at the musky taste of her arousal. My tongue circles her swollen nub, reveling in the immediate shake of her legs as they lift to clamp down over my shoulders.

"Oh, *fuck*." Her voice is loud. My hand reaches up until I feel the stretch in my side, smothering her mouth, pressing down harshly so she doesn't wake the kid and ruin what we've got going. Having her so malleable under my hands sends a rush of excitement through me—a tingle of power—and my cock thickens further, straining against my jeans, desperate to be let free.

With one palm still pressed against her mouth, the other

hand moves down until I reach the outside of her hole, playing in the wetness.

Fuck, she's sexy.

Two of my fingers plunge inside without warning, and she jerks, forcing them in deeper. I curl them upward, finding the spongy insides of her walls, my mouth alternating between quick flicks, and long, languid motions, paying close attention to how her body responds so I can pinpoint how she likes it. When I circle her clit again, and then suck it into my mouth, her body spasms and she moans, the sound vibrating against my palm, sending a shot of arousal straight to my dick.

There it is.

My fingers are drenched, her juices literally seeping onto my hand and down my wrist. I can tell she's close.

So I stop and lean back.

She groans, her head slapping against the couch cushion.

"Do you deserve to come, little bird?"

She says something, but it's muffled under my hand. I lean in toward her. "What was that? I can't hear."

Her eyes flare.

"Do I need to make you beg for it?"

My free hand, still by her thighs, rears back, and I bring it forward, smacking the top of her pussy. My eyes never leave her face, waiting for her to either say it's too much or to show a sign that she doesn't like it.

She whimpers, her hips thrusting against my palm.

My chest expands, my cock harder than it's ever been, and my hand comes down again.

Another moan, her eyes rolling back in her head.

I start up a slow and steady rhythm, her pussy lips swelling, blooming a beautiful shade of pink from the harsh sting of my hand. I alternate slaps with my palm rubbing tenderly against her mound.

Jesus Christ, she's so responsive.

She's close as fuck, I can *feel* it.

Leaning forward, my chest presses against hers. Her neck glistens with a light sheen of sweat, and I can't help but lick along the expanse of her throat before letting my lips skim across her ear.

"Do you like my hands on you?" I ask, my fingers rolling in a slow, circular motion on her clit.

She shakes her head no.

My stomach jolts with excitement.

"You filthy little liar." *Smack.* "You can act like you don't want me to touch you, but this—" my fingers dip down to her entrance, dipping them inside until they're slathered in her juices, before bringing them to her mouth. She tries to turn her head, but I grasp her jaw, locking her in place, smearing her cream over her lips. "This tells me different."

My fingers push so tight against her face I can feel the imprint of her teeth through her skin, and my tongue licks up the wetness coated across the seam of her lips. I pry her mouth open with mine, swirling her arousal between us, my balls tightening from the way her groan reverberates through my body. My hand dips down to her pussy, starting the slow torture of friction, and when her legs tremble around my hips, I lean back, raising my palm and bringing it down sharply in three quick slaps.

And that's all it takes. Her body bends like a pretzel as she shakes, her mouth gaping open. I dive down, my lips tangling with hers and sucking in her scream, keeping her as quiet as possible while she rides the explosion.

Slowly, she comes back down to earth, her body trembling in my arms, and mine aching with the need for relief. But, this isn't about me tonight. If she wants me to *take* it, I need to make sure she trusts me.

Still, I can't help the tendril of satisfaction worming its way inside at the way she's *finally* letting me in. The thought makes guilt slither around my spine, tightening like a constrictor.

She doesn't even know who you are.

I ease the feeling by telling myself she *does.* She may not know who I truly am or what I'm really here for, but in this moment, she knows me better than anyone else. Like she could draw up the innermost parts of me with a single look. And not the surface-level bullshit, like your hobbies or your favorite colors. Not even the past experiences or present struggles. I'm talking about that soul-deep shit. Where your energy connects with theirs and you twine together, riding the same vibration. Tuned into the same frequency.

That's rare.

That's something in the storybooks.

And that's something I was convinced didn't really exist. Only now, I'm finding it in her.

So even though I know I should pull back and get my head on straight. Either go through with what I'm hired for, or tell her the truth of why I'm here in the first place... I don't.

I can't.

And I'm not sure I ever will.

20

LILY

I 've never felt so vulnerable.

Which is saying a lot, because there have been numerous times in my life where I've been weak and at the heel of someone's mercy. But this… this feels *different*. Like sprinting through a marathon—exhausted and drained—yet completely satisfied.

Alex has moved behind me on the couch, both of us sprawled out, his arms wrapped around me, the warmth of his body fighting off the chill of revulsion that's trying to creep up my back.

"Why did you stop?" I ask, twisting to face him.

His eyebrow arches. "Because I wanted to hold you."

"But what if I wanted to return the favor?" My eyes glance down to his lap. Honestly, I don't think I have the energy for that, or the stomach. I've never *willingly* given head before in my life. Memories scream into my present just from the thought.

"You also wanted me to 'take it,'" Alex says.

My cheeks heat, my stomach flipping with disgust.

I shouldn't have said anything.

My fingers scratch at my wrist.

Alex's hand moves up, his knuckles tilting my chin until I'm staring into his eyes. "I want to give you what you want, little bird, but we need to talk about it more before I do. That's why we stopped."

I roll my eyes, scoffing, my face jerking out of his grasp. "Talking defeats the whole purpose. It was stupid anyway. I shouldn't have said anything." The words rush out of me, shame filling up every single cell in my body until I'm weighed down by regret.

Regret for saying something.

Regret for having something *to* say.

Regret for letting things happen to me in the first place.

My heart cinches tight, stomach heaving.

"No." His voice is sharp. "Don't do that. Not with me." He drags my face back again, his lips grazing mine on every exhale. "I don't want you to hide. I don't want you to cower away. I want you to look me in the eyes, and tell me what you need."

My body trembles, a sharp pain swelling my throat.

"I *want* to give it to you." He presses a chaste kiss to my lips.

I suck in a breath, my already over-sensitized body sizzling from his touch.

"There's nothing wrong with role-play, Lily. Nothing wrong with liking things. With *needing* certain things."

My chest burns, the sudden need for something to be swimming through my veins like a visceral itch, slinking beneath my skin, unable to be scratched.

His breath ghosts across the skin of my cheek, but he hesitates before saying the next part. "You have a rape fantasy."

The word rape sends me into a tailspin, defensive shackles rising up and slamming back down. Revulsion and shame slice through my veins, bleeding onto the floor, until I'm sure he can see how absolutely fucking pathetic I am. "No, I —"

Alex's grip on my body tightens. "There's nothing wrong

with it. It's hot as fuck." Another kiss. "We just need to be clear about things before we dive in." His eyes glide down my body before rising back to meet mine, the fire in his gaze enough to re-spark the match lying in the pit of my belly.

"I would die a thousand deaths right now to get inside of you," he continues. "But I want to make sure we do things right. I *need* to make sure you're taken care of."

Swallowing, I try to form words around my suddenly parched throat. "I don't like calling it that," I whisper.

He nods, his eyes spearing into me. "Okay, but…" He pauses, his thumb brushing against the underside of my jaw in a repetitive caress, lulling me into the feeling of comfort. "That's what it is, right? That's what you like?"

I nod, but then panic seizes my chest, a sharp ache radiating through the cavity. "I'm not uh… I'm not sure. I've never—"

His grip tightens again, and my heart rate slows down. "You've never actually done it?"

I shake my head.

"But you'd like to." His eyes don't lose contact, staying locked on mine the *entire* time. And there's something about the way he's handling everything, the way he's controlling the situation, and making me feel like I could tell him my darkest, deepest secrets, that has me wanting to tell him *everything*.

But I won't.

I can't even admit them to myself most days.

"Yeah." I nod.

He sucks on his lips, his cock twitching from where it's pressed against the back of my leg. "We need a safe word."

My nose scrunches. He's so direct and at ease, acting as if we're doing something completely mundane, like making a grocery list. Like he's done this a thousand times.

Maybe he has. My stomach jolts as a ghost of a thought sits in the back of my mind, reminding me that I don't really know him.

"I want to give you what you need, but I want you to know you're *always* in control of the situation, okay?" His voice pushes the whisper of caution from my brain.

Emotion clogs my throat, and I swallow around the lump. I don't know what that's like—being in control. My fingers tear at my wrist, my mind spinning so fast, I couldn't pick a word if I tried.

"How about bunny?" he suggests.

Satisfaction settles over my body with the word, and I nod. "Okay."

My face heats and I break our stare. *Does he think this is stupid?*

His fingers lift up my chin again. "Hey, don't do that. Talking about things is important." He leans in and peppers my cheek with kisses. "Are you thirsty? Hungry?"

I nod, my insides swirling with an unknown feeling. I feel... safe. Calm. Protected.

Cherished.

Alex stands and leans over me, his palm wrapping around the back of my neck. He pulls me until the top half of my body is lifted from the couch, held up solely by his grasp. His nose brushes mine. "I just want to make something *extremely* clear."

My heart pounds against my ribs.

"Now that I've had you. Now that I've *tasted* you, no one else gets to touch you." He slips his tongue in my mouth, branding me with ownership. I shouldn't like the way it feels.

But I do.

"You're *mine*."

And then he releases me, my body bouncing off the couch cushions as he walks into the kitchen.

I stare after him, my fingers tracing my lips, wondering where the hell he came from, and what the hell I'm going to do once he leaves.

21

MASON

"Where the fuck have you been?" Don's voice is gruff, and my first instinct is to bite back, remind him that I'm not a fucking kid anymore, but I resist the urge because I know he has the right to be pissed.

He's still technically my boss, after all.

"My bad, old man. I've been busy."

There's a pause, the line so quiet it makes me shift in my chair. I can picture Don with his slicked-back graying hair, probably in some tiki bar on the coast while his girl soaks up the luxury that years of working on the edge of the law has provided her.

"Define 'busy.'"

Sighing, I run a hand through my hair. I grab a toothpick from where they're stockpiled on the desk in my motel room and shove it in my mouth, the edge pricking my lip. "Just busy. Working. You know."

"Mmhm," he grunts. "You still hanging around the mark?"

"Lily."

I cringe as soon as I say her name, knowing my slip of the

tongue is equivalent to a giant red flag, waving in front of Don's face.

He groans. "I know her name. For fuck's sake, Mase. What the hell are you doing? Are you fucking her?"

My jaw clenches, stomach turning. "Don't come at me with bullshit. I just… I know it looks bad, okay?"

"It does look bad. It makes *me* look bad. I may not be there in person to run things, but it's still *my* name you're representing. My company that cashes your checks. It's still *me* this all comes back to when things don't get done."

My teeth grind. "I know."

"Then do your fucking job."

Irritation snaps at my back like shark teeth, puncturing my insides until my defenses are rankled. I know that he's right. I'm *not* doing my job. I haven't been since the moment I saw her—the moment I found her—and didn't immediately wrap things up and let her brother know where she was.

"When have you ever known me to not do my job, Don?"

He blows out a breath. "That's what has me worried. Up until now, you always have."

"Right. I always have. And I *always* will, so just let me do things my way." Guilt slams into my stomach. "This girl… she's different. I just want to make sure we're not sending her and her kid back to a bad situation."

He huffs. "You've never cared before."

"Yeah, well…" My chest pulls tight. "I care now."

"We don't get paid to *care*, Mason."

Nodding, I roll the toothpick from one side of my mouth to the other, frustration welling up inside of me. It feels almost dirty to talk about Lily like this, like she still means nothing to me.

Like she's a means to an end.

I *know* I need to wrap this shit up. Need to make a decision about what the hell I'm planning to do.

"What do you think's gonna happen here, Mason?" Don

continues. "You're gonna tell her brother where she is and then stick around? Quit working for me and start a brand new, fresh life, less than twenty-four hours away from the one you've been running from all these years?"

I run my hand through my hair, tugging on the roots. "No, *fuck*."

"You gonna come clean to her then?"

My stomach jumps to my throat. "I don't—I haven't thought about it."

"I'll answer for you. You are *not* going to tell her. You're gonna get your head out of your ass, and do your fucking job, or else I'll come and do it for you." He heaves a heavy breath down the line, the seconds stretching until they feel like hours, his words sinking into my skin and mixing into my veins, making me nauseous from the invasion.

"You watched the news yet?" he asks.

My brows furrow at his question. This is the second time we've talked, and both times, he's brought up the news. "No, should I?"

"Yeah, Mase... you should." He pauses. "Listen, sort your shit out, okay? Forget about the job for a second, and just consider the decisions you're making, and the effect they'll have on your future. And if you can't do that, then think about hers, and her kid's."

"Yeah." My stomach rolls.

"There's a reason why you came to me ten years ago."

Nausea teases my throat as we say our goodbyes, because he's right. I'm making shitty decisions. But I just got her. I'm not ready to lose her yet. Still, I know I can't keep living this lie, so that only leaves one option. I have to figure out a way to come clean. My stomach churns at the thought, anxiety creeping along the edges of my nerves and making them fray.

Maybe she'll forgive me.

Maybe she'll let me stick around.

My brain replays Don's words on repeat as I lean back in

my chair, Lily's taste from earlier still on my tongue, my eyes bouncing from the computer with her files to the TV on the dresser.

You should watch the news.

Something breezes across my back, causing a chill, and I already know that whatever is on there is something I won't want to see. But Don wouldn't have brought it up if it wasn't important. Reaching over, I grab the remote, the sound of the screen flicking to life loud in the otherwise silent room.

My body is tense, every muscle coiled tight, preparing myself for something that, deep down, I've been expecting for a long time. The past ten years have been nothing but a waiting game, and I know without even looking that this is it.

The moment I've been dreading.

I should have moved out of the fucking country when I had the chance.

Flipping through the channels, I pause when I get to the nightly news, my heart dropping into my stomach like a bomb.

"The presidential race is heating up, and although we won't be hearing the parties' official nominees until later this year at the national conventions, there are two names that stand above the rest, being touted as the clear frontrunners. Congressman Ron Damoine for the Democratic ticket. And Senator Thomas Wells, as the presumed nominee for the Republicans."

"That's right, Diana. Senator Wells has come out strong in the Iowa caucus, and people believe his base of family, faith and constitutionalism will easily win over the votes needed."

I turn the TV off, throwing the remote, the cracking sound as it hits the black screen dulled from the pounding in my ears. My fists clench and unclench as I try to rein in the rage that's boiling in my veins. My body is physically shaking, and the toothpick in my mouth splits in two from the force of my clenched jaw.

Family.

Faith.

Thomas Wells wouldn't give a shit about his family if it came up and bit him on the ass.

I should know.

I'm his son.

22

LILY

I've given into the fact that I have feelings for Alex, and I don't know where the hell they came from. I haven't felt anything for anyone in years. Not since I was an impressionable fourteen-year-old girl, confusing manipulation from a narcissist as true love.

But with Alex... I've never felt the type of security and safety I do with him. The level of trust—not the type that's earned—but the type that's intrinsic, like my soul is reaching out and twining with his.

I've never been able to share the dark parts of myself. Never had someone who asked to see them.

But he does. He asks, and it makes me feel everything.

And *everything* is scary. After years of using every tactic possible to avoid facing emotion, the feeling is overwhelming. Old habits threaten like a thundercloud, looming over my blue skies without the promise of a rainbow after the storm.

Which is why I'm on the phone with Derek.

"So. Alex, huh?"

My heart flutters at the mention of his name, and I have to bite back the smile blooming across my face.

"Yeah," I sigh. "Alex."

Chase's head pops up from where he's building Legos on the living room floor and I cringe, worry seeping through my happy moment, realizing how attached he's grown in such a short amount of time.

"But… I don't know, Derek."

Derek hums. "What don't you know about?"

I huff out a laugh. "When it comes to Alex? A hell of a lot, actually."

"So ask."

I scoff. "Like it's that easy."

"Lily… it *is* that easy."

Anxiety swirls from the middle of my stomach, wrapping around my chest and squeezing. "What if I don't like his answer?"

Derek hums. "Well, at least you'll know. Better to find out now than down the road, right?"

I scrunch my nose, my gut twisting. "Yeah, I guess."

He's silent for a few strained moments. "Lily, you deserve happiness. You don't need to punish yourself for the rest of your life. That's no way to live."

My throat swells. "I'm *not*."

He chuckles, but it's an empty sound. "Whatever helps you sleep at night."

I stick a fresh piece of cinnamon gum in my mouth, holding the phone between my shoulder and ear, my fingers rubbing against my wrist.

"I'm just sayin'," he continues. "You've worked extremely hard to get yourself to where you are. If this Alex guy makes you happy, then figure out whatever you need to, and just go for it."

I chew on my lip. "I don't know."

"Let yourself be happy, Lily."

"You don't think it's like… too good to be true? Because that's how it feels. Like he's some mysterious knight in shining armor, equipped with a Harley and trips to IHOP, and I'm sitting here in my low-income apartment, hiding in plain sight, waiting for the other shoe to drop."

Derek laughs. "You've gotta stop tryin' to find the bad in every situation. You look hard enough, you'll always find it."

My heart stutters when I glance toward the living room where my baby boy is playing with his toys. "And what happens when Chase gets attached and things don't work out? He doesn't even *live* here, Derek."

"So find out where he does live. If you can't have open and honest communication, then you don't have much anyway." He pauses. "Have you told him anything?"

My body tenses. "No," I whisper.

"Well." He blows out a breath. "If you can't tell him about you, and he isn't tellin' you about him… what do you both really have, anyway?"

My chest tightens because even though I call Derek to talk me down, and keep things in perspective, that doesn't mean I always like to hear what he has to say. "Yeah, you're right."

"Give yourself some grace, Lily. And when things get to be too much, you know to call."

A knock on my front door interrupts us. "Hey, someone's at my door. But thank you. You always know how to get me straight."

"Yeah, yeah. You're a pain in the ass, but for some reason I love you, anyway."

Smiling, I hang up, keeping an eye on Chase in the living room as I head to the front door. My stomach tenses, picturing Alex on the other side.

Derek's right. I need to talk to him. I learned a long time ago that I'm not a good judge of character. And there's a niggling in the back of my mind that reminds me of it every time I think about letting go of all my reservations and diving in one hundred percent.

Opening the door, my breath sticks in my throat, because it isn't Alex on the other side, it's Susan.

"Wow, Susan! Hi." I smile, trying to ignore the weight of disappointment that's sinking in my chest.

"Hi, honey." She waves. "Just thought I'd pop over and let you know I'm back in town."

"How's your sister? Do you want to come in?" I move to the side, gesturing behind me, but she shakes her head, running a hand through her graying hair. "No, sugar, I'm fine, and so is my sister, thank the lord." She puts her hands out to the sides.

I smile. "I'm glad to hear she's doing better." My stomach tightens as a thought drops into my head. "So you're all good to watch Chase again?"

"I've missed that boy." She nods, chuckling. "Who would have guessed a toddler would be easier to care for than a grown-ass woman."

"Wow. Your sister must be a treat," I joke.

I'm happy to see Susan, but even as relief flows through my veins, my gut sinks to the floor, because if she's here then Alex doesn't need to be. And I can't help but wonder whether he'll stick around.

Derek's earlier words flow through my brain, telling me to just "let myself be happy," but as much as I wish it was that easy to give in and just *be*, it isn't. There's no magic switch to flip that changes the wiring of your brain, or the caution that has poisoned your blood. And I learned a long time ago there's no such thing as a happy ending. There are only temporary falsehoods—illusions that shatter once you're pushed from the ledge, eyes uncovered to watch yourself fall.

But Derek *is* right in one thing. I'll never get anywhere if we don't talk. And if Alex is going to brand his ownership with a kiss on my lips, then I need to make sure he's in it for the long haul.

For my sake, *and* for my baby boy's.

"Hey, do you think you can watch Chase for a few hours tonight?" I ask Susan.

Susan's eyebrows rise but she bobs her head. "Of course. I'm back for good, honey, so I'm here whenever you need. Just bring him on over." Her hand reaches out and squeezes my forearm.

She turns to leave and I close the door, telling myself that everything will be fine. That Susan coming back is a sign, letting me know I need to make a decision regarding Alex. Either I let this *thing* we're doing continue, or I put a stop to it before it becomes even harder to walk away.

The butterflies erupting in my stomach let me know which way I *want* things to go.

But if that's going to happen, then I need some answers.

And tonight, I'm going to get them.

23

MASON

I was planning to go see Lily today. I'm not needed, it's her day off, but there's an anticipation that sits low in my gut, making me want to spend every free second with her. It's an odd feeling, wanting to be around someone just to soak in their presence.

But that was before I saw my shitbag father on TV, smiling for the cameras like he isn't a snake in sheep's clothing. That's all anybody ever is, isn't it? Millions of people hiding who they truly are behind fake smiles and happy faces. No one ever tells the truth. What you see is almost never what you get.

I guess in the end, we all have our secrets.

Glancing at the clock, I hop up, grabbing the unopened pack of Parliaments and a lighter, my body vibrating with volatility, pushing me out the door to give into the numbing buzz that only nicotine can provide.

I need time to process, to figure out what the hell I'm going to do. *Where the hell I'm going to go.* Just as my fingers grasp the doorknob, there's a knock on the other side, the sound so jarring it makes me step back a few paces, my chest jolting.

My brows draw in. *Who the fuck?*

Opening the door, my stomach clenches tight when I

come face-to-face with Lily. The temper inside simmers, doused by a calm that only she provides.

"Hey, little bird." My eyes drink her in, allowing the sight of her to wash away the worries of my past.

"Hiya." She grins, her hands in her back pockets. "Hope it's okay to stop by like this. I had to uh…" She looks around, reaching up and brushing the hair from her eyes. "Had to ask the front desk which room was yours."

My brow quirks. "And they just gave it to you?"

"They did." Her smile grows. "You don't really blend in."

"I'm glad you came by." I lean against the doorframe, my eyes glancing behind her. "Where's Chase?"

"He's with Susan."

My heart stutters. "Susan, the babysitter?"

She nods, and it's in this moment—in the way her confirmation is a straight shot to the chest, that I realize how attached I've become. I shouldn't be upset about Susan being back.

But I fucking am.

I open my mouth to respond, but the words stick on the back of my tongue, my brain registering her words. It's just her. My cock twitches and I straighten off the frame, stepping into her, the heat of her small body sparking off my skin, her neck craning to maintain eye contact.

"You telling me you came here all alone?" My voice is deep, a rasp that reveals how enticing it is to finally have her to myself, without the worry of a kid that's asleep or someone seeing who shouldn't.

"I did." Her eyes flash with her smile.

My heart kicks against my sternum as I step forward, my arm wrapping around her waist before she can protest, dragging her into me. She blows out a breath, and then my mouth is on hers, stealing the air for myself. Who needs nicotine when my new favorite vice has shown up instead?

I walk backward until we're in the room, closing the door

and shoving her up against it, the lightweight jacket she's wearing slipping off her shoulder from the impact. My hands go under her ass and lift, her legs wrapping around my hips, her hot center pressed against my growing erection. One hand runs up the center of her chest, reaching behind and tangling in the strands of her hair, the other keeping her locked around my waist, my lips never leaving hers.

Our kiss is messy. Teeth that bite and lips that slip. But we've never really done soft and sweet. My cock grows as I imagine her mouth slurping on my cock the way she's sucking on my tongue.

Fuck.

I lose all sense of myself with this chick, but I can't help it. I *need* her. This isn't about logic, it isn't even about satiating a carnal desire. This is about deep-diving inside of her and never coming up for air. An addiction I can't seem to kick. All I can do is surrender to the moment. Let myself become so lost in her I forget there was ever a reason to be found.

I pull back, my eyes drinking every delicious inch of her in. Her lips are puffy and red, her chest heaving with deep breaths. She looks like sex and sin and just fucking *everything*.

"My kiss looks good on you, little bird." I lean in, running my nose along the expanse of her neck, wanting to smell her skin and commit it to memory. Collect every piece of her like a snapshot for rainy days.

She giggles, smacking my chest and pushing me back. I allow her, enjoying the carefree energy she's bringing into the room, a stark contrast to two hours ago, when I found out the man who created me is running for President of the United States.

"I actually came here to talk," she says.

I groan, adjusting my hard-on, a smirk creeping on my face. "That sounds ominous. I thought you came to ride my dick."

She scoffs. "Jesus, with an attitude like that, who can say no?"

My grin widens. "As if you'd have the option."

Her smile dips the tiniest bit, heat flaring through her eyes.

"What are we doing?" she blurts, pacing in front of the bed.

"I thought that was pretty obvious." My brows wiggle.

She huffs, her arms crossing over her chest. "I mean... are we like, together?"

I force my body to stay relaxed, even though my heart is beating my chest like a battering ram, and I walk to the corner, sitting down in the desk chair. "Do you want to be?"

"I mean... I don't know." Her fingers scratch at her wrist. "I *want* to, but Alex. I don't even know what you do for a living. I don't know where you live. I don't know how long you're staying or..." She trails off, her arms raising before falling helplessly to her sides.

My heart twists and tangles around the lies that sit heavy in my chest, and I know this is it. This is my opportunity to come clean. Tell her I've known her far longer than she can imagine. That I was hired by her brother to hunt her down. That even though she may not know everything about me, she's uncovering all the parts that count. That every second spent in her presence is a second farther away from where I don't want to be.

But if I tell her, I'll lose her. And the thought of that is a serrated knife slicing through my middle, carving out a hole for my bleeding heart to break on the floor.

So I bite my tongue instead.

"I just... you keep telling me to trust you." She walks closer. "To let you in, let you keep my secrets. But, Alex, I can't jump into this without knowing. I don't even know if there's anything to jump *into*. How long are you even gonna be here for?" Her eyes glance around the motel.

I shrug, my mind trying to come up with something that straddles the in-between. "I can do what I do from anywhere," I say carefully.

"Ugh!" She pulls at her hair, then points a shaky finger at me. "See? That isn't a real answer. And *this*—" She gestures between us. "It isn't fair to me and it sure as hell isn't fair to Chase, and… look, I'm used to being disappointed. I'm used to heartbreak." Her eyes gloss over and my chest squeezes. "It's all I've ever known. But *Chase*, he… he fucking loves you, okay? You worked your way into his heart and he's never had that before." Her voice cracks. "And here I am, letting you stomp into our lives when I don't know the first fucking thing about you and it's *scary*." Her hand smacks her chest. "It's terrifying. It makes me feel like a shitty mom and a bad judge of character."

She's pacing, so close I can easily reach out and grab her. So I do. Without thinking, I react, my arms gripping her tight, pulling her onto my lap until her legs surround me and her face is directly in front of mine.

My hand grasps the back of her neck and brings her in, our foreheads touching. "You're not a shitty mom."

I mean the words when I say them, but the weight of my secrets press down on my chest, threatening to shatter me into a million pieces.

I've fucked so many faceless women. Told them pretty words and meaningless facts. But with Lily, it's something more. Something deeper. Something that, if I'm honest with myself, I've felt since the moment I laid eyes on her months ago, when I was taking her pictures from a distance and planning to hand her off to her brother.

And maybe that's why I never passed on what I found. Maybe that's why I've stayed here, less than a day's drive away from where I promised I would never go back.

Maybe that's why I don't want to leave.

Because drowning in Lily is better than wading in a life without her.

I can't lose her yet.

24

LILY

"*You're not a shitty mom.*"

"Easy for you to say." My hands reach up, scruffing along the edges of Alex's five o'clock shadow, the pale of my skin contrasting against the dark tan of his. "But I will be if I just let you slip in and out of our lives without getting answers. You're always so evasive, and I just *can't* let it happen anymore."

His jaw clenches under my palms, the muscle so tight the tension seeps into my fingertips.

My hips jerk into him farther when his arms squeeze my waist. "The answer is *yes*, little bird. We're together. I told you yesterday that you were mine. But you'll have to work with me here." He blows out a breath. "I'm not used to having anyone to answer to. I..."

My stomach dips and twists, knotting around the anxiety this conversation is giving, but I'm not leaving until I figure out what's going on. Until I'm sure about what decisions I need to make going forward. So I'll sit here, allowing my edges to continue to crack, hoping his answers will be the glue that binds them back together.

My gaze slips to the desk behind us. There's an expensive

looking laptop, wireless headphones, and a small mound of toothpicks. My lips twitch, realizing how completely *Alex* it is, but then my gaze snags on something next to it, and the realization is a rock being hurtled a hundred miles an hour into my gut, punching so fast I lose my breath.

A gun.

My vision spins, twisting and turning until all I can see are memories blending into my present.

Driving around town, Darryl's eyes are lazy while he talks on his phone. "Yeah, I'll be there. I'm out, runnin' errands with my girl."

His hand grips my knee, tight enough to where I know there will be a bruise. I wince but don't tell him it hurts. He doesn't like it when I push him away. My eyes fall to his gun, lying haphazardly in his lap. The sight of it makes a sick feeling swim through the bottom of my belly, and I don't like the way it feels.

Reaching into the center console, my hand fumbles until I feel the cool glass of the pipe hit my fingers. Pulling it out, I glance through the car windows, making sure it's a safe place to take a hit. The rough edges of the lighter, and the sounds of the igniting flame, create an almost calming sensation—a precursor to the buzz that overtakes my body moments later, making me float above the worry.

My hands grow clammy, my lungs squeezing so tight I gasp for air as I'm catapulted from one moment into another.

"What the fuck you lookin' at?"

My stomach jumps into my throat, my eyes trying so hard to focus around the fuzzy edges of my high. I think I'm at Amy's, but I can't be sure. I glance around for Darryl, but the living room is empty, soiled beanbags and mismatched chairs strewn against the stained carpet. I've been so out of it, I didn't even notice he left me here with this douchebag of a friend. The one who has now moved closer to me on the couch, his gaze wide and pupils dilated, hiding the color of his eyes.

My brain is muddled, but the cool press of metal between my eyes pulls it from the fog. "Watch your fuckin' eyes, bitch. I don't like the way you look at me."

My mind snaps back to the present, legs scrambling to

move off of Alex's lap. My heart careens against my ribcage. *Who the fuck have I let in my house?*

His grip tightens around me, not allowing me to move. "What just happened?"

My gut twists, head shaking back and forth, my body revolting against his hold.

I can't go back. I won't go back.

I fight against him, arms thrashing as tears burn behind my lids, my stomach heaving so hard bile teases the back of my throat. "Stop, stop, let me go, *please.*"

I *am* a bad judge of character. Years of lying with dark beasts clearly weren't enough to show me all the ways a manipulator can trick you into thinking they're the light. There's a grasping of my jaw, my neck twisting, and suddenly my eyes clash with a golden gaze. My heart calms slightly.

"Lily. Stay with me, baby. Talk to me." His voice is as firm as his hold and I swallow down more of the panic.

Alex isn't Darryl.

He isn't here. He won't find you.

"Al—Alex," I stutter. "Why do you have a gun on your nightstand?"

His eyes widen slightly, but his steady grip on my body never leaves. "I'm an investigator." His voice is strong and quick, like he knows that in order to calm me down, he can't beat around the bush.

Like he realizes that *this is important.*

My heart falters, my brain attempting to wrap around his words. "A *what?*"

His fingers twitch on my jaw. "An investigator."

"Like a cop?" My nose scrunches, the fear ebbing back to its dark corner, hiding in the memories I try so fucking hard to erase.

Alex chuckles, his hand moving to tuck a strand of hair behind my ear. "No, little bird, definitely not a cop." He pauses, his eyes shifting back and forth between mine, maybe from him deciding what to tell me, or maybe searching for some understanding.

Relief pours through my veins, and I take a few deep breaths, centering myself.

He's not here.

I lean my forehead against Alex's, our breaths mingling, hot and sweet, allowing myself to sink into his embrace. Letting his tight hold surround me until I feel the safety of his arms.

"Are you okay?" he asks, his hand moving to the back of my head and smoothing down the strands of my hair.

I nod, an explanation in the back of my mouth, but I *can't* find the courage to push it off my tongue. So I change the focus to him instead.

"Give me all your secrets. I promise to keep them safe," I whisper, echoing what he always says, my body trembling from the aftereffects of being thrown into my past.

He blows out a shaky breath, pausing for long moments before he gives in, following my lead and letting me change the subject. "I can't tell you why I'm here. Not because I don't want to, but because I *can't*. I sign NDAs. I'm in contracts. I could lose everything if I do."

Nodding, my eyes glance around again, my fingers squeezing the material of his shirt as I contemplate what he's told me… and what he hasn't.

An investigator.

I let the word flow through me, settling into my psyche, and I replay every moment since he's come into town. "Okay. Okay, that makes sense."

His lips tic up in the corner, a small grin that doesn't reach his eyes, and he leans in, pressing a kiss against my lips. I dive into the moment, desperate for his taste—for the feeling that only he has ever provided.

I stop suddenly as another thought hits. "Where do you live again?"

"Colorado," he mutters against my lips. "But I can work from anywhere. I travel... *a lot*, so it's hardly what you would call a home."

His words stick to my insides like glue, remembering that Raindale is just a short stop on his way to somewhere else. "So... how much longer are you *here* for?"

He exhales, his nose flaring, his gaze once again searing through mine. The moment is strained, and my heart aches, desperate to claw its way out of me and sink into him, to soak up the secrets he won't show.

"I'm not sure," he admits.

My stomach twists.

Both of his palms come up to grip my face, his thumbs brushing along my cheekbones. "But I know that I want to be wherever you are."

My chest warms. "Well, I'm here."

His hands tighten even further, our noses skimming with every inhale. "And I'm here, too, Lily."

"But for how long?" The words catch in my throat.

"For as long as you want me."

And then he leans in and steals my words with his mouth. I surrender to the feeling, swept away by everything he makes me feel. A moan slips out of me as his tongue tangles with mine, and I sink deeper into his hold, feeling him grow hard underneath me.

I move my hips forward, pressing my body weight down, and he groans, his fingers bruising against my jaw. I love the way he molds my body, the way it feels like as long as I'm in his arms, he'll protect me from the world. The thought lifts me up like a rollercoaster climbing up a hill, the view more beautiful with every rising inch.

And then, for the first time in my life, I truly surrender.

I *let* myself fall.

I just hope he's there to catch me when I land.

25

MASON

The second her taste hits my mouth, I'm lost. Maybe I should pull back, maybe the *right* thing to do is stop whatever this is and try and get to the bottom of why she saw my gun and freaked the fuck out. But, the truth is, I don't want to bring it back up. Don't want to talk about me again, or how she was so panicked I knew that nothing less than the truth would pacify her.

Guilt threatens to sink its way into the moment, but I push it back.

Call me selfish.

Call me a prick.

Both of these things are true. Neither of them change the fact that when it comes to Lily, I'm weak. A slave to my vices, just like I always have been.

My hips push against her as she grinds down on my lap, all the blood leaving my brain and rushing to my cock. The steady friction has me physically throbbing, my dick straining underneath the fabric, desperate to know what it's like to slide inside of her.

With one hand around her waist, my other slips her jacket off her shoulders, the sound of the light thump when it hits the floor muffled from the way my heart pounds in my ears. My fingers tease the hem of her tank top, exposing her silky skin, making me dizzy with the need to see her bare. To soak her in like sunshine, and store up her rays, hoping they'll get me through the inevitable dark days to come.

She raises her arms, and I push the fabric up and over, letting it fall somewhere on the floor, leaving her braless and beautiful before me.

I've seen her bare breasts before—had the taste of them on my tongue—but it still doesn't prepare me. It's a visceral experience, her half naked and panting on top of me. I take her in, my chest squeezing as I wonder how the hell I got so lucky, and how the *fuck* I'm going to keep her.

I cup her breast, the weight of her in my hand making my mouth water. My arm wraps back around her waist, and I bend down, sucking her areola into my mouth. She moans, her fingers tangling in the short strands of my hair, her hips moving in a torturous rhythm on my lap.

Heat collects at the base of my spine, and I stifle a groan.

My lips move across her chest, dipping in the valley between her breasts, and I lave kisses along the ridges of her chest bone until I reach her other nipple, twirling my tongue around the hardened peak, her fingers tightening in my hair.

"Alex," she moans.

That name from her lips flips a switch, desperation oozing from my movements, wanting to be closer. *Needing* to inhale her until she coats my lungs, infusing my heart with her essence. My mouth releases her nipple with a pop, and I surge up, my hand gripping the back of her neck, jerking her into me until our mouths collide.

The kiss is harsh and greedy, my tongue prying her lips open, desperate to show her with my actions what I feel for her with my soul.

She moves, her palms sliding down my chest until they reach the hem of my shirt, lifting the fabric. My lips break away to help her, and she rips the material over my head. She sits back, stilling her movements, her eyes widening as she gazes at the colorful patterns swirling from my shoulder to my chest, covering almost every inch of free skin.

My body burns from her stare.

Slowly, she reaches up and traces the patterns, goose bumps sprouting under her touch, every slide of her fingertips a straight shot to my cock.

"Do these all mean something?" she asks, her voice low and raspy.

My heart falters, and I nod, hoping she doesn't ruin the moment by asking. She doesn't, choosing to lean in and press soft kisses to my chest instead. A shiver works its way up my spine and wraps around my body, a knot clogging my throat when her lips linger on the area above my heart. Her hot breath coasts across my skin, making my abs clench, and I swallow, forcing the emotion back down.

Her fingers work their way down until they reach the button of my pants. She pops it open, slipping her hands underneath, tugging. My hips lift to give her more access, and she slides them off my body, my cock springing free. When her hand wraps around the shaft, my eyes roll back, pleasure skittering along my insides. I suck in a breath as she slides her palm from root to tip.

"*Fuck*, Lily."

My hands glide down her curves, fumbling with her jeans, the desperation prodding my nerves and making me clumsy. She helps, lifting her hips until she's hovering, and once I get them off, it's just her pink, panty-covered pussy directly in front of my face. Precum bubbles from my engorged head and her fingers swipe over the liquid, coating her palm as she slips it back down with ease, twisting once she's at the base.

I groan, gripping the front of her underwear and pulling until I feel the flimsy fabric give way. Her mouth parts, and the sight of the red marks left on her hips makes my stomach churn with heat.

The pink fabric is soaked through with her juices and I take the opportunity to shove them in her parted mouth. "Taste yourself, baby."

The fingers of her free hand wrap around my wrist, and she moans through the cotton.

Jesus.

Her hips drop back down, resuming her earlier rhythm on my lap, only now I'm transfixed by the sight of her pussy lips splitting open, her clit sliding up and down the length of my cock. It's erotic as fuck, and my balls tense, sending a coiling sensation spiraling through me.

Leaning in, I grab the panties from her mouth with my teeth, spitting them on the floor and replacing them with my lips. Her hand leaves my dick, moving to grab the back of my head as she sucks my tongue. And then *she's* the one positioning my length at her entrance, and *she's* the one pushing down inch by tortuous inch until I can't see straight from the blinding pleasure.

My head lulls back as she sinks fully on top of me, the warmth of her pussy gripping me like a vice, my abs tensing from how fucking perfect she feels with me inside of her.

She mewls, lifting herself up and slamming back down *hard*, working her hips in a figure-eight motion before repeating the process, and I'm... fucking lost in everything that she is. Praying to a God I don't believe in that somehow I'll get to keep her.

But it isn't long until I feel a shift. Her movements become stiff—robotic—the heat being sucked away by a sudden chill. My eyes pop open and notice her staring blankly at the wall behind me.

I grab the nape of her neck again, forcing her face to mine so I can look into her eyes. But it's like she isn't there.

What the fuck?

I push her sharply, stopping her movements, my heart stuttering when her facial expression barely changes as her eyes move from the wall to me.

She's no longer with me.

And that just doesn't work for me.

Moving both palms to her hips, I pull her off me, standing up and throwing her on the bed. She gasps, a bit of life flashing into her eyes. My hand grabs her throat, fingers squeezing the sides so tight the tendons bend from the pressure. And then I pull until her back is bowed off the bed, her nose brushing against mine.

"Come back to me, little bird." Her eyes flicker and focus, and my chest loosens, relief dousing the worry.

"Are you okay?" I loosen my grip.

She gasps for breath, nodding.

"Do you want to stop?"

She shakes her head.

"Do you remember your safe word?"

She nods again.

"Good."

I dive down, my teeth sinking into her lower lip until tangy copper floods my tastebuds. "You think you can ride my dick and *not* be here with me while you do it?"

She groans, her hips lifting off the bed, her slick cunt rubbing against my swollen cock. My free hand circles her nipple, rolling the bud between my fingers and pinching. She gasps, her chest pushing into my palm.

"Answer me."

She shakes her head. "No. I'm sorry, I—"

I chuckle. "You *will* be sorry." Gripping my shaft, I stroke up and down, spreading the juice from her pussy until I'm coated in the wetness. "You don't want to give it to me the way I want." My fingers twitch against her neck, her pulse thrumming erratically under my thumb. I position myself at her entrance. "Then I'll take it the way I need."

Her eyes blaze to life, and the uncertainty floats away, satisfaction clicking into place like a puzzle piece. *This is what she needs.*

"No," she whispers.

Smirking, I thrust inside of her, shoving my cock so deep I see stars.

"No," she says again, pushing against my chest. Her nails dig into my pecs, like her tiny body is enough to move my six-foot-seven frame. Arousal stabs at my insides, spreading through my limbs, so sharp it feels like needles. Moving from her neck, I grab her hands, ripping them off me and pinning them above her head.

"You can act like you don't want this." I thrust harder on the word, my eyes cataloging her face, attuned to her every motion, making sure she likes what I'm giving. "But your pussy can't lie the way your filthy mouth does."

My cock is so hard it feels like it might rip her in half. "Should I make you come to prove it?" I move both her wrists into one hand, sliding my other down her body until my fingers reach her swollen clit. Her body jolts, and she gasps, her knees pressing into my stomach, trying to push me back. My hips piston in and out of her, punishing her for making me feel so *fucking* much.

She moans again, her body arching as I rub her pussy, and my balls tighten, tendrils of pleasure spiraling through me until I worry I'll pass out from the feel of her walls fluttering around me.

And then... she explodes, a scream leaving her mouth as she creams my cock. The rhythmic massage is all I need and it pushes me over the edge, my balls tightening, shooting cum so deep inside of her, I can almost feel it painting her womb.

Jesus Christ.

Collapsing on top of her, I lay my head in the crook of her neck, pressing soft kisses to the side of her throat where pink marks from my fingers have left an imprint. I come out of my haze, my chest rising and falling as I try to catch my breath, my hand smoothing down the hair on the back of her head.

She gazes up at me, an indecipherable look in her eyes, and it's only then I realize her body is trembling. I lean in, pressing a kiss to her lips. "Are you with me, baby?"

She nods, sucking on her teeth.

One of my arms wraps around her waist, the other stays on her head, and I pull her closer, her leg wedging between mine.

Tears slip silently down her cheeks and my chest squeezes. I cup her face, wiping them away with my thumb. I want to say something, but I'm not sure what *to* say, so I stay silent, cradling her as she processes her emotions. I'm not surprised she has them after what we just did.

I sure as fuck do.

I'm feeling all kinds of things.

And as I lay here, holding the only woman who's ever made me ache for something more, my chest cracks in half, knowing that one day she'll find out the truth, and then I'll have to leave her, and all of these *feelings* behind.

26

LILY

I'm embarrassed. It flows through my veins like lava, heating my core and spreading through every limb.

It's been twenty minutes since Alex brought me back from the brink, and he hasn't moved from his spot. One arm is wrapped tightly around my waist, the other cradling the back of my head, our naked bodies intertwined as I break apart in his arms. And now that the heaviest of sobs have been wracked from my body, I feel… drained. Disgusting. Vulnerable.

Seen.

Lifting my head, I look at Alex, my heart rubbing against my raw edges with every fractured beat. I thought I could do it. Be normal. I thought that with him, maybe it would be different, because I feel so different. Turns out, I'm just as broken as I've always been.

Only, I've never had someone who *cared*. Never had someone pull me back from the darkness to give me what I need. And now he's staring at me like I'm precious. Holding me like I'm *important*. It makes my insides cramp, old wounds aching, because I didn't know. I never realized that this is what it could feel like. *This* is what it should have felt like all along.

Alex felt me missing and he brought me back. The sharp sting of his cock splitting me open, and his hand squeezing my throat until I couldn't breathe, lifted me from the fog.

He gave me what I asked for, and by doing so, gave me something I didn't know I needed. *Him.*

But I feel sick.

"Thank you," I whisper. "I'm sorry."

His hand smooths down the back of my head, his fingertips continuing until they trace the edge of my jaw. Chills trickle through my body at his touch. "For what?" he asks.

My throat swells and I choke out the words, tears blurring my vision. "I don't know."

"I've never had anyone cry after I gave them an orgasm," he jokes.

A giggle bursts out of me, chipping away small pieces of my shame, disintegrating them to dust.

His thumb brushes my cheek. "Do you want to talk about things now or later?"

My lungs squeeze tight, because the truth is, I'd rather not talk about it at all. But I'm realizing that when it comes to Alex, avoidance isn't a subject he's willing to entertain. And it's in this moment that full realization hits.

I trust him.

He pulls out the darkest parts of me and loves them until they sparkle.

"Is never an option?" I peer at him from under my lashes.

He chuckles. "Not if you ever want me to touch you again."

My stomach pulls like taffy, twisting and tearing, while I try to reach deep and find the strength to explain why I am the way I am. "Sex is..." I swallow. "Hard for me."

He nods, his hand going back to my head, pulling me farther into his embrace. I rest my cheek on his chest, the sound of his heartbeat pumping courage through my veins.

"No one has ever cared before." My insides blaze, flames

licking up my throat, making me want to stop the words. But I push through the fire, allowing myself to feel the burn. Because Alex deserves to know the whole truth. Because, for the first time, I wonder if sharing some of the burden would stop it from crushing my bones beneath its weight. "My mind's fucked up."

His body shifts, his palms soothing as they trail along my body. "So is mine."

Shaking my head against him, my fingers tap a nervous rhythm on his torso. "No, I mean… I had—there have been a lot of things happen to me that I prefer to forget. And I… sometimes sex recreates those memories, and my brain turns off like a switch."

His hands stop their caress, and after a tense moment he asks, "So that you don't remember?"

I shrug. "I guess. I don't really know."

"And the role-playing?"

I shrug again, the claws of shame threatening to rip old wounds and drown me in their blood. "I don't know. I just… it's the only way I've ever been able to come, so…"

"I thought you told me you had never actually done it."

Nausea rolls deep in my stomach, shooting up my throat like a gunshot, souring my mouth. I curl into him tighter. "I haven't," I whisper.

His body tenses, but otherwise, he shows no reaction. He doesn't push for more than what I'm able to give, and it makes my chest swell with warmth, so fucking thankful that he gets what I need without me having to speak the words.

"And what we did," he continues, his voice rumbling in his chest, and sinking into my bones. "That was okay?"

My cheeks heat, arousal curling through my womb at the memory. "That was *more* than okay. It was… incredible." I pause, anxiety forming a thought in my head, and trickling through my body like a leaky faucet. "But if it was too much for you then we—I can try harder to like the other way too. I get that it's not n—"

His mouth presses against mine, cutting off my words. "Stop speaking," he mutters against my lips. He rolls over until he's hovering on top of me, keeping us connected with his tongue.

I've rarely been kissed, but the few times I have pale in comparison.

Alex kisses me like he's reaching inside my chest and stealing my breath for his own. Like he'd let the world burn, if only I'd ask him for the ashes.

Finally, he breaks away, his eyes roaming over my face, the weight of his body pressing on mine the only thing tethering me to the ground.

"I'm going to say something, and I need you to listen to me." His palm runs down my hair again, and I lean into his touch. His other hand grips my chin, his thumb pressing into my bottom lip. "Being with you is what I like. However you need. However you want. Getting you off gets *me* off. Feeling you... learning all the different parts of you—" He swallows, his Adam's apple bobbing. "It's a fucking gift. I'll be whatever you need me to be."

My chest spasms, stomach warming. Emotion swirls in the center of my gut like fog, unfurling through my body, filling up the empty space. My hand lifts, fingers scratching against his stubble. "And who gets to be what *you* need?"

His eyes flash with heat, his lips turning up in the corner. His hand moves from my chin, skimming up my cheek and wrapping around the back of my neck. Leaning in, his nose brushes against mine, the moment thick with a tender energy.

"You're the only thing I need, little bird."

He says it like a promise, and he seals it with a kiss.

LILY

Moving from table to table hurts—the most delicious type of throb—the kind that reminds me of who it was that put the ache there in the first place. It's been three days since that night with Alex, and still, my body pulls and pinches, the whisper of his touch in every twinge.

I would be lying if I said I didn't love it.

Somewhere along the way, despite my intention to *not* let it happen, I got attached. It happened before the sex, stupidly letting myself sink into the comfort of seeing him in the mornings, and again when I got off work at night.

Now that things have gone back to "normal," I'm not quite sure what to do with myself. He comes into the diner most days, sitting in his signature corner booth, a notepad or his worn copy of *The Art of War* in his ring-covered hands. The ones that glide over my body and leave imprints on my skin.

But today he wasn't here, and I'm lost in the worry that creeps through my psyche, wondering where he is and what he's doing. *If he'll be back.*

"Lily."

I jump at the sound of my manager's voice, spilling a bit

of the salt that I'm pouring into the shaker. My hand shoots to my chest. "Jesus, Johnny, you scared me."

He grins. "You've been a little out of it today. You okay?"

"Yeah, I'm fine." I wave him off. "Today was busier than usual, right?"

"Yeah, I don't know what was up with that, but I'm fucking tired as hell."

I nod in agreement, scooping up the salt, the grains tickling the palm of my hand.

"Listen, you still got the keys to lock up?" Johnny asks, scratching at the hair behind his head.

I lift a brow. "Yeah, why? You leaving?"

He smiles, his hand gripping the back of his neck as he glances at the floor. "Yeah, I've got some places to be if you're alright with closing."

I bob my head even though the idea of being alone makes me uneasy. But Johnny is notorious for pawning off his duties to whichever server is the closer, and I'm a big girl. I'm no stranger to things that go bump in the night.

It's twenty minutes later when I finally finish, grabbing the drawer from the cash register and locking it up in the safe for Johnny to balance in the morning. Closing the office door, I walk through the kitchen, making my way to the back exit. I'm almost there when I feel it.

The heat at my back.

I spin around, my eyes straining through the dark, but there's nothing there other than the sudden chill running through me. Turning toward the door, I start to move again when I hear another noise, my heart kicking up a notch in my chest, adrenaline pumping through my veins.

Fucking Johnny, leaving me here alone.

My fight-or-flight response kicks in, the deepest recesses of my mind gaping wide like an open wound, pouring fear into my veins. Visions of who it could be run through my mind until suddenly, I'm absolutely fucking terrified that it's *him*.

That somehow, despite me disappearing four years ago, despite me never reaching out to anyone from my past; he's found me.

And if he's found me, he's found *Chase*.

Pure and icy dread freezes me in place, my worst nightmares playing out like a preview in my head. But as soon as I feel a body press against my back, my muscles ease, breath bursting from my lungs in relief because I know it isn't him.

I can feel the difference.

"Stupid of you to be all alone in a place like this." Alex's voice is a rumble, vibrating through my bones, mixing with the adrenaline that's still flooding through my system.

"Al—"

His calloused palm smacks over my mouth, muffling my words. The sting radiating through the bottom of my cheeks. His body presses farther into me. "Shut up."

My pussy throbs, fingers trembling from leftover fear as they dig into my thighs.

"You don't get to speak unless it's to ask for my cock in your mouth, do you understand?"

I nod, my chest pulling tight.

His free hand wraps around my waist and skims up the middle of my chest, my stomach tightening in anticipation. "You've been teasing me for *days*. I've been fucking dreaming about these tits." His grasp is rough as he squeezes a breast in his palm, sending a shot of arousal spiking through my middle.

"Ale—" I mumble against his hand.

His fingers tighten against my jaw. "I didn't come back here for your mouth. I came back here for this." His touch rustles the fabric of my shirt against my skin, his hand gliding from my chest, over my stomach, and down between my legs, cupping my pussy through my black pants.

His other palm moves from my mouth, resting against the front of my throat.

"Please," I whisper, my heart rate accelerating when he kicks my ankle, making my knee jerk from its position until my legs spread.

"Put your hands against the fridge."

I shake my head, anticipation thrumming through my insides until my pulse throbs in time to the arousal that's seeping through my veins. "No."

He chuckles against my ear, low and raspy, before his large frame pushes into mine, pressing me against the cool metal of the stainless steel. I try to move, but he has me pinned—completely immobile. I suck in a gasp, biting back the moan that tries to slip free at the thought of me not being able to stop him. Of him doing whatever he wants with me, in the middle of the diner, with or without my permission.

His breath is hot on my skin as he leans in, whispering in my ear. "Is there anyone else here?"

There's a squeeze on my hip, his grip almost bruising in its intensity. Excitement filters through me.

"Yes," I say. "Someone's in the back office."

"You filthy little liar," he tsks. "I *know* you're alone. I waited outside until every last person left. And then I watched you from across the street, prancing around in these little pants, this tight as fuck shirt." He thrusts into me, his erection pressing against my ass. I bite my cheek to hold in the moan.

"You really think having someone here would stop me?" he rasps, his fingers working the button of my pants open and shoving them off my hips. "I'd fuck you in a roomful of people, forcing you to look them in the eyes as you come around my cock."

I thrash against his hold, my hands flinging behind me, fingernails digging into any piece of him I can reach. He sucks in a breath, and then my wrists are caught in his grasp, my arms twisted behind my back and locked in place by his bruising grip.

"Go ahead," he sings into my ear, his hand trailing down

my stomach and slipping underneath my panties, stroking my swollen clit. "Try to get away. I like it when you fight."

My heart kicks against my ribs, and I rear my head back, throwing my entire body weight into the motion. But it's useless because he doesn't even budge. My five-foot-two frame is nothing compared to his stature. His size alone incapacitates me.

He tightens his grip on my wrists, lips skimming across my collarbone before his teeth sink into my skin, a rush of heat shooting through me like a gunshot.

I gasp at the harsh sting. *Is he marking me?*

"Please, Oh my God," I cry.

"God can't hear you." There's a clink of a belt buckle. "And I'm not listening."

A sudden burn blazes across my hips as he rips my panties down the middle, and shoves himself so deep inside me I scream out.

"Jesus, *fuck*," he groans, his grip becoming loose on my arms. Not that it matters. I'm too lost in delirious pleasure as it scratches along my skin. I like being under his control.

He starts a punishing pace, his cock sliding easily, because despite my resistance and my fake cries of no, my pussy is soaking, the juices from his abuse dripping down my legs.

My clit throbs as I push back against him, acting like I don't want him anywhere near me. It only makes him hold me tighter, pistoning his hips against my backside, my breasts smashed against the unforgiving metal of the refrigerator.

He releases my wrists, tingles rushing through my fingers as the blood flows back into them, and he wraps his arms around my middle, crushing our bodies together. My hands dig into his forearms, no longer fighting as I give into the shakes of my body, pleasure spiraling through me. Soft moans slip from my mouth with every thrust, his dick hitting so deep I swear I feel it bruising my womb.

"What happened?" he rumbles in my ear. "No more

crying? No more screams for help?" He slips out of me and I bite my lip from the loss, my body buzzing so hard I feel like I'm floating.

His hand cups my jaw, twisting my face to his. "Say no again. *Lie* to me. Give me a reason to palm that ass until it breaks."

He spins me around, forcing the breath from my lungs at the sudden movement, and slams me on top of the salad bar countertop, my elbows smashing into the stainless steel. I swallow down a cry, the ache radiating up my arm, even as my pussy throbs from the sting.

The bite of pain is a reprieve from the fog that usually descends.

That, combined with the sensation of him pressed against me, pinning my body in place while he wraps my hair around his fist, has me spiraling so fast it's blinding.

And then he's sliding back inside of me, thrusting his cock so deep his balls slap against my clit. The root of my hair pulls until it burns, wrapped around his fist, his other hand squeezing my shoulder, using my body as leverage to fuck me raw.

Heat coils deep in my gut, spiraling upward, spreading through my insides and reaching every single limb until even my fingertips sizzle.

The pressure on my shoulder eases, and suddenly there's a sharp sting followed by warmth, spreading across my ass cheek, making my pussy spasm around him.

Smack.

I gasp, my stomach clenching as he spanks me.

"You dirty fucking slut."

Smack.

It's not the first time I've been called a slut. I've always been disgusted with the word, but the way he says it, like he's picked it out of the dirt and made it sparkle just for him, sends me reeling. Like he's taken away the degradation and given me the power.

Because I know that all I have to say is one word and everything will stop.

I'm in control.

"I'm going to come inside you," he grunts against the skin of my neck. "Make you feel me for days, so you're reminded with every breath who you belong to."

My eyes roll back at his filthy words, my core contracting at the thought of him coming undone inside of me, *because* of me, and that's all it takes. I explode into a thousand pieces, my body shaking violently, my throat being rubbed raw from my scream as I collapse against the cold metal of the kitchen counter. Vaguely, I'm aware of a groan behind me, his cock pulsing as he presses as far into me as he can get.

When I come back to myself, it's to the feel of soft kisses being laid up and down my spine. I lay still, waiting for the shame to reach up and grip me in its claws. I know it's on the way, it never leaves me completely.

But when you spend years with your body being used a certain way, you become conditioned.

I don't know any other way to be.

I'm sick.

I'm broken.

And I'm fucking disturbed.

But Alex *sees* those pieces, and nurtures them like they're worthy. Like they're *his*. And while I know I'll never be whole again, for the first time, I wonder if it's possible to fall in love with jagged edges.

"God, Lily, you're fucking incredible. What do you need, baby? Are you thirsty? Did I hurt you?" His voice brings me back to the present and I straighten, my body sore and satiated, reveling in the feel of being worked over by him.

I look around, realizing we'll need to sanitize the area before we can leave, but feeling so vulnerable in the moment that I don't want to put forth the effort. What I *really* want is to have him hold me for the rest of the night, to keep the nightmares at bay and remind me that what we just did doesn't make me less of a person.

I bite back the emotion that's surging up my throat.

"We need to clean this place back up." Spinning around, I look into his eyes. "And hi, by the way."

His eyes sparkle as he leans in, pressing his lips to mine. "Hi, little bird."

He kisses me again, his tongue twisting with mine until I feel the tangle in my heart. Backing away with a wink, he runs a hand through his hair. "Okay, now where's the cleaning shit? Let's do this and then go get our boy."

Our boy.

Fireworks dance through me like the fourth of July, and while the feeling is scary, the sparks making my insides jump with nerves, the view is too beautiful to step away.

So I'll stand in their shower and risk getting burned.

28

MASON

I'm fucked.

There's truly no other way to put it. But when I'm with Lily, I get crazy ideas in my head. Ideas that make me think maybe I *don't* have to do anything drastic. Maybe her knowing I'm a PI is enough. Maybe "one day" never has to come.

I could refund Chase his money, tell him I had no luck, and then stay. For good. Don would give me hell, but he'd get over it. Eventually. I think.

The longer I sit with the idea, the more merit I give it in my head, visions of carving out a new future here with Lily and her son taking root and growing branches around my soul.

A place where I can belong.

A family.

I know running from your problems isn't the healthiest thing in the world, but it's worked well enough for the past decade.

My brain has been a seesaw, the weight of my decisions tottering back and forth—a lot like the one on this playground where I'm standing with Lily, watching Chase run around like a maniac.

The truth is that I could get used to this, and that's a concept I've spent the past ten years avoiding like the plague. But it's happened anyway. The pull to Lily is too strong for me to ignore, and while it terrifies the living shit out of me, the thought of leaving them scares me more.

So, I guess it just comes down to what I'm willing to live with, and what I'm willing to lose.

There was once upon a time when I thought my life would end up differently. When I was still a young kid, thinking I was grown, wading through murky man-made waters. Back when I chirped like a parrot about family and faith. But even back then, deep down, I knew it wasn't the truth. How could I when I had spent my life watching snakes worshiped as gods?

Chase jumps off the monkey bars, running toward the slide, and my heart lurches as I watch him. I take the free moment to sidle up to Lily, dragging her into me until she molds to my side like a missing limb. She only comes to the middle of my chest on a good day, and yet somehow, she fits me better than anyone else ever has. The thought makes my lungs squeeze tight.

"Hi." Lily smiles.

"Hi back." I press a kiss against her forehead.

"Careful." Her arms wrap tight around my waist. "A girl could get used to this."

My muscles tense when my heart skips, and I press another kiss to her head.

"Mommy, Awex, are you watching?" Chase's little voice soars across the air, and while it hits my ears first, it settles deep in my chest, spreading warmth through me like a heated blanket.

We both turn toward the slide, and I move Lily in front of me, pressing our bodies close together, my arms wrapping around her waist. Her fingers squeeze my forearms, and I swear I feel it in the depths of my soul.

How can I leave this?

My phone vibrates in my pocket, and she shifts, turning quickly to glance at me. "You need to get that?" she asks.

I do, but there's no chance in hell I'll answer it in front of her. Still, with every ignored buzz, our harsh reality drops back in, reminding me that she's a job. A mark.

A paycheck.

I shake my head, my hold tightening against her stomach. "Nope."

She smiles, leaning back against me, and that's where we stay for the rest of the afternoon, until Chase is so tired he falls asleep in my arms on the walk to their apartment.

It isn't until later, when I'm at the motel, that I check my missed calls and texts.

Most from Don. My brows furrow, irritation wringing my insides dry because I *just* talked to that motherfucker.

There's also a missed call from Lily's brother, Chase.

His name tugs on the chains binding me to the job I've been paid for, reminding me that I'm sitting here living a fucking lie. I've been avoiding him, stupidly hoping that maybe he'd be patient long enough for me to come up with a plan.

I pull up my voicemail and press play, Chase's sharp voice coming through the line.

"Mason. It's Chase Adams. Look... it's been a minute since I've heard from you, and I get that this shit takes time, but *fuck*, man. Can I get an update? I'm driving myself fucking crazy over here. My girl is losing her mind with me, and I'm..." He blows out a breath, and guilt works its way through my insides at the desperation that leaks from his voice. "I'm starting to lose hope. I just... It's been almost a year, and if you're really the best—if you're *really* the fucking best, and even you can't find her, then...." He clears his throat. "Maybe there's nothing left to find."

There's a higher pitched voice whispering words I can't make out before he speaks again. "Anyway, call me back. *Please*. Just give me *something*."

Click.

I lean back on the bed, swallowing around the burn from the crater that's just been ripped open in my chest. Chase deserves to know his sister, but Lily obviously doesn't want to be found.

And I still have no idea why.

Blowing out a breath, I call back Don, ignoring the anxiety that's already brewing in my gut like a storm.

"Mase. *Jesus*, finally. You know I'm really not a fan of this whole 'you avoiding my calls' thing. I'm still your fucking boss."

I smirk, amusement lining my lips. "That's only a technicality."

"Technicalities exist for a reason," he grunts.

Laughing, I unwrap a toothpick and roll it between my lips. "If you say so, old man."

"What the hell are you doing down there still, Mase?"

I cringe, drumming my fingertips on the desk's top. "You won't like the answer."

"Then don't fucking tell me. Just get your shit together and handle it, okay? I've been giving you time, but it's about to be out, boy." He sighs. "You wanna talk about your dad?"

My entire body tenses. "What's there to say? We knew this day was coming, and my dumb ass should have been watching for it."

"What's your plan?"

My brows lift to my hairline. "What do you mean?"

"Come on, Mason. You aren't stupid, so stop pretending like you are. There's no way your face won't be plastered all over."

"I've stayed hidden for this long," I grumble.

"You can add all the muscle and tattoos you want, kid, but someone will recognize you eventually. This isn't the senate. This is the fucking presidency. Your ghost is gonna be in the limelight again whether you like it or not. They'll *use* your story to snatch the vote. I advise you to think about that when you do whatever the hell it is you're doing right now." He pauses. "Think about *who* you're involving."

My insides pull tight, the need for a cigarette raging through my system like a stampede. "Yeah..." I clench my jaw, my teeth biting into the wood of the toothpick.

"Besides that, you have a job to do, and if you can't do it, then you need to tell me right now. I swear to God if I was there I'd bash your head against the wall until you got it through your thick head."

"Don, be real." I laugh. "We both know you'd never beat me in a fight."

"Fuck you."

I smile. "Don't be bitter."

"Don't be stupid," he hits back. "Actions have consequences. What's going to happen if he wins, Mason? This isn't going away."

My heart trips and stutters against my sternum. "I know."

"Then *be smart.* Finish this job and get the hell out of the country. Come to the beach and stay with me."

I roll my eyes, my stomach twisting. "Who'd keep the business going?"

"You let me worry about that."

Cringing, I sit back, pulling up the pictures of Lily I took the first time I saw her, across the street of her apartment, hidden behind sharp bushes that bit into my skin.

Nausea churns in my gut. *Fuck.*

"Do you hear me, Mason? This is serious."

"Yeah..." I run my hand through my hair. "I hear you. I'll take care of it."

"Make sure you do."

He hangs up, and I put my head in my hands, his words stabbing my skin and sinking into my bones, causing an ache I know will never leave. Pushing back from the desk, I curse, standing up and grabbing the still unopened pack of cigarettes and heading out the front door.

The flick of a lighter, the singe of paper, and a deep inhale is all it takes for my body to unclench, nicotine flowing through my veins and wrapping me in its embrace, dulling the whisper of regret and the prodding of heartache that's nicking my insides.

Pulling out my phone, I Google Senator Wells, my blood icing over in my veins.

Senator Wells campaign stays strong as he makes his way to Phoenix.

He's coming to Arizona.

29

LILY

"I'm kidnapping you this weekend."

My eyes widen and I giggle, looking over at Annabelle and shaking my head. "You can try, but you won't succeed."

"Come on, girl," she whines. "Dish to me! I just started hanging out with you, and then *my* dick of the week jumped ship and got lost in *your* vagina, so the least you can do is go out with me."

My stomach clenches when she so casually mentions the fact that she's fucked Alex. *My* Alex.

I'd be lying if I said it didn't bother me. It does, but I remind myself that we all have our pasts, and while I can't fault him for his, it's hard not to wonder if everyone else experiences him the same way as me.

If everyone gets to know what it feels like to be consumed by him.

Annabelle sips on her Styrofoam cup, placing it above the drink station. "Oh, no, uh-uh, don't give me that look. I already told you, it's *fine*. You don't need to deny it. Besides, even if you did, I wouldn't believe you. Every time that man walks in here, he looks more pussy whipped than the day before."

A laugh bursts out of me, and I spin, peeking around the corner to where Alex sits in his signature corner booth, reading his worn copy of *The Art of War*, so reminiscent to the first time we met.

Who would have thought that it would only take a couple months until I'd find myself willingly falling into some fucked-up reality where my head is filled with visions of possibility.

I've made plenty of mistakes in my past, left behind my family in pursuit of numbing pain I can't outrun, but with Alex, maybe I can start fresh. It won't replace the history of scars. It won't heal my broken soul, but maybe it can be a balm, and I can find some peace in the happiness he provides.

Derek is right, I can't keep punishing myself forever.

"I don't know, I think I have plans." My eyes drift toward Alex again.

She rolls her eyes but a smile lights up her face. "Fine. But I'm taking a rain check. You owe me."

Smiling, I make my way over to Alex's table, plopping down in the booth opposite him. He glances up from his book and grins. The weight of his stare is heady, causing an ache to flare between my thighs and my heart to skip every other beat. It's impossible to come to work without remembering how he fucked me raw on the counter, and having him here now, looking at me the way he is…

My stomach clenches, arousal spiraling through me at the memory, followed closely by the comfort in knowing he offers what I need and never asks for more than I can give. The mix of emotions twist and turn like a cyclone. When the storm passes and only the dust remains, it settles around *him*. Because with Alex, everything I've been running from feels a little less dark. A little less scary. A little less suffocating. Because I know he'll help me take the breath.

I pop a cold fry from his plate into my mouth. "I'll have you know I just turned down girls' night for you."

He grins. "Oh?"

I nod, chewing slowly. "That's right. So what are we doing on Friday?"

His head cocks to the side. "You don't work?"

A smile splits my cheeks as I shake my head, my ponytail brushing along the top of my back. "Nope. I'm all yours if you want me."

His eyes flash. "I always want you."

My veins heat at his words. "Good."

He watches me silently for a few moments. "I'm taking you out."

"Like a date?" I ask, excitement buzzing in my stomach.

His lips tilt up. "Is that not okay with you?"

I shake my head. "No, it's perfect. I've never been on one."

His smile drops and he does that thing he does—that penetrating gaze that strips away my smile and sears beneath my skin.

"Don't look at me like that," I mumble.

He smirks, unwrapping a toothpick from his pocket and popping it in his mouth. "Like what?"

"All sad eyes and sexy."

He chuckles. "I don't know any other way to look at you, little bird." He leans in close, his hands resting flat against the table. "You're sexy as fuck."

I suck in a breath, butterflies erupting in my stomach.

The bell chimes above the door and I hop up quickly, not wanting anyone to see me eye fucking another customer. But I can't wipe the smile from my face.

A date.

It's Friday night. Chase is with Susan and I'm... *nervous*. I've done a lot of things in my life, but a date has never been one of them.

There's a knock on my door just as I finish smoothing down my blouse, looking at myself in the mirror one last time and cringing at what I see.

It's a far cry from the fashionista I always dreamed of becoming, but when you don't have two cents to rub together, you get used to making do with what you have. And the closest I have to a nice outfit is a ruched black halter style top and my nicest pair of Goodwill jeans. Blowing out a breath, my fingers swipe against my opposite wrist as I make my way to the front.

When I open the door, heat rushes to my cheeks, nerves tap dancing in my gut. Alex's dark hair is slicked back, his teeth gleaming underneath my porch light with his smile. He holds a giant bouquet of red roses.

His eyes change as he drinks me in, his gaze burning me alive, and suddenly, this outfit doesn't feel so ratty. Not when he's staring at me like he wants to devour me whole.

"Hi," I breathe. "Are those for me?" I point to the flowers.

He clears his throat, and he steps into me, having to duck slightly under the frame of the door. His lips skim my cheek as he hands me the bouquet. "Pretty flowers for a stunning girl."

I grasp them, my fingers brushing against his, the simple touch sending my stomach flying into my throat. "Thank you, they're beautiful," I say, bringing them to my nose and inhaling the sweet fragrance.

"*You're* beautiful," he rasps, pressing a kiss to my lips.

A smile blooms on my face while I kiss him back, and suddenly a giggle escapes, forcing us to break apart and totally ruining the moment.

He leans back, a hint of a grin cracking his face. "What's funny?"

"Nothing," I laugh. "This is all just so cliche."

His lips turn down like he's offended, and I pull him back into me by his face, my fingers scratching against his jaw. "It's perfect." I rise up to kiss his pouty lips. "I've never had cliche before."

His lips land on mine again and I sink into him, lost in his taste—in his attention. His arms lock behind me, and I break away, locking my gaze in his as I skim my fingers along his biceps. "Where are you taking me tonight?"

"It's a surprise." He grins, his eyes sparking.

My insides quake with possibility, and for the first time, I feel excited for the unknown.

And I fall a little deeper.

30
MASON

I've never been the dating type. Never been one who wooed a woman and promised them the world. Dating gives hope, and hope is something I've never had the urge to give. There's only been one other person I've called mine, but even then, there wasn't this *need* to make her feel cherished. Not the way there is with Lily.

It pisses me off that no one has ever taken care of her before now. When I show up to her place with a bouquet of roses I picked up at the corner store—the same one she goes to every week for groceries—her eyes light up like it's the best gift she's ever received.

I want to put that look on her face every day for the rest of my life, and that thought terrifies me more than it should, because I still haven't figured shit out, and I know I'm running out of time.

"You ready to go?" I ask her.

She nods, and I grab her hand, pulling her behind me to the parking lot where my Harley sits.

"Are we going on that?" She waves her hand at my bike.

"Yeah, why?" Amusement sprinkles through my chest at the way she fidgets. "You've never been on one?"

She shakes her head, a small smile breaking over her face. "No, I have. Just don't like them very much."

Grabbing a helmet off the back and walking over to her, I place it in her hands. "Then you haven't been riding them right." I wink.

Her chest brushes against my stomach as she sucks in a breath and I close my eyes, willing my cock to calm down until after we get back. I'm determined to give her a night she'll remember. *Clichés included.*

Truthfully, I don't have anything spectacular planned, I just want to dote on her. Take her out and show her how she deserves to be treated.

I've reserved us a table at a small French restaurant right outside of Phoenix, next to a small lake where I plan to take her after, just to sit outside by the water and talk. A nice, normal night where she can let go of the weight she always carries on her shoulders and enjoy her time with me. *Hopefully.*

She climbs onto the back of my bike, and the heat of her body pressed against me sends a shot of desire curling through my insides. I look back and smirk. "Ready?"

She nods, the black helmet hiding her eyes from my view.

It's a thirty-minute ride, and she's silent, only the tightening of her arms around my waist reminding me she's there in the first place. Pulling into the lot, I park and turn off the engine, my hands coming down on top of hers and squeezing.

She climbs off my bike, and I'm struck by the sight of her, unsure why it is that every moment spent in her presence makes me want to dive a little deeper. How is it that she gets *more* attractive the longer I stare? She pulls off her helmet, her dark locks mussed and tumbling down her back, giving her a freshly fucked look that makes my stomach flip and blood rush to my cock.

"What are you looking at?" She glances at her outfit,

running her hands over the front of her shirt and down her dark jeans.

I stand up, walking to her, and draw her into me, running my tongue across her lips and reveling in her taste. "You, little bird. I'm always looking at you."

She smiles against my mouth, her hands reaching up and wrapping around my neck. "You know, you're much more romantic than I gave you credit for."

I quirk a brow. "I'm not romantic, Lily. I'm just in——" The words stick on the back of my tongue and I clear my throat as I realize what I was about to say.

In love.

She tilts her head, her eyes gaining a curious sheen, and my heart spasms in my chest. My thumb brushes against the underside of her jaw, the smoothness of her skin making my mouth water, wanting to feel it under my tongue.

I smile, running my hands down her arms and grasping her palm, locking our fingers together. I bring her hand up to my mouth, pressing a kiss to the back. "You must bring it out of me."

Her eyes dim, and she inhales heavily before pasting a grin on her face and twisting to stare at the restaurant. "Wow, Alex, this place looks really nice." She fidgets as I lead us through the doors. "Is it okay for me to wear *jeans* in here?"

I smirk and tap the top of her nose, turning my attention to the blonde hostess as her head pops up from her stand with a big grin. We *are* underdressed, but honestly, I don't give a fuck. The only thing places like this care about is the money. If you act like you belong, then you do. I grew up living and breathing in this type of environment, and if I have to adopt the air of my past in order to give her a night to remember, then that's what I'll do.

Besides, fuck these people. It isn't about what they think, it's about my woman. And that's what Lily is.

Mine.

"Alex Calhoun. We have a reservation."

The hostess nods and leads us to our booth. When we sit down, I can feel Lily's stare burning a hole in the center of my chest.

"What?" I ask.

She blinks a few times then shakes her head. "Nothing, I-I never knew your last name is all. Crazy because it's never even crossed my mind to ask." Her eyes haze over, and my stomach tenses as I force a smile on my face.

It's not my last name. It's Don's.

She picks up a menu. "Jesus, how'd you even find this place?"

I raise my fingers and wiggle them. "Magic."

"Alex." She giggles, rolling her eyes. "The entire menu is in French."

I shrug. "And? I'll order for you if you want."

"There's nothing under fifty bucks!" she whisper-shouts.

I shrug again. "Don't worry about that."

Her eyes slide behind me and she shrinks a little in her chair, making my stomach sink. I glance around, realizing for the first time that there are servers in the corner glancing over at us, whispering in hushed voices. *Fuck.* Suddenly, I'm second-guessing the entire evening. I was trying to show her a nice night, give her things that she's never had, but I don't want her to spend all of her time being uncomfortable. With people judging us for tattoos and jeans when they're used to suits and pretty dresses.

My leg reaches for hers under the table, my foot grazing up her calf.

Her eyes flash to mine. "Stop it," she mouths.

I smirk. "Or what?"

The waiter interrupts our moment, and I order without thinking, allowing the names of the items to roll effortlessly off my tongue.

"Parles-tu français?" I ask him. I need to tell him to keep his coworkers in check, but I don't want to embarrass Lily.

His eyes widen with his nod, and I swallow, my eyes flashing once again to the girls in the corner. "Demandez à vos collègues d'arrêter de regarder ici comme si nous étions le divertissement et j'ajouterai une centaine de plus à votre conseil." *Get your coworkers to stop watching us like we're the entertainment, and I'll add a hundred to your tip.*

"Oui, Monsieur."

He takes our menu, and it isn't until I take a sip of my sparkling water and look back to Lily that I realize she's frozen in place, eyes large and round, glass of water frozen halfway to her mouth.

I grin, even though panic starts to leech my nerves. *This was a stupid idea.*

"Who *are* you?" she asks.

I lift my shoulder. "I'm not allowed to speak French?"

She shakes her head. "No, I'm just... surprised."

"Well, maybe I like surprising you."

"Hmm," she hums. "What did you say?"

My foot brushes against hers again under the table, heat flaring in my veins when her leg wraps around mine.

"Doesn't matter," I say.

Her eyes narrow. "Do you speak any other languages?"

I nod. "Learning languages wasn't a negotiation when I was growing up."

My heart beats the fuck out of my chest because we're dangerously close to wading into territory that I'm uncomfortable talking about.

"And where'd you grow up?" She bites her lip when she asks, her fingers tapping against her wrist like she's nervous to ask.

Swallowing around the baseball-sized knot in my throat, I lean back in my chair, my eyes assessing her silently for long, stretched moments. I may not be able to give her everything, but I can give her this.

"Oregon," I force out.

"Oh, that's right." She nods, pursing her lips.

A small grin tilts my lips as I watch her. She's so fucking cute. "Go ahead."

Her brows raise. "What do you mean?"

I wave my hand in the space between us. "Ask away. I can see you're dying to know more."

Her head cocks to the side. "And you'll answer?"

I shrug. "Only one way to find out."

We're interrupted when the waiter brings our food, but she doesn't miss a beat, her eyes gaining a fire and her shoulders straightening, looking like she's preparing for battle now that I've given her the green light.

"Do your parents still live there, in Oregon?"

My chest pinches as I cut into my steak. "Yes."

"Do you speak to them?"

Nausea rolls in my gut. "No."

"How come?"

I place my fork and knife down, sadness tightening my muscles until I feel like they might snap. "*That* is a long story."

She exhales and I can see the disappointment swirling in her eyes. I reach across the table and cover her hand with mine. "One that I'll share, but not here."

She nods, looking at the table. I tap the top of her fingers with mine, leaving my chair to lean halfway across the table. "Don't hide from me, little bird."

She looks back up and then meets me in the middle, brushing a kiss across my lips, lighting up my insides.

"Give me all your secrets," she speaks against my lips. "I promise to keep them safe."

31

LILY

He speaks *French*. He walks in the room and everyone turns to stare, but not because he's out of place—although he is. It's because he commands the power, effortlessly inserting himself in the center like it's his God-given right to be there.

I've seen him in *my* element, but I've never seen him like this, and there's something intoxicating about dominating the thoughts of the man who dominates the room.

Dinner is different than I expected, not that I have much experience to go off of. But it never crossed my mind he'd take me somewhere so fancy. And maybe that's why he didn't tell me, because he knew I'd say no, too uncomfortable to even think about going somewhere with several sets of utensils and crystal wine glasses for your water.

But somehow, he makes me feel comfortable in spite of that, and the sprouts of trust budding just under the surface root deeper into my chest. With every side he shows, it feels more and more like he's trying to ground me in something permanent.

I think I'm ready to be kept.

Now we're at Sumner Lake; a small body of water right outside of Phoenix. And even though I've never been here before, its familiarity rushes through my veins, memories throwing me off balance.

Lakes bring flashbacks of my past. Of times with people who I thought were friends and family. Times when I tried, *really* tried, naively perhaps, to be the best version of myself. Before I accepted the fact that there are some demons you can't outrun.

I've worked hard to get where I am, to *not* be the type of mother who birthed me. To not allow the things that happened to me to fuel the fear that could tarnish my son's childhood. But when I stare out at this lake, soaking in the glow of the moon kissing glossy waters, my sorrow bleeds through the cracks, suffusing the peace with a pain so intense it steals my breath.

And just like that, my body *craves* to find the numb.

Tinkling laughter fills the air from a group of teenagers down the way, and my heart squeezes in my chest, replacing their distant blurred faces with those of my past.

Of Becca.

Lee.

Chase.

"What are you thinking so hard about?" Alex plops down behind me, his legs lining my sides and his arms wrapping around my middle.

I shake my head, sighing. "I just haven't been to a lake in a long time."

"You used to go a lot?"

Goose bumps sprout along my skin, but it's not the outside that creates the chill. It's the type of cold that seeps from your soul, spreading like molasses until the frost coats every bone, causing an ache that even the sun can't take away. My head twists to gaze up at him, wondering if it's even possible to spill my secrets. I've been burying them so long, I'm not sure I can find their shallow graves. But there's something prodding me to dig up the skeletons, hoping the rot of pain doesn't suffocate me under its stench.

"Yeah," I speak slowly. "The town I used to live in surrounded a big one. We used to go all the time as kids."

He hesitates before speaking. "Who's we?"

My brows angle down. "What?"

"You said 'we', who else are you talking about?"

"Oh... my friends." My nose scrunches in distaste as their betrayal rises through my throat and settles on my tongue, tasting just as sour as it did so many years ago. "And my brother, I guess."

He nods. "What's your brother's name?"

My chest stings, the thought of him like a brand seared into my heart, the burn radiating through my middle and settling behind my eyes. "Chase," I force out.

I expect surprise, a moment of realization that I named my son after my brother, but he simply nods, almost like he's known it all along. "Do you still talk to him?"

"Does it matter?" I shrug.

Tingles race down my neck when his lips skim along my shoulder. "Yes," he mutters against my skin.

"I don't—I don't talk to him anymore." A tear drips from the corner of my eye, and I quickly wipe it away with the back of my hand, not wanting to show how much it truly affects me.

"How come?" he presses.

"How come you don't talk to *your* family?" I retort.

His body stiffens behind me, and he lets out a sigh. "My upbringing was different. You already know about the pressure I felt..."

He trails off and my heart falters, sickness swirling through me when I think about him as a little boy, slicing his skin in order to feel.

"Yeah, I remember." I run my hand along his forearm, feeling the raised flesh underneath the pads of my fingers.

"We all have our stories," he says. "My parents aren't good people. Narcissism at its finest. They manipulate *everyone*, weaving an image so tight-knit and perfect, no one would believe anything other than their lie."

My chest tightens.

"*Every* day more of my character was stripped away, cut to fucking pieces by their expectations." He shakes his head.

"And the French?" I ask, unable to stop the words from rolling off my tongue.

He chuckles, pulling my body tighter against him, his breath hot against my ear. "Est-ce que tu aimes ça?"

Shivers skate down my spine. "What does that mean?"

"I asked if you liked it," he rasps.

My cheeks heat. "I don't know a woman who wouldn't."

Arousal spikes through my core when I feel him harden against my back. "Is French the only language you know?"

His grip loosens. "It's the one I'm most fluent in, but I'm passable in others. My parents... they had international guests frequently, and it was important to my father for his child to hold conversation."

I try to picture what Alex's childhood must have been like, but I come up blank, the bits and pieces he's provided not enough to paint the image. Or maybe it's so far removed from anything I've known, it's not able to even exist in my imagination.

"Is your father a businessman?" I twist to see his face.

He nods, the muscles in his jaw tensing. "Yep. For the biggest corporation in the world."

"Oh." I'm dying to know more, but don't want to push him. I can tell this is a sensitive subject, and I know if he prodded *me*, I wouldn't react well.

He blows out a breath. "There, I told you one of mine. Now tell me one of yours."

"My what?"

"Your *secrets*."

My stomach churns. "I don't know where I'd even start."

"The beginning seems like a good place."

My insides wage war between breaking down my walls and reenforcing them, making tears pool in my eyes. I close them to ebb the burn. "I don't know if I can."

He pulls me tighter against him, rocking us in time to the sound of small waves lapping at the rocky shoreline. "Try."

Try.

One syllable. A thousand different emotions.

"My mom was a junkie," I burst out. "She abandoned my brother and me when I was little. I don't—" I shake my head when a tear escapes, annoyance squeezing my stomach because I'm crying over a woman I barely remember. "I don't know much about her. But she fucked my brother up."

"She *abandoned* you?"

I puff out my cheeks. "Yep. Got so high she left us at a gas station in Nowhere, Tennessee." A forgotten wound starts to throb in the center of my chest. "Chase always swore up and down that she didn't mean it. That she just... forgot." I clap my hands together before dropping them to my sides. "But there were only so many nights he could keep the faith, you know? Eventually, he realized she wasn't coming back." I pause, thinking back to how Chase's eyes grew vacant, his personality hardening into stone.

His faith in a woman who never deserved it grew sharp edges that chipped away his childhood piece by piece. "He was never the same after that."

Alex huffs, the wispies on the back of my neck blowing from his breath.

"We were placed into foster care," I continue. My insides squeeze tight, hands growing clammy at even thinking the words, let alone speaking them out loud.

"They split you two up?" he asks.

I shake my head. "No, we were kept together, and he... Chase... he was my biggest protector." My nose burns, throat swelling. "He was my stable ground in a world that always shook beneath my feet."

"He sounds like a great brother."

Before I can stop it, my cheeks are wet from the tears trailing down my face. "The best," I mutter under my breath.

"What was foster care like?"

I lean my head against his chest. "Some places were fine. Others were... not." The wave of shame surges through my insides, dousing me in blackened memories. "One in particular, he—" My voice gets stuck in my throat, snapshots of a past I've trained myself to forget rolling in like fog. I shake my head. "It doesn't matter."

Alex's arms flex on my stomach. "It *does*."

I ignore his words. "The last foster parents we had were amazing, though. They actually adopted us." A soft smile graces my face. "Sam and Anna Adams."

Alex chuckles. "Sam *Adams?* Like the beer?"

I giggle, a sliver of light creeping through the heavy moment. "Yep. They were everything I always dreamed of having. And after years of being touted around place to place, being treated as a paycheck from the government or a... a *toy* to be used—" My teeth clench so hard I'm afraid I'll crack a molar. "It was nice to have the picture-perfect family."

His fingers skim under the hem of my shirt, and the touch alone is enough to ground me. To keep me in the moment. It's difficult, but it feels good to be able to talk about this with someone.

"So what happened?"

I shrug, not knowing if I can put it into words. I *want* to say that sometimes broken pieces are ingrained too deep. That no matter how many times you sweep them up, there are fragments left behind. And eventually, those shards become part of you, the thought of digging them out too painful to bear.

"Sam and Anna were amazing. But they were afraid of pushing us away, most of their focus went to Chase because *he* was the problem child. I wasn't." My lips lift slightly as I shake my head. "I figured out at a young age that when you pretend like nothing is wrong, people believe you."

"Act weak when you are strong, and strong when you are weak."

I twist to face him. "What?"

"It's a Sun Tzu quote from *The Art of War*."

My chest pulls as I hum.

Act strong when you are weak.

"Yeah, that was me, I guess. Always weak." Another tear slides down my face, hot and salty as it hits my lips. My tongue peeks out to wipe the moisture away. "But people believe the face you show them. The more I talked, the less they asked. The more I smiled, the less they cared."

"That's sad, little bird."

"Why do you call me that?" I turn in his arms.

He smiles softly, his hand coming up to run down my cheek. "Birds are social animals. They live in flocks, and flourish in the skies. But when they're put in captivity, they become lonely. Depressed. Aggressive. Sometimes, they show their trauma by never singing again."

My chest aches at his words.

"When I first met you, *you* seemed lonely. Depressed. Aggressive. It made me want to hear you sing."

My breathing thins.

His thumb presses into my bottom lip. "Birds aren't meant to be caged." He leans down and presses a kiss to my lips. "What stole your song, little bird?"

My heart stutters. "I don't think I can talk about that."

His nostrils flare, his eyes searching mine. "I'm afraid I already know."

Alex isn't a stupid man.

A sob breaks out of me, and he catches it with his lips,

sucking in my cries and letting them rest on his tongue. I don't say any more about it. I can't. But I don't need to, because Alex brings me in close and lets me shatter in his arms.

And for the first time I'm not worried about sweeping up the pieces.

3 2
MASON

W hen you know something, you just know.

She doesn't have to say the words, I can piece things together well enough. It's unexplainable, the feeling of wishing like hell you could erase someone's pain, but knowing there's nothing you can do. She cries in my arms, and I breathe in her hurt, hoping that somehow letting her relieve her burden and place it on my shoulders will help her find some peace.

But the shadows of monsters linger long after they're gone. The best we can hope for is to pull ourselves from the darkness.

I didn't intend for the date to end up this way, and then suddenly, *boom*. Just like that, some of the information I've been dying for since I first walked into *Dina's Diner* fell into my lap. None of it explains why she ran away. If anything, it makes indecision flare even stronger in my gut, because more than ever, it's clear that Chase isn't the bad guy. He seems to be one of the best.

And it's that realization which makes a small piece of me think about giving him the information he's desperate for, jumping on my bike and getting the hell out of Dodge before my father even steps foot into Arizona. Giving Lily back to someone who will love her unconditionally. Who won't keep things from her that she deserves to know.

But as soon as the thought starts to grow, I rip it out from its root. I can't do *anything* until I tell her everything.

I have to come clean.

Leaning in, I press another kiss to the top of her head, her sobs dying down, slight hiccups the only thing that remains. It's ironic, how she was running toward the vision of the perfect family I was trying to escape.

"I'm s—sorry," she stutters. "I ruined the date."

I smile, my hand smoothing the flyaways of her hair. "Little bird, without you, there *is* no date."

She sinks lower until she's lying with her head in my lap, her gorgeous hazel eyes peering up at me with all the trust in the world, and I know that now is my moment. I could lay it all on the line and beg for her forgiveness. Wipe the slate clean and tell her that I swear to fucking *God* I'll never abuse her trust again.

But selfishly, I want more time, even though I know I don't deserve it.

I run my hand through her hair, peppering her face with kisses instead, and she giggles, the sound lighting up my chest like a strobe light.

"I didn't think it would be this easy," she sighs.

My brow quirks. "What would?"

She waves her hand between us. "*This.* I mean... it's not easy. Saying things out loud has never been my strong suit." Her nose scrunches. "Not the words that really matter, anyway. But it feels nice to have someone who knows about my past."

I continue smoothing her hair. "What made you leave?"

Her brows raise and my heart slams against my ribs, hoping I'm not wading into dangerous territory. But I need to know. Maybe if she tells me what I want to hear, the guilt will loosen its choke hold around my neck.

"What made me leave my family? Drugs." She raises her arms, showing off her tattooed-covered scars. "What made me leave Tennessee entirely? A psychotic ex-boyfriend who I'm terrified will find out about his son."

Her brows draw down, her fingers scratching in a staggered rhythm against her wrist and I... feel like a piece of shit at how relieved I feel that I finally have a reason to not give her up to her brother.

For her safety. *For Chase.*

Another tear seeps out of the corner of her eye, and my chest burns at the sight. I don't have nice words to say or anything that can lessen the sting of her memories, so I stay quiet instead, hoping that holding her through it will be enough.

"Let's talk about you now." She gives me a sad smile. "What do your parents do?"

I smother my cringe, the craving for nicotine suddenly flowing through my veins, more potent now that the taste of tobacco is fresh on my tongue. "My mom runs charities."

Her eyes widen. "Oh, that's... noble."

A small grin makes its way onto my face. "Yeah, that's why she does it."

"Because she's noble?"

"Because she wants people to *think* she is."

Her lips turn down in the corners. "Oh."

I run a hand through my hair. "My dad is a politician."

There. I said it. Ripped it off like a Band-Aid. I don't know how the hell to come clean about Mason, but I can start here. I can give her this—can give her the truth about *Alex.*

Her brows shoot to her hairline. "I did *not* expect you to say that."

I chuckle. "I don't know why you would. It's not information I offer up in normal conversation."

She sits upright, facing me, her legs brushing against mine as she settles into a new position, curiosity lining the edges of her eyes. "How come you don't talk to them anymore?"

The sutures holding my heart together start to fray, but I push through the pain of the tear to give her what I can. "I didn't want to be part of their fucked-up family anymore, so I left."

Her head tilts to the side. "Just like that?" She snaps her fingers.

"Just like that." *Just like you did.*

"I get that. I can see it." Her head bobs.

"Can you?"

"Yeah, you don't really look the part of a politician's son."

Her words are a poisoned arrow splitting my chest in half, the venom spreading through me until it unlocks all the whispers from my past.

Stand up straighter.

Work harder.

Be a man.

You're an embarrassment to this family.

Get rid of it or marry her.

It's the last one that haunts my every moment, the ghost who never leaves, reminding me that she's right.

I'm no politician's son.

I gave up that title on the night he killed my child.

33

LILY

I'm broken. I know this.

There's nothing I can do to change it, but it feels nice to let somebody else in. I never thought I would have someone in my life to share the weight with. I was always led to believe that fucked-up people don't deserve good things. And while I'm definitely *fucked up*, Alex is the best thing I've ever had.

Tonight turned into so much more than I expected, and the aftereffects of our talk have left me reeling, the bond between us pulsing as it strengthens.

Storm clouds rumble in the distance, and Alex hops up, leading me to his bike so we can outrun the rain. Pulling into a gas station on the edge of downtown, he pulls up to a pump. Standing up, I unlatch my helmet, pulling it off my head. I don't mention the fact that while he makes sure I'm wearing one, he never does himself.

He wraps his arm around my waist and kisses my temple. "Do you want anything from inside?"

I shake my head, smiling like a loon as I imagine all the filthy ways I want him to take advantage of me when we get home. After such an intense conversation, it's a visceral need, the want spinning a web inside of me, hoping to catch his soul and entangle it with mine. I *need* to feel him close.

He nods, leaving to walk inside the station, and I take the moment to stretch my legs, glancing around. There aren't many other cars here, a dented red Toyota a few spots away and an expensive black car, the back windows entirely shaded from view. It looks like a car you'd see in the movies, and I squint my eyes, nosy enough to try and see through the tinted glass, wondering what kind of person it could be.

I snort, imagining what life in that type of luxury would be like. What it must feel like to be driven around without a care in the world. Idly, I wonder if what they say is true. If money really *can't* buy happiness. To me, it seems like financial stability would allow space to focus on the things that bring you joy, but I guess I don't have much experience in the matter. Here I am, excited over the fact I just had a full meal and won't have to make rice and beans for the next month to make up for it.

Shaking my head, I let out a chuckle and close my eyes, breathing in the fresh nighttime air, reveling in the fact that while I may not have money, this is the best my life has felt in years. And no matter what happens tomorrow or otherwise, I know I'll take this night with me forever, living in the memory of my happiness, using its strength to help keep away the nightmares.

Alex walks out of the gas station doors, and a grin lights up my face as I take him in, a heavy ache throbbing between my legs. He makes me *crazy*, and alive, and free. It's like nothing I've ever experienced.

The only time I've ever come close is the first time I got high. But that type of elation is artificial and fleeting, leaving you lower than you were before.

I got sober for my son.

I'm *staying* sober for me.

Alex is looking down as he walks toward me, slipping his

wallet in his back pocket, and I'm transfixed on the sight of him, lost in visions of the future.

That is, until the back door to the fancy car opens and steals my attention away.

Red bottomed heels pop out of the door, my gaze sliding up perfect legs, over toned curves, and into the face of one of the most stunning women I've ever laid eyes on. Like a goddess, she emerges, and I feel small simply standing in her view.

She's tall enough to tower over me, and I briefly wonder if she's a supermodel. And then all of my thoughts freeze in place when her eyes zone in on Alex, her perfectly manicured hand covering her mouth. Even from a distance, I can see it's trembling.

"Alexander?" she gasps.

My head whips to Alex and he freezes in place, his head snapping so fast it makes *my* neck hurt.

I watch, my gut somersaulting, my mind screaming to turn around, to not witness whatever is about to take place. But I'm rooted to the spot. Unable to do anything but watch as this beautiful woman walks up to *my* man as if she has any right.

Only, he's not looking at her like a stranger.

He's looking at her like a ghost.

"Alexander?" she asks again, her voice shaky.

My heart drops to my stomach.

His eyes swing to me, widening slightly, like he's asking for understanding, but how can I grant understanding when I don't know what the *fuck* is going on?

He turns his attention back to her and a curtain is pulled, his entire demeanor changing; jaw tensing, spine growing rigid. Such a difference from the carefree man who walked out of the store less than three minutes ago.

"Olivia." His voice is as cold as the foreboding chill that's coasting over my skin. I reason with myself that she's obviously from his past. He said he grew up in luxury, that his father is a politician. My eyes trail over her form, envy stewing in my gut at how *effortless* she is.

Maybe she's a politician's wife. She looks the part.

Her gaze is stuck on Alex, her eyes soaking in every inch of him like he's the water made to quench her thirst. "I can't —" She takes a step closer. "You look..."

His muscles tense, and he takes a giant step away from her and toward me. I straighten, matching his movement. I have no idea what's going on, but it's clear he doesn't want this woman around him.

"What are you doing in Phoenix?" he cuts her off.

A shadow flashes over her eyes, the corners of her lips turning down. She glances at her driver and then back to Alex. She doesn't notice me once. I might as well be wallpaper, just another neutral shade, blending into the background.

She sighs, her hand rubbing at her temple. "I'm here for your father."

My heart slams against my chest.

His father?

He scoffs, sneering at her. "Of course you are. Always hopping to attention whenever he calls your name, aren't you?"

She rears back like his words are a gunshot, and my eyes jump between them, trying to keep myself on steady ground. Even though I'm nothing but a bystander, watching their obviously tortured history play out before my eyes makes my insides quake.

"That's not fair," she whispers, her arms wrapping around her waist.

He takes another step toward his bike, his eyes softening when they land on me.

And then for the first time, *Olivia* looks my way.

I stand tall as she takes me in, trying like hell to appear unaffected. But I feel... *small.* Useless. Like I would never be able to compare.

Apparently she agrees because she dismisses me as quickly as she saw me. "Alexander, can we talk?" She looks back to him. "I had no idea you... I just—"

His jaw clenches. "We have nothing to say."

She huffs. "There's *everything* to say! You left me. Right before our wedding. There are things you don't know." I stare in horror as tears trickle from her eyes and track down her cheeks. "I thought you were *dead.*"

My stomach twists, barbed wire wrapping around my chest and squeezing, walls that he spent so much time meticulously taking down being resurrected again in nanoseconds.

Memories from earlier tonight, every word said between us flying through my brain. He didn't tell me this. And *this...* this feels like a big thing not to say.

Maybe it's the look on my face, or maybe it's the way he always seems to feel what's happening with my soul, but either way, Alex's head snaps toward me.

"Fuck," he curses under his breath and rushes over.

I coach my legs to move, but they don't obey, frozen in place. Rooted to the spot. He steps directly into me, his hands reaching out, and for the first time since meeting him, my stomach churns violently and I lurch out of his grasp.

He's always been my exception, but right now he feels just like every other lying jerk.

He tries again, gripping my chin, his gaze searing into mine. "No," he commands. "Let me explain."

I scoff, breaking eye contact, gulping down the burn that's swelling my throat. I don't want to make a scene in front of his *fiancée.*

His body grows rigid, and he turns, dragging me with him to his bike. "We're done here."

"Alexander, wait," Olivia begs.

Jealousy rears up and bites me in the chest, spreading its poison through every limb until the green is oozing from my pores. This woman has parts of his history that I never will. Parts he never intended to tell me.

As I hop on the back of his bike, the tension coiling inside of me breaks, anger flooding through my system.

"I can explain," he rushes out. "This isn't what it seems like, I swear to fucking *God*, Lily."

My mouth opens but I have no words to say. All I have are questions, and so I'll wait until we get to where we're going to ask for answers.

Just a few minutes ago, I was fine. I was reveling in the fact that he was mine and that finally, *finally*, something seemed to be made just for me. That the universe finally gave in and was going to let me be happy.

I know better. When something is too good to be true, it usually is.

He should have told me. I don't mind that he had a past. I mind that he's kept it from me, when he's had plenty of opportunity to bring it up. I've given him every piece of me, and still there are parts to him that remain cloaked from my view.

The realization nicks at my insides like a thousand paper cuts, and I hate the way it feels.

So I decide not to feel it.

Like a light switch, I click it off, allowing a blanket of calm to take over. My eyes unfocus from where they were locked in Alex's gaze, and I paste a smile on my face. "It's fine, Alex."

His nostrils flare. "No."

No?

"Don't you do that with me, little bird. You stay *with me* when you're with me."

But it's too late. I'm already gone.

34

MASON

Her eyes glaze over, growing unfocused, and my rapidly pounding heart ceases to beat.

Fucking Olivia.

This is why I don't come to the West Coast. And this is why I've always, *always* listened to my gut. Until now. Until Lily. She rolled in like morning fog, thick and muggy, skewing my vision and making things unclear.

I ignore the fury that's cycling through my veins at seeing Olivia's face and focus all of my attention on my girl. On getting us back to her place so I can talk her down. Explain. I was going to tell her. Just not tonight. We had enough heavy tonight to last a lifetime, and Olivia is a part of my past that is so raw it hurts to even think about.

But I won't let Lily hide from me.

Part of me is terrified by her reaction. If she can't handle this information, how the hell do I expect her to stick around after she knows it all?

I breathe deep and talk myself down, ignoring the heat of Olivia's stare on my back, and her voice that's still calling out, raking down my insides like heated metal, reopening scabs that are far from healed.

But I don't look back. Olivia ceased mattering to me the moment she decided to play by my father's rules instead of doing what was best for us.

But Lily...

We can come back from this.

It's everything else she doesn't know that I'm still unsure about.

My insides tighten, and once again, I'm reminded of what a clusterfuck I've created. *I can't lose her.*

I straddle my bike, my eyes meeting Olivia's glassy gaze one last time, bile burning the back of my throat. I don't buy her tears, and even if I did, I don't care to clear them. Reaching my hand back, I palm Lily's thigh, blowing out a breath of relief when she doesn't jerk away.

And then I peel out of the parking lot, choosing to deal with the fact my past has come back to bite me in the ass *after* I explain things to Lily.

We beat the rain, but just by seconds, heavy drops splattering on my head and sticking to my eyelashes right as we pull into her apartment. I ride all the way to the back of the lot, parking under one of the spots that's covered by a worn awning. I hop off the bike first, turning toward Lily with my hands on my hips, watching to see what she does.

She takes her time, slowly and methodically standing up, taking off her helmet and placing it on the seat. It's silent other than the sound of rain smacking against the metal cover, and blood whooshes in my ears as I think about where to start. How to bring her back in order to actually *hear* what I have to say.

She disassociates better than anyone I've ever seen, and since I don't want to fuck her while I know she's upset, I'll have to find a workaround.

"Lily."

She locks her gaze on mine, but her eyes are like a mirror. I see nothing in them but my own reflection.

"Lily," I repeat. "Don't do that."

She cocks her head. "Do what?"

I lift my hand and wave it at her. "Whatever the fuck this is." The nerves inside of me rise through my vocal cords, making my voice tense.

She shrugs. "I'm tired. Think I'm just gonna go grab Chase and call it a night. Thank you for the dinner."

My heart palpitates as she moves to walk by me, like it knows that if she walks away now, this will be it. She won't open back up. And I *need* her to open up so I can figure out a way to tell her everything else. "No."

She pauses, her back stiffening. "No?"

I move forward, small puddles splashing under my feet until I reach her, gripping her waist and dragging her into me. My hand grips behind her head, tangling in the strands of her hair, my other palm cupping her neck, fingertips grazing along the bottom of her jawline. I wrench her head back sharply so she looks me in the eye.

A small gasp escapes her perfect lips.

"You can stop singing for everyone in the world, little bird, but not for me." My grip tightens on her neck, her pulse skittering underneath my palm. "You want to be mad? *Be mad.* But you stay here with me and you *fight.*"

Her eyes flicker, and my chest tightens. "Are you going to let me explain?"

I pull her hair by the root, strong enough where I know she'll feel the sting, and her eyes flare, raging back to life. Relief worms its way through the beats of my heart.

Her hands curl into fists and her pliable body grows rigid.

"Explain what, *Alexander?*" she spits. "How I opened up and shared things with you tonight and thought you did the same only to find out you were *engaged* to be married?" Her hands smack against my chest, the heat of her hurt singeing through my skin.

"I don't need this." She pushes against me. My grip on her tightens. "I don't even know who the *fuck* you are."

Thunder claps loud enough to make her jump, and I take the opportunity to grasp her waist, pulling her until every inch of her body is flush against me.

"You can lie to yourself all you want," I say. "But don't lie to me. You want to know the truth? I'll tell you. You *know* I will. So what is it that you're so afraid of hearing?"

She scoffs, ripping out of my arms, and rushing into the downpour. I let her, my heart banging against my sternum as harsh as the storm that booms in the air.

"God *damnit!*" I race after her, ignoring the way the rain blinds my vision and chills my skin. "Yes, okay? I was engaged."

She ignores me and keeps moving toward the staircase.

"Yes, I thought I loved her."

Her steps falter, but only for a moment.

I follow her, irritation at the way she's not even willing to *hear* me, propelling me forward. "Yes, I was going to tell you."

She pauses halfway up the stairs and turns toward me, lightning striking across the sky, highlighting the wetness on her face. Her hair is matted, stuck against the side of her cheek, drenched from the rain, and her eyes are paralyzing with their intensity.

My heart ricochets off the walls of my chest cavity, echoing the sound of my footsteps on the stairs as I make my way to her. I stop when I'm one step down, my face level with hers. My hands reach out and cup her face, leaning in until our noses brush together.

"No," I whisper. "I never felt a fraction for her what I feel for you."

She sucks in a breath, and I lean so close I can taste the raindrops on her lips.

I hold her face tight, keeping her locked in my gaze. "I love *you*, Lily."

Her eyes well with tears, her breath stalling in her chest. I see the moment my words click into place, and it makes relief douse the panic that was coiling tight inside me. She leans in, pressing her lips to mine, and I promise myself right there, that after tonight, I'll tell her the truth.

The whole truth.

And then I'll beg her forgiveness and pray to whatever God exists that she'll keep me in her life.

The first time a man told me he loved me I was nine
years old.

He said to keep it a secret. To be a good girl. That people
wouldn't *get it*. He said all the things I was too young to understand but desperate to feel. My chest pulls tight, the thought
threatening to tear into the present. But that son of a bitch has
taken enough of my happy moments, so I'll try like hell to
make it so he can't take this one too.

Debris crumbles off the walls I've built, knocked down by
the stampede of emotion coursing through my veins. There
are a thousand different things to feel, and I don't know which
one to grasp onto, so I surrender to all of them instead.

Alex loves me.

I dive into his mouth, hoping to show him everything I
don't know how to say. Like always, thoughts creep in the back
of my mind, but I let the echo of his words bat them away,
sinking into the moment, desperate to feel his skin on mine.
To prove to me that my worries were unfounded.

I'm choosing to believe him.

I'm choosing to *trust*.

We're both soaking wet, our bodies sticking together, slippery from the water that's coating our skin. But it doesn't matter. All I care about is losing myself in him.

Because the truth is, I think I love him too.

My tongue skims along the inside of his lips, his taste flooding through every sense until I'm delirious with need. His fingers dig into the sides of my face, a rumble vibrating through my body as he groans into my mouth. He moves, stepping up until he's level with me, twisting us until my back slams into the metal railing of the staircase, a twinge shooting up my spine.

He pushes his hips into me, his hard cock grinding into my stomach. Arousal spears through my center, my insides clenching around nothing, craving for him to fill all my empty space—for him to show me through action what he said with his words.

Because I need to know what it's *supposed* to feel like.

My hands cup the sides of Alex's face, relishing in the feel of his stubble as it scratches against my fingers. Letting his stature wrap me in its strength and ground me in the present.

"*Fuck*, Lily," he moans. "I was so worried you—"

"Ssh." I cut him off with my lips, not wanting to hear him speak, needing for him to fuck away the nightmares that come along with tender touches.

His palms leave my cheeks, working their way down my body until he grips underneath my ass, hoisting me up, my legs wrapping around his waist. My core clenches when I feel his thick erection settle between my legs. My arms wrap around his neck and I lean back as he thrusts against me, the rain beating down on our bodies the same way his love beats down on my soul.

"Let me take you inside," he rasps.

My legs squeeze against him tighter as I start to grind my clothed pussy on his cock. He groans, his hand cupping the back of my head and pulling me into him.

"Take me, then," I say, my tongue licking along the seam of his lips.

"Jesus *Christ*, Lily."

And then he's moving, jumping the stairs two at a time and rushing down the hallway. I giggle into his neck when we reach my door, and he fumbles, trying to maneuver my body to grab the keys from my back pocket. He pulls them free, the lock clicking just as I take his mouth with mine, our tongues tangling, a balloon of *want* expanding deep in my stomach. His fingers curl into the cheeks of my ass as he stumbles through the door, kicking it closed behind him, and walking us through the living room.

He breaks away from our kiss and throws me onto the couch, my body bouncing off the cushions. Wasting no time, he rips his soaking wet shirt over his head, his tatted muscles rippling from the movement.

My eyes glaze over, warmth spreading through my chest.

Maybe after the passion has died down and I come back to my senses, I'll feel embarrassed at the fact that we're relegated to trysts in living rooms or in his motel. That I don't even have a mattress for us to sleep on.

But that's the thing about Alex. He *sees* me for what I am, and here he is loving me anyway.

He wraps his arms around me, my stomach somersaulting as he picks me up and lays me on the floor, his hands making quick work of my clothes. Once he has me stripped to my panties, he leans down, hovering over me. Chills dance across my stomach as the rainwater dries off my skin.

His mouth presses against mine, desire spreading through me like a heatwave. He moves, his lips and tongue making pathways down my body. Lust swims in my veins, my chest heaving, and my head growing foggy. And then I make the mistake of looking down. The vision of his head between my legs flipping a switch, my mind retreating so I don't have to remember the past. Of a time where *another* dark head of hair was dipping between my thighs, back when I was too young to know what it meant.

Numbness coasts over my body, and I float just outside of it, watching things happening but not *feeling* it. A bystander to my own experience, everything muted from where I'm watching behind my darkened shield.

A sharp sting on my inner thigh slices up my insides, sling shotting to the forefront of my brain, bringing me back. I let out a squeak of pain, my eyes lasering in on where Alex nipped the skin with his teeth. It pulses and throbs, blood rushing to welt under the surface, my eyes watering, but my pussy spasms from the pain.

"Eyes on me, baby," Alex says, his palms rubbing the inside of my legs. He presses a kiss to where his teeth left a mark, soothing the ache. "It's just you and me, yeah? I need you to stay with me."

I nod, emotion swelling in my throat because he's asking for something that I don't know if I can give. "Alex, I don't think I can—"

His body moves upward quickly, eyes peering into mine, his breath skating off my lips and penetrating every pore. "You remember your safe word?" His fingers smooth the wet strands of hair away from my face.

I nod again.

"If it's too hard for you, if it's too much... use it. But stay with me, Lily. Just *try.*" He brings my hand to his chest, his fingers weaving through mine as he places them over his heart. "It's you and me, little bird."

And then he moves back down, his breath hot as it blows over the fabric of my panties, his tongue teasing along the lips of my pussy. He presses a kiss right where I want him most, the sensitive bundle of nerves swelling underneath his touch.

His mouth skims back and forth, torturing me with the light pressure, driving my brain into a frenzy until I feel like I'll implode from the tension. "Alex, *please*, just..."

He glances at me, his eyes flaring as he dips his fingers underneath the fabric and pulls harshly.

I stutter out a moan, the sides of my hips rubbed raw from where the fabric ripped. "Always ruining my underwear," I gasp.

He smirks. "I'll buy you new ones."

And then he dives in, his tongue sliding between my folds and curling inside of me, his finger pressing down in a circular motion on my clit.

"*Fuck*," I whimper.

He groans when my hands reach down, tugging on his short strands, pushing him farther into me, waiting for... I don't know what. My mind feels almost feral, consumed by molten lava that's slowly carving its way through my insides, my body the volcano waiting to erupt.

For the first time, my brain isn't dying to escape, too high in the clouds for me to focus on anything other than the way he's making me feel.

He loves me.

And I can feel it with every swipe of his tongue. Every imprint of his fingers as they bruise my fragile skin.

I'm not an optimist. There's no healing for me. Most days it hurts to breathe, and most nights the sleep never comes. But maybe tonight I'll be granted some relief.

A respite from the traumas that have shaped my entire life.

Maybe tonight, Alex can be my drug.

MASON

She's fucking beautiful like this; spread out before me, soaked from the rain and her arousal. My eyes glance up every few moments, making sure her gaze is glossy from how *I'm* making her feel, not from her disappearing somewhere I can't reach.

I suck her clit into my mouth, my cock jerking when I feel it pulse against my tongue

Her legs tremble from where they're wrapped around my shoulders, small moans coming from her perfect mouth as she thrashes against the carpet. My teeth bite down slightly, and the scrape is all she needs, her body shaking violently as she moans through her release.

I suck up her pleasure, reveling in her taste until I feel like I'll die if I don't get inside her. The wet material of my jeans sticks to my skin as I rip off my pants, sliding up her body so my mouth can tangle with hers.

"Do you like the way you taste on me, baby?" I whisper into her mouth.

She moans, her lips pressing harder against mine.

My cock throbs against the heat of her pussy, precum dripping from my hardened shaft and mixing with her wetness. I thrust my hips, sliding the length of me against her, watching her eyes roll back when I hit her overly sensitive clit. Pleasure races up my spine at the friction.

My hands grab hers, pulling them until they're suspended above her head, her wrists gripped tightly in my hold. She leans into our kiss, her back arching, teeth biting into my lower lip until blood floods my mouth.

She mewls, and my cock slips down, splitting apart her pussy lips and gliding inside of her.

Goddamn.

I push in farther, burying myself to the hilt at the same time my eyes lock onto hers, emotion swirling through her gaze. The sight makes my heart skip and my hips jerk out of rhythm. Her walls flutter around me, massaging my shaft on every stroke, and my abs tense up, knowing I could come immediately from how amazing she is. From how *personal* this feels.

Tingles pulse inside of me like an electrical current, her hardened nipples brushing against my chest, our breaths mingling in the space between us.

My grip on her wrists relax, moving from where they were pinning her down and intertwining our fingers. I'm balls deep inside of her, hitting her cervix on every stroke, and still, it doesn't feel like enough. I'm not sure it ever will with her.

Her eyes are slightly unfocused as my cock massages her insides, heat coiling at the base of my spine, welding our energies until they fuse together.

Pleasure races up and down my body, goose bumps covering my legs. I continue my deep thrusts into her body, grinding my pelvis against her clit on every forward motion, my stomach tensing every time her back arches as she fucks me back.

She's so fucking perfect.

Her body stiffens, pussy molding around me, and I groan as sparks shoot through my middle. What looks like surprise flickers through her eyes, and she sucks in a gasp, turning her head away. I release one of her hands, moving to grip her jaw, bringing her gaze back.

"Look at *me* while you fall apart on my cock, baby."

And she does, her body squeezing me so tightly it makes my balls tighten, the vein on the underside of my dick physically throbbing as my vision goes white, and I shoot my cum deep inside of her.

Holy shit.

I collapse on top of her body, my head resting in the crook of her neck, the wet strands of her hair tickling my nose. Her heart is racing under mine, our beats syncopated like we're two harmonies of the same song, and I can't remember sex *ever* being like this.

"I love you," I mouth into her skin. My stomach clenches with the silence, but I don't expect to hear her say it back. I just... *need* her to know.

Her breathing is low and deep. "I love you too," she whispers.

My heart stutters before dropkicking me in the chest and beating double time, happiness suffusing every single cell.

She loves me.

And with those words I know, without a shadow of a doubt, I want to have a life with her.

I will never find another love like Lily. She's my *person*. My little bird. And I'll do everything I can to help her find her song.

A FEW HOURS later and I'm back at the motel. Anticipation careens through me as I realize that once I clear the air and explain things to Lily, I'll be able to give her everything. And in order to give her *everything*, I need to make a plan.

First, I'll call Don and explain what's happening. I'm sure

he'll be pissed at the lost income, but he can get the fuck over it. Deep down, he only wants the best for me, and once he realizes there's nothing he can do to change things, I think he'll back down.

Then I need to come clean to Lily; tell her everything she doesn't know, and introduce her to the real me.

Mason.

She has to understand. She *will* understand.

My mind is whirling, anxiety eating away at my insides as I try to envision the best possible outcome. I'm a planner. Someone who knows that in order to ensure success, you have to plot things out. Make sure there are no ways it can fail, and have backup plans just in case.

This... this has failure written all over it.

But I know I need to try.

Nerves jumble my stomach until I can't focus, my legs bouncing underneath the desk. I grab the pack of Parliaments off the corner, not even trying to fight the urge, and head outside to light one up, allowing myself to sink into the relief of nicotine.

I lean against the side of the building, the brick scratching against my back. One of my legs rests behind me on the wall, the flick of the Zippo flaring in the darkness for a split second. But that's all it takes to see the blacked-out Suburban in the lot.

My body freezes, the hairs on the back of my neck rising, warning me that something is *off*. Slowly, I bring the flame to the end of the cigarette, and I inhale a drag, letting it settle in my lungs. My jaw tightens as the Suburban pulls from its spot and slowly makes its way to where I am. I push down the feeling of panic that's swirling through my middle, taking another drag and flicking the ashes on the ground.

But I already know.

If I'm being honest with myself, I knew the moment Olivia's voice scratched against my eardrums.

The Suburban pulls up to the curb, the back door opening. I watch, my chest squeezing tight, as shiny black shoes
clack onto the pavement. When I see his face, the reality of
my situation bears down on me like the weight of a thousand
missed decisions.

My father's brother.

My uncle Frank.

He's always been my father's lapdog, realizing early on he
didn't have what it takes to make it to the top. So instead, he's
dedicated his life to riding coattails. Doing the dirty work.
Being the muscle behind the scenes.

My stomach twists, but I make sure to keep a passive look
on my face. He closes the door, leaning against the car, his
right leg crossing in front of his left.

The silence is tense, but I don't give a fuck. I'm not
breaking first. Words from *The Art of War* run through my
head. The entire reason I've memorized that damn book
staring back at me from the face of family.

*"Move swift as the Wind and closely formed as the Wood. Attack
like the Fire and be still as the Mountain."*

So I stay still and silent, the burning sizzle of paper from
my cigarette harsh in the air as I bring it to my lips and
inhale.

"Get in," Frank finally says.

I smirk, taking another drag. "Get fucked."

His lips thin. "It's not a *request*, Alexander. Your father
wants to speak to you. In private."

My heart stutters, nausea roiling deep in my gut. "That's a
shame because there's nothing I have to say to him."

He sighs. "You're making this more difficult than it needs
to be."

My brows rise and I flick the butt to the ground, stomping
on it with the bottom of my boot. "*I'm* not doing anything.
I'm simply saying no. How did you find me here?" I ask the

question, but I already know the answer. And I'm so *fucking. Stupid.*

The moment we left the gas station, I'm sure we were followed. It's what I would have done. It's what I *have* done a hundred times, when I tracked my marks. You can *always* find someone, and that's why I've been diligent in covering my tracks for years.

Until Lily.

Frank tilts his head down, huffing out a laugh. *"Mason."*

The name slams into me, but other than the slight rising of my chin, I don't show the upheaval spinning inside.

He smirks. "Your father is President of the United States. You really think we wouldn't find you?"

"Not yet, he isn't."

His grin widens. "Semantics." He straightens off the car. "Olivia is losing her fucking mind. We don't want to make things... difficult."

"That sounds like a *you* problem, Frank."

"Maybe it is." He nods, running a hand over his mouth, his flashy watch glinting off the yellow lighting from the street. "But a lot of *problems* can be caused by other people, Alexander."

My spine straightens. "What's that mean?"

He shrugs. "It means whatever you think it means."

My jaw clenches, bile rising through my esophagus and burning the back of my throat. This is the exact type of shit I ran away from. Once you sip from the fountain of power, it's easy to become greedy for the taste, and my father and his goons are desperate to quench their thirst.

Thomas Wells *makes* the laws, but that doesn't mean they apply to him.

My chest pulls.

Frank walks over to me, and my muscles tense, forcing myself to stay in place—to not jerk away. The closer he gets, the easier I can see the deep frown lines that mar his face, more defined than they were a decade ago when I saw him last. When I was little, he used to pull me to the side, place his hand on my shoulder and squeeze tight, leaning in close to whisper advice in my ear. Like the snake to Eve; manipulation in its highest form.

He does the same move now, and it takes everything in me not to rip his arm from the socket. But I stand stoic, letting him say whatever it is he wants to say. I've learned from my mistakes, I won't ever show emotion around any of them again.

"It's a shame, you know?" His voice is low. Quiet. "Single parenting is hard. It's so easy for kids to just... slip away."

My heart stalls in my fucking chest, lungs compressing, terror *pouring* through my insides at the thinly veiled threat. My nostrils flare, teeth grinding so hard I feel a molar start to crack.

He leans in closer, his breath blowing across my face. "Get in the fucking car, Alexander."

Don's repeated warnings scream in my head; all the times he reminded me what would happen if I continued to be so goddamn stupid.

And now I've put Lily and Chase on their radar.

I'll do anything to protect them.

So for the first time in a decade, I do as I'm told, and I get in the fucking car.

MASON

The Hoppenstein Hotel is one of the nicest in Phoenix, and as we walk through the back entrance, making our way to the presidential suite, I scoff at the predictability. Over a decade, and still, nothing has changed.

There's security at the entry, and my breath sticks to my lungs as Frank pushes open the door, leading me into the main sitting area. My eyes glance around, heart smacking my ribcage, as I look for signs of life. My mother. My father. Olivia. But they're nowhere to be found.

I'm not sure what I expected, but an empty room wasn't it.

"Your father is in the boardroom," Frank says. "Let me check if that's where he wants to see you." He smiles, blinding me with his chemically whitened teeth. "Make yourself at home."

I shake my head, walking to the couch in the center of the room and taking a seat. There's an unlit Cuban resting on a crystal ashtray, and I take it upon myself to light it up. I sit back and enjoy the flavor on my tongue.

If I'm here in Hell, I might as well take advantage of the hospitality.

"Alexander."

My gut twists so tight it steals my breath. His voice is just as I remember it, sending a chill down my spine. Anger brews in my stomach as I resist the natural urge to sit straighter and call him sir.

But that boy was stomped from existence the night he ripped out my heart and ground it to dust.

Fuck him.

I'd rather die than let him know the lifelong tools he beat into me are still ingrained.

I lean back on the couch, rolling the stogie between my fingers.

He moves to stand in front of me, hands in his pockets, and I take the moment to soak him in. I've seen him on television, but it's different, getting to stare at the man who shaped your nightmares up close. His hair is still dark, grayer now at the temples, and he looks as polished as ever in a pair of dress pants and a crisp white button-down.

He nods toward the Cuban. "Those were a gift."

I puff on the cigar, letting the embers sit heavy on my tongue, before blowing it directly into his face.

He grimaces, moving to sit in the chair opposite me, his eyes trailing along the ink on my arms. Crossing his legs, his hand comes up to rub at his chin. "Ten years and you have nothing to say?"

There are a thousand things I *want* to say. A million questions I'm desperate to ask. My chest fucking *aches* with the need for answers. But I arch my brow, keeping silent. Deep down, I knew that I would end up here. I just didn't know it would be so soon.

I puff on the cigar one more time before placing it back on the ashtray, leaning forward and blowing out a heavy breath. "We said everything we needed to say ten years ago."

He scoffs. "Come on now, Alexander. You were a child back then. *Barely* an adult. Are you still upset about that?"

Fire rages through my blood, my stomach churning in

disgust. I inhale deeply to calm myself, bringing up memories of the books I read back when I was trying to rid myself of the pain from losing family.

"Never expect a narcissist to admit their wrongdoing. They'll paint themselves as the hero or the victim, but they'll never be the villain."

I bite back the retort that's sitting heavy on my tongue.

His eyes peer into mine, calculated, like he's weighing his options and trying to figure out what to say. "Why did you leave?"

"Why didn't you come find me?" I retort.

He chuckles, standing up and walking to the corner of the room, pouring himself a brandy, the smell hitting me before he even makes it back to his seat.

It's *that* smell, that oaky, pungent scent; the type that permeates the air and sinks into your pores without even trying. It makes my stomach heave, remembering the times he'd spit his words with the stench of whiskey and disappointment on his breath.

He meanders back, sitting down, the crystal tumbler dangling from his fingertips. "You didn't want to be found."

My chest cramps, heart squeezing at the monotony of his voice. A leopard never changes his spots, and my father has always been an empty shell, waiting to rule the world.

"I found you the moment you left," he continues. My breath whooshes out of me. *What?*

"Surprised?" He grins. "Had people tracking you from the second you packed your bag and ran away like the foolish kid you've always been." He sips from his tumbler. "But… people love a sob story. So as much as it pained your mother and me, we let you go. We pulled back our guys." He lifts a brow. "You wouldn't have been agreeable anyway."

I expected the callous answer, but I *didn't* expect for it to punch me in the chest, knocking the breath from my lungs and bruising my twisted heart.

"You killed my child." I grit my teeth, my anger simmering like water in a pan. "I think I had the right."

He rolls his eyes. "So I gave Olivia a little incentive to go get things taken care of. Big deal." He shrugs.

"Bold stance." I smirk. "Your constituents know you feel that way?"

His eyes flare. "You don't worry about what my *constituents* feel."

"I know what *I* feel," I burst out. Regret immediately sinks into my bones, and I pull my emotions back in, clamping them tight to my chest.

His spine straightens. "That's always been your problem, son. You *feel* too much. Don't blame me for stepping in and making sure things were taken care of."

I scoff. "That's rich. You didn't care about me and you know it. You only cared about how it would make you look."

"You're damn right," he snaps. "It looked bad enough having my nineteen-year-old son *engaged* like some pussy-whipped bitch."

I huff a laugh, shaking my head. He hasn't changed at all. "You *told* me to marry her."

He lifts his shoulders. "A miscalculation." He takes another sip. "We thought it would look better in the polls."

I grit my teeth, grief seeping through the fresh wounds on my heart. "It wasn't your decision to make."

"It was the *only* decision to make. Do you have any idea how it would have looked? If I can't control my son, how can I control a country?"

My stomach churns. "Well congratulations, *Dad*, you lost anyway."

His eyes narrow. "I won't this time."

A smirk lines my mouth, hatred flowing through my veins and making my tongue sharp. "How can you be so sure?"

He smiles wide. "Because now I have you."

My chest rattles, confusion burning a hole through my insides. "You really don't."

Frank comes out of the woodwork, stepping from the shadows and into our line of sight. I should have known he was listening in the wings. It isn't like Thomas Wells to ever have a sincere face-to-face conversation without some backup.

"Alexander, you're a smart man," Frank says. "Finding a lost son a decade after he went missing will be worldwide headline news. You can imagine what that will do with the voters."

My father's eyes sparkle. "You're my ticket into the White House, son."

Panic wrings my insides. "God forbid you let your merit and ideals get you there."

Frank shakes his head. "People don't vote on ideals. Not anymore."

I stand up. "This is ridiculous. There's a reason I stayed away all these years. I have no interest in helping you."

My father's brows rise to his hairline as he leans back in his seat. "I don't remember giving you a choice."

"I'm not a kid anymore. I won't just jump and say how high."

He hums. "Rumor has it you spend a lot of time around kids these days."

My blood freezes, his insinuation spreading through me like a sickness. "What the fuck is that supposed to mean?"

He shrugs. "Collateral."

Fear grips my heart and squeezes. "You wouldn't," I rasp.

"I'm just a father willing to do *anything* to get back his child." He takes another sip from his glass. "Surely, you understand."

The jab doesn't go unnoticed, grief pulsing hot and sharp through my chest. But I tamp it down, knowing that a reaction will let him know where I stand. And the quickest way to lose the battle is by showing all your cards. But I'll be damned if I let him do anything that would put Lily or her son in harm's way, and he knows it. I was so stupid to touch her in public, *right* after running into Olivia. There's no way they didn't follow us home.

"Appear weak when you are strong, and strong when you are weak."

Sighing, I sit back down, running a hand through my hair and nodding. And with my agreement comes the knowledge that every plan I made revolving Lily is now nothing more than a dream. A "what could have been" moment.

They drop me back off at my motel room a few hours later, reminding me once more what's at stake if I try to disappear. I grab *The Art of War* that's propped on the corner of the desk and open it, my eyes scouring for words of advice— something to calm the storm that's raging through my body.

"All warfare is based on deception. Hence, when we are able to attack, we must seem unable; when using our forces, we must appear inactive; when we are near, we must make the enemy believe we are far away; when far away, we must make him believe we are near."

As long as Lily is here, as long as she's alone, she'll be vulnerable.

She can't stay. But she can't be with me either.

So with my heart cracking from the weight of my decision, I pull out my phone, and I make the call I didn't want to make.

My chest burns deeper with every ring.

"Mason." His voice is sharp.

Blowing out a breath, my stomach churning more with every breath I take, I force the words from my lips.

"Chase. I found her."

I haven't heard from Alex in two days, and it has my nerves on edge. It's not like him to just disappear, and the fact that it's happened after what I thought was a monumental night sends tendrils of unease curling around my spine.

Maybe he's sick.

It's times like these where I wish I had a cell phone, so I could send him a text, or *something*. But instead I'm just here, floating in limbo, waiting for him to either put me out of my misery or for the other shoe to drop.

Where is he?

"Mommy, I wanna pway ball." Chase comes from his room, a bright orange ball wrapped in his tiny hands.

"Okay, baby. Just give me a minute and we'll head out." My plan is to take him to the park, then stop by the Motel Eight and check to make sure everything's okay with Alex.

He wouldn't just *leave*. He promised.

"But I wanna pway now!" Chase screeches, hopping through the living room.

I lean over, massaging my temples, trying to soothe away the pulsing between my eyes. "I'm gonna grab some medicine and then we can go, okay? Do you need help with your shoes?" I ask.

He shakes his head, the ball pressed up against his red and blue Spider-Man tee. "Nope. I got 'em."

I smile at him and walk down the small hallway into our cramped bathroom, the light flickering as I open the medicine cabinet, grabbing the Excedrin. Normally, I stay away from medicine, anything that numbs pain is a slippery slope, but every once in a while I cave, knowing the migraine will incapacitate me if I don't get it under control.

"Okay, baby boy, are you ready?" I holler, moving back to the living room. I open my mouth to speak again but my words cut off when I realize Chase is nowhere in sight.

"Chase!" I yell, my heart banging so fast it's liable to burst through the center of my chest. My eyes scan the living room, noticing the front door is ajar.

I run toward it, my fingers jamming into the doorframe as I pass the threshold and look for him. My stomach is in knots, my breathing choppy, panic squeezing my insides. But then I see him, skipping after his ball across the road. My heart shoots to my throat when I see him approach two men, and I sprint down the staircase to chase him across the street, terror gripping me from the inside out.

Chase turns around, grinning wide when he sees me. "Mommy!" he yells, waving me over.

I pick up the pace, desperate to get him away from strangers. *Who are these guys?* And what the hell are they doing standing in an empty parking lot behind the bushes?

My vision blurs, eyes laser-focused on my baby boy. On making sure I don't lose sight of him for a second. As I close the gap, relief trickles through my veins, and it's only then that I look up.

I stop short, feet stumbling and my lungs squeezing tight. Anxiety shoots up my middle, lodging into my throat and expanding until I'm sure if I tried to speak, it would explode out of me in a guttural sob. I put my hand out, silently urging him to come closer.

He runs over and slams into my legs, wrapping his arms around my knees, and my rigid body sways but stays locked in place. Tears burn behind my eyes, my nostrils flaring to try and ease the heavy ache in my heart as I stare into a face so similar to mine.

So similar to my son's.

My brother, Chase.

"Lily." His voice is a whisper, but it's enough to break the dam, and I swallow the pain that's surging through my insides.

How did he find me?

I have no clue how I'm supposed to react. I wasn't prepared. I haven't planned. My fingers scratch against my wrist, nerves wringing tight, twisting until they're about to snap. I *want* to run into his arms. I *want* to tell him how much I've missed him. How the little girl inside of me went missing when I did, and how for the first time I can feel her coming back to life.

"No, this is *Mommy*."

I smile down at my son, hoping like hell that the way my heart slams against my ribs doesn't show on my face.

"That's right, baby." I smooth his hair from his forehead.

Sucking in a deep breath, I look back up and I meet my brother's gaze.

"Hi," I mumble.

His eyes gain a glossy sheen, his jaw muscles tensing.

"Hey, Lily. Long time." A voice to Chase's right steals my attention and I glance over, taking in the charming smile and hypnotic green eyes of Jackson Rhoades. My brother's best friend. He's seemed to have only grown *more* handsome over the years, and my heart stutters when I realize if he's here with Chase that means they're still as close as ever. Jealousy flares along my edges, knowing that life went on as usual in Sugarlake without me.

Still, even through the twinge of envy, my mouth lifts as I soak him in. Jackson's always had an effortless charm that exudes from his pores, the way a rainbow breaks through stormy clouds.

"Hi, Jax." I smile.

His eyes move to my son while mine float back to my brother. Chase is frozen in place, his brow furrowed, gaze bouncing from me to my baby boy. The scar through his left eyebrow is still as prominent as it was when we were kids, and a pang of hurt slices through me, remembering how he got it.

From protecting me. Like usual.

He doesn't speak and familiarity lights up my insides at the brooding. Some things never change.

But what does one even say to a sibling they haven't seen in over ten years?

I'm sorry?

I've missed you?

This doesn't change a thing?

"Lily," he says again, his voice catching on my name.

"You know my mommy?" Baby Chase's voice breaks through the tension, his eyes big and round. Pain spreads through my sternum, regret sloshing around my stomach, heavy and thick, that *this* is his first introduction to family.

My brother's face breaks into a soft smile, his eyes leaving mine. "Yeah, kid. I know your mommy."

"What's your name?" Jax cuts in, kneeling on his heels.

I blink slowly, preparing for the onslaught of emotion, not wanting to look in my brother's eyes when he hears my son's name.

"I'm Chase." He beams, puffing out his tiny chest.

My brother's nostrils flare and Jax's mouth gapes open as both of their gazes swing to mine.

I swallow around the knot in my throat and run my fingers through my baby's hair to keep myself calm and grounded.

"Do you—" My voice breaks, and I clear my throat and try again. "Do you guys want to come inside?" I point behind me at the apartment complex.

Chase waves his arm. "Lead the way, Lil."

The nickname spears through my chest, rupturing the stitches that have held me together over the years, and I turn around to hide the tears forming behind my eyes. It's an odd feeling, being so happy to see him, but wanting him to disappear.

They follow us across the street and up the stairs, my stomach tightening as memories from the other night with Alex flash through my mind, reminding me that he's been MIA ever since. But I can't focus on that now, not when my past has forced its way into my present.

The front door is still open from where I ran away in a hurry, and I see Chase's eyes follow my baby boy as he runs across the living room, plopping down in front of his play area.

I walk straight to the kitchen counter, ripping open my purse and grabbing a stick of cinnamon gum, my wrist being rubbed raw from the pads of my fingers. Breathing deep, I roll my shoulders back, turning toward Chase and Jax. They're both standing in front of the couch, taking in their surroundings.

Judging, I'm sure. "Do you guys want something to drink?"

A low laugh rumbles out of Chase, his thumb flicking over his bottom lip. "I want a lot of things, Lil, but a drink definitely isn't at the top of my list."

I swallow, glancing down at the worn carpet. "I was just trying to be hospitable."

Jax pats Chase on the back, moving farther into the living room and sitting down on the couch, an easy smile gracing his features. "I'd *love* something to drink, Lily. And then we should catch up." His eyes glance over to my baby boy. "But... maybe not in front of such sensitive ears?"

It's not a bad idea to send baby Chase to Susan's, so we can talk in privacy. But the part of me that knows this is my only day of the week to spend with him holds on tight, not wanting to give up such precious moments. Still, I know they're right. I can feel the anger floating through the air, wrapping around my neck like a noose, and he doesn't need to be around to see the hanging.

Sucking down my pride, I nod. "Hey, baby boy, you wanna go play with Susan for a little bit and let Mommy get our new friends settled?"

Baby Chase sits up a bit straighter, the blue Lego dropping from his hand as he chews on his lip. "I want Awex."

My heart thunks against my ribs, my stomach splitting down the middle. "Alex is busy right now, honey, but maybe later."

His lips turn down in the corners, but he eventually nods, standing up and putting his small hand in mine. My eyes slide to our guests, Chase's fists clenched so tight I'm surprised his fingernails aren't breaking through the skin of his palm.

"We'll be right back. Just..." I glance around, unease flowing through the space between us. "Make yourselves at home, I guess."

I don't know why they're here, but the fact of the matter is they *are*, so I need to deal with it. All I can do is hope that after we talk, they understand all of the reasons why I stayed away. Why I have to *continue* to stay away.

Because I'll do anything to protect my child.

39

LILY

It's been silent for ten minutes. Shortly after I got back from Susan's, Jax said he would give us some space, pulling his phone out of his pocket and smiling wide as he walked out the front door. Ever since, it's just been Chase and me, his eyes boring into the side of my head.

My fingers tap out an unsteady rhythm on my wrist, my legs crisscrossed underneath me and going numb from lack of blood flow. But I don't want to move, afraid that if I break whatever weird stasis we're in, I'll cave first.

I want to talk, but *I'm* not the one who showed up out of nowhere, and I have no idea what to say. I'm having a hard enough time trying to keep from flinging myself into his arms just to soak up his embrace; to remember what it feels like after going so many years without.

Chase groans, leaning forward and resting his elbows on his knees. The way he stares is the exact same as it always has been, like his eyes are stripping me away piece by piece, finding the truth even when I hide it behind thick layers.

Growing up, he always read me like a book. But eventually, when there are things you want to keep from prying eyes, you learn how to hide the message.

His gaze slides down my arms, watching the way my fingers tap against my forearm.

"What are they of?" His voice is raspy after so many minutes of silence, and I look down, my heart shooting to my throat when I realize he's asking about my tattoos.

Swallowing, my fingers stop their incessant rubbing to glide over the ink, appreciating the artwork instead. I move closer, holding out my arm for him to see. I skim the dates inscribed on the inside of my wrist first. "This is the day Chase was born."

His nostrils flare. "Nice name."

A small smile breaks its way onto my face. My fingers move. "And this is—"

"Wiggles," he interrupts. "I'd recognize that bunny anywhere." He smirks and lightness weaves through my insides, hope sprouting wings, tempting me to try and soar. But the higher you fly, the harder you fall, so I temper the feeling.

I scoff, rolling my eyes to hide the emotion that's lying behind them. "Do *not* disrespect Wiggles. He was everything to me."

"He was disgusting."

"He was *home*."

That word quiets the space between us, filling it with a thick tension that pulls tighter with every second.

"Where the fuck have you been, Lil?" Chase whispers, his voice cracking.

My stomach rages with unease, unsure of how to answer him. I've *been* a lot of places. Beaten and left for dead by my shit ex-boyfriend. Feeling like I was going to die while I went through withdrawals on Derek's guest bed; pregnant and scared. But those are conversations I don't think he's ready to hear, and honestly, ones I'm not sure I'm ready to tell.

"I've been living, Chase." I shrug.

"No," he says sharply. "You don't get to do that. You don't

get to shrug your shoulders and brush this off like you didn't return a fucking phone call. You *disappeared*, Lily."

My chest constricts. "I know," I whisper.

"Do you?" he shoots back. "Do you have any idea what that was like for me?"

Irritation snaps at my spine with his words. What it was like for *him*?

"No, Chase, I *don't* know. Because believe it or not, not everything is about you. I was fucked up, okay?" Tears burn my lower lids, my heart slamming against my sternum with every breath. "And I'm *sorry*." My hands cover my chest. "I'm sorry that I left. I'm sorry that I never called. I'm sorry that you wasted a trip out here, trying to find answers for something that I don't have answers *for*." Wetness drips down my face, falling on my upper lip, and I swipe it away angrily, emotion dancing around my insides like it's the first time it's felt freedom in years.

"It was my job to take care of you." His voice cracks.

My stomach flares, old wounds bleeding like they're newly formed, and I reach out, my palm covering his. "No, Chase. It wasn't."

He scoffs, ripping his hand out from under mine before standing up and pacing the floor.

"Are you clean?" His words sting as they slap across my face, and my body leans back from the impact.

The pads of my fingers trace over the raised flesh on my arms. "Yeah. A little over four years now."

He whooshes out a breath, running his hands through his hair and nodding. "Four years," he mutters. "Four years." He walks to the wall where pictures of baby Chase are hanging, his eyes bouncing from one to the next like he doesn't know where to look first. "How old is he?"

"He's three and a half."

He tilts his head to the ceiling and nods. "He's beautiful, Lil."

My heart stutters, more tears escaping from the corner of my eyes. I've *dreamed* of this. Of having Chase meet his nephew. Of them loving each other. I can't help the seed that's planted in the middle of my chest, threatening to tear through the soil of my melancholy and hope they get a chance.

"Thank you." I bite back what I really want to say.

Aren't you proud?

Can't you see?

I didn't end up like her.

"How did you find me?" I say instead.

He spins to face me. "I've been *desperate* to fucking find you, Lily, for ten goddamn years."

My breath stalls in my throat. "I didn't want to be found."

"Clearly," he deadpans. "A few years ago, Sam and Anna hired a PI to look for you."

My chest tightens, the two letters echoing through my chest cavity, reminding me of Alex and his sudden disappearing act. A chill skates up my spine.

"They did?" The thought of Sam and Anna makes sadness wind through my muscles, the tendons tearing from the weight of my guilt. They were good to me, and I loved them. *Love* them. But they were easy to manipulate. Some mistakes are ones you have to live with for the rest of your life. Taking advantage of Sam and Anna is one of mine.

Not everyone is meant for redemption. Some of us are destined to live in purgatory, hoping we get a chance to repent in the next life. I've made peace with that, but it doesn't make the want to right my wrongs any less potent.

Chase nods. "About a year ago, I decided to hire him again."

"You should have just stopped looking," I mutter.

"Do you have *any* idea what you put me through, Lily? What life was like once you were gone?" He steps closer, his eyes blazing with his heartbreak.

"I know, I—"

"No," he interrupts. "I don't think you *do*. You have no clue."

A tear drips down my face and I wipe it with the back of my hand, biting back the sob that wants to tear through my throat. "I'm sorry, Chase. I don't know what you want me to say."

He blows out a breath, his hands resting on the nape of his neck. "It's okay. I mean..." He shakes his head. "It's *not* okay, but once you're back home, we'll have time to work things out."

Shock cramps my stomach. I've never seen a situation that Chase has wanted to tackle head-on, and this change in his personality is jarring, a stark reminder that he continued to grow while I was gone. I don't know the man standing in front of me, and that makes grief stick to my lungs. It's heavy, weighing down each breath with the reality that lost years can never be found.

I swallow around the thick saliva pooling in my mouth. "Wait, what do you mean 'when we go home'?"

His hands drop to his sides. "Back to Sugarlake, Lily." His brows draw in. "Did you really think I was coming all this way to *not* take you back with me?"

I scoff. "I'm an adult, Chase."

"Really?" he sneers. "Wish I could have been around to see it."

I wince. "I deserve that."

He huffs out a laugh, plopping down in the seat next to me. I can feel the shift of energy, the anger draining away, releasing its gripping hold on the air as he breathes deep and mouths silent words to himself. My eyes widen as I watch him gain control, in awe of the man he's become without me. The Chase I remember would have lost his shit and asked questions later.

He turns toward me, pasting a smile on his face. "We can work out the details later, I just..." His hand rubs his chest. "I *feel* so fucking much right now, and it's overwhelming. I don't want you to think I'm not ready to hear you."

My mouth drops open.

"What?" He cocks a brow.

"Who *are* you?"

"It's your fault for not knowing." His eyes cut me with their glare.

A knock sounds on the door, and my heart jumps to my throat, hope swelling in my chest that it's Alex. But when the door swings open and Jax walks in with a smile on his face, that hope deflates.

"Everyone still alive in here?" He meanders in with a smile, instantly easing the tension in the room. "What'd I miss?"

Chase sighs. "Just filling in Lily on how we found her."

A sick feeling settles heavy in my gut. *What are the odds a PI would show up in my life right when Chase comes back?*

My hands grow clammy, nerves making my skin pull tight. "Hey, what was the name of the PI you used?"

Chase looks over to me, running his hand through his hair. "Mason, why?"

Relief trickles through my veins. *Thank God.*

I shrug. "Just curious."

My heart aches at Alex's silence, but I swallow down the pain, reminding myself that I chose to trust him. But I don't think a simple phone call is too much to ask.

Jax walks over and settles between us, throwing his arm around my shoulder and winking. "As cozy as this is, we should probably find a place to stay." He looks around. "I don't think there's room for us here."

I cringe at the reminder of everything my life is lacking. At the small apartment that can't even comfortably fit baby Chase and me, let alone visitors. "There's not much around Raindale, other than the Motel Eight on the edge of town."

Chase nods. "That will work."

"I don't have a car, but I can walk you guys there." I perk up at the opportunity to go see Alex, anxious energy popping like kernels in my stomach.

Chase smirks. "We have a car."

My brows rise. "Oh, right."

"You can still come, though," he continues. "Give us directions."

I smile. "Only a few roads in this town, and the motel is on the main stretch.

He blows out a breath, his eyes growing dark, looking like he's searching for the words to say. "I want you to come, Lil."

Warmth spreads through me at his tone and I nod. "Okay, I will." My fingers tap against my wrist. "Wait... so if you hired a private investigator, does that mean that someone has been watching me?"

Nausea curdles my gut. At the fact that I didn't know—wasn't aware of my surroundings. *Anything* could have happened.

Chase twists his lips. "I'm not gonna apologize for doing what I needed to do to find you." He shakes his head, nostrils flaring. "I'll be outside by the car. We can talk more about this later after we get settled in."

My lips turn down as he walks from the room, the piece of my heart that cracked when I left him throbbing.

Jax sighs, tapping his fingers on his knee. "He *is* happy, you know? He's just hurt."

"Yeah, well." I tense my jaw. "Some things never change, I guess."

"With all due respect, Lily." Jax leans toward me on the couch. "You've been gone for ten years. You have *no* idea what's happened while you were gone. No *clue* how much your brother has truly changed."

He stands up, stretching his arms above his head, my eyes catching on the thin sliver of skin peeking between his jeans and his shirt. *How can someone be so... pretty?*

"Now, come on, Mama, we've got a motel to get, and a brother's broken heart to soothe."

My chest squeezes as I stand up and follow him out, pushing my feelings down and focusing on the moment.

Chase is here.

Alex is missing.

And I have no idea what the fuck to do.

40

MASON

"Well, Mase, you really went and fucked things up."

I chuckle at Don's words, even though humor is the last thing I'm feeling. I rub a hand over my brows and light up a cigarette. "Yeah, tell me about it, old man."

"So, what now? You gonna make a trip to see me?"

My stomach clenches because I know what he's doing. He's asking if I'm going to run. He's telling me that's what he thinks I should do, and while that may have worked for the past ten years, it won't now.

It never really did, if I'm honest. I didn't hide successfully because I *ran*, it was because my father was choosing not to find me.

But now Lily and Chase are in the mix. And I'll do anything to protect them.

"I'm gonna stay here." I suck in a drag, my eyes scanning the motel parking lot. My bags are packed and I'm headed out, but first, I need to go to Lily and try to explain.

"I mean... not *here* in Raindale," I continue. "I finished the job, there's nothing left for me here." My chest tightens at the lie. "But I'm going to stay with my father."

"What?" His voice is incredulous. "Are you out of your mind?"

I glance down at the worn copy of *The Art of War* resting on top of my bag, reminding myself why I've kept it on my person all these years. So I could soak in the words like gospel in case I ever had to face my enemy.

"Let your plans be dark and impenetrable as night, and when you move, fall like a thunderbolt."

The truth is on the tip of my tongue, but I don't trust my phone to not be tapped, so I swallow down the words and let him think what he wants.

"Yeah." I cringe, my stomach turning. "Just like that. It's useless to keep running, Don. Listen..." I squeeze the phone tighter to my ear. "I'm sorry to leave you high and dry like this, I just—"

He exhales heavily down the line. "I get it, kid. I don't like it, but I get it. I'll figure it out." Even through the phone, I can feel the emotion seeping through the cracks in his voice. "You always have a place with me, okay? Take care of yourself, Mase."

There's a click, and I take the final drag on my cigarette, melancholy swirling through my chest.

I haven't been able to sleep since I called Chase, my mind plagued with guilt. But I have to let her go.

At least temporarily.

Keeping them safe is the *only* option, and the only chance for me to take care of my father is to be in the belly of the beast. He has to think I'm agreeable, that I'm *willing* to do whatever he says. That's the thing about narcissists, they're always so caught up in themselves, they don't see anyone else for what they truly are. And out of everything that's wrong with Thomas Wells, *that* will be his biggest downfall. Even if I lose Lily in the process.

One day, when this is all over, maybe I can come back and set things right with her.

When I talked to Chase, I told him not to make any rash decisions—to wait for word from me before showing up. I may be a piece of shit for what I've done, but I won't just leave without giving her the truth. She deserves to have an idea of what's coming.

My back straightens as I pick up my duffel bag and head to my bike, my stomach heavy and my heart fracturing more with every beat.

A car pulls into the lot and parks a few spaces down, and my eyes glance over as I load up my bag. When my eyes meet the gaze of the driver, my lungs seize, and I choke on air, because behind the steering wheel is none other than Chase Adams.

That *motherfucking bitch*.

I should have known better than to think that he would listen to me. My eyes move across the car, noting the blond guy in the passenger seat and the pixie of a girl in the back. *Lily*. My heart plummets to my feet, the fissures tearing until they're gaping holes.

This isn't how I wanted this to go down.

But sometimes life doesn't give you what you want, so I suck in a breath and prepare for the explosion, hoping there's enough of me left to sort through the debris and find my bloodied pieces.

Chase's eyes find me immediately as he opens the driver's side door. I tip my chin in greeting.

My eyes flash to Lily as she steps out of the car. *Does she already know?*

Her eyes lock with mine and her posture softens, like seeing me is a relief. But like watching a train wreck, it happens in slow motion, and I can do nothing but brace for the impact.

My gaze stays on her, unable to break away. But I'm speaking to her brother. "I thought I told you to wait for my call."

Confusion flickers through her gaze and my stomach twists, nausea simmering deep in my gut.

"What are—" she starts.

"Remind me when the fuck I asked for your permission to do anything, Mason?"

My eyes glance to Chase, my teeth grinding at what a gigantic pain in my ass he is.

"Mason?" Lily's voice grabs my attention. "No, this is... I —*what?*"

Chase spins around, his head tilting. "Lily, this is Mason. The PI I was telling you about."

Her brows furrow, her head moving back and forth like her brain's been rattled and she's trying to shift it back into place. "No. No, it isn't."

With every shake, our foundation crumbles, our trust having been built on top of sinkholes. And even giants fall when the ground collapses beneath their feet.

"This is *Alex.*" She waves her hand toward me. "Tell them, Alex. Tell them who you are."

I bite my lip, nostrils flaring to stem the burn behind my eyes. "Little bird," I whisper.

"No," she snaps, her voice cracking. "No." She walks closer to me, her fists clenched so tight her knuckles are white. "You *tell* them."

I glance down, because I can't physically stand watching as our love shatters. My tongue swipes across my bottom lip.

"Lily," Chase interrupts. "I don't know what the fuck he told you, but his name is *Mason.*" My eyes swing to him, and then to his friend who has been silently watching, like he paid for tickets for the show.

Lily walks even closer, her rising ire branding me with its heat, singeing through my clothes. I welcome the burn, knowing it's only a small part of what I deserve. The toes of her shoes hit mine and she gazes up at me, her eyes brimming with unshed tears.

My chest caves, my fists clenching to keep from gripping her face.

"Tell them," she hisses through her teeth.

I shake my head slowly, my stomach churning. "I can't."

Her hands come up and shove at my shoulders, my body jostling from the unexpected pressure. I close my eyes, knowing if I watch her break apart then I'll break along with her, and I need to keep it together so I can bring my father to his knees.

"You fucking *asshole!*" she screams, shoving me again. "You look me in the eyes and you *tell* me you lied." Tears stream down her face. "You don't get to do this. You don't get to *do* this to me."

The energy between us flares, my throat clogging with things I want to say, but knowing there's nothing for me to defend. There are no words that will make this better. I already *did* do this to her.

Arms wrap around her waist and Chase drags her back, leaning down and whispering in her ear. She lets out a sob that slices straight through my sternum, and she turns, collapsing in his embrace. Chase's eyes are dark and murderous as they glare at me from above her head, his hand smoothing down her back. *Comforting* her. The way I always promised I would do.

"What the *fuck* is she talking about, Mason?" he spits.

I ignore him, my vision laser-focused on Lily, and I take a step forward, overcome with the need to explain. To make her understand.

Things weren't supposed to happen this way.

"Little bird."

Her head snaps to me, her fists gripping her brother's shirt as his arms tighten around her. "Don't call me that, you son of a bitch. You don't *ever* get to call me that again."

I take another step forward. "Just let me explain."

"You don't get to explain shit to her, Mason," Chase inter-rupts again. "You did your job. You can go now."

My jaw tenses, panic wrapping around my jugular and squeezing. "Lily," I try again.

She ignores me, burying her face in her brother's chest. I bite back the burn that's scorching my esophagus and nod, blowing out a breath.

Maybe this is for the best.

If there's at least one thing I can take comfort in, it's that she isn't alone. Calling Chase was the right thing. He'll catch her when she falls. So, instead of causing more grief, I back away, straddle my bike and fire it up.

And I ride away from the best thing that's ever happened to me, terrified that she'll never happen again.

41

LILY

My wrist is rubbed raw, but it doesn't stop me from scratching at its surface, deepening the wound until it burns as sharply as my insides. Luckily, I'm well versed in boxing emotions and shoving them to a corner. And when they get too big to handle, or they break out of their shell, I take their place, closing my eyes and slipping into the darkness, muting everything around me so I don't have to feel the lockjaw of their bite.

Alex… Mason… whatever the hell his name is, *lied* to me. He's a liar.

I've had a lot of people take advantage of me in my life. A lot of trauma I'm not sure I'll ever truly overcome. A lot of abuse at the hands of men who said they loved me.

Love.

What a bullshit word. What a bullshit concept. If this is love, I'd rather drown in someone's hatred. At least then, I'd know what to expect.

As I sit in Chase's motel room, adjacent to the one Jax has for himself, my mind replays every moment. My rose-tinted glasses are shattered, eyeballs bleeding from the memories. His smiles turn sinister in my mind when I realize the entire reason he introduced himself was because he was being *paid* to.

He never loved me. He just used me, like everyone else before him.

Shame bubbles under my skin at how easily he manipulated me into believing he was different. That he was someone I could trust. Bile teases the back of my throat, my head growing dizzy when I think of all of the things I told him. Things I've never told another soul. All of my fragile vulnerabilities held in the palm of his hand, being stroked into a false security before he goes in for the kill.

A bird with broken wings still believing they can fly.

Fuck him.

Idly, I wonder if he passed along my secrets. I stare across the motel room at my brother, questioning whether I should feel ashamed for the things he may know.

And *my* Chase—my sweet baby boy—who will be absolutely devastated to lose the only man he's ever had in his life. The only other person who's ever shown him love.

Guilt slashes through my middle and threatens to swallow me whole. I'm so gullible. My entire life has been shaped by men who lie and cheat and *manipulate*. And there I stand, in the eye of the hurricane, not realizing I'm surrounded by a storm.

Was everything a lie? The girl at the gas station called him Alexander, so for my sanity, I hold on to that small thread of hope that at least that one thing wasn't a complete fabrication.

Confusion swims in my veins, making an ache pulse between my eyes, stomach heaving at the way my thoughts scramble. Like a ride at a carnival, I'm strapped in and spun around with nowhere to go but in circles.

"Do you wanna talk about it?" Chase asks, sitting in the desk chair, his phone hanging from his hand.

I shake my head, not trusting myself to speak. I feel stupid and reckless. Like I'm stuck in a nightmare, my conscience shaking my shoulders and screaming *"wake up!"* but unable to actually force myself awake.

I need to call Derek.

I need to hold my baby boy.

What I *don't* need is to talk.

"Did he..." Chase swallows. "I'm sorry I sent him if he hurt you." His eyes look up to meet mine. "But I'm not sorry for tracking you down."

My teeth grind as I try to hold back the pain of my broken heart.

I stand, the stiff mattress creaking from the sudden movement. "I'm gonna head out." I wipe my clammy hands on my thighs.

Chase jerks to his feet, moving toward me. "What? No, you should stay for a while. We've barely talked."

I grace him with a small smile, but I don't have the motivation to hold it for long. "We'll have time to talk. You guys are staying for a few days, right?"

He nods, his lips pursing. "I just... you promise you won't run?"

My chest cramps at his question, realizing the scars he wears are ones I've caused. I was selfish back then, lost in the bottom of my addiction.

"I promise." I say the words softly, walking over and squeezing his shoulder.

While I was caught off guard by him showing up, and I'm still off-kilter from him shoving his way back in my life, I'm grateful he's here to hold me through the hardship.

You and me against the world.

My throat swells and I back away, heading to the door. "Tell Jax I said bye. You guys can come over tomorrow night, but I work all day."

"Where do you work?"

"Dina's Diner. I'm a waitress."

He blows out a breath. "God, it's so wild to have you in front of me. You look so..." He shakes his head.

I cock a brow, twisting to face him. "So, what?"

"Healthy." He sucks on his teeth. "I always thought you did before, but you never looked like *this*. You just—I didn't pay enough attention back then."

His words slam into the center of my chest, forcing the breath from my lungs. I swallow down the hurt, pasting a smile on my face. It's thin and it causes the muscles in my cheeks to cramp from the effort. "Yeah, well... you were busy with other things."

The sour tang in my words doesn't go unnoticed, his eyes narrowing the slightest bit. "You have *no* idea wh—"

"It doesn't matter," I cut him off, not wanting to get into another conversation. My soul can't bear the weight.

When I reach the door, a sharp throb in my chest has me leaning my head against the door. "Look," I speak into the wood. "I didn't ask for you to come here. I know I've made mistakes." My voice cracks. "I know I hurt you." I suck in a shaky breath. "But you stopped seeing me long before I left. You stopped caring first."

"I *never* stopped caring."

"Bullshit!" I snap, anger rushing through my veins and flushing my cheeks. I spin around. "You were so focused on perfect fucking princess Alina that I could have cut a line at the dinner table, and you would have turned the other way."

His body deflates and he falls back into his chair. "That's not fair."

"Life's not fair." I shrug. And then I twist the handle and walk out the door, stumbling through my feelings, trying like hell to keep my head above ground.

I make the long trek back to my house, wiping stray tears from my eyes, and trying to pull it together before I get to Susan's. And even though I'm breaking—tearing apart at the seams—a small wisp of hope dangles like a hangnail, jagged and sharp but too painful to pull.

For the rest of the night, my ears strain, longing to hear the rumble of an engine and a knock at my door.

But the sounds never come. And I'm left with broken dreams and disappointment.

MASON

S talking in silence is one of the many skills I've acquired over the years of being a private investigator, and right now, I'm executing with precision, parked in the shadows of the lot across the street from the motel, waiting to see where Chase ends up.

The three of them appear from the main office, Lily walking next to her brother, the long-haired blond heading into a different room than the two of them. Swallowing down the sharp stabs that pierce my chest as I watch her disappear behind closed doors, I roll out of the lot and head to Lily's apartment complex.

There are things I need to take care of. Things she'll hate me for, but will ensure she isn't left here in Raindale, unprotected.

I'll revel in her hatred as long as it's keeping her safe. I'll let her think the worst of me. Let her believe that everything between us was forged from my lies, even though the reality is that with her, I'm the realest I've ever been. And honestly, I'm not sure how I'll recover from the loss.

But my father knows where she is. Worse, knows *who* she is to me, and as long as she's by herself, working every day of the week and having baby Chase stay with Susan, they're vulnerable. And I'm not willing to take the risk.

It's long after the hot Arizona sun has fallen beneath the horizon, the full moon rising in its place, that I head back to the motel and knock on Chase's door.

The red wood swings open, Chase's eyes widening before they turn into slits, his arms crossing over his chest. "What the fuck do you want?"

I raise a brow. "I think you say fuck more than any person I've ever met."

His jaw clenches. "Do you honestly *fucking* think that joking with me is something we do now?" He shoves his finger into my chest, and I have to temper the urge to rip his hand off me. "I was nice to you because I *had* to be, but that was before you fucked with my baby sister."

His anger spirals off him like steam in the cold, and my respect heightens, because despite my size and the fact I could break all his fingers before he could throw a punch, he's standing up for Lily. Making sure I know my place. He has the type of loyalty most people dream of having, and it makes my attitude toward him warm, just a little.

"It's because of your sister that I'm letting you get away with talking to me like that." I take a step forward until I tower over him. "But do it again and we'll have problems."

I grab a toothpick from my pocket, my body screaming for a cigarette to calm the nerves. But there's no time for that right now. "Listen, I don't have much time. Can I come in?"

His eyes are calculating as they size me up, his jaw muscle tensing as the seconds tick by.

"*Please,*" I bite out, the urgency I feel in my veins bleeding into my voice. Time is running out for me to say what I need to say; my father expects me in Phoenix within the hour.

Sighing, he runs a hand through his hair, tugging at the roots before opening the door and walking away. I blow out a breath of relief and follow him in, glancing behind me, making sure there are no wandering eyes. I wouldn't put it past my father to have someone watching me, even though he knows he has me by the balls.

My stomach somersaults at the idea of being in the public eye. Of being *scrutinized*. Nausea churns at the mere thought, and I realize that if Lily hates me now, things are going to get a lot worse when she turns on the news and realizes who my father really is. Another thing I never got around to telling her.

I follow Chase into his room, anxiety making me jumpy as I shove my hands in my pockets and bounce on the balls of my feet.

"So what is it?" he says, sitting on the edge of the bed.

"I'm in love with your sister."

His nostrils flare, and he opens his mouth, but I keep talking, rushing out the words so I can get to the point. "I just thought we should get that out of the way. I didn't mean for it to happen, but it did. And maybe it's unprofessional—"

"It's unprofessional as *fuck*, you sleazy prick," he cuts in.

I smirk. "I won't deny it. But I love her, and she loves me too."

His eyes narrow. "How do you know?"

My hand presses against my chest, hoping that the weight of my palm will help subdue the ache. "Trust me." My voice pinches. "I know. You can hate me for it all you want, but it doesn't change the truth."

His brow quirks. "And what truth is that?"

"That I stalked her for a paycheck, and then we fell in love, and now I need your help to keep her safe."

"I have *always* tried to keep her safe," he hisses.

I nod, my eyes softening at the defensiveness in his tone. "I know."

He pinches the bridge of his nose. "Just how long did you know about her being here before you actually told me?"

I purse my lips. "A while."

He huffs.

"Honestly, you can get upset about that shit later. But *listen* to me, Chase." I slap my hand into my open palm. "There are people in my life who will use her to hurt me."

"Of fucking course there is." He glares, rage swirling through the hazel center of his eyes.

"My father is Thomas Wells, he's running for president and he's..." My jaw tenses as I try to figure out the best way to say it. "He's not a good man. He found out about Lily and now he's using her to make me his bitch."

Chase's elbows rest on his knees, his hands pressing into his eyes as he groans. "Jesus, what the *fuck*, dude?"

"I know it sounds crazy. But, Lily isn't safe here. Not if she's alone."

He looks to the side, his face trying to hold back the pain that's clear as day in his features. "She won't come back with me."

I shake my head. "She will. She'll find out tomorrow that she's being evicted."

Chase's eyes widen, and he jerks forward in his chair. "*What?*"

Running a hand over my face, I cringe. "I may have talked to her landlord. It didn't take much to convince them, she's three months behind on rent." My heart thunks against my chest, knowing she didn't have the money but was too proud to ask for help—knowing I'm taking advantage of that fact now. "I did what needed to be done."

Chase's eyes are wide and he shakes his head. "I thought I was an asshole, but you really take the fucking cake."

I shrug. "I don't want to live in this world if she's not in it. And I'll never forgive myself if something happens to her or Chase."

He nods, exhaling through his nose. "No, I get that."

Relief floods through me. "Look, she has demons in

Tennessee. Ones she's afraid of meeting." Our eyes lock. "I'm trusting you to keep her safe."

He nods.

"I need to be sure you understand me." I step forward, tilting my head. "She *isn't* safe here."

"I won't leave without her."

Blowing out a breath, I turn to walk out the door, but something makes me pause at the threshold; words on the tip of my tongue that I'm dying to get out.

"Her son... He——" I pause, praying for my heart to settle from where it's twisting violently in my chest. "He loves pancakes. But not the boxed ones. The fancy ones with chocolate chips baked in, and whipped cream with chocolate sauce on top." My voice breaks and I clear my throat. "He'll throw *back* some bacon, but only if it's crispy, and he hates sausage."

I peer at Chase from the corner of my eyes. His nostrils flare, tongue running over the front of his teeth.

"He likes it when you make a smiley face with ketchup on top of scrambled eggs, and..." I continue. "And he's *so* fucking special." I exhale a shaky breath.

I thought my heart was already broken, but it isn't until this moment that the final pieces rip and tear away, shriveling as they fall to the ground. I'll never get to hold his hand, or see his chubby cheeks break into a smile. I'll never hear him squeal with excitement when we play Spider-Man on the walls. I'll never get to tell him that for all the ways I love his mother, I love him just as much.

It's that last thought that breaks me, my chest splitting from the pain, organs spilling to the floor.

"She's a good mom, Chase."

His chin lifts, and he jerks his head, his Adam's apple bobbing with his swallow.

I nod, sniffing back the burn of tears.

And then I turn around and say goodbye to Raindale, Arizona, leaving my heart behind with it.

43
LILY

"What do you *mean* I have thirty days?" Panic grips my throat as I stare at my apartment manager, the eviction notice crumpled in my hand.

"Lily, I'm sorry, there's nothing I can do. The orders came directly from the big boss."

My stomach drops to the floor. "There has to be *something*, Alice, please."

She shakes her head, her lips turning down in the corners. "Honey, you're three months behind on rent."

My cheeks flush from the shame that surges forward at her statement. "I know, it's just... it's been slower than usual at the diner, and..." I trail off.

I was supposed to be at work fifteen minutes ago, but honestly, I'm having a hard time caring since without a place to live, there's really no point. Not to mention that nowhere else is going to rent to someone like me, especially not with an eviction on my record.

My fingers scratch at the scab on my wrist. "I get it, Alice. I'm sorry, I know it's not your fault."

She smiles, her eyes softening. Her hand reaches out and

squeezes my arm. "I really wish there was something I could do, Lily, but you know there isn't."

"Yeah." I sigh. "Thanks, anyway."

Three hours later, and I feel worse than I did before. My stomach is tossing like a ship in stormy waters, and there aren't enough customers coming in to keep my mind occupied. Still, I serve the ones who do with my biggest smile, hoping my friendliness might solve the issues their one-dollar tips won't.

"So what are you gonna do?" Annabelle asks as we roll silverware in the corner booth.

I groan, resting my forehead against the table. "I have no idea."

"Well, I'd let you move in with me, but I don't have enough space for you *and* a kid."

Lifting my head, my gaze catches hers, and I smile softly, warmth surrounding the hollow hole in my chest, thankful for her friendship.

The bell above the front door rings, and I twist to look as Chase and Jax walk in. Their faces light up when they see me, and I turn back around, finishing my roll up and moving to stand.

Annabelle's eyes widen as she takes them in.

"Oh no." I wag my finger. "They are *off*-limits."

Her bottom lip sticks out. "What? Why?" she whines.

"Because that's my brother."

She glances back at them. "*That's* your brother?"

I nod, popping my gum. "Yep."

"His friend looks familiar." She cocks her head as they reach the table, her eyes sliding down Jax's frame. "Is he off-limits too?"

"Taken, I'm afraid," he pipes in, a blinding smile spreading across his face with a wink.

I roll my eyes at his flirting, wondering what kind of a woman ends up snagging a man like Jackson Rhoades. The two of us were never close, by the time he moved to town I was already wading the murky waters of drug abuse; lost in the manipulation of my ex, Darryl.

My stomach curdles, dread racing through my veins at the thought of him.

Chase leans in for a hug. His embrace is strong and I find myself sinking into his hold, allowing the little bit of comfort in an otherwise cold and unforgiving world.

This has been a *shitty* week. But I've endured a lot of bad days in my life, and comparatively, this one isn't even close. I have air in my lungs, my baby boy by my side, and for all of the times I've been sad over losing Chase; now I have him too.

My chest aches when I think of him leaving—of not knowing when I'll see him again.

"Thought we'd come and see where you work." He grins.

Annabelle clears her throat. "Don't be *rude*, Lily. Introduce me."

I smirk. "Annabelle, this is Chase and Jax."

Her eyes light up in recognition. "*Jax*. Jackson Rhoades?"

My eyes narrow, suddenly untrusting of how she knows him. *Is everyone in on some big secret?*

His smile widens. "That would be me."

"You're dating Blakely Donahue!" She points at him. "I *knew* you looked familiar. Well, shit," she laughs. "There goes my chances."

My eyebrows draw in. "Who's that?"

"She's my fucking rock is who she is." Annabelle's hand goes over her heart. "Her story was featured on the cover of Vogue last month, and the way she's so open about her eating disorder really..." Her eyes well with tears. "I just appreciate her candor, is all."

My stomach sinks, wondering what shadows Annabelle hides behind her sunny disposition.

Jax's smile softens. "She'd be really happy to hear that."

Annabelle stares for long moments before snapping herself out of it, waving her hand in the air and shaking her head. "Ugh, well, I'll work for you tonight, *obviously*. You spend it with your family. You didn't tell me they were in town." Her eyes narrow to slits.

Refusal is on the tip of my tongue, about to tell her that I can't afford to *not* work the shift, but then I remember I'm about to lose my home anyway, so I might as well spend some time with Chase and Jax while I can. Maybe they can help me think of a solution.

"Okay, thanks." I turn to face the boys. "You guys hungry?" I ask, leading them toward a booth closer to the front. "Let me finish up and I'll come join you."

Plopping down two menus, I force a smile and turn to finish my side work.

It's thirty minutes later when I finally squeeze into the booth next to Jax.

Jax tilts his head. "All done?"

I smile at him. "Yep."

He grins, wiping his hands on his napkin. I stare across the table at Chase, who has an unreadable expression on his face, so similar to the ones he used to constantly wear when we were kids.

"Good to see your brooding nature hasn't changed," I tease. "Why are you looking at me like that?"

"No, I..." He shakes his head, clearing his throat. "How's your day been?"

It's a simple question, but it's one that burns a pathway through my tender insides, like a dragon breathing fire on scorched earth, making sure everything is crumbled to ash.

I pop my gum. "Shitty, to be honest."

He bobs his head, and something flashes through his eyes, almost like he knew that would be my answer. My stomach twists, the reality of my situation stringing me up like Christmas lights, heartbreak and homelessness flashing for the world to see. I hate having my problems so glaringly on display.

I drum my fingers on the table, resisting the urge to scratch at my wrist. "I got an eviction notice on the door this morning."

Jax takes a drink of his water, and Chase shifts in his seat before leaning forward and pushing his plate away. "What are you gonna do?"

Their reaction is lackluster, but maybe they assumed my life was shit anyway, and so this isn't a big surprise.

"I really have no fucking clue." I chuckle. "I've always tried to do my best, you know? Believe it or not, I've worked hard to get here." My throat swells. "*So* hard. And now..." I lift my shoulders in defeat.

Chase leans against the booth. "You can always come back with us."

I consider it for a moment, but then memories of what *else* is in Tennessee hit me like a freight train, the force as strong as the memory of fists, striking against my bones.

I can't go back.

If I do, then I'll be less than thirty minutes away from a man who I'd rather die than see again. From a man who kept me beaten and bruised, doped up and hidden from the world.

If I go back, then I'll have to face Darryl.

Chase's father.

But with no home and no viable options, I don't know if I have any other choice.

*

"You like Spider-Man?"

I take a sip of water, washing down the hint of cinnamon flavor left over from my gum. Chase and Jax are both in the living room, listening intently as baby Chase explains how to play Spider-Man. It makes my glued-together heart twist, the tattered edges fraying because this is something Alex and he always played. But then again, everything seems to remind me of Alex. Mason. *Whatever his name is.*

A sharp pain spears through my chest.

"No, cawwy me on the walls, like this!" Chase squeals, picking up his Spider-Man stuffy and placing it against the wall, then soaring it into the air.

"He likes to pretend he can stick to the walls, and then swing by his web to the next spot," I jump in, trying to help explain. "Like Spider-Man."

Baby Chase nods. "Yeah, like Awex does."

My insides ache, anger welling up inside of me, for A —Mason to have the fucking audacity to come into my life and make my child fall in love with him.

Breaking my heart is one thing. Hurting the reason for my existence is quite another.

The landline phone rings and I head to the kitchen to answer it, the giggles floating from the living room making a small smile break across my face. Warmth kindles in the center of my chest, fighting against the icy storm of heartbreak that's freezing me from the inside out.

"Hello?"

"Lily," Derek breathes down the line. "Sorry I missed your call."

"Yeah, I just..." I bite my cheek, trying to stem the sudden flow of tears that want to break free. *Get it together, Lily. You're stronger than this.* "I'm being evicted."

"*What?*" His voice is harsh, like he's just as surprised as I was. "Why?"

I cringe, not wanting to tell him. "I've been a little behind on rent for a few months."

"Lily—"

"But it's never been an issue before," I rush out. "And I *always* pay the late fees. I just..." Swallowing, I glance into the living room, watching my baby boy swing from the walls in the arms of his uncle.

My chest burns.

"You should have called and told me you needed help."

"I didn't want to be a burden."

He sighs. "You never are."

I pause, pinching the bridge between my nose "There's more."

And then I lay it all out. I tell him everything about *Mason*, everything about my brother, and all the ways I'm confused, and broken, and have no idea what to do. Derek is the only person who knows everything about Darryl, and *no one* knows about Derek, which is why he's always been my safe space.

I'm surprised when he tells me he thinks I should consider coming back to Tennessee.

"What? I couldn't..." Sharp pains shoot across my sternum from the thought, my nightmares coming to haunt me in the day, reminding me of everything that could happen.

"Look," he croons. "I know it's scary, and it's not ideal, but... you'd be in Sugarlake. With family. Tell 'em about Darryl and they can help protect you."

My heart stutters. "It's not that simple."

"Life never is, Lily. What else are you gonna do? Move place to place, hopin' you can somehow make it work on your own?"

The muscles in my jaw strain. "It's worked for me so far."

"Aren't you tired of runnin' yet? Come home. Let the people who love you *help* you."

Fear swirls in my gut, the urge to shut it down raging through me. But then I hear a shriek from the living room, and peer around the corner, the words stalling on the back of my tongue. My baby boy's smile is blinding, but it's my brother who steals my breath. He's laughing, his eyes gazing at my son like he's the greatest gift in the world.

My chest pulls tight.

My baby deserves a family.

I ignore the sick feeling whipping through my middle, my fingers clenching the phone so tight I'm afraid it may break. "Okay." I nod. "Guess I'm going home."

44

MASON

I t's been two weeks and I've had no way to check and make sure that Lily is safe. I've texted Chase, but so far, they've gone completely unanswered. It makes my insides tighten whenever I focus on the "what-ifs", and right now, I can't afford the distraction, so I remind myself the only way to ensure her safety for good is to make sure my father can't reach her.

I've been a good little lapdog, but ever since we came back to the estate in Oregon, they've been keeping me private, dropping tidbits into the press slowly, making people salivate with the questions. *What's going on with Thomas Wells? Why did he postpone his campaign trail? What could possibly be more important?*

The longer I stay here, stowed away like a prisoner, the more I come to terms with the fact that I've never really been hidden. They chose to let me live out my life, allowed me the illusion of believing that I was successful. But now I know they've just been waiting for the opportune moment to strike. For the moment when I could be used as a tool. But I'll bide my time, even if I have to do it lying in my child-hood room, the memories of my misery echoing off the walls. They may have kept track of my physical whereabouts, but they don't know my mind. They can't know that I spent years of my time, forging my mental state into a fortress. One that they can never penetrate. One they can never win against.

"He who is prudent and lies in wait for an enemy who is not, will be victorious."

But I would be lying if I said I wasn't going a little stir crazy. It's been two weeks and I still haven't seen my mother. I haven't spoken to Olivia. My only points of contact have been my uncle Frank and my father, two pieces of a whole.

Their plan is to play it like I ran away, a troubled teen who crumbled under the pressure of being a Wells. Afraid of marrying so young, and what it meant to live in the shadow of my father.

They're not wrong. On any of those facts. They just left out the part that my father went behind my back and destroyed my chance at happiness. I might not have anything to help bring my father down yet, but I'll wait patiently in the wings, even if it takes years. Even if he makes it to that seat in the White House. I'll expose him for what he is.

I make my way downstairs to get a glass of water. It's been years since I've been here, yet everything comes back to me quickly. Absolutely *nothing* has changed, even my room is the same as it was the night I left. Walking into the kitchen, I stop short at the sight of my mother, her hands gripping the edge of the island as she tosses back a pill with a glass of wine.

Typical.

Like I said, nothing around here has changed.

I clear my throat and she gasps, turning around. My heart clenches at seeing her, so polished and perfect, looking every bit the Stepford wife, and for just a moment, I'm thrown into the past. To a time when I craved her love and was always left wanting.

Thinking about how shitty my mother is makes me think of Lily again, and all the ways she thrives in the role. My stomach flips at the thought of her, grief rising up and sticking to my insides.

My mother's eyes widen, something akin to sadness flickering in her gaze before she smooths out her disposition. She walks over to me, her hand reaching up to cup my face. I let her, my jaw muscle jumping underneath her frail palm. She shakes slightly, her skin cold and clammy, and if I didn't know better, I'd think it was from seeing me again. But I know it's the Sunday morning cocktail inside of her that makes her tremble, not the sight of her long-lost son.

"Alexander," she whispers. "He said you were back, but I—"

She cuts off her words when my father's voice floats down the hall and he walks in, followed closely behind by his bitch, Frank.

And then, in walks Olivia.

It's the first time I've seen her since the gas station, and the anger I felt for her then is tenfold, my rage grasping onto her, needing somewhere to place the blame.

She looks away, glancing down at the ground.

"Oh, good, you're here already," my father says. "We have media training today. All of us together, so we can answer questions appropriately when asked." He walks over and smacks me on the back, a Cheshire grin creeping over his face. "Next week is the big day, are you ready?"

I force a smile, biting back the smart-ass retort that's laying thick on my tongue. Better for him to think I'm agreeable. "Ready as I'll ever be."

His grin stays painted on his face as he walks over and kisses my mother on the cheek. My eyes glide back to Olivia as she glances around the room, actively avoiding my stare. Fire races down my spine. Officially, she has the role of my father's "personal assistant." Betrayal runs hot, knowing that after everything, she stuck around. Accepted a *job* offer from him like he didn't ruin fucking everything.

It infuriates me that this whole time she's been at my father's beck and call, and I can't, for the life of me, figure out why. It can't be for money. Olivia is an oil heiress, her portion of her family's inheritance alone is more than what our entire family will make in a lifetime.

Ten years ago, I thought she stayed around for me. Foolishly, I thought that what we had was love. But now that I've felt what love truly is, I know that's not the case. Olivia and I were just photo ops, strategically placed and forced into decisions that neither of us had the spine to fight against.

The media training is monotonous, and a few hours later, I'm lying back in my childhood room, my phone on my chest as I silently wait for a text message I know will never come. My body starts to tense, insides jittery with the need for nicotine, so I walk to the patio and light up a cigarette, staring up at the sky.

"Alexander."

Olivia's voice floats from the room behind me, and my muscles stiffen, wondering how I was so lost in my thoughts I didn't hear her come in. I turn around, my eyes narrowing. Her lips are turned down in the corners, a heaviness to her gaze that didn't exist ten years ago, like her experiences have started to darken her soul until they bled through her eyes.

"Olivia." My voice is sharp, my walls rising immediately around her. I don't *trust* her.

"I thought that we could take a minute and talk." She walks in farther, and I move to go inside, but she shakes her head, her eyes shining with a warning. My insides clench, my steps stuttering to a halt. She closes the patio door behind her, walking to the lounger and perching on the corner.

My head cocks as I watch her, wondering what the fuck she's doing.

"Fewer prying eyes out here on the patio." She smiles, pointing toward the ceilings. Realization settles like a rock in my gut. *Cameras.* Of course.

I stare at her, crossing my arms and occasionally taking drags of my cigarette, waiting for her to spit out whatever she came here to say.

"How are you?" she asks after long minutes of silence.

I huff out a laugh, snuffing out the butt of my cigarette on the banister. "How do you think I am, Olivia? I'm peachy."

She nods, her hand running through her hair. "I'm surprised you're going along with all of this."

I shrug. "Yeah, well. Why fight when you can't win?"

She nods, her mouth twisting. "Yeah, I get that."

There's a sadness to her features, and maybe if I was a better man I would try to find the cause, but the days of me wasting *any* of my goodness on her is over.

"Do you have a point to being here, Olivia? Or are you just forcing inane conversation to torture me?" I raise my brow.

"No, I—" She shakes her head. "I just wanted to talk. To apologize, I guess."

My stomach twists. "Apologize for what?"

"For my part in everything. I know you must think the worst of me." Her voice shakes.

I chuckle. "That's an understatement."

Her eyes are wide and glossy as they gaze up at me. "Alexander—"

"I stopped being Alexander the moment you killed our child."

She swallows and glances down, a single tear falling down the side of her face. Slowly, she lifts her head and locks me into her stare.

"She wasn't yours."

4 5

LILY

Jax left Raindale after the first weekend, but Chase stayed for the next two weeks. It's been an adjustment to having him back in my life, but a nice distraction, nonetheless. Still, I can't help feeling like we're circling around each other's orbit, unsure of how to break into the atmosphere. Maybe he's too afraid to push, not wanting me to change my decision on going home, and I'm too afraid of being vulnerable enough to tell him that I don't have any other choices. So instead, we keep it surface level.

I finished my last shift at Dina's two days ago, and said a tearful goodbye to Annabelle, who wrote her number down on a sticky note and shoved it in my hands, making me promise to get a cell phone so we could text.

And now, all three of us are packed into his black Ford truck; equipped with a brand-new car seat, and driving down the main stretch of Sugarlake. Baby Chase is at the age where he doesn't quite grasp what's going on, but I've been thankful that he's had his uncle here to help mute Mason's absence. But the past week he's started to ask when he's coming back.

Mason. It's hard to think of him that way, but any time I remember his soft words or the rough grip of his hands, I repeat the name like a mantra—a whip cracking against my back, lashing me with the reminder of his lies.

My forehead presses against the cool window, my eyes soaking up the town that changed my life forever. The place I never thought I'd see again. It's thriving, businesses on Main Street open and beautiful, the sentimentality of the small town bleeding through the air and suffocating my lungs. My mind goes foggy, flashbacks of a similar moment, years ago, when Chase and I first moved here with Sam and Anna.

"Tennessee is so pretty. I bet it's the prettiest state in the whole universe," I say, watching the vibrant colors of the landscape pass by the window as we drive to our new home.

Chase smirks. "That's just because you don't remember living anywhere else."

He's right, I don't. The memories of our time in Chicago, back when we lived with our birth mother, is murky at best.

"Whatever, doesn't matter. I'm sure it wasn't like this." I point to the mountain range through the window, a sense of peace filling up my chest, the calmest I've ever felt in my whole entire life.

Anna, our new foster mom, glances back from the passenger seat. "I've always loved Tennessee, too, Lily." Her accent is thick, but after years of living in Tennessee, I've gotten used to the twang. "I think you'll really like it in Sugarlake. You know, that's where I grew up as a little girl."

My mind fills with visions of a young Anna, with two loving parents, and her wide smiling face as she played in her front yard and waved hi to all her neighbors. It's all I've ever wanted is to have a home like that. Maybe now, I will.

She glances at her husband, Sam, and my eyes fall to where he squeezes her knee, my heart clenching at the movement.

"I'm so happy you two are here with us to experience it."

Emotion ricochets off my insides at the memory, back when I truly believed there was light at the end of the tunnel. Of course, back then, I hadn't realized what happened to me wasn't okay. My body felt the trauma that my brain couldn't yet grasp. It was only as I started to mature, that I realized it wasn't *normal* for a forty-year-old man to touch me between my legs and tell me how much he loved me. That it wasn't *normal* for my body to tear and bleed, making it difficult to hide the pain when I walked. That it wasn't *normal* for me to like the way it felt when he rewarded me for keeping quiet.

Disgust crawls up my throat, wrapping around my neck, and I push the feeling aside, not wanting to face the shame that is my past. But being back in Sugarlake makes it hard to ignore.

Chase looks over at me, his fingers tapping against his steering wheel.

"You doing okay?" he asks me.

I nod, swallowing around the emotion. "Yeah. Being back here is a trip, though." My fingers scratch at my wrist. "I guess I'm a little nervous."

He bobs his head. "I was too when I came back for the first time."

My brows draw in, my gaze snapping to him. I had assumed he never left. "What do you mean *come back?*"

His brows lift. "It's been a long time, Lil. Life still happened even when you were gone. And things happened here that I—" He grips the roots of his hair. "I had to leave for a while. It took a lot of work, *personal* work to get to a place where I could come back. Where I felt whole enough to be here."

"Did—" I pause, the question heavy and sticking on my tongue. "Did Lee go with you?"

My heart beats double time in my chest, unsure what I want the answer to be. Years of separation and life experience may have dulled the pain of them hooking up behind my back, but their betrayal still exists like scars that twinge when touched.

Chase blows out a breath. "Goldi is the love of my life, Lily."

Amusement bubbles in my chest at that *stupid* nickname. "She still hate it when you call her that?"

He smirks. "She *loves* it when I call her that."

I giggle, and it makes him smile, and I grab onto the lightness of the moment, hoping beyond hope that there's a trail being blazed for our healing.

His chuckles die down, and he sighs as we roll to a stop at a red light. "I wasn't the man that Goldi deserved for a long time, so when I left... I left without her."

My heart falters as I watch the pain flit through his eyes, his forehead wrinkling. For the first time, I wonder about the stories my brother has to tell, and there's a hollow ache inside of me—a missing piece that won't ever be found, knowing I missed being around to hear them.

"But you got her back," I state.

"I got her back," he agrees, a blinding smile blooming on his face. "And now she's gonna be my wife."

My brows rise, but the words themselves aren't that surprising. "Honestly, shocked you aren't already married," I mutter.

He blows out a breath. "We had a lot of work to do to get to that point." He glances at me. "Losing you, it fucked me up, Lily."

I glance at baby Chase, making sure he's still asleep, before moving my attention back.

"I'm not blaming you," he continues. "But I wasn't healthy after you were gone. Honestly, wasn't healthy before. I had to work on *me* before I was able to be there for her. And you know how Goldi gets."

I roll my eyes, because *yeah*, even though I haven't seen her in years, there are pieces of personality that are fundamental. And Alina May Carson has stubborn in spades.

"Selfish?" I ask, unable to keep the barb in.

His jaw muscles tic, his grip tightening on the wheel. "She's been through a lot."

I lift my shoulders. If he's looking for sympathy, he won't find it in me. "Haven't we all?"

The fact of the matter is that Lee was my best friend for years, my first *real* friend. And from the moment she stomped into my front yard and introduced herself, we were inseparable. Which is why it hurt so bad to find her with Chase. The two most important people in my life, loving each other so hard that they didn't leave any love for me.

It's what made it so easy to slip away.

I blow out a shaky breath, my fingers tapping against my tattoo of Wiggles. "Is she gonna be there?" I wave my arm toward the front window of the car. "At your place, I mean?"

His brows furrow. "I mean… yeah, Lil. She lives there. I'm not gonna ask her to leave."

I force a smile onto my face. "No, of course not. It's fine." Anxiety snaps like rubber bands against my stomach. "We're gonna have to get it over with, eventually, right? Sooner is better than later, I guess."

He grins. "Exactly."

We pull into a driveway. "This your place?"

He smiles. "Only for a couple more months while I build our house."

I nod, not surprised at all that he's working construction. Our adopted father, Sam, owns Sugarlake Construction Company. He always wanted Chase to follow in his footsteps. "You work for Sam?"

"He wishes." The side of his mouth tilts. "No, I run the company now. He's retired."

Nerves simmer low in my belly at the thought of seeing Sam and Anna. There's so much I missed out on. So many people who I know I hurt when I left.

I see the front door open from the corner of my eye and I glance over, my heart beating so hard it jumps to my throat. A bright-eyed, blonde-haired woman stands in the doorway, a gigantic smile splitting her face in half. Chase's entire demeanor softens as he takes her in, and I can't help the pangs of envy that bang against my insides.

He turns to me. "You ready?"

I swallow, my hands shaky from the nerves. "As I'll ever be."

Taking a deep breath, I unbuckle my seat belt and get ready to face my past.

46

MASON

I 've only had a few life-changing moments, ones that become integral in forming who you are as a person, and *this* is one of those moments.

Olivia stares at me, her eyes rimmed red with what I'm assuming are tears of guilt, telling me the child she carried for five months, the child I envisioned holding in my arms, the child I *grieved*... that child wasn't mine.

"I'm sorry, say that again?" I ask, cocking my head to the side, a fire growing steadily in the pit of my stomach.

She swallows, the pale skin of her neck blossoming a deep shade of red. "She wasn't *yours*, Alex."

"Don't call me that." The nickname is too tender, whispers of it slipping off another woman's tongue too fresh. My mind is racing, reframing everything I thought I knew from my past, a tendril of intuition prodding at my back. "Whose was it?"

Her eyes drop, the cerulean blue growing glassy as she stutters out a shaky breath. She purses her lips. "I think you know."

My chest caves in.

No.

"Are you..." I rub my forehead with my fingertips. "Are you telling me you were having an affair with my father?"

She bites her bottom lip, breaking eye contact and looking to the side.

"You were *eighteen!*" I snap.

"Fifteen when it started."

Bile rolls through my stomach, the nausea so overwhelming my mouth sours.

My chin lifts, teeth grinding to keep from spewing the acid off my tongue. I shake my head. "No, that's... that's before we started dating. That's—" My eyes widen, my hand coming to cover my mouth. "That's the first time he invited your family around."

Another tear drips down her face. "I thought he loved me," she whispers.

"My father doesn't love anyone."

She scoffs, her eyes blazing as they lock on mine. "I know that now."

I collapse against the railing of the patio, shock and disgust warring for first place inside of me. I always knew my father was a vile man, but I never knew his sins ran this deep. He took advantage of a fifteen-year-old girl. He *groomed* her. He stuck her to my side so he could keep her close.

This is *evil*. This is...

Illegal.

Not that it matters, without proof, it would still just be my word against his. And my word doesn't hold weight like a man who is first in line to run the country.

My mind replays Olivia's words, and I stand up straighter. "Wait a second. Wait... wait." I pace back and forth, my chest cavity collapsing from the weight of her truth. "Are you telling me that the baby—*my fucking baby*—was actually his?" My fingers press against the numbers tattooed on my arm. The one that Lily's son asked about—the due date for a baby that apparently was never mine to begin with.

She chokes out a sob, her hand coming up to cover her mouth, black tears smearing down her face. "I'm sorry, Alexander."

Pieces of my heart that I didn't know still existed shatter, proving there's always more to lose. Always deeper to fall. Always more to grieve.

"I wanted to keep her!" she bursts out. "I wanted to keep her," she cries again. "But Thomas knew that people would question the timing."

I tilt my head. "The timing?"

"Of the baby," she whimpers, gasping through her tears.

"So, let me get this straight." I run my hands over my face and light up another cigarette. "He wanted me to marry you to cover up *his* mistakes, and then when he realized having a grandkid made out of wedlock could hurt him in the polls... you both just decided to just rip it out at the source? Because fuck what anyone else thought, right? Fuck what *I* thought."

She looks up at me, her eyes flaring. "There is no *we* in that scenario. He didn't give me a choice. He swept me away for a weekend. I thought he was being romantic," she scoffs. "But then a doctor came to the hotel, and—" She sniffles, her hands covering her stomach as she collapses in on herself. After a few moments, she lifts her head, staring me in the eyes. "And then, after you left, he told me you were dead. And I have..." she pauses, breathing deep, her eyes closing. "I promised myself I wouldn't stop until I could make him pay."

My heart clamps down, squeezing in my chest. "So why haven't you?"

She shrugs. "Because I'm pathetic? Because I'm weak?" Her hand trembles as she runs it through her hair. "Because I'm a coward."

I run my tongue over my teeth, flicking the ash from my cigarette. "Did you ever love me?"

She swallows, looking down at the ground. "Eventually."

Huffing out a laugh, I raise my head to the sky. "You're unbelievable."

"I'm sorry, I—" Her voice catches, and she stands up, walking over and grabbing the cigarette from my hand, bringing it to her lips and inhaling. "If there was some way I could go back in time, I would. But Alexander, I thought he *loved* me." More tears fall from her eyes. "I didn't know."

My hands go to my hips, and I breathe deep, trying to calm the storm that's raging through my insides. "Yet, here you are."

She walks to the banister, gripping the edges so tightly her fingertips turn red. "I'm a prisoner in Thomas's world, the same as everyone else. I hate him," she whispers, so faint I have to lean in to hear. "I want him to pay for what he's done."

"He will." The words escape me before I can draw them back, and I cringe, cursing myself for being so fucking stupid. I don't know if I can trust her, but *if* I can—if there's even a small chance—it would help to have her on my side. So even though it might be a colossal mistake, I continue. "I'll make sure of it."

Her eyes harden as she stares at me before her gaze scans the area.

"Are you okay?" I ask.

She rubs her lips together. "Yes, I'm just… do you think they can hear us?"

I shrug, because the truth is, I'm not sure if they can. I wouldn't put anything past my father, and the fact that she seems to think there are cameras in my room, tell me everything we do is most likely under scrutiny. "I guess we'll find out, huh? He probably wouldn't like you telling me all his secrets."

"You're right." Her teeth sink into her lower lip as she straightens from where she was leaning over the balcony. "Can I see your phone?"

Slipping my cell from my back pocket, I hand it to her, my heart beating out a staccato rhythm against my ribs. She types furiously, her eyes scanning the screen before her lips tighten, and she walks over, placing the phone in my hand.

"Thank you for listening," she mutters, her lips soft as they skim the stubble on my cheek. And then she turns around and walks inside.

Energy bounces through my muscles, my stomach somersaulting as I look down and read the words.

He liked to take pictures.
He keeps them in his safe.
I know how to get them.

47
LILY

I can't remember a time in my life that was more uncomfortable than this moment right here, sitting across the table from Lee while she sips her tea, staring me in the eyes, not saying a word. My hands wrap around the hot mug placed in front of me, hoping the warmth can seep through my body and stop the chill that's racing down my spine. I'm having a hard time keeping it together. Seeing Lee in person sends pinpricks of irritation stabbing along my sides until the wounds from years ago feel like they're fresh slices on my skin.

She takes another sip, her mouth slurping as she drinks from her cup, the sound grating on my nerves.

Finally, she sets down her mug, a soft smile blooming across her face as she looks at me. "Hi."

Annoyance rolls like a ball in my chest, and I struggle to tamp down the urge to bite out a smart retort. But this is *her* home, and regardless of our personal relationship, I'm grateful she's letting us stay. But if she thinks we can just pick up where we left off a decade ago, then she's in for a rude awakening.

"Hi," I force out.

Her nails tap on the tabletop, faint giggles floating from

the living room, baby Chase having stolen his uncle away immediately, demanding a tour of his new home.

When we first walked in, his eyes widened, and my already bruised heart squeezed tight, knowing he'd never seen such a nice house. But we've never had the luxury of a comfortable life. My baby hasn't been graced with stability, and guilt spins me around in its tornado, ripping me up from the roots.

What if he grows up and resents me?

What if I can't provide him the life he sees here?

What if, what if, what if?

I swallow back the burn rising up my throat and meet Lee's eyes. She looks as good as she always did, but there's a melancholy sheen to her gaze now, one that wasn't there when we were kids. We were always different. Where she was truly the embodiment of innocence, like sweet cherry pie at the end of a meal, I was just an expert at *presenting* it, my insides rotted and sour. But somehow, her light attracted the darkest parts of me, making me want to embody everything she was. Lee was *living* the life I always dreamed of. She was the girl I always wanted to be. And she made me feel like the weight I constantly carried in my heart wouldn't always feel so heavy.

Odd, how you can be so close to someone, and then suddenly, they're nothing more than a memory. Soul sisters to strangers, in the blink of an eye.

"He's adorable," Lee continues, her head tilting in the direction of my son.

I force a smile. "Thank you."

My voice is strained, but I don't know how else to be. It's difficult for me to pretend, I just don't have the energy, my emotions drained dry from the past few weeks. I don't *want* to hate her, but I'm having a hard time finding any peace with what she's done.

She puffs out her cheeks. "Dang, Lily, this is crazy."

I tilt my head. "What is, exactly?"

She waves her hand toward me. "*Seein'* you here. I never

thought we'd—" She cuts off mid-sentence, clearing her throat. Her hand reaches out to cover mine on top of the table.

My eyes lock on where we touch, my stomach tensing at the feel.

"It's real good to have you home again."

My eyebrow quirks. "Is it?"

She withdraws her hand. "I know it makes Chase happy."

"And you?"

She swallows. "Of course I'm happy, Lily. You were my best friend, even if at the end, things weren't so great."

I scoff, and her eyes narrow.

"I still missed you when you were gone. Before that, if I'm honest."

"Honesty," I spit. "What a concept."

She bites into her lower lip, chewing until it's red. "Do you really wanna talk about this right now? I mean, I'm game." She puts her hands out to her sides. "I'm ready to dive in whenever you are, girlfriend, but you *just* got here, and I know things ended up bein'..." She trails off, and my insides tense.

"Ended up being what?"

"*Different* than you expected. You know, with Mason and all."

My hurt flares to life like a diamond glinting in the sun, and I snap before I can think better of it. "You know nothing about Mason. And you know nothing about what I've been through. All you know is the girl I let you know, which, fucking news flash, Lee, wasn't real."

Lee's eyes harden as she leans back in her chair. "Don't you sit there and pretend like you weren't true with me, Lily Ann Adams. I know you were."

My lips curl. "I wasn't. But you were so busy with yourself you never took the time to see it."

"Ouch," she whispers.

My hand presses into my stomach, trying to ease the ache. "Yeah, well." I shrug.

"Everything okay in here?" Chase's voice comes from the hallway, a beaming toddler dangling from his hip.

Lee's eyes bore holes into my face, and I clench my jaw, refusing to meet her gaze, the wounds too fresh from everything that's gone unsaid. She sighs and stands up, walking next to Chase and squeezing his arm. "Everything is peachy keen, jelly bean. I'm gonna start supper." She turns toward me. "There are some people who wanna come see you tomorrow for lunch, but if you're more comfortable with me tellin' them no, then I will." She puts her hand on her hip. "I know you may not wanna believe it, Lily, but I love you. I always have, even when we hurt each other. And more than anything else in this world, I want you to feel welcome here."

Guilt spears my middle, her words slamming against my wall of hurt and making it shake, the edges starting to crumble. But the word love stopped mattering when *Mason* shattered what it meant.

I don't feel like it's my place to tell them *not* to have people come over, so even though the thought of seeing everyone at once makes my nerves tighten and my veins beg for the kind of numb only drugs can provide, I don't tell them no.

"They can all come. I don't mind." I paste a smile on my face. "It will be good to see them. I'm sure we all have things to say."

*

A FEW HOURS LATER, baby Chase and I have settled into the guest bedroom. It's a temporary situation, obviously, but until I can figure out what to do for money, I'm thankful for the place to stay.

I lean down on the bed, kissing my baby boy's head as he sleeps, knowing the excitement of the day has knocked him out. After that disastrous first meeting with Lee, I've tucked myself away, trying to find some silent moments. But the calm doesn't stop the thunderclouds from rolling in, and tonight promises rain.

There's a knock on the door and I walk to it, putting a finger to my mouth when I see Chase, letting him know to stay quiet. I step into the hall, leaving the door slightly ajar.

"Hey," Chase whispers. "You okay?"

I nod, pulling my hair back into a ponytail. "I'm good, dude. Who all is coming for lunch tomorrow?"

Anxiety pools low in my stomach, not wanting to face everyone, but knowing I don't have a choice.

Chase's eyes flash, the space between his brows wrinkling. "Becca and Jax of course. And then Lee's brother and Blakely, Jax's girl."

"Oh." My fingers rub against my wrist, insides winding tight. *What the hell have I gotten myself into?*

"I just wanted to check in and make sure everything was okay. I don't..." He sighs, resting his hands on his head. "I don't want to overwhelm you, but I figured it was just best to, I don't know."

"Rip the Band-Aid off?" I raise my brows.

He smiles. "Yeah, I guess."

I wave him off. "Really, Chase, it's fine. I'll have to face everyone at some point anyway, right? I just..."

"Just what?"

My heart clenches tight, my chest aching from all of the heavy emotions that have played out in my life over the past few weeks. "I just don't want everyone to hate me."

His lips turn down. "Nobody *hates* you, Lily. We're all here because we fucking love you."

Love. There's that goddamn word again.

"Listen." He lowers his voice. "I wasn't going to bring this up until later, but, I have this therapist."

I choke on a cough. "A *therapist?*"

He smirks. "Yes, a fucking therapist, Lily. One you probably should pay half the damn bills for considering you're a big subject of conversation."

The guilt wraps around me like a ribbon.

"Anyway, I'd really like us to go together and have group sessions, if that's something you'd be willing to do?" He breaks eye contact, his cheeks flushing slightly as he asks, and my heart stutters, knowing how difficult this must be for him.

Therapy. I've never thought about it before, but there's nothing I want more in this world than to heal the divide between us. My brother was the most important person in my life at one time, and I've missed him every day. If he asks me to go to therapy, if he thinks there's a chance for healing between us, then I'll follow his lead and do what he wants. Even though the idea scares me shitless.

I nod. "Of course."

He blows out a breath, a smile breaking across his face. "Okay, Yeah. Yes. Great." He bounces slightly on the balls of his feet. "Okay, I'm gonna go see if Goldi needs help with anything, you good?"

I smile bright until the muscles in my cheeks pinch. "I'm good."

And when he walks away, I head back into my room and slink inside, collapsing against the back of the door, and muffling the scream. Pushing it back down, where no one can hear it.

48

MASON

The rest of the afternoon is a blur, my mind racing in a thousand different directions, unsure where to focus my attention. The only way to calm my thoughts is to make a list and tackle things one by one. Don't leave any room for miscalculation.

First, I take a walk, chain-smoking cigarettes, while I scope out the camera's blind spots around the perimeter of the house. Then, when I make it back to my room, I let myself mourn.

I mourn the loss of a daughter I never really had.

I mourn the loss of a sister I never got to know.

And I mourn for Olivia, her body wearing memories that she didn't make by choice.

My anger toward her has morphed into sorrow. It's confusing, because years of hurt feelings don't just disappear overnight, but she was a victim, not a villain, subject to crimes I wouldn't wish on my worst enemy.

By the time dinner comes around—the first "family" meal since I've been back—I've decided that I'm going to take a chance, trusting that Olivia means it when she says she wants to make my father pay. Selfishly, I want to take him down, and while I know it would happen eventually with or without her, Olivia deserves justice, whichever way she chooses to seek it.

We're all just lions at Thomas Wells's circus, desperate to feel the earth under our feet; our paws chained to cold metal.

It's hard to sit through dinner when you're expected to eat across from a man who lives his life as though he hasn't tattooed people's hurt on his skin and worn it as his shield. He kisses my mother like she's the only thing he sees, but her stare is vacant, and my heart squeezes, knowing they're really just two hollow pieces to an empty shell.

Olivia is also here, although God knows why, silently twirling her pasta methodically around her fork. My head cocks as I take in my mother. *Does she know?* I assume she'd have to, what with the fact Olivia is always around.

And then another thought hits me, wondering if Olivia was the first.

If she was the last.

My blood boils even hotter, my fists clenching so tightly the silverware cuts into my hand. I've never wished death on anyone, but even if the life drained from his body under my hands, it wouldn't feel like enough.

After dinner, we all separate, prisoners dismissed back to their cells. But instead of heading to my room, I walk outside, lighting up a cigarette and hiding in the shadows, waiting until Olivia leaves for the night.

It's forty minutes later when she appears out of the side door, adjusting her top and wiping the smeared lipstick off her lips. My stomach tosses, again questioning whether I can trust her. *Is she setting me up? Testing my loyalty?*

Reaching out, I grip her by the shoulder, my hand covering her mouth to stifle her gasp as I push her against the brick wall.

"Ssh, it's me," I whisper.

Her body softens as she realizes, and she nods her head.

My hands drop to my sides as I back away. "What do you need?" I ask.

She tilts her head. "For..."

"To get them?" I lower my voice even more. "The pictures. What do you need?"

Her eyes spark in understanding. "*You* need to get them."

A warning tingle rushes up my spine, my brows shooting to my hairline. "And how do you expect me to do that?"

She licks her lips. "I've known his passcode for years. It never changes, and he's never taken me seriously enough to think I was a threat." Her nostrils flare, jaw clenching. "I'll distract him, and you can slip into his office and grab what we need."

"What about the cameras?"

Her forehead wrinkles. "We'll just have to make sure and do it right before we turn them in."

I suck in a breath. It's risky, but not impossible. "You're sure they're there?"

She nods. "He adds to them all the time."

My stomach sours.

"But he has favorite ones. Some from when I was..." She doesn't finish her sentence, but she doesn't need to, I get the gist.

"And you'll... go public?" I tilt down my head to meet her eyes, my palm gripping her arm. "You're truly okay with that?"

"If I said I would do it, then I'll do it, Alexander," she hisses, ripping herself out of my hold.

I raise my hands. "I'm just making sure. It's not like you're making fucking cookies, Olivia. I don't want to start this unless you're one hundred percent in. This is *important*. This could change everything."

Her eyes soften. "This could set us free. Both of us."

Her hand comes up, fingers grazing against my stubble,

and I jerk back, my mouth twisting at her touch. "What are you doing?"

She shakes her head. "I'm sorry, I just thought——"

"Well you thought wrong." I harden my gaze, my fingers gripping at the roots of my hair. I turn toward her, pointing my finger. "Are you fucking with me right now?"

Her eyes widen. "What? No."

Running my tongue over my teeth, I step in closer. "You better not be, Olivia. We have a past, but if I find out you're playing me, I will fuck your world up, do you understand me?"

"I understand." Her throat bobs with her swallow, her cheeks flushing. "You never used to be so callous."

My lips twist. "I used to be a naive fool."

"That girl you were with at the gas station, is she..."

My lungs seize, thoughts of her bringing up Lily, yet another warning bell going off in my head. "She's none of your concern."

I try to stop the thoughts, but her name was enough, and the ache sharpens in my solar plexus, spreading until it feels as though I'll bleed out from the pain.

Olivia's lips purse. "Fine. I'm sorry I asked, I was just curious." She lifts her shoulders.

"I don't want to talk about her." *I can't.*

She gazes up at the sky, running a hand over her face. "We can do it at the press conference next week."

My heart rate picks up, pounding in my ears. That would work perfectly. As long as I can get the photos before we leave, there's nothing he can do to stop it once we're in front of the press. It's our best shot.

"You'll speak? You're sure?" I ask again, anxiety slithering around my spine like a constrictor.

Her eyes darken. "I'm sure."

"Okay." I blow out a breath, energy billowing inside of me like a smoke cloud, knowing I'm *right* there.

On the edge of freedom.

49

LILY

C hase and Lee have a nice back patio, string lights above our head, tiki torches around the perimeter, and an outdoor table that seats ten. Right now, I'm sitting smack dab in the center, coloring dinosaurs with my baby boy.

Lee brings out a few platters, setting them in the middle of the table, and I feel useless. Like an intruder. I glance up, watching as she stumbles, resting her hands on the back of the chair across from me, closing her eyes and gulping in deep breaths. Her face drains of color.

"Are you alright?" I ask.

Her gaze snaps open and she looks up at me, painting a smile on her face. "I'm fine, I've just been sick with a stomach bug that won't quit!" She presses her hand against her stomach. "Some days I think it's better and then *boom!* I can't get outta bed."

My eyes trail down her form, gaze resting on where her palm cradles her stomach. My heart skips. I'm a firm believer that sometimes your subconscious can relay information through body language you aren't willing to acknowledge. And if that's the case, Lee's relaying *all kinds* of information.

Picking up a glass of water, I take a sip. "Interesting."

Her eyebrow cocks. "What's so interestin' about it?"

I shrug, picking up a blue crayon and helping baby Chase color in his dinosaurs.

Chase saunters out, whistling, embodying a laid back and easy demeanor. Never in my life would I have guessed that I would see him whistling while he works, but here he is, busting out of his cocoon, having transformed into a beautiful butterfly.

He walks over to Lee, his arm wrapping around her waist as he presses a kiss to her head. "Hey, baby. You okay?"

She smiles faintly at him, her skin still pallid. "I'm fine, babe. Just queasy."

His brows furrow. "Still? Have you called the doctor?"

She waves him off. "Psh. Ain't nothin' a doc gonna tell me other than to take it easy and sleep it off."

I snort under my breath. "And to take a pregnancy test," I mutter.

Chase snaps his head to me, and so does Lee, her eyes narrowing. "If you've got somethin' to say, Lily, you can just come right out and say it."

Dropping the crayon, I raise my hands. "I didn't say a thing."

"Pwegnanc-eeeeeeee," a tiny voice to my left croons.

Shit.

Chase's eyes grow wide, his head twisting back to Lee.

"Nope," she says, throwing her hands up. "Nope. Nope. We are *not* havin' this conversation right now. I'll be inside."

She hustles away and Chase sits down across from me, running a hand through his hair. "Do you really think...?"

I shrug. "That's between you and her. I just know when I was pregnant with this one." I point to baby Chase. "I was throwing up *constantly*." My fingers scratch at my wrist. "That being said, I was also going through heavy withdrawal, so who's to say? Your fiancée done any hard drugs lately?" I smile wide, attempting to lighten the mood.

It doesn't work.

"That's not funny, Lil."

My stomach tenses, but I soften my smile. "Sometimes humor is the best way to cope."

He blows out a breath, his eyes glancing around the patio. Leaning forward, his elbows rest on the table. "Listen, no one who is coming knows about us being engaged. We were thinking of announcing it today. So until we do, mind keeping it quiet?"

My brows shoot up, shock circling through my insides. "*What?* No one knows yet?"

He smiles. "It happened the same day I found out where you were. I've been a bit preoccupied."

Guilt spirals through my center but I ignore the heaviness. It's not a *new* feeling, after all. "Well." I mime zipping my lips. "Mum's the word. Your secret's safe with me."

Ten minutes later, the doorbell rings, making my body jolt. I grip the purple crayon in my fist, taking deep breaths. My nerves are frayed, my mind having had all evening to run through the ten thousand different ways this reunion could go.

Mainly, I'm scared of Becca.

While she was never as close with me as Lee, at the end of the day it was still the three of us. But Becca never held on to friendships quite as tight, especially when someone else was already letting go. And I pulled away first, I won't deny it, which made it easy for her to wash her hands, firmly aligning herself to Lee's camp, becoming protective of her and pushing me to the side.

Speak of the devil, and she'll appear.

Becca walks through the back patio, her curly red hair bouncing with every step, and an *extremely* attractive blond guy with his hand around her waist. My hands press against my thighs, and I swallow down the anxiety, preparing for the worst. Becca isn't one to hold back her sharp tongue and her opinions.

Chase walks over, his eyes bouncing from me to baby Chase. "Hey, man, you want to come learn how to flip burgers on the grill?"

Baby Chase's eyes light up and he squeals, scrambling off his booster seat. I reach out to help him, but he barely touches my hand before he's off and running to his uncle. My heart spasms against my sternum at the sight of them.

I'll go through whatever steps I need, and face off anyone from my past, no matter how terrifying and hurtful. Because my baby boy deserves to have his family.

"Well, look at what the cat dragged in." Becca stands at the head of the table, her hip cocked to the side, as she stares me dead in the eye. Immediately, I can sense a difference from the girl I knew; a softness surrounding her like an aura. It makes me slightly less on edge.

I force a grin. "Hi, Becca."

Her lips twitch. "Is that all I get? A 'hi'? After you up and disappeared, leavin' us all here in shambles?"

My insides squeeze tight, nerves racing through my insides. *I don't know if I can do this.*

Her arms open wide and her lips curl up. "The *least* you can do is get over here and give me a hug." Shock floods my chest, drizzling down through my extremities like a watering can, dousing the nerves with relief.

I stand up slowly, a flush rising on my cheeks as I move toward her. She pulls me in, wrapping me in her arms. I sink into her hold, trying like hell to stem the tears from where they're burning behind my eyes. The Becca *I* knew would never have done this. She would have strung me up with her cutting words, and beaten me blue out of spite. It makes me wonder what happened to make her able to lead with love instead of fire.

"It's so good to see you, girlfriend. You look..." She pulls back, her hands gripping my forearms, her emerald green gaze soaking me in. "You look damn good." Her eyes zone in on my tattoos, and she smirks. "I always wanted to get a tattoo, but I've never had the nerve."

She smiles wide, and a deep chuckle breaks out, the tall guy from earlier appearing next to her, a smile on his face. I take him in, wondering who he is and why I can't place him, but there's a tingle of familiarity that niggles at the back of my brain.

"Baby girl, you never told me you wanted a tattoo." His blue eyes sparkle as he grins at her.

A beaming smile breaks across her face and she twists to look up at him, her eyes warming. The love flows *effortlessly* between the two of them, and it makes my stomach cramp, wondering if that's how I looked at Al—*Mason*.

"Yep." She pops the p. "A big number thirty-three, right on my ass."

He chuckles again, his palm reaching down and gripping said ass cheek, and my face flushes, feeling like a third wheel.

She smacks his chest but lets his hand linger as she turns back to me. "You remember Eli, Lily?"

My brows shoot to my hairline, surprise slamming into my middle, making me lose my breath. "Eli as in Elliot Carson? Lee's brother?" My eyes take him in, recognition flaring to life. Last I heard, he had one foot out the door, ready to make it big in the NBA.

He grins, his dark blond hair bobbing with his head nod. "The one and only. How you doin', Lily? You're much older than the last time I saw you."

A laugh bursts out of me, his demeanor instantly putting me at ease. Honestly, the two of them combined have an energy that reaches out and wraps around me, making me feel comfortable in their presence.

I grin. "Back at ya."

He leans in closer, his arm moving from Becca's waist to her shoulder. "Take deep breaths, everything will be okay."

My brows draw in.

"You look nervous," he continues. "I know, more than anyone else here, what it's like to be terrified of coming back home. But I promise, we don't bite."

I huff out a laugh, embarrassment that my nerves are that obvious rising to my cheeks. "Famous last words."

Eli winks, and I lose my breath just a little, caught off guard by his charm.

Becca's still smiling at me, her eyes wide and friendly. *Am I in an alternate universe?*

"I heard you went and had yourself a baby while you were gone. That true?" She cocks a brow.

I turn around, looking for my baby, finding him in Chase's arms, standing in front of the grill. I point my finger, that same warmth from earlier rising up through my chest and squeezing my heart. "Yep," I say. "The only good thing I've ever done with my life."

Becca's eyes spark. "Well, now, I don't think that's the truth. You look like you've done some good things for yourself too, girlfriend."

The corners of my mouth twitch. "Debatable."

Eli smiles warmly before leaning in to kiss Becca. "I'm gonna go find my sister."

I watch as he walks away and then turn back to Becca, my heart thumping against my ribcage. "You don't hate me?" I ask softly.

Her finger curls into her wild hair as she appraises me, her eyes squinting. Finally, she sighs, shaking her head. "I don't hate *anyone*. Life is too short, and I've learned that hate won't do anything but keep you from learnin' how to love. Everyone makes mistakes." Her eyes grow dark as her eyes flit past me to Eli. "Everyone deserves second chances."

My chest spasms and I nod my head, biting back the emotion surging from her words.

Becca steps farther into me, her hand resting on top of where my fingers are skating along my skin in a nervous

290 BENEATH THE SURFACE

rhythm. "No one here has any right to judge you for your past. We're all just a big ball of *fucked* up, and learnin' how to make the most of what we've got. Was I mad at you for a long time? Yes. But... life has a funny way of makin' you see things from different angles. And your choices are your own, Lily. I'm just happy to have you back, and get to watch you raise that little boy." Her head tilts. "You *are* stayin', right?"

The burn explodes from the back of my eyes, tears slipping down the apples of my cheeks, acceptance bleeding into my skin from where it seeps out of her pores. I nod. "Yeah." I look around, feeling a bit of hope in the desolation that's been my life. "I'm staying."

She backs up, smiling. "Well, good." Her eyes flicker behind me again. "But just so you know, Eli is *mine*."

I purse my lips to hide my grin. "I could tell."

She giggles. "Well, I'm just makin' sure. I worked long and hard to get that man back in my life, and I'm still tryin' every day to prove myself. I don't need a cute little spritely thing like you comin' in here and tryin' to fuck up all my hard work."

Amusement bubbles from deep in my stomach, true laughter floating out of me for the first time in what feels like forever.

More voices filter in through the patio doors, and I look toward the noise. Jax saunters in, followed closely by a pretty brunette.

Becca glances toward them. "You saw Jax already when they went to find you, right? That's Blakely, his girlfriend."

"And she's... a model?" I ask, remembering Annabelle talking about the cover of Vogue.

Becca smirks. "Kinda. She's a social media influencer. Her dad is some bigwig in Cali, and she moved out here to be with Jax and just kinda... never left? Sometimes, paparazzi even comes around, but it's died down a lot in the past six months or so."

I suck in a breath. "*Paparazzi?*"

Becca nods. "Yeah. Can you believe it? In *Sugarlake*. The old biddies down at the market have a day with it all." She chuckles, springing a curl around her finger. "She's good people, though, and she's good as hell for Jax."

"Mommy! Watch!" Baby Chase's voice floats across the back patio, and I look over, his little hand holding a spatula, helping his uncle flip burgers. My heart flips. "Wow, baby, that's *incredible!* Good job!"

He beams and squirms to get down from Chase's arms to run over. He wraps himself around my legs, realizing there's another person here and looks up at her with a shy smile.

Becca's grin widens and she squats down. "Well, aren't you the handsomest little man I've ever seen."

A dimple pops in his cheek as he peeks at her from behind me.

"I'm Becca. What's your name?" She tilts her head, holding out her hand.

He grips my legs tighter. "I'm Chase."

Becca sucks in a sharp gasp, her eyes flickering up to me. *Okay, guess they didn't tell her that yet.*

"Well, that's just confusin' havin' two Chases. What's your middle name?"

I swallow harshly.

"Dewek."

"Hmm. Nope, that won't do either. I'm gonna call you Baby C."

Chase makes a face, his hands letting go of my pant leg. "But I'm not a baby."

"No?" Becca's eyebrow quirks. "You sure? You kinda look it."

He comes out from behind my legs entirely, his little fists resting on his hips. "I do *not*! I'm a big boy, just ask my mommy."

She makes an o shape with her mouth, looking toward me. "Is that true, Lily?"

I nod, holding back a giggle. "It is. He's a very big boy."

Becca sighs. "So, what about just C? I can't be callin' you both Chase, I'll wind up confusin' myself."

Baby Chase contemplates it, his teeth working into his bottom lip before he nods. "Okay."

"We've gotta spit shake," she says. And then Becca straight up spits into the palm of her hand and holds it out to him.

He bursts into giggles, his nose scrunching. "Ewwwwww, I don't wanna touch that!"

She grins wide, her green eyes sparkling. "You're no fun. But I'm still holdin' you to it."

"I am too fun." He smiles and steps closer to her. "Do you know how to pway Spiduh-Man?"

Her eyes flashing to me in victory. "Nope, can you teach me?"

He reaches out to grab her hand but pauses, most likely realizing she just spit in it, and walks around to her other side instead. "Mommy, I'm gonna teach Becca how to pway. Bye!"

Then he's off, taking what's left of my heart with him.

And for the first time, I sit back and let myself imagine what it will be like letting him grow up in Sugarlake, with all of these people treating him like family.

50

MASON

The conference is in two hours, and I'm trying like hell to keep my nerves under control. *Everything* is riding on this moment. On Olivia being who she says she is.

Olivia, who I watched park in the driveway fifteen minutes ago, walk in like she owns the place, and make her way to *distract* my father until it's time to leave.

I walk through the house, making my way to the office, my body on edge from the blood sizzling through my veins. I pause when I pass the formal living room, my mother staring at the family portrait hung in the middle of the gallery wall.

My chest pinches, and even though I know I should walk away, that time is short, and there are *important* things that have to happen, I can't stop my feet from moving in her direction, part of me aching at the thought of upending her world in just a few short hours. She'll never win any mother of the year awards. My nannies were more viable candidates, but she's still *my mother*.

My insides quake, the little boy in me never quite being able to let go of aching for her love and attention. "Are you okay?"

She snaps out of whatever daze she was in, her perfectly

manicured hand coming up to touch the pearls around her neck as we lock gazes. "I'm just fine, honey. Do you remember when this portrait was done?"

I nod slowly, my eyes taking in her posture, not wanting to look at the picture that houses memories from that time of my life. "I do," I say carefully.

The truth is that I remember this day well.

In the portrait, I'm wearing a long sleeve maroon sweater over khaki pants. But that was a secondary choice made by my father's assistant. Originally, I was in a polo, picked out by a team of stylists who were preparing us for this *picture-perfect* moment. When I came downstairs to the living area, the outfit was short lived. My mother walked over, her eyes appraising me before lingering on my arms.

I remember the feel of her stare as it burned into the fresh scabs from the night before. I had tried to sneak into her room, steal concealer to cover them, but there was only so much I could do, and the job was spotty at best. My insides cramped, trying to hide them from her view, not wanting anyone to know what I did late at night in the corner of my bathroom. I was worried that if she found out, they'd somehow figure out how to take *that* away from me, too. My only form of release. The only thing I had control over doing.

Her lips thinned, pressing so tightly against each other that the edges turned white, and then she snapped her fingers, calling over one of my father's many assistants. "He can't wear this shirt. We need long sleeves. Find something."

And then with one last sweeping gaze over me, she turned around and walked away.

The cuts from that night were my deepest yet.

Snapping out of the memory, I look over at my mom, my stomach churning with pain. *Is she really going to bring this up, now?* I'm not sure what I expected to see when she asked the question, maybe some remorse sneaking through her features, an apology poised on the tip of her tongue.

But I don't get either of those things.

I just get a small, wistful smile, and her ever vacant stare. "Those were the days, huh." She sighs.

Her words punch through my chest, my teeth grinding until I feel the tension radiating up my jaw.

"I'm having brunch with the ladies, so I'll meet you at the press conference." She walks over, pressing a chaste kiss to my cheek before walking out of the room.

Pushing down the ache of wanting a narcissist's love, I focus back on what's important.

This is my chance.

Glancing at the time, I see that we have a little less than an hour and a half before we're due at the Capitol's steps in downtown Salem, where my father has decided the grand gesture will be. "*A strong statement from a strong family.*"

I make my way down the long hall, my stomach somer-saulting with nerves. This is a gigantic risk. There are cameras. *Everywhere.* And while the house isn't bustling with people yet, in less than thirty minutes it will be, and if someone has any suspicion whatsoever that something is going on, then this is all fucked. Then *I'm* fucked.

This can't fail. There's no other option.

My heartbeats stampede through my chest, pounding so loud I worry someone will hear as I approach his office door. It's locked, of course, but I've spent years getting into places that should be impenetrable, so it only takes a flick of my wrist and a paper clip for me to hear the click of the door, my stomach jumping at the noise.

I make my way in, eyes scanning the area for where Olivia said the safe would be. Hidden behind a picture frame. But when I look around, my heart drops through my stomach like a rock, because the entire fucking room is lined in photos. *Fucking, great, Olivia.* Again, my mind questions whether this is all a setup.

I've set a timer on my cell, to make sure I'm in and out of

the room in less than five minutes, my brain replaying the code for the safe. Olivia slipped it to me after a media training session yesterday.

35-0-72-16

Sucking on my teeth, my stomach knotted so tight I can hardly breathe, I make my way to the photo closest to me and work my way down the line. Skimming my hands along the portraits, I attempt to lift up the bottom of the frames, my fingers running on the wall behind. *Not it.*

I move to another one, so similar to the one my mother was just staring at in the living room, my hand sliding under the ornate gold rim. It lifts easily, and my heart jumps into my throat as my fingers touch metal. I glance around, my vision searching for the cameras. I can't see them in here, but I know they exist.

My heart bangs in my eardrums, my hands sweating from nerves as I lift the photo, revealing the safe underneath.

Holy shit. She was telling the truth.

I've just reached forward to enter the code, when the sharp crack of wood slats sound from down the hallway. My blood turns to ice, my lungs being punched from fear. I hold my air in, like even the sound of my breathing will alert someone that I'm here.

Did they see me? Is all of this about to go to shit?

I wait for a few moments, but when I don't hear anything else, I turn back toward the safe, my stomach lighting up like fireworks, sparking off my insides and shooting down my legs.

35-0-72-16

A lock unlatches and I blow out a shaky breath, my stomach as tight as a fist. A chill skates over my back, goose bumps sprouting along my arms, and I pause again, my saliva thick as it coats my mouth from the anxiety.

The safe itself is filled to the brim. Gold coins, a few stacks of hundred-dollar bills, files of paperwork. But then, in the back corner, there's a box, and my gut just *knows*. Breathing deep, my gut tenses, and I reach behind everything else, grabbing it and unlocking the latch.

Bile immediately churns at the contents. Because Olivia was right. There are pictures. Lots of them. And they aren't all of her.

My heart squeezes as I sift through the images, my vision blurring with anger from the snippets of depravity that this man who created me caused. On innocent souls. On girls who weren't even old enough to know better. My phone vibrates in my pocket, alerting me that my five minutes are up, but I stay rooted in my spot, unable to move. Lost in the horror of what he is. Of *who* I've been created from.

Noise from the hallway, louder than before, creeps through the walls and my heart jackhammers against my ribs, spurring me into movement. Grabbing all the pictures, I stuff them in my jacket pocket, latching the box and shoving it to the back.

Footsteps grow closer, and my brain whirls, stomach dropping to the floor, hands slippery as they stumble to close the safe and pick up the heavy frame to hang back up on the wall.

Fuck. Fuck. Fuck.

I get it back in place, and my eyes furiously scan the room, dread pumping like caffeine through my veins as I try to find a spot to hide, praying like hell that whoever it is, doesn't try to come in here.

Even if I *do* hide successfully, they'll know that the door shouldn't be unlocked. *Fuck.*

"Hey, where are you going?" Olivia's muffled voice flows through the door, and my heart ceases to fucking beat. It must be my father. *Shit.* I'm frozen in my spot, afraid that if I move, the noise will let him know that I'm here. Their bodies create shadows that filter through the bottom of the door, and I suck in my breath, holding it in my lungs.

My stomach is in knots, tightening further with every second, my forehead collecting beads of sweat like treasure.

"I told you to get presentable, Olivia. We have somewhere to be," he snaps.

"Well, yeah, but..." Her voice trails off, and I hear something thud, the doorknob jostling from the movement.

My stomach twists.

She giggles. "I wasn't done with you yet. Come back to the room." She whispers something else, her voice too low for me to understand.

He groans slightly, and nausea churns in my gut, but it soon turns to relief as I hear footsteps walking away.

Jesus fucking Christ.

I collapse against the edge of his desk, my body shaking from the adrenaline.

Waiting a few more minutes until I'm sure the coast is clear, I blow out unsteady breaths, *dying* for a cigarette to calm the nerves. Walking to the door, I crack it open, looking both ways to make sure the coast is clear, and then walk as fast as possible out of the hallway and back up to my room.

And now, I just pray that no one checks the security footage or notices anything is amiss before we leave.

I look at the clock.

One hour to go.

LILY

Lunch goes surprisingly well, but even without the animosity I expected, even though they're welcoming me back, kid in tow, there's still a gaping hole that's throbbing in the middle of my chest from being all alone. Surviving heartbreak, while being surrounded by loving relationships.

It's hard to not feel like the odd man out.

I can't help the punch to my gut, realizing their lives moved on without me, as if I wasn't here to begin with. Pleasant looks and polite smiles come my way, but I don't get to laugh at the inside jokes. I don't get to feel like one of their puzzle pieces; the way they all seem to effortlessly click together. A well-oiled machine they've had years to perfect.

And then there's me, surrounded by love but never really getting to know it.

Although, if I'm honest with myself, that's not quite true.

I've known love. I've felt it in the depths of my soul. Laid it in the palm of somebody's hand while they held my broken fragments and pretended I was whole.

Even if it was all a lie.

Grief claws at my insides, the memory of the way he felt

—the way *life* felt with him, causing a sharp pain to radiate across my chest, settling low in my gut.

As mad as I am, as disappointed and betrayed as I feel, part of me still had hope he would at least try to explain himself. But maybe he was waiting for the first excuse to leave.

Or maybe he knew there was nothing real worth saving.

I sit at the outdoor table after putting Chase down for a nap, the baby monitor gripped tightly in my hand. Clinking glass draws my attention.

Chase stands behind Lee at the head of the table, a grin on both of their faces. "Everybody listen up," Chase shouts. "You guys already know my long-lost baby sister is finally back home." His eyes narrow. "Where she *fucking* belongs."

My cheeks flush as I grin, raising my water glass in a toast.

His face breaks into a smile and Jax lets out a giant whoop, making Blakely burst out in a fit of laughter. It spreads around the rest of the table, a ball of warmth bouncing around in the middle of my stomach.

"But, that's not the only reason we wanted everyone to get together," Chase continues. "I'd love to say you're all gonna be the first to know, but we already told our parents… and Lily, so… you're *almost* the first to know."

"Saving the best for last!" Jax cuts in again.

"Exactly." Chase's hand grips Lee's shoulder, and I cock my head, thinking about Lee's parents for the first time in years. I wonder how they are. Her mom was always one of my favorite people. Always doling out life lessons like they were pieces of her famous banana bread.

Lee's eyes sparkle. "We're gettin' hitched, y'all!" She takes a ring out of her pocket and slips it on her finger, beaming from ear to ear.

Becca shrieks, jumping up from her chair. "Holy *shit!* The bastard finally asked!"

Everyone bursts out laughing again, even me, and for the

first time all night, I feel like I'm part of something. Like this is *family*.

I didn't expect everyone to be so forgiving. So... grown. So matured. Becca rushes over to grab Lee in a hug, and I don't miss the way Lee's mouth tightens and her skin pales.

Not pregnant, my ass.

Blakely clears her throat. "Well, I know I'm the newest member of the group, but I just want to say how happy I am to be part of this. Anyone who stands next to you guys for even a second can see how absolutely in love you are. How you're meant to be together." She presses a hand to her chest, and Jax smiles at her, his heart pouring through his eyes as he leans in and kisses her right on the mouth.

My eyes tear up at Blakely's words, my gaze swinging over to Chase and Lee, watching them together. At the way whenever she moves, he follows. Like they're two halves of a whole, complementing each other in perfect harmony.

Suddenly, realization smacks me in the face.

I feel like the villain.

I've never wanted to make my brother choose between who he loves and me, and looking back now, I realize that's exactly what I did. My chest cramps and I decide that whatever I need to do, whatever I need to work on, I'll do it. So I can come to a place of understanding. Of acceptance. Because I'm *tired* of being angry.

Becca sits back down next to Eli, and Lee stares up at Chase with a smile, her diamond glinting under the sun. My heart squeezes.

"I don't want anything fancy," she says. "Just all of y'all there. I only wish——" Her voice cuts off, infusing the air with melancholy.

Lee's eyes meet Eli's across the table, and I follow her gaze, watching as he swallows, gripping Becca's hand tight.

"I just wish Mama was still here to see it."

Her words steal the breath from my lungs; my gasp

audible enough to where all eyes turn on me. I cover my mouth with my hands, feeling stupid as fuck that I drew their attention, but I can't help it. Hearing about Lee's mom not being here anymore; someone who was a second mother to me...

I wasn't here.

Because of my choices.

Lee's eyes soften. "Oh, I guess that's right, you wouldn't know."

My fingers scratch at my wrist, trying to ease the pain from the new strike against my heart. "I'm so sorry," I say.

She smiles and shrugs. "It happened a long time ago. And over the years, I've learned that she's never really gone." Her eyes land on Eli's again, her palm pressing down on her chest. "She's right here, livin' on through all of us."

"Now that I believe," Blakely pipes in. "I never had the pleasure of knowing her, but I still feel her in everything you do. From all the stories I've heard, it sounds like she was an amazing woman."

"She was," I say, everyone's gaze turning toward me. "I mean." I clear my throat. "She was amazing. She was... she was everything." The tacky tendrils of sorrow for yet another person lost, for another thing I missed, wraps around my heart, its iron grip bruising. "I wish I had been here to say goodbye."

Lee's lips turn down in the corners, and she stands, walking over to where I am, plopping down in the seat next to me. She covers my hand with hers, the heat of her palm sending warmth up my arm. "She loved you, Lily, and she would be proud of the woman you are now."

I scoff, tears bubbling up through my throat. "You don't even know what kind of woman I am."

"I know enough," she says. "I know you're a good mama. And I may not know what you've gone through, but I know you came out on the other side. *Stronger.* Mama would be proud of you." She pauses, worrying her bottom lip. "We can go visit her grave, if you want to."

My insides toss, not sure if I can. Not sure if I deserve to say goodbye after I left without it in the first place. I shrug, pulling out of her grasp. "Yeah, maybe. I think I'm gonna head inside."

Jax stands up and stretches. "That's a good idea, let's all go inside, watch a movie or something."

My head pounds from the events of the day, but I don't want to wake up baby Chase so I stay in the living room with everyone else. Lee clicks on the TV and raises the remote to change the channel, but Jax interrupts her.

"Hey, wait a second, Lee."

He leans forward, his eyes narrowing on the news station that's playing. "I swear I've heard about this before."

We all turn our attention to the screen, watching the news-casters talk about the presidential campaign.

"Hey, Chase, what was that PI's name again?" Jax rubs his jaw.

My heart stalls in my chest, them talking about *Mason* so openly ripping open my middle, my bleeding heart exposed. My muscles pull tight, the craving for something to numb the pain so overpowering it causes a physical ache to spread through my body.

"Mason, why?" Chase responds.

Jax's eyes flicker to me as he shakes his head. "I don't know. I thought he looked familiar when we saw him in Arizona, and now." He pauses, pointing at the TV, where they're talking about the Republican frontrunner. A man named Senator Thomas Wells, from Oregon.

"Senator Wells is set for a press conference this afternoon at three p.m. This comes after weeks of speculation over his disappearance. Experts say they think we may have another instance of withdrawal from the candidacy. Ten years ago, Senator Wells dropped out after the devas-tating disappearance of his then nineteen-year-old son, Alexander Wells."

A picture pops up on the screen, and Jax smacks his knee, his finger pointing again at the screen. "I *knew* he looked familiar."

My heart crashes into my sternum, ricocheting off the walls and landing at my feet, nothing more than chewed up dust.

Because even though the young man in the picture is polished and proper, I would know him anywhere.

That's...

"His name was Alex," I say.

And then I stand up, my vision blurring, as I race out of the room.

52

MASON

There's a nervous energy swirling through the car. We're in a limo, of course, Thomas Wells wouldn't be caught dead in anything less than prestige. My father sits next to Olivia, Frank next to me. My mother is meeting us there, coming straight from her brunch.

My leg bounces as we pull onto the side street of the Capitol, the photos I've tucked away in this *ridiculous* suit burning a hole through my pocket. Olivia chews on her bottom lip, her eyes nervous and wild as they flicker between me and the windows.

I sympathize with her position. It takes a lot of guts to do what she's about to, but at the end of the day, she still used me as a tool. She still never really loved me. She still *lied*.

Just like I lied to Lily.

Although not quite as extreme, it does put things in perspective. Both were a breach of trust where your entire foundation of belief is rocked to the core. When all of this is over, when my mind quiets from revenge and allows me to reflect instead, I know I'll feel the regret for not telling her the truth as soon as I knew I loved her.

My gaze snags on Olivia's, anticipation weaving through my system, knowing that we're *so fucking close.*

My father smiles, laughing at something Frank says before looking over at me. "You ready for this, son? Need to go over what to say again?"

My lips twitch as I look him dead in the eye, knowing that I've never been more ready for anything in my life than I am for this moment.

For *ten* years I've been running from this man. And it ends today. "I know what to say."

"Let's hear it." His teeth gleam. "Just to be sure."

I lift my brows. "There's a lot of story behind the past decade, and not enough time to tell you all the details of what went on. I was young and scared, and in the process of me running away, I hurt the people who loved me most, and I regret my decisions that brought us here today."

"Perfect." Frank's meaty hand grips my shoulder tight, and I bite on the inside of my cheek to keep from ripping his arm off of me and breaking all of his fingers.

The car jolts to a stop, and we exit, making our way through the controlled crowd of people, cameras blinding with their flashes as we walk to the steps of the Capitol where the podium sits.

As I sit down next to my mother, my eyes scan the crowd, imagining what their reaction will be when everything comes out into the open. Frank goes up to the podium first, thanking people for coming and answering a few questions.

And then it's my father's turn.

Olivia's knee shakes next to me, the motion making my stomach tense and jump faster than it already was. I pull a toothpick out of my pocket, my fingers brushing the edges of the photographs, and pop it in my mouth, wishing it was the sweet release of nicotine instead.

"Thank you all for coming. I've been a man of family and faith my entire life," my father speaks.

I hold back the snort.

"And I know many of you, as is your right, have been wondering why I've gone off the grid for the past two weeks." He pauses dramatically, with practiced precision that would make the Oscars proud, pulling a handkerchief and dabbing it underneath his eyes. *Fucking prick.*

"Well, folks, a blessing has fallen on our family. Many of you know that ten years ago, my son Alexander went tragically missing after the night of his engagement party to the lovely young woman you see right there." My father turns and waves at Olivia.

My jaw clenches as she smiles, waving back. Murmurs start rumbling in the crowd.

"It is my absolute joy to tell you that after years of desperation, of never giving up the faith—the faith that is not only the foundation of our family, but our country—our boy is home. Alexander, come on up here, son."

He turns toward me as the murmurs grow rampant, cameras being raised along with hands flying in the air, hoping to be called on for a question. The entire spectacle makes me sick to my stomach, but I push down the nausea and I move forward, knowing that these next few steps are my steps to freedom.

We did it. This is going to happen. And after it's done, I'm going back to Tennessee, finding Lily, and begging for a chance to explain. I'm going to actually live for the first time in my life, and I can't fucking wait.

My father leans into the microphone. "We'll take just a few questions now."

He points to the woman in front, who I already know is Sandy from WSNC Oregon; the first person on our approved list of people. She was given the appropriate questions to ask before this event started. See, what most people don't realize is that the majority of these conferences are nothing more than shows. A play put on for the masses. Unfortunately, for everyone else up on this stage, I'm not planning on following the script.

My stomach flips, nerves racing through me until my hands physically shake, hoping that Olivia doesn't back out now. She was truthful up until this point, so all I can do is hope that she'll stand strong with me up here and say what she needs to say.

"Hi, thank you, Senator. Sandy from WSNC. Wow. Alexander, HI."

I chuckle, grinning. "Hi, Sandy."

"I guess we'll start with... where have you been?"

I lean in, running a hand through my hair. "There's a lot of story behind the past decade and not enough time to tell you all the details of what went on. I was young and scared, and while I made decisions in my life that I regret, other people's decisions are what I'd like to talk about today."

My father tenses as he stands next to me, his nostrils flaring.

"And I'm planning to answer all of your questions. I am," I continue. "But first, I'd like to invite Olivia Sanderson to join me up here."

My father's spine goes rigid, his head snapping toward me.

I cover the microphone with my hand and let loose the first *genuine* smile since being in his presence. "Careful, Father, your mask is slipping."

Olivia comes to stand next to me, her hair falling on the side of her face, curtaining her eyes from my father's view. Her fingers tremble as she grips onto the podium. The press box is so quiet you could hear a pin drop, the tension spiking higher with every second.

Olivia clears her throat. "When I was fifteen years old, Thomas Wells brought me into his home, took me up—"

My father springs forward, ripping the microphone from

in front of her face. I push her so she isn't hit by his elbow, my arm forcefully shoving him back.

Gasps sound from the audience, and I hold back a grin, because if anything, he's making the situation worse. The innocence card is much harder to play when you try to steal the microphone to silence the girl.

From the corner of my eye, I see his security moving forward, but he seems to collect himself, running his hand down the front of his suit and slicking his hair back before he turns and shakes his head, waving them off.

"Are you kidding me?" he spits. "What the hell do you think this is?"

I smile wide. "This, Father, is justice."

Olivia's eyes are wide as they stare at us, and I nod my head, encouraging her to continue. "Olivia, go ahead. I won't let him touch you."

She nods, her teeth chewing her bottom lip. "Thomas Wells invited me into his home under the guise of wanting to match-make me with his son," she starts again. "It wasn't much later that he brought me into his room, supplied me with alcohol and pills, and stole *everything* from me." She turns her eyes to him. "Thomas Wells *raped* me when I was fifteen years old and took pictures of the tearing. He..." Her voice chokes, tears streaking down her cheeks. She lifts her chin higher. "He made me pretend to be in love with his son so he could use me as his *toy*. He convinced me that what we had was love, and when he got me pregnant, he held me down, and he had a two-bit doctor *cut her out.*"

My chest burns from her words, sorrow swirling in my gut.

Olivia stands strong, her shoulders back and her head held high.

My father is stoic, his eyes blazing fire, but a mask still on his face. Ever the perfect fucking politician.

The press explodes, the sound of yelled questions and

clicking of cameras so violent it makes my insides jump. Olivia ignores it all, turning to face her abuser, black tears marring her face. "I hope you rot in prison, and they show you all the mercy you showed me."

And then she walks off stage and disappears into one of the cars.

I clear my throat, trying not to let the emotion show on my face as I make my way back to the mic. "There is evidence in my possession that I will be turning over to the appropriate authorities. Thank you for your time."

Before I step off the stage, my eyes flash to my father one last time. His mouth is gaping, eyes wide and frantic. He has to know there's no coming back from this.

Victory swims through my veins, and justice has never felt so fucking sweet.

"Let your plans be dark and impenetrable as night, and when you move, fall like a thunderbolt."

53

LILY

I've lived constantly on edge.
   On the edge of my sanity.
On the edge of my life.

My trigger has always been emotion. Or rather, the lack of being able to control it. The guilt. The shame. The fear. The reason I dove into drugs in the first place was because of the numb they provided.

And being *numb* was the only thing I cared for. After we were removed from the last foster home before Sam and Anna, I was angry. I didn't understand why we had to leave again. I did everything my foster father told me to do. I never spoke a word. It was *him* that got sloppy, it was *him* who got caught sneaking into my room by my brother.

I don't know what happened after, but I know it took months to convince Chase that nothing ever happened. I didn't want my foster father to get in trouble. But as I got older, I started to realize that what he did wasn't normal. It wasn't okay.

I can't even think his name without falling into the darkness he created.

My biological mother did a lot of unforgivable things, but

it was *him* who fucked me up for life. He conditioned me into believing that the pain was pleasure, and that his dirty body splitting mine apart was love. I was nine and too young to know better. Eventually, I grew attached to the way he could make me feel. I craved his approval.

He turned me into something shameful.

Something twisted.

Something *sick.*

I remember driving away from their home, in the back seat of my social worker's car, and being absolutely terrified.

He had always warned me that if we were taken, Chase and I would be separated. And it was always supposed to be Chase and me against the world.

We weren't, of course. We were put with Sam and Anna.

And when we moved in with them, I stayed up late at night, waiting for a new stranger to sneak into my room.

But the stranger never came.

And oddly, I felt a sense of loss. Like *I* had done something wrong.

As I grew older, I began to understand what truly happened to me. The rage bubbled like witch's brew until it overflowed from the cauldron, burning through my insides like acid, allowing the shame to plant roots in the holes it left behind.

Because what was wrong with me if I enjoyed it?

What was wrong with me for not knowing and not speaking up?

What's wrong with me for still not speaking?

I tried to mask it at first with laughter and light, but eventually the mask became too heavy to wear. I so desperately wanted to be normal. To be accepted. To be loved. I didn't want people to look at me and say the same things they always said about my "troubled" brother. But the truth was that I was miserable, standing in a roomful of people, my own hand muffling my screams.

It wasn't until I met Darryl at the airport, coming back from our first "family" vacation that everything changed. Looking back, I realize now that Darryl was just another predator, preying on weak and vulnerable children, looking to get his kicks.

He was twenty. I was fourteen. He was *exciting*. So when he pulled me aside as I came out of the airport restroom and had us exchange numbers, I was giddy for the adventure.

I had never given Sam or Anna any reason not to trust me, so when I told them I was going out with Becca and Lee, they didn't second-guess it. Besides, most of their energy went into making sure Chase was acclimating appropriately. *He* was the problem child, not me. And that's what made it so easy.

Darryl fucked me the first time we hung out. I hadn't wanted it, but I didn't know that what *I* wanted mattered. So, I let him use my body the way it was used before, and I convinced myself I liked how it felt. And when he cut my first line of coke, teaching me how to snort, it made the pretending fade away, a glorious bliss taking its place.

He was my foster father two point oh. He told me I was special. Told me I could trust him. That he'd never steer me wrong. He was popular because he was everyone's drug dealer. He was dangerous, which made me feel safe. He was a wolf in sheep's clothing, and by the time I figured that out, it was too late. I was too gone, too dependent. My self-worth had been whittled down to a nub, shattering at the slightest touch.

But where he'd tear me down one day, he'd build me up the next, and so started the toxic cycle.

The thing about active addiction is that you're a slave to the drugs that flow through your veins. You become someone else entirely. You'll hurt, lie, cheat, steal. *Anything* to get that next fix. It becomes the only thing that matters.

One night, when I was seventeen, Darryl decided to share me with his friends. I did what had become normal for me, letting my mind drift away and float above my body, watching as if it was a movie on the screen so I wouldn't have to feel the pain. But when it was over, the shame wrapped around my insides and squeezed, creating an agony so deep I thought I'd never be free. Alone, on a dirty mattress in an otherwise empty room, I freebased to the point of overdose. And nobody there cared enough to save me.

The *only* reason I survived was because it was Anna's birthday, and I wasn't where I was supposed to be. Chase hunted me down and found me half dead on the bedroom floor.

Some days, when I'm living in my regret, I wonder what that must have been like for him; finding me in the same position he so often found our mother. I don't even remember it happening. I don't know whether he screamed, or cried, or even stayed by my side in the hospital.

I just remember waking up.

And I remember running.

"ARE YOU READY FOR THIS?" Chase asks, turning toward me as we sit in Sam and Anna's driveway.

I take the moment to glance around, nerves pricking under my skin, making my movements jerky and painful. Baby Chase sits in the back seat, and I swallow down my nerves, knowing that if anything, I have to do this for him. So he can know his grandparents. So they can love him the way he deserves to be loved.

My heart clenches, and I blow out a breath, nodding.

Stepping out of the car, the memories spin around me like a sandstorm. The front yard looks the exact same as it did when we first moved here. My eyes glance three doors down to the single-story house with blue shutters. *I wonder if Lee's dad still lives there.*

My mind takes me back without preamble to our first day

here, when my brain was filled with possibilities. Sometimes, I wish I could reach out and grab the hope I used to have tattooed on my skin. Wrap it around myself again, and wear it like a cloak.

I've never hula-hooped before. But Anna gave it to me as a gift, a "housewarming" present, and so here I am, standing in our new front yard, doing my best to swing my hips and let the plastic swirl around my body. I'm so invested in making sure it doesn't drop that I don't see the girl coming our way until she's at the edge of the yard.

I stop in my tracks, the hula-hoop falling to the grassy ground, excitement at seeing another kid making a smile beam across my face. I'm so antsy from being here, from feeling a sense of normalcy for the first time that I can't stop myself from running over to greet her.

Her eyes widen as I approach.

"Hi! I'm Lily! Do you live on this street? I'm so excited that you came over. I've been so worried about not making any friends, but then here you are, and oh! Your eyes are so pretty, they must be the bluest things I've ever seen."

My heart pounds in my chest and I gulp in a breath of air, realizing that I probably just scared her away with my rambling. But it doesn't stop me from leaning in close to stare at her big, blue eyes. I can't help it. She's like a magnet. She just has this light about her, and I can't help but try and take a closer look, wanting to know how to emulate it within myself.

"How do you talk like that?" she asks, stuffing her hands in her back pocket. "You know... just goin' and goin' for so long without havin' to breathe?"

Her accent is thick, and a pang of jealousy weaves through my chest at the innocence that glows around her like an aura. It seems effortless for her, and I have to try so hard.

I force a laugh out. "You'll get used to me. My mom used to tell me I had enough energy to light up all of Chicago."

It's not true. I don't even remember much of my mom, but sometimes, telling stories like she cared—like she loved me—dulls the absence of her memory.

"I think I believe her." She grins wide, her eyes sparkling. "Well, I'm

Alina May Carson, but my friends call me Lee. I live three houses down that way." She points down the street, and when her eyes come back, they float behind me to where Chase is brooding on the front steps, watching us in silence.

I should have known at that moment she wasn't really there for me. Her eyes only spared me a second glance, but they were glued to Chase forever. And his were stuck on hers.

My heart spasms in my chest, my stomach turning from the memory.

I turn, opening the back door of the car and reaching in to unbuckle baby Chase from his car seat. "Okay, baby, you ready to go meet some new friends?"

He beams and nods, his arms reaching out as I lift him from the car and prop him on my hip. I grin down at him, his right hand coming up to rest on my cheek. "It's gonna be okay, Mommy."

Tears burn behind my eyes, guilt for showing my emotions raging in my gut. But I'm not surprised he picked up on my struggle. Children can feel things that adults choose to ignore.

I smile. "I know, baby. Thank you."

He reaches his small arms around me, his Spider-Man stuffy dangling from his fist, and he hugs me tight. "I'll wove you fowever, I'll wike you for always."

My nostrils flare, and I take the moment, gripping my baby boy tight, and breathing him in. No matter what happens, no matter how many mistakes I've made, this right here in my arms is the greatest thing I've ever done.

"As long as I'm living, my baby you'll be," I whisper into his hair.

And then I open my eyes and walk to the front door, ready to tackle my past head-on.

For him. And maybe a little bit for me.

5 4

LILY

M y baby boy clings tightly to my hand as we make our way into Sam and Anna's house.

I may not ever be able to heal my internal traumas; may spend the rest of my days waking up in cold sweats from the nightmares. But if I can't heal mine then the best I can hope for is to heal the ones I've caused in others.

Besides, dealing with other people's pain is a distraction from the betrayal of the man who I thought was the one.

Alexander Wells.

Part of me wants to believe, so badly, that he was planning to tell me everything. After all, he gave me his real name. Told me his father was a politician. He shared intimate moments that I refuse to believe were lies. I *have* to believe that at least some of what he said was honest.

Chase unlocks the front door, and my stomach jumbles like a shuffled deck, nerves wracking through every cell. The walls bleed with a familiarity that assaults my senses, and my muscles tense, preparing to see the closest people I've ever had as parents for the first time since I ran away.

We make our way into the living room, and my feet stop short when I see them sitting on the couch, their heads huddled together as they speak in hushed voices. Anna reacts first, her face snapping to Chase, her eyes lighting up as she sees him. And then her head swivels to me, her strawberry-blonde hair swishing behind her as her hand covers her mouth.

"Lily," she breathes.

Her voice is infused with a warmth I don't deserve, and it stabs at my heart like a hooked knife. We walk farther into the room, my baby boy silent as a lamb, gripping my hand tighter than before.

"Hi, Anna. Sam."

I *want* to call them mom and dad, the way I used to, but I don't feel like I deserve it. I'm unsure if they'll even want me to use the titles, after treating them as nothing more than two strangers who were only in my way.

Anna bursts into tears—loud, heaving sobs racking her body as she collapses against Sam. He rubs her back, his eyes on me, wide and glossy.

Baby Chase fidgets, stepping closer.

I pull him along as we take a seat on the couch facing opposite them. And then we wait. I don't know what to do or say, so I follow Chase's lead who is just sitting in silence, letting them cry.

After a few moments, Anna straightens, her shaky hands wiping under her eyes, focusing her attention on me. "I'm sorry for the outburst, it's just..." Her palm covers her heart. "I never thought I'd see you again, and now that you're here…" Her forehead wrinkles. "And you look so good, and your baby boy." Her voice cuts off as she shakes her head. "It's just a bit overwhelmin' is all."

Sam clears his throat. "We've been dreaming of this day for a long time."

I swallow around the lump in my throat, my stomach twisting like a pretzel. "Sorry it took so long," I whisper.

"We're just glad you're here now." Sam's eyes move to my son. "And who's this?"

I smile, peering down at my baby boy. "This is Chase."

Anna sucks in a breath. "That's a beautiful name for a beautiful boy," she says, her voice wavering.

"Chase, this is Sam and Anna. Your grandpa and grandma."

His eyes grow big and round as he looks at them. "*Mine?* Like... to keep?"

My throat clogs, my heart cracking from the simple statement. Sometimes, as an adult, it's easy to forget how a child views the world. And I've never once thought about the fact that he may see grandparents in his cartoons and wonder why he doesn't get to have them.

I nod, chewing on the inside of my lip and squeezing his hand. "You bet, baby. They're all yours." I bop his nose.

He slides off the cushion and walks to the middle of the room, gripping his Spider-Man stuffy to his chest. Anna and Sam's faces mirror each other, eyes wide and teary, anticipation lining all their angles.

"Hi," Chase says.

Anna's hands come up to her cheeks, and Sam's grin is so wide it spreads from ear to ear. "Hi back."

My baby nods his head, walks over to them, climbs up on the couch, and plops himself right between them.

Always so brave.

Anna's eyes spark to life, the happiness shining through her blue gaze, soaking us in her joy.

Chase, who's been sitting in the corner of the room silently up until now, chuckles. "You can't say he doesn't have an outgoing personality." He looks toward me, smirking. "Wonder where he gets it from?"

Anna laughs, her hand smoothing down my baby's head, and the sight of them together makes my heart somersault in my chest, aching for all of their missed moments, hoping they'll get to make up for lost time.

✦

Two hours later and baby Chase is officially comfortable. He's gone through the entire history of Spider-Man, and then Anna brought out the family photo albums. They're flipping through them as she tells him stories. My eyes snag on one photo in particular of Lee, Becca, and me lying in the grass with cherry popsicles, all three of us grinning ear to ear.

My stomach cramps, grief at the loss of our friendship winding through my muscles. *What I wouldn't give to go back to simpler times.*

Chase walks over, grabbing my baby boy at the waist and swinging him up on his shoulders. "Okay, I'm taking this little beast outside to play. Gotta show him the lay of the land, teach him all the good hiding spots." He grins and winks, walking down the hallway and out the back door.

I know he's doing it to give us the time alone, and while it needs to happen, it doesn't make the reality any easier. With both Chases gone, there's no buffer, and immediately the air in the room grows thick with tension.

Finally, I break the silence. "Thank you," I say, my fingers twisting around my opposite wrist. "For being so kind to him."

Anna tilts her head, her lips turning down in the corner. "He's your baby. And you're *ours.* You don't need to thank us for lovin' on our family."

That one sentence is enough to break down my wall of emotion, and tears blur my vision, my hands coming up to cup my face. "I'm so—so sorry," I stutter through the hiccups.

Sam and Anna move in tandem until they're flanking me, their arms embracing me like a cocoon. I can feel their breath on the back of my neck as tears seep through my fingers. Anna sniffles next to me, and I relax into their hold, allowing us to have the purge of emotion, for all the things none of us know how to say.

And it's in this moment I know, that even through all the bad choices I've made, all the trials and tribulations I've been through; that God shone a light when he chose them as my parents. I'm lucky to have them, and I promise myself to never take advantage of that knowledge again.

It's a while later that we finally wipe our faces dry, the weight on my shoulders feeling less burdensome than it has in years.

Anna sighs, sitting back, and running a hand through her strawberry locks. "I have so many things I wanna know, Lily, I won't lie and say I don't. And you hurt us when you left. You..." She purses her lips. "For years, I've felt like we failed you as parents. That maybe we selfishly made the choice to adopt you, because we wanted you so badly. Because we loved you so much. I've struggled with the idea that we weren't what you needed. And I'm so sorry if we ever made you feel like you couldn't come to us."

My chest tightens, and I reach out, gripping her hand in mine.

"But I want," she continues. "I *need* you to know we aren't mad at you, honey. We're so, so proud of who you've become, and we're so happy to have you back."

Her love and acceptance wraps around me. "It's hard for me." I pause, glancing down at my lap, trying to find the right words to say. "It's hard for me to talk about things, but I want to. I do. And I'm sorry I made you feel like you weren't good parents. You've *always* been the only parents I've ever dreamed of having. My demons are from before our time together."

Anna squeezes her eyes shut, her jaw clenching. Sam's hand stops on my back. "And I can't talk about it out loud. Not yet. But I want to try."

"Okay," Anna nods. "Okay."

"I'm..." My voice catches on the knot in my throat, and I

swallow, trying again. "I'm gonna go to therapy with Chase. And I thought… I thought maybe you two would like to come sometime?"

Anna smiles as wetness lines her lower lid, and Sam's hand comes up to smooth down my hair. "Of course we will," he says.

They don't ask any more questions, even though I'm sure they're dying to know.

They don't badger me with guilt, or with blame.

They just surround me with their love, and for the first time since I was that little girl hula-hooping in the front yard, I feel a little bit of hope clinging to me like a second skin. And I like the way it feels.

55
LILY

I've finally worked up the courage to visit Derek. I had to borrow Lee's car, and I told her I was job hunting, not ready to reveal his existence to anyone yet, some part of me still wanting to hold things close to my chest.

Since Chase and Lee don't have a landline, and I didn't want to call from their cell phones, I've decided to just surprise him, and hope that he's there when I arrive.

But I *need* to see him, not only because I miss him, but also because what Mason did for all those women, the way he brought down his father to bring them justice, has my body craving drugs in a way that it hasn't in years. It was triggering, in a way I didn't expect it to be. But it also lessened my anger toward him, knowing that while he lied to me—while he broke my heart, my trust in him being a good man was on point.

Bad men don't bring down pedophiles.

Bad men don't lift up survivors and help them find their peace.

The thought of driving into the heart of Sweetwater has my nerves severely on edge, jitters racing through my veins like horses, but I know that if I don't face my fear, it will eventually overwhelm me. I can't avoid it forever.

Sam and Anna are babysitting Chase, so now is the perfect time.

I'm pulling off the highway and onto the exit ramp when the gas light comes on, so I make a pit stop, my stomach souring when I realize I only have three dollars to put in the tank. *Shit.* Hopefully it will be enough to get to his place and back home.

My cheeks flush even though there's no one around to witness the embarrassment, and worry nags at my gut, wondering what I'm going to do for cash. I feel like a freeloader as it is, and I refuse to stay and mooch off of Chase and Lee for much longer. Especially since Lee and I haven't had an honest conversation since the first day I arrived.

Sighing, I unbuckle my seat belt and open the door, glancing up at the pump number before I walk inside. As I reach the door, a tingle shoots up my back, something screaming at me to turn around and go. My steps falter, hair swishing against my face as I look around, but I don't see anything out of the ordinary. Just two other cars, and the butt of a cigarette, still smoking on the sidewalk.

Brushing off the eerie vibes, I make my way inside to pay. There's no one at the counter, and after a few minutes of waiting, I search for a bell or something to ring.

Does anybody even fucking work here?

Finally, a woman walks to the front, adjusting her red and yellow shirt and smiling at me. "Sorry about that, you walked in right at the shift change."

I grin, the icy chill still lingering at my back.

Paying for the gas, I walk back to Lee's car, the sound of the beep as I unlock the doors loud in the air. The hairs on the back of my neck stand up, and I flip around again, scanning the area.

Nothing.

Get it together, Lily.

While the gas pumps, my fingers scratch at my wrist, anxiety eating through my muscles until there's nothing left but bone. My heart jumps when someone slams their car door.

I don't like being here.

It was stupid of me to come.

Getting back in the driver's seat, I glance in the rearview mirror, reaching over and locking the doors when I get that shiver skating up my spine again. *What the hell?*

I shake it off, *again*, and continue my way to Derek's. I'm excited to see him, knowing that it will help ground me. He's never been one to mince words, and he has plenty of experience in talking me off the ledge.

Pulling into Derek's driveway, I frown, my heart sinking at the fact that his car isn't here, but I decide to try the keypad, see if it's still the same as before. I can wait for him inside, I doubt he'll mind.

Excitement winds around my chest at the thought of surprising him.

Walking to the front door, I grip Lee's keys tight, the pink pepper spray holder jostling against the side of my hand.

I try the combination. *Beep.*

Smiling as the door opens wide, I waltz inside, immediately sighing a breath of relief. This place felt like home when I had no place to call my own.

I walk down the hallway and through the living room, my fingers dusting over the fireplace that houses pictures of Derek and his family through the years. My steps falter, my forehead wrinkling as I come across a framed photo of me, my pregnant belly the size of a watermelon, my head thrown back in laughter. My stomach clenches as I pick up the frame, my finger tracing over my face. I was so broken back then, and somehow, this picture I've never seen catches the very moment that I found my purpose. *Being a good mother.*

The craving for the high fades away, replaced with rein-forced steel, this photo reminding me that I will *never* do to my baby boy what my biological mother did to me. I'm touched the photo is here, and I make a mental note to ask him to send me a copy. I'll carry it around for whenever I'm feeling weak.

The front door creaks open, and I smile, excited that he got home so fast. I move to place the photo back on the ledge, but freeze when I hear a voice behind me.

"Look who it is."

That same chill from earlier skates up my spine again, wrapping around my middle, and robbing the breath from my lungs. I stay locked in place, terrified of moving. Petrified that he'll walk over and take the photo from my hands, see that Chase exists and try to take him from me. Try to *hurt* him. My stomach rises and falls like a rollercoaster.

I close my eyes, trying to center myself even though every-thing in me is telling me to run as fast as I can. But I know that won't work. Now that he's seen me, I doubt he'll let me go.

"Darryl," I say in a shaky voice.

I set the photo face down, hoping to fucking *God* that he doesn't take notice, and spin around slowly, my heart beating in my throat.

His hair is greasy and standing in different directions, the icy blond tips he used to wear replaced by the dirt brown of his natural color. His face is marred with pockmarks, much worse than when I knew him, and even though he's the reason behind a majority of my nightmares, I feel a pang of regret, sad that he's never crawled out of the hole of his drug abuse. Gold metal chains dangle from around his neck, and a red and yellow shirt hangs loosely off his frame. The same shirt the lady at the gas station was wearing.

A shift change.

He smiles, the sight sending shivers down my arms and a rolling feeling through my gut.

"Hi, sugar. Long time." His thumb comes up to rub at his bottom lip, his eyes glazed and unfocused even as he peers at me. It's *very* clear that he's high.

"You look good," he continues, his gaze raking up and down my form, making me feel stripped down and naked under his gaze. My stomach churns.

He moves closer, his hands tapping against his thigh in a nervous rhythm. "Where ya been, Lily baby? We've sure missed you around here."

My mind races, not knowing what to say. Not knowing what will keep him calm and what will set him off. I force a smile on my face, resisting the urge to vomit. "I had to leave, Dar. I didn't want to." My eyes track his shaky hand as he pulls a Glock from his back pocket.

My heart stutters, stomach squeezing tight. "But I *had* to. I was messed up, you know? Had to get my mind right."

"Hmm." His eyes bounce between mine, and he rubs his temple with the tip of his gun. "Did it work?"

My smile is so wide, my cheek muscles pull. "Yep. I don't have a phone, or I would have tried to find you sooner."

My eyes fall past him to the open front door, and suddenly panic seizes my lungs, hoping like hell that Derek doesn't come home. I don't want him in danger because of me.

I slowly start to move toward him, hoping that his high will keep him from realizing what I'm doing. Maybe if I just do it slowly, one step at a time, I can make it. I glance to the entry table where I stupidly left the keys to Lee's car. With the pepper spray.

"How did you get in, Darryl?"

He grins. "You left the door wide open for me, baby." He grabs his junk and thrusts into his hand. "You that desperate to see me again?"

Bile teases the back of my throat as I take another step closer. I'm right in front of him now, my eyes darting from his face to his gun and back. My heart pulses in my neck, my breathing sharp and heavy.

I move to take another step while his eyes are bouncing around the room, but his head snaps toward me and he rushes over, his hand gripping my hair until it feels like I'm being scalped, the barrel of his gun slamming down on the side of my head.

My stomach rolls, dots blurring my vision. Wetness drips down the side of my face, red blots falling on the wood floor off my chin.

"You stupid *bitch*, you don't think I see you trying to get away from me? Come over here and have a seat. Let's catch up." He shoves me forward by the head, the cut on my temple throbbing, and my stomach rolling like waves in the sea. He throws me down onto the couch cushions and sits next to me, his foot crossing over his opposite knee.

Mason's voice filters through my mind, whispered words he spoke into my skin flowing through me like a prayer.

Appear weak when you are strong, and strong when you are weak.

I shove my trembling hands under my thighs, hiding the shakes from his view.

He shifts, pulling something from his pocket, and I squint my eyes, realizing it's a snuff bottle filled with cocaine. They're small containers with holes in the top, easy access for when you're on the go. He puts the bottle up to his nose, his other hand, gun and all, plugging the other nostril as he inhales deeply, snorting up his high.

The muscles in my body stiffen, having drugs so close to me for the first time in years. As strong as my mind has become, I don't think the physical cravings will ever leave. My eyes flick to the picture frame that's placed facedown on the fireplace lounge, reminding myself what's at stake.

I need to play along. I need to do whatever I need to do in order to make it out of here and get back to my son.

"You don't mind, do you?" He smirks as he sniffs from the

snuff container again and then holds it toward me in offering. "You want?"

My jaw clenches, swallowing the saliva that's pooling in my mouth. My fingernails rip into the couch cushion underneath my legs, holding on for dear life as I try to maintain control over my revolting body. My nerve endings light up, begging for the thing I trained it to need for years.

"Nah." He cackles, smacking his knee. "I forgot. You got your 'mind right.'"

My head grows dizzy, and I breathe deep through my nose, hoping to stem the nausea.

He sighs, scratching his head with the butt of his gun, and setting the container down on the ground next to him. He leans in, his putrid breath sticking to my skin, making the insides of my stomach curl. "You think you're too good for me now? Is that it?"

My middle clamps down so hard that bile races up my esophagus. "No, I—"

Before I can finish the sentence, his gun whips out, cracking me across the face, blood flooding my mouth as I fly off the couch and onto the floor. I swallow the copper taste, my nails digging into the wood, the sharp ache in my jaw sparking a fire that rages through my chest.

I stay hunched on the ground, climbing to my knees and spitting the extra blood from my mouth. "Darryl—"

He looms over me, his thick boot pressing in the middle of my back until my body collapses on the floor, the pressure of the ground causing a throb to spread through my chest. My heart is staggered in its beating, my mind whirling, praying like hell I'll make it out of this.

That somehow, this won't be the end for me.

He reaches down, his fingernails jagged as they slice into the skin of my arm, flipping me over until I'm flat on my back, blood pooling in the back of my throat from the position. He snarls and spits, his thick saliva dropping on my cheek and slowly dribbling down off my chin. I dry heave, turning my head to the side.

"You caused me a lot of fuckin' problems when you left. And for *years* I had your family comin' here, sniffin' around and askin' me questions like they had any right to you. Like I didn't strip you of everything you were and replace it with my brand." His face is so close to mine, his lips skim against my cheek with each word. "Your shithead brother came to my work and *threatened* me. Made me tell him where you were. Fucking runnin' away to Arizona like some ungrateful bitch."

My eyes widen, shock pouring through me at the fact that he knows where I was. That he *knows where the fuck I was.*

"You knew?" I manage to rasp out.

He smirks. "Amy."

My heart stalls in my chest. *No.* Amy *helped* me. How could I have been so damn stupid? I never should have trusted her. *Did she tell him I was pregnant too?*

The thought sends terror pumping through my veins.

He laughs. "Don't worry, you weren't worth the trip. But then I see you walk into my gas station, lookin' the way you do. And well..." He smiles, his teeth chipped and stained. "Old habits die hard, I guess."

His hand comes down and grasps my jaw, making it crack under the pressure. "You made me look like a fool, leavin' me after everything I did for you. Didn't I do enough for you, baby?" He straddles my hips, his knees on either side of my body. He leans in and licks up the side of my face, his fingers tightening on my jaw. I hold my breath to keep from throwing up.

"Didn't I give you the world?"

I try to nod, but my head is held firm by his grip.

He stands up, pulling my face with him until the top half of my back is suspended from the floor. "Don't you fuckin' lie to me."

He slams me back down, my head bouncing off the

ground, my vision blurring. My stomach somersaults and twists, rising into my throat from the blinding pain.

"You think you're so much goddamn *better* than me?" His boot flies into my ribs, the force behind his kick knocking the wind from my lungs, a stabbing ache radiating up my side.

With all the force I can muster, I jump up, shoving him off me, a burst of adrenaline fueling my movements.

Clunky and unfocused, I run, my head spinning from the sudden shift in posture. *If I could just get to the pepper spray.*

But I never make it. A loud crack sounds through the air and I fall back to the ground. The air is silent as I wait for the pain, shock flowing through me as I cup my shoulder, wet liquid seeping through my fingers. I gasp in air, a burn starting in my upper arm and spreading slowly outward, until all I feel is fire ravaging my insides.

I try to hang on. Try to live through the knowledge that I've just been shot. That my stupid mistakes have led me here. But I can feel the blackness crawling up my spine and begging to take over, promising me a warm safe place to hide until it's over. The way I've always known to protect myself.

So I close my eyes and surrender, my last thought of my baby boy, praying he remembers how much I love him.

I'll love you forever, I'll like you for always.

MASON

Child Pornography.
Statutory Rape.

Lewd and Lascivious Acts on a Minor.

These are just some of the headlines running rampant all over the world as the former frontrunner for the United States Presidency is shamed and held without bail. The satisfaction thrums through my veins, and I lean back, inhaling the scent of the Cubans that I kept as a token.

After Olivia came forward, others followed. So far, five women have said that Thomas Wells coerced them, raped them, or made unwanted advances. Three of those five were under the age of eighteen at the time.

I suspect that as time goes on, more will speak out. But I don't celebrate that fact, because the sad reality is that while he'll get locked away—while he'll lose everything—those women will wear reminders of him on their souls for eternity.

I haven't heard from Olivia in the few days since the conference.

My uncle Frank knew, of course, no surprise there. My mother... I'm not sure what to think about her. She acted devastated, but I've seen her performative tears many times over the years, and they're always strategically placed in front of cameras. I think she's very convincing at *playing* the victim, but I'm not convinced she really is one.

She came home to me walking out the door, my bag packed and ready to go.

Unsurprisingly, she didn't try to stop me. I barely got a goodbye. And as I rode away from my childhood home, I let go of every last drop of expectation. Every last bind that tied me. With each mile that ticked by, my chains loosened, and by the time I made it past Tennessee state lines, they broke off and were left behind.

"Well, Mase, how's it feel to be back in Nashville?" Don's voice comes down the line, and I smirk, leaning back on my leather couch.

I sniff the Cuban in my hand, setting it down on the table beside me.

"It feels like freedom, old man."

"Well, lucky for you I haven't hired anyone else to take your place."

I grin. "That's because I'm irreplaceable."

He chuckles.

Sighing, I run a hand down my face. "To be honest, Don, I don't know that I'm gonna come back and work for you."

"Why the hell not?" His voice is sharp.

"I don't know, it depends, I guess. I'm just over the whole traveling all the time and hunting people down thing. Everything that happened with Lily put things in perspective for me. I don't want to be responsible for upending people's lives. They don't deserve it."

He groans. "I've told you before, Mase, we don't get paid to care."

Irritation swells in my middle. "Well, that's the problem, Don. I *do* care. I spent the past decade running, only to end up back in the place I despised. I can't find it in me to keep doing it to other people."

"Other people aren't the heir to the Wells legacy," he scoffs. "Hardly a good comparison."

"Yeah, well... it doesn't make their issues any less valid."

He sighs. "Listen. Why don't you sit with it for a little bit? There's no rush, we don't have any active jobs lined up right now, anyway. If you feel like it's really your time to retire, you let me know. Hell, we'll save you a room out here on the ocean. It's beautiful here."

Nodding, I swallow down the emotion that his words cause. Don is the closest thing I have to a father figure. The only man who has *ever* taken me under his wing and shown me all the ways of the world. He guided me down an otherwise blind path.

He taught me to look a man in the eyes to see his character. And when I was a grieving nineteen-year-old still trying to overcome my demons, he plopped *The Art of War* in my hands and taught me preparation. To learn that even if I can't control people's actions, I can always control my *re*action.

I miss Don, and I feel a sense of loyalty to him that tugs on my insides, urging me to continue to do what I've always done. To run his company for him—repay him for all the ways he bettered my world. But I'm not destined for this life anymore, just as I'm not destined to live out the rest of my days on some island, tucked away from the world.

I've done enough hiding.

"Yeah, I'll let you know."

He grunts and we say our goodbyes, hanging up. There's a sense of relief at the phone call, and I think we both know, that while he can tell me to think about it all he wants, there's no going back for me.

Only forward.

Sitting down in front of my computer, I stare at the Google map that's been haunting my every thought since I pulled it up the other day. Sugarlake is a little over one hundred miles from where I am. And it's taking every ounce of me to not jump on my bike and make the trip to see if Lily is there.

Now that the distraction of revenge is gone, it feels as though there's something intrinsic missing, like a vital organ my body is trying to compensate without. My heart, already smashed to pieces, fractures more whenever I think of Lily's son, knowing I made him promises I had no right to make. Gave him visions of a future that, deep down, I knew probably wouldn't come to pass.

I haven't left my apartment since I've been back. Free but lacking purpose. Where I used to long for solitude, now I find the loneliness stifling, missing the giggles of a screaming toddler, and the song of a little bird.

My phone vibrates from across the room, and I jump up to grab it, my brows furrowing when I see the name on the caller ID.

Chase Adams.

My heart stutters.

"Hello?"

"Mason." His voice is low and gravelly, and my stomach squeezes at his tone.

"What's wrong? What happened?"

My mind races, zooming through a thousand different scenarios, immediately wondering if somehow my father still got to her. *That's impossible.*

"Can you... I don't——" He pauses, blowing out a shaky breath. "It's Lily, she..."

My heart ceases to fucking beat. My insides burn up, needing him to spit it the fuck out, whatever it is. "What about her?"

"Just get here, man," he rasps. "She's gonna need you."

LILY

I wake up in an ER hospital bed, and there isn't a single part of me that isn't aching.

"Lily, Jesus fucking Christ." Chase's voice pulls me out of the inventory I'm taking of my body, and rushes to my side.

I open my mouth to speak but sharp pain radiates through my jaw. I close it slowly and wince, my right hand coming up to soothe the ache. Burning scorches through my arm, my mouth popping back open. "Ow, *fuck*."

Chase smirks. "Yeah, I bet that hurt."

"What happened?" I force out, tamping down the agony searing through the right side of my body.

Chase sighs, picking up my left hand. His eyes dark and murderous. "Your asshole ex is what the fuck happened."

My body jerks and I stutter out a whimper from the pain of suddenly moving.

Chase stiffens. "Do you need me to call someone in here? They said they'd be back in a minute, but if you need something for the pain relief..."

"No." My voice is sharp. "No drugs."

Chase's eyes fog over as he nods. "Right. Right, *fuck*, of course not."

"I had just gotten home and saw your car." Another voice cuts in and my eyes flicker to Derek, his hair mussed in different directions, his blue eyes sharp and penetrating. "And another one parked haphazardly in my front yard. The front door was slightly ajar, and something just felt off. I was already on the phone with 911 when I heard the gunshot."

My insides clench tight, my left hand squeezing Chase's tighter. *Gunshot.* I was shot. By Darryl.

That motherfucker.

"I'm so glad you're okay," I mutter, trying not to move my jaw too much.

"Fuck, Lil, we're glad *you're* okay," Chase says.

"I went to go after him, but when I saw you bleeding on the floor..." Derek exhales a shaky breath. "My mind went blank and you were all I could focus on."

"So he got away," I conclude.

Derek cringes, nodding.

Chase squeezes my fingers. "He will *never* get to you again, Lily."

Smiling softly, I ignore the throbbing ache that spreads across my temples. "You can't promise me that, Chase."

I have to wonder if I'll ever truly escape the choices of my past, or if I'm destined to live in their shadow for eternity. I've been here for less than a month, and already I'm turning other people's lives upside down.

Darryl knows where I am. He knows I'm back. He fucking knows where Derek lives, and it's only a matter of time before he comes to finish the job.

My life was just *fine* before all of this. Before Chase sent his goon to come find me. Before Mason entered my damn life.

Mason.

Alex.

My heart squeezes tight, even through my anger, wishing more than anything that he was here. That he'd hold my face

in his palms and wipe away the prints of Darryl's grip. Tell me
he'll never let another thing come between us.

That he'll protect me and my baby boy.

There's nowhere I've ever felt safer than with him.

Chase's jaw muscles tic. "I *can* promise it. I won't let him
get away with this shit. I should have killed him when I saw
him last."

The curtain surrounding the bed swings back, and a man
walks in with a nurse at his side, white lab coat and a stetho-
scope around his neck. He smiles gently, pushing glasses up his
nose.

"Well, look who's awake." His grin widens, but my mind is
too rattled from the day's events to pay too much attention.
"How are you feeling?"

"Like I've been hit by a truck."

He nods. "The bullet used was a 9mm, and luckily, stayed
intact when it entered the body."

Lucky.

What a concept. Nothing about my situation feels lucky. It
feels like I've been beaten half to death by my drug-addled ex.
It *feels* like he tried to kill me. It *feels* like I've made things worse
for everyone, just like I always have.

"It was a clean exit, and didn't hit any nerves or tendons."

Chase stares at the doctor, his hand never leaving mine.
"So what does that mean?"

The doctor's eyes focus on him. "It means that after a
quick antibiotic drip, and some X-rays, she'll be free to go."
His gaze comes back to me. "She'll need to be monitored
closely over the next few days, to make sure there are no
complications."

He taps the side of his head.

"From the gunshot wound?" I ask, my brain muddled. I
don't understand what he's saying.

"From the blunt force trauma to your head." His lips turn

down. "Any confusion, problems breathing, loss of conscious-
ness… you need to bring her back in immediately."

"I'm right here," I hiss through my teeth, grabbing on to
the irritation of him talking like I'm not in the room to keep
myself from falling apart at the seams.

He looks over to me and grins slightly. "My apologies, Ms.
Adams. Do you have any questions for me? Would you like
something to manage the pain?"

For just a split second, I consider saying yes. But then
Darryl's face flashes through my mind, the deep scarring on
his cheeks, the glazed and empty look in his eyes, and disgust
churns in my gut.

"No," I say, just like earlier. "No drugs." I turn my gaze to
Chase, suddenly desperate for them to understand. "Don't let
them give me any drugs."

Chase's lips turn down in the corner, his fingers squeezing
mine. "I won't let them, Lil."

The doctor nods. "Alright, then we'll get you taken care of
and you should be out of here within the next couple hours."

THREE AND A HALF HOURS LATER, Chase pulls into his
driveway, turning off the engine and sighing as he looks over
at me. "You're not gonna run again, are you?"

Gritting my teeth, I shake my head. "I can't take Chase
away from the only family he's ever known."

He nods, sucking on his teeth. "Good. I'd just find you
again, anyway."

I stare down at my hand, the urge to scratch at my wrist
strong, but as I go to move, a stinging pain in my shoulder
reminds me that my arm is in a sling, and I can't.

"Are you gonna be okay?" he asks.

I shrug. The past few weeks combined with the events of

today coagulating until they're a giant blood clot, forcing my heart to work double time in order to simply beat.

He swallows, his Adam's apple bobbing. I continue to stare at him, the haze creeping up over my mind, whispering that it can protect me. Keep me safe from having to deal with these pesky emotions.

"I called Sam and Anna. They wanted to come to the hospital, but I told them I wasn't sure if you would want C to see you like this."

My chest squeezes at the nickname that everyone in the family has taken to using for my baby boy.

"You're right. Thank you." The throbbing intensifies in my head. I'm sure I look like a complete disaster, but I'm scared to look in the mirror, not wanting to see the sins of my past showing as bruises on my face. I try to move to open the car door, but forget *again* that my arm is in a sling, and *every-thing* hurts. Tears burn behind my eyes, frustration making me grit my teeth. "Can you... can you help me open the door?" I stutter out.

Chase's lips draw down as he nods. "There's one more thing." He cringes. "You're probably gonna want to kill me, but he deserved to know. He would have *wanted* to know."

My insides freeze. "Who is 'he'?"

"Mason. He's here."

His hand waves in front of us, to the black Harley Davidson that's parked off to the side—the one I didn't take time to notice when we first pulled in. My lungs cramp and I suck in a breath, hurt clashing against visceral need, my vulnerability not knowing which one to cling to.

I lean my head back against the headrest, unsure how to feel. Part of me is still so angry with him. But the bigger part of me craves his comfort, knowing he's the only person who has ever been able to bring me back when I'm feeling lost in the wind. Blowing out a slow breath, I nod.

"Well, let's go in and greet him."

58
MASON

Car doors slam and my body jolts upright, my heart banging against my chest cavity, body tensed and itching to get close to Lily. I have no idea how she's going to react to me being here. And maybe it was stupid. Maybe it was selfish to come when she's been through so much. Especially since she most likely wants nothing to do with me.

But I couldn't *not* come.

I'm up and out of my seat before the front door even opens. Alina—who has been the picture of southern hospitality—is on my heels, as we move to the hallway that leads to the entry. My footsteps halt when the door opens and Chase walks in, his arm wrapped around Lily's waist.

My stomach tenses as my eyes soak her in. Her right arm is in a sling, but it's overshadowed by her face, which has been turned into a canvas of blacks, blues, and purples. The entire right side is swollen, a giant contusion sitting on top of her forehead. Both of her beautiful eyes are surrounded by rings of color, and my body rages at the need to find the motherfucker who did this. Show the stupid son of a bitch what happens to people who think they can *touch* her and not have any consequences.

Her eyes glance up and lock on mine, my chest pulling so tight I feel faint. The blood vessels have ruptured in her right eye, bleeding into her iris, and I bite back the anger that's sparking in my veins at seeing my little bird look so broken.

I can't help but feel like part of the responsibility for her ending up like this falls on me. After all, it was *me* who ensured she'd come back here. It was *me* who was so lost in the threat of my father, that I didn't even consider the threat waiting for her in Tennessee.

It was *me* who was a coward and ran without talking, instead of letting her be a part of her decision. And it was *me* thinking I knew best, instead of consulting her on the safety of her own life and that of her son's.

Regret is a hell of a thing. It's heavy as it presses down, forcing me to my knees. I'm ashamed of myself for allowing Lily to leave my life so effortlessly. For not fighting to make her understand.

My heart twists as she steps out of Chase's arms and walks slowly toward me. The air is silent and thick, tension curling around us like a thick fog, pulling us together the way gravity moves the earth toward the sun. My hands clench at my sides to keep from ghosting along her face. I want to kiss every single part of her. Spread my apologies along her body, and pray for forgiveness. But I hold back, allowing her to do what-ever it is she needs. I'm at her mercy, and whatever she chooses will be my penance. I'll accept it willingly. It's nothing less than what I deserve.

She stops when she's right in front of me, our connection flaring to life as our eyes lock. The tendons in my arms flex.

And then she collapses into me. My heart stutters, drag-ging her until she's cradled completely in my arms. She breaks, guttural sobs leaving her body as she sinks to the floor, sliding down my torso. I follow, my arms never loosening their grip, trying to keep her battered parts from being jostled. My legs surround her crumpled form, her face in my chest, tears soaking through the fabric of my shirt.

"Little bird," I murmur. "It's okay, baby. I've got you." My hand comes up and smooths down the back of her head gently, afraid of hitting a wound, but knowing she needs the comfort.

My eyes glance up and lock on Chase, his eyes red-rimmed and glassy as he takes us in. He jerks his chin in a nod, and then walks around us, grabbing Alina's hand and leaving the room.

And this is where I stay, holding the other half of my soul, soaking up her pain and letting it settle on my skin. I'll bear the weight for now, and hope she lets me stay to help her weather the storm.

It isn't until my legs are numb, and my shirt is soaked with tears that she calms down, her cries turning to hiccups, and her breaths coming in even. I rock us back and forth gently, my mouth peppering kisses on her head, my heart fucking *aching* with the need to take it all away.

"You're an asshole," she mumbles against my shirt.

"I know."

She sighs, turning her head to look up at me, her swollen cheek pressed against my middle. Even battered and bruised, she's the most beautiful thing I've ever seen.

"I should hate you." Her voice cracks.

I bite the inside of my cheek and nod. "I know."

"But I'm really, *really*, glad you're here." She hiccups again, her body shivering in my arms.

My arms squeeze her tighter and she yelps. "Sorry, sore ribs."

Anger flares in my gut. "I'm going to *kill* that moth-erfucker."

She yawns, her eyes fluttering. "Can you do it later? Right now, I just want you to hold me. I'll be mad at you again tomorrow."

A chuckle bubbles from my chest, and I press a kiss to the top of her head again, hope swelling my heart. "Where's your room?"

She closes her eyes. "Second door on the right."

I stand up carefully, one arm slipping under her legs, and the other cradling her back as I carry her down the hall and into her room. She lies on the bed, her head propped by pillows, watching as I untie her shoes and remove them.

"I'm gonna take off your clothes, okay? Tell me if I hurt you."

She nods.

Slipping off her socks, I run my hands softly up her legs, along the outside of her thighs, unbuttoning her jeans, and moving one of my hands underneath to slide them off her hips. They roll down easily, but I have to hold back the curse as I take inventory of the blood spatter on her jeans.

Once her pants are off, I lean forward, my hands slipping under the hem of her shirt and lifting. My chest pulls when her bruised side comes into view. My fingers ghost over the area, and Lily sucks in a breath.

My eyes flicker to her face. "Am I hurting you?"

She shakes her head, a pained smile spreading on her face. "Only my heart."

My stomach twists and I lean down, pressing my mouth softly to the contusion on her side. "I didn't mean to."

Her breathing stutters and she raises her left hand to gingerly wipe under her eyes. "Didn't you?"

I shake my head, my chest caving in on itself as I rise up to meet her gaze. "I never meant to fall in love with you. And I never meant to hurt you. I was *going* to tell you, Lily. I was trying to protect you."

She turns her head to the side. "I don't want to talk about this now."

I nod, sucking my bottom lip into my mouth. "Okay."

Gingerly, I move the straps of her tank top over her

slinged arm, then lift her shirt the rest of the way off, my stomach tensing with worry that I'll graze her hurt shoulder.

I reach behind her and unhook her bra, repeating the motion of the straps and letting it fall to the floor beside us. Unable to stop myself, I lean back in, pressing another kiss to her chest, right over her heart. "You can hate me, little bird. I can live with that. Just as long as you promise to stay alive."

Glancing up, I expect a response, but her breathing has evened out, her eyes closed.

I allow myself a few minutes to soak her in, and then I lay down beside her, wrapping her in my arms, and whispering that I'll keep her safe.

Tonight, I'll hold her.

Tomorrow, I'll find that motherfucker and make him pay.

59

MASON

Despite Lily's battered body, she sleeps through the night, and I'm able to slip out of her bed in the morning before she wakes up. I stretch, making my way down the hall, the smell of fresh brewed coffee and the need for a cigarette tweaking my insides. Walking into the kitchen, I stop short when I see Alina staring at the pot of coffee like it insulted her.

"Morning," I rasp, my voice still gravelly from sleep.

She spins around, a smile lighting her face. "Mornin'!" she chirps. "You want some coffee?"

I nod, rubbing the back of my neck. "I'd love some, actually. Thank you."

She grins and gets down a cup, sliding it over to me. "I'll get you a mug, but the rest is up to you. Your legs ain't broke."

I laugh, enjoying her candor. Her gaze flicks past me, her eyes sparkling as Chase walks into the room. He moves to her, his arms wrapping around her waist, bending her backward and diving his tongue into her mouth, obviously not giving a single fuck that I'm in the room.

Chuckling, I walk out to their back patio, and pull a cigarette from my pocket, inhaling the sweet relief. The sliding door opens a few minutes later, Chase sipping his coffee as he stands next to me.

"So, when do we leave?" he asks.

I look at him, quirking an eyebrow. "You'll need to be more specific."

"I assume you're going to find this fuckface, right?"

Taking a deep drag off my cigarette, my head tilts toward the sky as I blow the smoke. Licking my lips, I nod, my insides tense with the anger I'm holding back for when I find the piece of shit. "Yep, that sounds about right."

Chase's eyes darken. "Good. I'm coming with." His hands rest on top of his head. "Derek called, said there's a warrant out for Darryl's arrest for attempted murder."

I huff a laugh, smoke flowing from my nose. "That won't do shit unless he turns himself in or they find him."

"Yeah, well. I won't let her run away again, Mason. She's here and she's staying. And I *need* her to feel safe." His arms rise to his sides. "So let's do what we need to do to make that happen."

Determination winds its way through my insides, and I nod in agreement. "Okay. Be ready in an hour. You're driving." I put out the butt of my cigarette, walking inside.

When I make it back to Lily's room, she's awake, frustration lining her features, her brow drawn and lips pursed.

"Need some help?"

She snaps her gaze to me. "I need to clean the wound, but..." She shakes her head. "Do you think it's okay to take a shower?"

My chest spasms. "Yeah, little bird. Do you need help?"

Her chin lifts, eyes hardening. "No, I can do it. I just... I want my baby back here with me, but I—" She waves her hand down her body. "What will he think?"

My heart stutters, stomach tightening as I walk over to her, crouching down until I'm staring up into her face. Her hair falls in a curtain, and I reach up, brushing it behind her ears, before gently cupping her chin in my hand. "He'll think that his mom is a fighter. A warrior. A *survivor*."

Wetness trails down her cheek and drips over my knuckles. Unable to take the sight, I surge up, kissing away her tears, my mouth trailing over her bruises and landing on the corner of her lips.

She inhales a shaky breath. "I'm still mad at you."

I nod, my hands framing her face. "That's okay."

"I don't forgive you."

"That's okay, too."

Her gaze flickers between my mouth and my eyes. "Does it make me weak if I want you to stay anyway?"

My heart jumps in my chest, spreading hope like ivy. I swallow, trying to find the right words to say. "I think that's your decision to make, little bird. I could tell you a thousand reasons why I did what I did, but they'd all be excuses."

"Just tell me the truth," she whispers.

"The truth," I repeat, something tugging my stomach up through my middle. "The truth is that I've been a PI going by the name Mason since I was nineteen years old. Your brother hired me, desperate to find you. The truth is that the moment I saw you, I *needed* to know you. And the first time we met, I knew, even then, I wouldn't go through with the job."

Her nostrils flare. "But you did go through with it."

I lean my forehead against hers, careful to avoid her right side. "My father found me. Threatened you and Chase." Emotion explodes from my chest, the memory of fear freezing my insides, as visceral now as it was then. "I would rather *die* than let anything happen to you."

Another tear drips from her eye, and I wipe it away with my thumb.

"The truth is that I needed to handle my father before coming back to you. That Olivia was my fiancée and pregnant with who I thought was my child, but turned out to be his." Her eyes widen and I suck in a breath. "The *truth* is that I paid off your landlord to force you out. I went to your brother in his motel and made him promise to take you home." My stomach churns with my confession.

Her eyes flare and she jerks her head away, wincing. "You did *what?*"

My eyes burn. "My father *threatened* your son, Lily. He isn't an amateur. He was a powerful man. He could have done anything to either of you. So yeah, I'm the bad guy." My voice cracks, my fist slamming against my chest. "I'm the asshole who fucked up your world. But I would do it a thousand times over if it kept you safe."

She opens her mouth, but I keep going, desperate to get everything out in the open.

"The *truth* is that you are anything but weak."

She sniffles, her palm smacking her thigh. "I don't even *know* you."

I grab her hand, pressing it against my chest, a tear finally escaping, hot as it trails down my cheek. "You know me. Little bird, you fucking *know* me."

She shakes her head. "I just… are you Alex or are you Mason? I don't know. I need some time."

Blowing out a breath, I nod, my insides tossing. "The people who named me Alexander are dead to me. Mason is the name *I* chose—the name that makes me feel free. But a name is *just* a name, little bird. You can call me whatever you want." Kissing her lightly on the lips, I stand up and wink. "In case that was the last one I ever get."

The corners of her mouth twitch. "You're a prick."

I move to the door, turning around to smile. "But I'm *your* prick, whether you claim me or not."

My heart pounds in my chest as I leave her to shower, hoping she chooses to let me stay.

TRACKING down Darryl was one of the easiest jobs I've ever done. He wasn't even hiding. *Mistake on his part.* His rap sheet is a mile long, all of it public record, and after a little digging I have a general idea of where I think he is.

So, three hours after I left Lily alone in her room, her brother and I pull up to the curb of a worn-down house, with chain link fencing around the perimeter, and a rusted-out car on stilts in the driveway.

I glance over at Chase, noticing his tense demeanor. "You good?"

His brows are furrowed, his fists white-knuckling against his legs. "Yeah, I've just... I've been to this house before. *Fuck.*" He rips at his hair. "I've driven by this place *so* many fucking times after she went missing, praying that she'd be around. But she never was." He huffs out a laugh.

Grabbing the gun from my holster, I pull the slide back to chamber a round, and click the safety off, just in case. "Well, it's not his house. It's registered to an Amy Landerson."

Chase shrugs. "I don't give a fuck."

I grin, anticipation thrumming through my insides. "Me neither."

Walking up to the door, I knock on it with my fist, before standing back and raising my leg, kicking it off the hinges. Perks of having a large frame.

"Knock, knock. Anybody home?" I yell.

A young woman pops up from the couch, her eyes half lidded and glossy, her body wavering as she tries to focus on Chase and me before landing on the broken door.

"Hi." I smile wide, my heart smacking against my ribs. "Your man around?" I ask, twisting my body.

"You the cops?" Her words are slurred.

"I'm the person your bullshit boyfriend pissed off. Where is he?"

She scratches her head. "I dunno who you're talkin' about."

Chase grunts before power walking down the hallway. My chest seizes in panic, knowing he isn't armed, and chances are that Darryl is. I start to follow, but my eyes glance back at who I assume is Amy, noticing the fresh blood on her hands, and the needle next to her on the floor. My stomach drops, knowing that at one time, this was my Lily.

Yelling comes from a back room, and I rush down the hall, my heart twisting in my chest. I find Chase, his fist in Darryl's face, his hand wrapped around his throat as he pins him against the wall.

"You think you can fuck with my sister, and I wouldn't come to fuck you up? You think I'd just let you go?" He slams his fist forward again, smashing into Darryl's nose, blood spurting from his nostrils and spattering across Chase's knuckles. "I've been waiting *years* for this."

Walking closer, I pull Chase back. He releases him, and Darryl falls to the floor in a heap, his hands coming up to cover his face.

I crouch down next to him, pulling the gun from my holster and tipping up his chin with the barrel, his eyes unfocused and hazy. *High as a fucking kite.*

"Darryl," I croon.

"What do you fuckers want?" he spits.

My eyes gleam, my chest burning with the rage I've been biting back until now. "It seems you're confused." I turn toward Chase who's rubbing his busted knuckles. "Does he seem confused to you?" I ask.

Chase smirks. "Yeah, he does."

"Yeah," I repeat. "You see, you *must* be confused, thinking that I'm here to answer any of your fucking questions." Removing the barrel from under his chin, I bring it back, slamming it across the side of his face, the crack sending a rush of satisfaction through my veins.

Darryl screams, whipping to the side, a chipped tooth

flying out of his mouth, and landing on the ground next to me.

"Doesn't feel so good when it happens to you, does it?" I lean in close, my hand grasping his head by his greasy hair, wrenching his neck up and back until it's bent at a ninety-degree angle. "You think you could touch her and I'd let you walk away?" I slam him face-first into the ground.

The carpet muffles his groan of pain. He rolls on his back and grins, his teeth stained red. "You talkin' about Lily? I shoulda fucked her 'fore I killed her."

"Don't say her name, you piece of shit," Chase seethes, coming forward and planting his boot into Darryl's side. He yelps, curling in on himself.

He coughs, spitting up blood, a maniacal laugh piercing through the air.

This guy is so gone he's barely human.

"Maybe next time I'll catch that bastard kid. She ever have it?"

Rage floods through my insides, and my vision goes black. Gripping him by the nape of his neck, I hoist him up and shove him into the wall, my gun to his temple, and my forearm against his throat. "You wanna test me, mother-fucker? Is that it?"

His eyes widen, his hands scratching against my arm as I press it against his windpipe, feeling it crush under the pressure. His mouth opens, gasping for air, his eyes bulging from their sockets. I push harder, enjoying watching the life drain from his eyes. His face turns pallid, blue rimming his mouth from lack of oxygen, and I'm gone. Determined to wipe this piece of shit from the planet so he can never reach them. So he can't even take a fucking breath to try and say their names.

A hand grips my shoulder tight and jerks, snapping me out of the haze. I turn, Darryl dropping to the ground, wheezing and clutching his throat, whimpers leaving his pathetic mouth.

"Don't kill him," Chase says.

I sigh, pinching the bridge of my nose, trying to calm the storm raging inside of me.

"If you kill him, *you'll* be the one who gets taken away." He runs his hand over his face. "And fuck it, man. They need you, okay? She loves you. She's gonna forgive you, and Baby C needs you too."

My heart swells.

I spin back around, peering down at Darryl's crumpled form. He struggles, pushing up on his skinny arms, attempting to stand. Chase and I are shoulder to shoulder, watching his effort. As soon as he gets himself upright, I move forward, coldcocking him across the temple again.

His limp body collapses to the ground.

Grabbing the zip ties I brought from my back pocket, I secure his hands and feet, picking him up and slinging him over my shoulder before walking out of the room.

Chase follows, his eyebrows at his hairline. "Came prepared, huh?"

I grin, adjusting Darryl's dead weight as we approach the car and throw him into the back seat. I revel in the sound of his head smashing against the door.

"Where the fuck are we taking him?" Chase asks.

"If you won't let me kill him, then we sure as shit can make sure he gets locked the fuck up and kept far away. Let's drop him on a street by the police station and we'll call in a tip. They'll pick him up. It's not like he can run."

Anger still swims in my gut for all the shit he caused, but I feel confident that justice will be served.

As we kick him out into an alley by the Sweetwater police station, I breathe a little easier.

I can't help but feel like this was a turn for the better with Chase. There's an acceptance that he never showed me before. A common cause that brought us together, showing us that in the grand scheme of things, maybe we're not so different, after all.

Baby Chase has decided that my life is a superhero movie. I go along with it, just happy he isn't traumatized by seeing me beat black and blue. I take a bite of cereal, smiling as he explains to the room how his mom was saved by Spider-Man. The girls all came over for a "spa" day, which was really code for "make Lily feel less like shit." But it's been nice having them around. Feeling like I belong.

Strange how tragedy can bring people together.

The front door opens, my eyes widening when Chase and Mason walk in, giggling with each other like schoolboys.

What the hell?

"Fucking *finally,*" Jax groans, walking in from the living room. "I thought I was gonna have to spend the rest of the day listening to them talk about fashion."

I snort into my cereal, and Blakely grins. "Jackson, I thought you loved when I share my fashion tastes." She grins, and his eyes darken.

"Ugh, gag me. I'm gonna go call Eli," Becca says, leaving the room.

"Where have you two been?" Lee asks, sipping from a glass of water.

Chase shrugs, and Mason takes off his jacket, one I have no clue how he wears in this heat. My insides flare as I take him in.

God, he makes it hard to be mad when he looks that good.

"Awex!" Chase squeals, scrambling off the barstool and running into his arms. The name is a shock to my system; already having gotten used to calling him Mason.

The biggest smile splits Mason's face as he scoops up my baby boy and brings him to his chest, his eyes closing as he holds him tight. "Hey, little man. I missed you."

Chase leans back, his little hands pressing into Mason's cheeks. "You pwomised me a pancake tower."

My heart expands, warmth flowing through my chest, and Mason laughs. "Yeah, buddy, I did."

He adjusts him on his hip, and walks farther into the kitchen, completely at ease in a roomful of strangers. His gaze locks on me.

I grin. "Sneaking off to bond with my brother, now?"

He smiles back, lifting his shoulder. "We found some common ground."

My brow quirks.

"Awex, did you know that Mommy was saved by Spiduh-Man?"

Mason's focus goes back to the boy in his arms, and my stomach somersaults. How could I make my baby live without a man like Mason, when it's clear that he's in love?

How can I live without him, when it's clear that *I* am too?

"Hey, Lily," Lee says. "I don't know if you're up for it, but next week I'm headin' to Mama's grave if you wanna go with."

My stomach tightens, but I nod, wanting to be able to face Mrs. Carson and pay my respects.

She beams at me. "Great!"

Blakely grins, excusing herself to follow Jax back into the living room.

"Seriously, where have you guys been?" I ask, taking in their rumpled forms.

Chase's eyes harden as he stares at me. "I told you that he would never get to you again."

My insides seize, the breath cutting from my lungs. My body jerks and a burn ravages my side, making me wince in pain. Mason steps forward, baby Chase still sitting on his hip, his eyes flashing with worry.

I put up my hand. "I'm okay, it's just easy to forget I'm immobilized." My chest squeezes. "Are you saying...?"

Mason nods. "He's in custody. He has *a lot* of warrants, little bird. More than just charges against you." He walks closer, stepping into me and brushing my hair behind my ear with his free hand. I lean into his touch, my eyes fluttering. "You'll probably have to testify."

I nod, sucking down the anxiety that swarms my veins like a beehive. "I'll do whatever I need to make sure he leaves us alone for good."

"Awex!" Chase interrupts the moment, bouncing in Mason's arms. "Let's pway."

Mason grins. "Okay, little man." He looks to me, and I wave them off. "That's fine, I'm tired, I think I'll go lie down."

I can see in Mason's face that he wants to go with me, but he respects our distance, waiting until I choose to let him back in.

"Hey, can we talk, Lil?" Chase asks.

I nod, my eyes flickering down to his busted knuckles. "You wanna clean those first?" My stomach spasms, visions of what they may have done to Darryl flashing through my head. It's probably less than he deserved, but either way, I can't find it in me to care.

He brushes his fingers across the top of his hand. "I just want to say a couple things, and then I'll let you sleep."

Standing up, we walk to my bedroom, Chase closing the door behind us. My body feels heavy and I go to lie down on the bed, hoping I can stay awake long enough for this conversation. I'm *so* tired, my body craving rest.

"I called Doc," he says.

My brow arches. "Who's Doc?"

He smiles, shaking his head. "My therapist. Well, he *was* my therapist, back when I lived in Nashville. But I think you'll like him best. For our family sessions."

Unease flickers through my middle. "Oh, okay."

"I was fucked up over you for a long time, you know? He helped me work through it."

I push down the nausea that climbs up my throat. "Listen, I..-I would say that I'm sorry for my mistakes, but the truth is that if I didn't make them, then I wouldn't have my son, and I would make the same decisions a thousand times over for him."

My stomach flips, hoping that he understands what I'm saying. He closes his eyes and nods.

"For a long time, Lil," he starts. "I felt like it was my fault."

My chest compresses, gut cramping. "*What?* Chase, nothing was your fault. *Nothing.*" I reach my good hand out to cover his on the bed. "You were the only person there for me through my entire life." Dread rises through me, trying to force out the words. But they still won't come. "I was keeping secrets from you long before we moved to Sugarlake."

His face shutters.

"I had demons of my own I didn't want anyone to see. I wish I could talk about them... I wish I—"

His hand flips under mine, twining our fingers together. "I have nightmares of that time we spent with Jason and Lydia."

Jason. His name reverberates off the walls and slams into my middle so fast, I cower.

"*Fuck*, Lily, are you okay?"

My eyes burn from the tears I try so hard to hold back, and I shake my head. "I can't talk about him."

Chase's entire demeanor stiffens, his nostrils flaring.

Finally, he sighs, his lips twisting. "I fucking knew it. I never wanted to see it, but I fucking knew it anyway. I wrote about it in my damn journal."

My insides cave, the darkness calling me like a siren as shame tries to pull me under its cloak. I don't want him to think less of me now that he knows.

Suddenly, he moves, wrapping me in his arms. It stings my side, my body stiffer than it was yesterday, but I allow him to hold me, silent tears dripping down my cheeks.

"I want to heal," I mutter. "I want to ge-get better. But I can't talk about it yet."

"Ssh," he soothes. "I know better than anyone what it's like to not be able to voice things." He leans back, looking me in the eye. "I just wish I could have done more." His voice chokes. "I should have cut that fucker's dick off."

My gaze goes to the raised flesh that runs through his left brow, and it brings an odd sense of comfort, reminding me that while my wounds run deep, we all have scars. Some more visible than others.

"You're the best brother a girl could ask for, Chase Adams," I whisper. "I wouldn't just name my kid after anyone."

His jaw muscle tics. "You and me against the world, right, Lil?"

My throat swells, my vision growing splotchy. "Forever."

He grins, and with a kiss to my forehead, he stands up and walks out the door.

Once he's gone, I weep for all the things I can't voice, and I cry for all the ways I want to heal.

MASON

It's been a week, and Lily hasn't told me to leave. Technically, she hasn't told me to stay either, but Jax and Blakely tipped me off about this bed-and-breakfast spot on the edge of town. So here I am, immersing myself in the small-town life whether Lily admits she wants me here or not.

I've spent every single day at Chase and Alina's—who has *finally* given me permission to call her Lee—and every day, I've been feeling Lily's eyes linger a little longer. Her icy walls melting a little more.

"You're lucky he wants to play with you all the time," Lily says, her voice startling me from where I'm watching baby Chase suck in deep, even breaths.

He fell asleep about twenty minutes ago, and I've been sitting here, soaking him in ever since, my gut twisting with worry over what the fuck I'll do if she decides she doesn't want me around. I know he's not mine, but... he *feels* like mine.

I smirk, standing up and walking over to her. "You sure it's not *you* who wants to play with me?"

She snorts, slapping her hand on my chest, and I grin, enjoying the light that's slowly starting to seep back into her eyes.

Lee walks into the living room, her gaze softening as she sees how close we're standing. "I can watch him if y'all two wanna go talk." She waves her hand toward Chase.

Lily's brows draw in, her head tilting. "That's not—"

Grabbing her hand, I drag her down the hall. "That'd be great, thanks," I holler behind my shoulder.

I follow Lily into the room and close the door, pushing her up against it, immediately crowding her space. "Do you forgive me yet?" I ask, my arms coming up to rest on the sides of her head, caging her in.

She sucks in a breath, her eyes darkening. Her face is still bruised, but the swelling has gone down significantly, and she's out of the sling they had her in. She's still sore, but she never complains, swallowing down the pain and refusing to take heavy meds.

She scrunches her nose. "You think you deserve to be forgiven?"

I nod, bringing my mouth close enough to brush against hers. "I'll beg if you want."

She smiles against my lips. "I don't want you to beg," she says. "I just want you to be honest."

My body pushes into hers, letting her feel the effect her closeness is having on my body, my cock growing as I press it against her belly. "I'm *honestly* tired of trying not to touch you."

She huffs. "God, but can you be serious for a second?"

My hands come down to frame her face, loving the way my palms feel sliding against her skin. "I *am* honest, little bird. I'm in love with you. Desperately." I press a kiss to the corner of her lips.

"Madly." A kiss to the other side.

"Deeply." I brush my lips against hers lightly, my stomach jumping when she doesn't push me away.

"And you don't have any other secrets?"

My heart skips in my chest, banging against my rib cage. I

shake my head. "No other secrets. Well, I never lived in
Colorado. But that's it, I swear." I brush my lips across hers
again. "Please, little bird. *Love* me back," I whisper.

Her eyes flicker, and then her hands run up my chest. "I *do*
love you. I never stopped. That's the problem."

I press my erection into her hips again, unable to stop the
way my body reacts to her touch. "Say bunny."

Our safe word. If she says it, I'll swallow my pride, and I'll
respect her choice.

She sucks in a breath but shakes her head. And that's all I
need.

I lean in and capture her lips with mine, months of
anxiety melting away at the taste of her on my tongue. She
moans and sinks into me farther as I lift her legs up to wrap
around my waist, pulling her farther into the room, and lying
on the bed so she rests on top of me.

She twirls her tongue with mine, my heart jolting against
my sternum, my cock straining to be let free. Her hair tickles
my neck as she moves, sitting up straight, her hot center
pressing down on me. I groan, thrusting my hips into her,
and she bites her lip as she peers down. "I forgive you," she
says.

A grin spreads across my face, my chest feeling like it
might explode from her words. I rise up on my elbows,
bringing her in for another kiss as she starts to slowly grind on
my lap.

"I don't think this is what Lee had in mind when she said
for us to talk," Lily gasps. "She's *right* down the hall."

My mouth leaves hers and moves to suck on her neck.
"Don't care," I mumble against her skin.

"I don't know if I can—"

My finger presses against her lips, already knowing what
she's going to say. That she doesn't know if she can *do* normal
sex. "You can, little bird. There's no one here but you
and me."

Biting her bottom lip, her eyes darken, making a shot of arousal pool in my stomach.

"I want you on top, because I don't want to hurt you. You're still healing." I lean back, my hands going behind my head. "Take control, baby."

I move to help her take off my pants, knowing she doesn't have full range of motion yet. Her pink summer dress flows around us, my cock springing free and resting against her damp panties. She mewls as she presses herself against me.

"Oh my *God*, I missed you," she groans.

My chest lights up like the night sky, soaking up the energy that weaves between us, binding us together. There was a time I thought that it would never happen again. That I'd already had my chance. That we'd have to wait until the next life to try again.

She slips her hand under her dress and moves her panties to the side, her palm grabbing my shaft and lining it up at her entrance. I pulse in her hand, precum bubbling at the tip and sliding down my length when her hand pumps me once. Twice.

My abs tighten and my head falls back at her touch. "*Fuck.*"

Slowly, she drops down on my cock, her heat enveloping me inch by glorious inch until she's seated fully on top of me. Her eyes flutter closed, her chest heaving as she sucks in deep breaths.

I twitch inside of her, ready to explode just from the feel of her walls hugging me. My palms grip her hips. "Are you okay?"

"It hurts a little." She moves her hips forward, making my eyes roll back. "But I like the pain."

She starts a steady rhythm, her hips moving slow and steady, the heat building between our bodies until it feels like an inferno. But I'm willing to burn alive as long as we get to be together.

Heat collects at the base of my spine as her walls flutter around me, her hand coming up to her mouth to stifle the sounds.

My hips start to move, working us into a slightly faster motion, wanting to feel her come apart around me. "Are you still with me, little bird?"

Her eyes look down, blazing into mine. She nods, and I thrust sharply into her, my thumb pressing down on her swollen clit. "Are you gonna come for me?"

She nods again, her legs tightening around my hips as she works her body the way she needs against my cock. *Fuck*, she's the sexiest thing I've ever seen.

My balls tense, my cock jerking inside of her.

Goddamn.

And then her body tightens up, her mouth opening on a silent scream, body trembling, and walls milking my shaft as she comes undone around me.

Her orgasm is enough to send me over the edge, my length throbbing as I release deep inside of her, my hips pushing in farther to be as close to her as I can get.

Spent, I collapse back on the bed, her body resting on top of mine, her mouth laving kisses along my chest.

My hand smooths over the back of her hair. "Are you okay?" My heart pinches as I think about her body still healing, and me, a fucking Neanderthal not able to keep my hands to myself.

She grins up at me. "I'm perfect."

And as we lie in her temporary bed, in her temporary home, my soul feels more satiated than ever. Because I know that *this* is forever.

I'm never leaving again.

LILY

I 've never been to a graveyard, and it's... *cleaner* than I expected. Prettier. I wanted to bring flowers to pay my respects to Mrs. Carson, but the truth is I don't have the money, so I ended up gazing at her tombstone, a heavy ache in my heart, whispering my words of gratitude for all the ways she taught me how to be a good person.

And I thank her for making Lee, for bringing her into my brother's life, because even though the hurt isn't fully healed between us, it's clear as day to see how happy she makes him. How absolutely *meant* for each other they are.

"So," Lee says, twisting toward me in the passenger seat of her car. "Where to now?"

My fingers twist in my lap. There's a cookout happening at her place later today, with *everyone* coming. Jax, who flips cars for a living, has some big production movie that's being released featuring his work, and Blakely managed to get an early copy. The plan is to eat dinner and watch it on the projector screen we've set up out back.

I shrug. "Don't we need to head back?"

She smiles at me. "We do. But I wanna talk to you first for a minute."

My stomach twists.

She reaches out and grips my hand tight. I let her, my heart growing heavy from the thickness in the air.

"I'm sorry," she says.

My chest pulls, my wide eyes glancing up to her. "Why are *you* sorry?"

"For a lot of things." She lifts her shoulder. "But mainly because I hurt you, and I know it."

I glance to the side. "That was years ago."

"Doesn't matter. Doesn't change the way my actions made you feel, does it? They're still valid, they're still..." She trails off, her teeth sinking into her lower lip. Blowing out a breath, she tries again. "The truth is," she continues, her eyes shining with unshed tears. "I've always been a little bit selfish." Her voice wavers and my lips curl up at her words, because *yeah*, she has been. "And over the past year especially, I've had to come to terms with a lot of the things I've done, and how they've affected the people around me." Her fingers squeeze mine. "The people I love most in the world."

The walls of my resentment shake as her words pelt against them.

"I'm sorry I didn't tell you about Chase and me." Tears roll down her cheeks and she wipes them away with the back of her hand, closing her eyes as she leans back against her seat. "But more than that, I'm sorry that I let you down as a friend."

"Lee, you—"

She shakes her head. "No, it's true, Lily. I *knew* there was somethin' wrong with you. I *knew* you needed help."

My throat tightens, memories of my teenage years causing the old scars to pulse like fresh wounds.

"And I kept pushin' it to the side, more worried about my damn self. And then..." She shrugs. "It was too late." Her hand comes up to cover her mouth, her forehead wrinkling as she breaks into sobs, her shoulders shaking. "You were already gone."

A ball blazes in my chest, surging up through my esophagus.

"I've spent *years* tryin' to come to terms with the fact that I let you down. But there's nothin' to come to terms with, other than the fact that I've always kinda been a shitty friend."

I bark out a laugh, her cursing catching me off guard.

"But we all have to learn from our mistakes, and try to grow from 'em, right? Ain't that the point of livin'?" She looks at me, her eyes red and watery.

I stare back at her, a sense of peace washing over me, realizing that she's right. Staying mad is staying in the past. And I don't want to live there anymore.

"What is it your mom always used to say?" I ask. "About forgiving?"

She sniffles, glancing down at her lap, swallowing around her tears. "Forgiveness is divine, Alina May."

My vision blurs as I nod, my eyes looking at the ceiling of the car. "Yeah. Well. I forgive you, Alina May. And I hope you can forgive me, too."

Lee chokes out a strangled noise, reaching across the console and wrapping me in a hug. It pulls at the wounds on my right side, but I ignore the pain, sinking into the grace of growth.

Wind whips through the open windows, blowing our hair into tangles, and Lee leans back, wiping under her eyes. She giggles. "I think Mama agrees with us. Whenever the wind blows here, I like to think it's her, givin' her seal of approval."

WE'RE SMACK dab in the middle of a barbecue. Chase and Eli are manning the grill, my baby boy is bouncing on Mason's lap as he sits next to me, his arm around my waist. Blakely is taking live shots to post on her Instagram, showcasing the spread. I've been enraptured by her today, watching her explain to strangers on the internet how she's been struggling all week, knowing she'd be surrounded by this food today.

She's young, but I'm envious of her strength.

Sam and Anna are chopping vegetables in the kitchen, and Lee's father, Mr. Carson, is sitting right next to me.

"This might not be my place," Mr. Carson says suddenly.

I turn to look at him, my brows rising. Mr. Carson and I were never super close. He was always heavily invested in Eli's basketball career, so it was her mom who I bonded with. But he was still there—still a part of my childhood. I can't even imagine what he's been through after losing the other half of his soul.

"But I know about your issues with drugs."

My stomach tenses. *Okay, blunt, but I'll take it.*

He leans in closer. "I'm an alcoholic."

Sadness weighs down my chest, a kindred spirit sparking between us, a sense of relatability that no one else here could possibly understand.

"I've made horrible mistakes. I'm sure you can relate." He smiles thinly. "But I go to meetin's three times a week, and you're always more than welcome to come with." He clears his throat. "If that's somethin' you'd wanna do."

I nod, swallowing around the lump in my throat. "I'd love that, Mr. Carson. Thank you."

He grunts, leaning back in his chair, and I grin as everyone is corralled for dinner.

Becca shoots up from her seat as everyone else sits down, her finger coiling around a strand of her red hair. "Wait, I have.... um... I have somethin' I wanna say before we all dig in, please and thank you."

Everyone's attention moves her way, and she swallows audibly, her hands visibly shaking as she turns to Eli, who's looking at her with a raised brow.

"My family never showed me the right way to love. They never taught me what it looked like."

My chest squeezes in sympathy, remembering her preacher father and her mom who never gave any of us the time of day. I wonder if they're still running the town.

She turns toward Eli, her hand caressing the side of his face. "But then *you* came along. And you showed me what it meant to be loved. To be cherished." Her eyes water and she smacks her hand against her forehead. "Damn, I swore to myself I wouldn't cry. My *point* is that you loved me when I didn't know what it meant, and I did a shit job at lovin' you back."

Baby Chase giggles from next to me. "She said a naughty word," he whispers loudly in Mason's ear.

Mason chuckles, his palm coming to rest on my thigh and squeezing.

Becca pushes back her seat and bends down in front of Eli. There's an audible gasp in the room, Lee's hand coming up to cover her heart. Blakely's holding up her phone like she's recording.

"I've spent every second tryin' to make up for my mistakes. And you, Elliot Carson, are the most amazin', lovin', most *forgivin'* man on the planet."

Lee's eyes meet mine and she winks.

Forgiveness is divine.

Becca reaches in her pocket and pulls out a ring box, opening it to what looks like a platinum band. "I'd be the stupidest woman on the planet to not make sure you're tied to me forever."

Eli laughs, his eyes watery as he cups her face. "Rebecca Jean, are you *proposing* to me?"

She shrugs. "I'm nothin' if not unconventional. Eli… if you stay with me, baby, I'll give you the world."

He grips her behind the neck, drawing her into a deep kiss, uncaring that the rest of us are around.

"I take it that's his yes," Jax says.

Lee wipes under her eyes, puffing out her cheeks, and squeezing Chase's hand on the table. "Well, I might as well add to the moment, and tell y'all that we're expectin'."

Eli pulls away from Becca, turning to his sister. "Expecting what?"

She puts her hands on her belly. "A baby, of course."

I knew it.

Anna squeals. "Two weddin's and a baby!"

Mason leans in, whispering in my ear. "We better get to work. Can't have your family showing us up."

I raise a brow, but my heart skips in my chest, my stomach flipping.

He leans in and kisses me, and I close my eyes, getting lost in everything that he is.

Baby Chase giggles. "Ewwww, stop it."

I grin, leaning over Mason, and smothering kisses on *his* face instead, before sitting back and digging into the food, a lightness suffusing its way through my chest.

Three hours later, the sun has set, and we're laid up in the makeshift theater out back, the baby monitor in my hand, my head lying in Mason's lap.

The movie is in its final scene, Jax's face beaming from ear to ear as we watch his life's passion play out in front of us. Getting his cars in the movies, the way his dad always dreamed.

Suddenly, his mouth pops open, his eyes growing glassy as he stares at the screen. I turn my head, curious what has him looking so emotional.

There's a dedication, right before the ending credits.

For James A. Rhoades.

Jax's father.

My gaze goes back to Jax as his hands grip at his necklace. He turns, cupping Blakely's face, tears streaming down his cheeks as he whispers words only she can hear.

My eyes continue moving along the backyard. Chase and Alina—his arms wrapped around her waist, his hands resting on her belly. Becca and Eli—his brand-new engagement ring shining on his finger. Sam and Anna—holding hands, watching the family they thought they'd never have, grow before their eyes. And Mr. Carson—a man who lost his wife, but somehow managed to find a way to come back stronger.

I relax in Mason's arms, feeling content. Peaceful. *Happy.* And happiness is a funny thing. When one person has it, it spreads like ivy, winding its way around everyone else; if only they let it grow.

And *this* moment right here, is happiness.

I close my eyes, knowing that this is just the beginning of a life full of joy.

And it starts right here, in Sugarlake, Tennessee, beneath the stars.

EPILOGUE #1

Chase and Lee's new home is finally done. Built from the ground up with Chase's own hands, it's stunning; the craftsmanship unmatched. But tonight, it's the backyard that takes my breath away.

Twinkling lights are strung from the patio, winding around the trellis that's covered in stargazer lilies.

Today is their wedding day.

Well, technically night, since they chose to have an evening wedding. It's an intimate affair. No bridesmaids. No rows of people waiting for the show. There's just Chase. And Alina. Pledging to love each other in sickness and in health, under the beautiful Tennessee night sky.

I tighten my arms around Gail Elizabeth, their four-month-old daughter, and press a kiss to her head, breathing in her scent. *Why do babies smell so good?*

Mason wraps his arm around me, bringing me into his side, baby Chase sitting in his lap, resting his sleepy head on his shoulder. "You look good like that."

I smirk. "Like what?"

He nods toward the baby, his grin growing. My chest swells. The past year has been more than I could have ever imagined. I finally opened up to Chase—and to Sam and Anna—about what happened in my past. It wasn't easy, especially on Chase. There's no getting rid of the protective gene that runs through his veins. But now he knows not to try and bear the weight alone, and so when we have moments of grief, we grieve together.

Watching him marry the love of his life is an honor.

We go to therapy once a month as a family, and I attend every week on my own. Until Darryl was locked away, my anxiety was through the roof. But three months ago, his trial finally came to an end. I thought that testifying against him would be traumatizing, and while it wasn't easy by any means, it also brought me peace. It's been cathartic to finally be able to work through my trauma. The scars from both him and from my original abuser, Jason, are branded deep. I won't lie, it hurts to remember. Some days more than others. But it's also cleansing for my soul.

Chase clears his throat, staring at Lee like she plucks the stars from the sky just for him. "Goldi, I once told you that your glow 'n stick stars lit my path to you, but the truth is, I could find you in the darkest night. Because you're my *person*. You're my one. I fell in love with your light. Your grace. Your ability to stand strong no matter what life throws your way."

Lee smiles, wiping under her eyes.

"I lived most of my life convinced I didn't deserve good things," he continues. "That a kid like me was just a tiny speck in the universe—a waste of everyone's time."

My heart squeezes in my chest.

Chase reaches out, cupping Lee's cheek. "You showed that kid he was bigger than the stars. You showed the man what it meant to love selflessly. And I promise to love you, cherish you, *honor* you for all of our lifetimes."

Tears stream down my face as the minister pronounces them husband and wife, and Chase pulls Lee in for a kiss.

"Promise to never leave?" Lee asks, soft enough I can barely hear.

Chase grins. "Cross my heart and hope to die."

Mason's palm rests on my stomach as he leans in close, whispering in my ear. "When do you want to tell them?"

I grin, shifting the sleeping baby in my arms, joy infusing every single pore of my body. Our family is growing. Not by one, but by two.

Because Mason and I are having twins.

EPILOGUE #2

FIVE YEARS LATER

"Mase, you better get in here and get your kids!" I holler through the back door of our home. "I gotta go!"

Mason comes rushing in through the back patio, being chased by my baby Chase, both of them doused with water and breathing heavy, knocking over Mason's easel on their way to the kitchen.

While I know Mason enjoyed being a stay-at-home dad, I convinced him to pick back up a paintbrush. Told him that it's never too late to live out your dreams. When you know, you know. And he knew he was meant to be an artist at eleven years old.

I laugh at the look on his face, adjusting our toddler on my hip, and glancing back at our twins, Kylie and Katie, eating breakfast at the kitchen table.

"You sure you can handle things?" I ask.

Mason scoffs, wiping his sopping hair back from his eyes. "Please. They're *my* kids, just because this one is a heathen, doesn't mean I can't handle the rest." His hand ruffles Chase's hair, who cackles next to him.

"Dad's just mad that I'm better at water gun fights."

Mason narrows his eyes. "I *taught* you everything you know."

Chase shrugs, walking over to me and taking Ashlynn, our two-year-old, from my arms, smooching her on the cheek. My chest pulls tight as I watch him love on his baby sister. "Don't worry, Mom. I'll help Dad manage while you're gone."

Mason grins as he walks toward me, kissing me on the lips. "How long are you gone for again?"

I smile back, scrunching my nose at how wet he is. "Just a few days. I'll be back after the runway show."

While I fit back in relatively seamlessly with almost everyone, Blakely was someone I had a hard time relating to. But then three years ago, when she was shopping for her wedding dress, things changed.

She didn't like anything she tried, so I stepped in and helped her create one, reigniting my forgotten passion.

Fashion.

After that, it was game over. She sat me down three weeks later, told me she was expanding her brand to include a clothing line, and she wanted me to be the designer. I resisted at first, feeling completely unqualified. But once I gave in, I've never looked back.

I work from home most days, and every once in a while, I get to travel to the greatest cities in the world, seeing my designs being modeled on a runway.

Blakely would normally be going with me, but she's busy at home with her and Jax's brand-new baby. A little boy they named James.

Derek and Mr. Carson have bonded, all three of us going to weekly meetings together, and sometimes we attend the Nar-Anon meetings that Chase runs on Sundays. I'm so grateful for the way Derek has seamlessly blended with everyone. One day, I'll convince him to move to Sugarlake.

As for Becca and Eli? They got married on a beautiful day

in May, in Florida of all places. Unlike Chase and Lee's wedding, theirs was an *event*.

NBA stars, college basketball teams, and hundreds of people I've never even heard of in attendance. Becca's parents weren't invited. It came out four years ago that her father was involved in *multiple* affairs, some with married women. And that was just more than this small town could accept, so after being publicly shamed, he and his wife left town, and Becca hasn't heard from them since.

She doesn't seem to mind.

Leaving one more peck on Mason's lips, I back away, throwing my purse over my shoulder and grabbing my suitcase. "Don't forget Becca's coming to pick the twins up at three, so they can go to cheer practice with her girls."

Mason groans. "They're *five*. Why do they need to be in cheer with Becca's crazy daughters?"

I grin. "Because they like it."

He rubs his hands over his face. "Okay."

After bringing in all my kids for hugs and kisses, I tamp down the melancholy that always wraps around my heart when I have to leave them, knowing they're in good hands while I'm gone.

After all, it takes a village to raise a family, and I've got the best damn village around.

Mason follows me to the entry, gripping my hips and pushing me up against the door. "*Miss* me while you're gone," he rumbles in my ear. Then he smacks me on the ass, making me jump. He was rough last night, our CNC role-play leaving bruises that will last the whole trip.

"Go sing your song, little bird. The world wants to hear it."

Grinning, I blow him a kiss and walk outside.

It's windy today, so loud it whistles as it blows through the trees, and I stumble just a bit as I make my way to the car. I smile as the strong breeze whips across my face, remembering when Lee told me she thinks of her mom whenever it blows.

It's always had a *different* meaning for me.

But that was another lifetime.

Closing my eyes, I soak in the moment, imagining that the breeze is collecting the love from everyone I know, and wrapping itself around me, carrying me through my trip. Reminding me of all the things I have to live for.

I look back at my house, warmth bleeding from my pores. And I drive away from Sugarlake, knowing what awaits me when I come back.

My home. My heart. My *life*.

And through it all, I'll remember the wind.

ALSO BY EMILY MCINTIRE

THE SUGARLAKE SERIES

Beneath the Stars

Beneath the Stands

Beneath the Hood

Beneath the Surface

THE NEVER AFTER SERIES

A COLLECTION OF DARK ROMANCES WHERE THE VILLAIN GETS THE GIRL

Hooked: A Dark Peter Pan Reimagining

Scarred: A Dark Hamlet Reimagining

Wretched: A Dark Wizard of Oz Reimagining

Twisted: A Dark Aladdin Reimagining

Crossed: A Dark Hunchback of Notre-Dame Reimagining

COMPLETE STANDALONES

Be Still My Heart: A Romantic Suspense

JOIN THE MCINCULT!

EmilyMcIntire.com

The McIncult (Facebook Group)

Want text alerts? Text **MCINCULT** to 833- 942- 4409 to stay
up to date on new releases!

ACKNOWLEDGMENTS

To you, the reader. None of this is possible without you. Thank you so much for reading my books, liking my words, and loving my characters. There isn't a single day that goes by where I'm not entirely overwhelmed and thankful for you.

To my best friend, Sav R. Miller. The person who is there reading every word as it's written. The only one who listens to my ideas and tells me whether I should go with it or let it go. The person who keeps me from spiraling, kicks away my imposter syndrome, and reminds me that I am *that bitch*. I am so grateful to have you in my life.

To my alpha readers: Lee Jacquot and Anne Lucy-Shanley. Thank you for keeping my characters in check, and fixing all my plot holes. You are invaluable.

To my beta readers: Ariel Mareroa and Michelle Chamberland. Thank you for reading on my ridiculous deadline, giving honest feedback, and being my hype team.

To my Editor Ellie and proofreader Rosa: You already know. One day I'll learn how to properly use farther and further.

To my Cover Designer: Clarise Tan at CT Cover Creations. From the very beginning, you have taken my vision and created absolutely stunning covers. Thank you so much for everything you do and for sharing your talent.

To my Street Team (who still doesn't have a cool name because none of you have thought of one): I honestly have no idea how to begin expressing my gratitude. You are the first ones I share things with, and I am SO thankful to have you by my side and loving my work enough to help hype it to the masses. You're all wild and I wouldn't have it any other way. (AND NO! It is NOT a cult LOL) So honored to have you by my side on this crazy ride.

To my ARC Team: You all are incredible, and my success is largely due to you. Thank you so much for all of the time and energy you put into reading, reviewing and hyping out my books. And thank you for enjoying my work enough to want to be a permanent part of the process.

To my Em-C Glammers: Thank you so much for being part of my Glam Fam. I love being able to hop into our Facebook group and laugh about our days, get book recs, and vent when things are tough.

To my family: The most supportive family on the planet. Thank you for all of your never ending support. And thank you for letting me use you to make jokes on TikTok which sell a lot of books. (LOL) Not every author who writes in this genre has family that is supportive, and words aren't adequate to speak on how thankful I am that you are.

To Mike: My amazing husband. Thank you for being you, for being an incredible husband and an amazing father. For letting me lock myself away for hours at a time to hide in my writing cave, and for making all of my swag, taking all my pictures, and listening as I flesh out my characters. None of this is possible without you.

To my daughter, Melody. You are now, and always will be the reason for everything.

ABOUT THE AUTHOR

Emily McIntire is a *USA TODAY* bestselling author known for her Never After series, where she gives our favorite villains their happily ever afters. With books that range from small town to dark romance, she doesn't like to box herself into one type of story, but at the core of all her novels is soul- deep love. When she's not writing, you can find her waiting on her long- lost Hogwarts letter, enjoying her family, or lost between the pages of a good book.